THE
LOST
KINGS

BRUNO HARE

SIMON &
SCHUSTER

London · New York · Sydney · Toronto

A CBS COMPANY

First published in Great Britain by Simon & Schuster UK Ltd, 2010
A CBS COMPANY

Copyright © Bruno Hare, 2010

1 3 5 7 9 10 8 6 4 2

Simon & Schuster UK Ltd
1st Floor
222 Gray's Inn Road
London WC1X 8HB

www.simonsays.co.uk

Simon & Schuster Australia
Sydney

Frontispiece and maps by Liane Payne

A CIP catalogue record for this book is available
from the British Library

Hardback ISBN: 978-1-84737-292-5
Trade Paperback ISBN: 978-1-84737-293-2

Printed in the UK by CPI Mackays, Chatham ME5 8TD

For Mona

CONTENTS

'Like all great travellers, I have seen more than I remember, and remember more than I have seen.'

Benjamin Disraeli

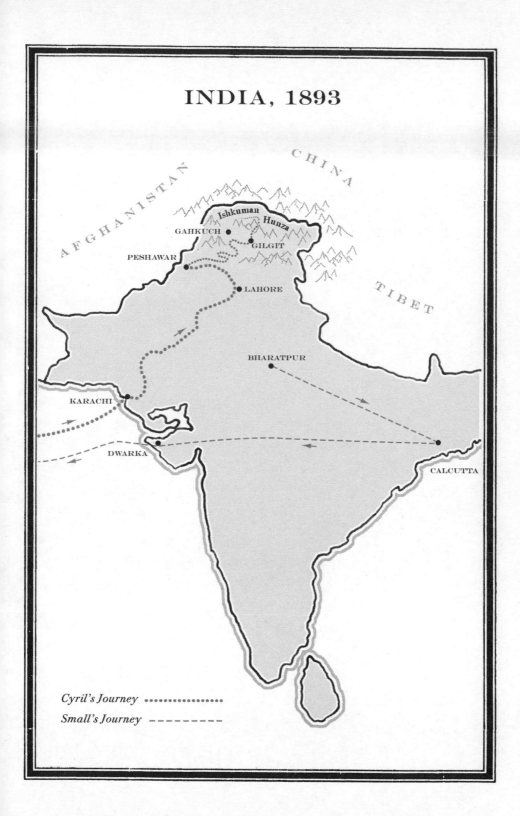

INDIA, 1893

AFGHANISTAN

CHINA

Ishkuman

Hunza

GAHKUCH

GILGIT

PESHAWAR

TIBET

LAHORE

BHARATPUR

KARACHI

DWARKA

CALCUTTA

Cyril's Journey ••••••••••••••

Small's Journey ----------

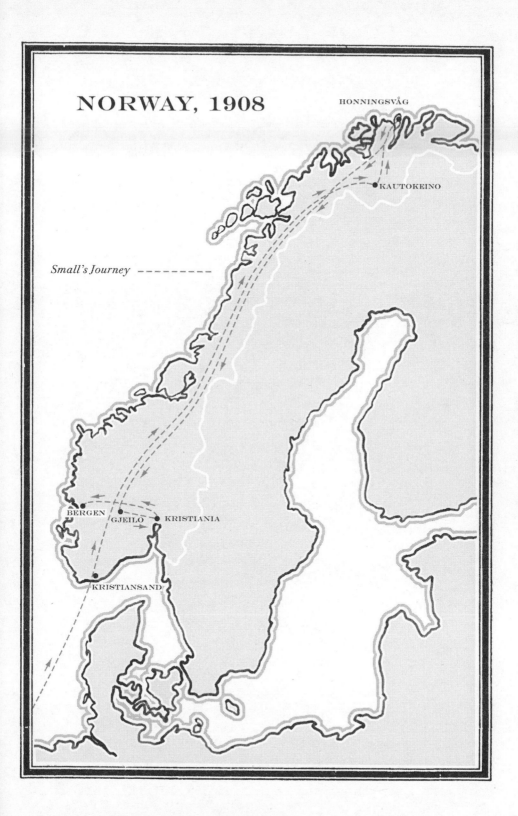

NORWAY, 1908

HONNINGSVÅG

KAUTOKEINO

Small's Journey ----------

BERGEN

GJEILO   KRISTIANIA

KRISTIANSAND

THE NOTEBOOKS OF CYRIL KING

1893

The Man Who Died

The world in which my body conducted its affairs was in every way different from the one my mind occupied until recently. I expect it is similar for most people – for every soldier or gambler who sees himself as an undertaker, there is a real undertaker who, in his head, is on the battlefield with his brothers-in-arms; or at the poker table, surrounded by gunslingers, an ace up his sleeve. Some must be permanently a soldier, a gambler or an undertaker in both body and mind, but not many. I am not one of them, and in truth I resembled the undertaker more than the soldier or gambler.

To the casual observer, I was all that you would expect a watch-maker to be – punctual, logical, meticulous and possessed of an exaggerated eye for detail. In my head, though, watches had no bearing on my calling whatsoever. The apprenticeship I completed in London at the age of sixteen had made time my trade for the last seven years, but at heart I was an explorer, a chap proud to discover new lands and peoples for the good of his nation and his beloved monarch, and I conducted my life as accordingly as my limited means would allow. Indeed, it was in the spirit of exploration that I had allowed my aunt to push the apprenticeship upon me in the first place. The move took me from the dull flats of the Fens to the throbbing heart of the Empire, and there I explored London's famous squares and monuments. When they were exhausted, I turned to its endless alleys and delved deep into its dark and forgotten corners. I encountered people and worlds lost to the city, but it was not until this February past that I left the country of my birth for the first time and embarked on the life for which I had been waiting so long. I did not discover any new lands or conquer any tribes, and what I have unearthed could not be presented to Her Majesty with pride. I suspect she would rather not know that such things went on within her borders, but what happened to me is certainly worth recounting. It is stranger than any of the tales I heard from the mouths of gin-soaked Londoners, and it led briefly to the paths of my imagination and my daily existence joining, before they split once more and continued on their separate ways.

Of course, the word of this watchmaker alone may not be sufficient to convince you that what I am about to tell you actually occurred. Fortunately, you do not have only mine to take. Small was with me, and though he is not altogether an honest fellow, he has lived a sufficiently long and eventful life to qualify as an identifier of the remarkable. So, though I am no wordsmith, I take up my pen in the hope that I do not need to be – that events such as those I relate shall speak for themselves.

Apart from the blue sky that replaced the sleet and rain which had been greying the city, at first that morning followed the routine of any other. I rose at seven, bathed, shaved and dressed. I brewed a cup of tea, buttered a piece of bread and consumed them both as I pored over the morning paper. It contained the usual colonial news and descriptions of honourable parliamentary debates; tales of great Englishmen furthering the knowledge of mankind both at home and in the far reaches of the Empire; and also reports of lesser countrymen awaiting trial in Her Majesty's London courts for crimes encompassing everything from the theft of the Lord Mayor's horse to the murder of an English professor in the souks of Cairo. At half past eight, I departed my rooms on Amwell Street and walked along Rosebery Avenue until I joined the Gray's Inn Road. I turned right onto High Holborn, left onto Chancery Lane and unlocked the shop at nine.

When I opened the door, the morning sun threw my shadow onto the sea of clocks and watches that occupied the shop's surfaces. I entered and raised my hand to retract the blind on the door, but a dusty shard of sunlight was streaming through a tear in it, hitting a replica Earnshaw that did not work, but remained hanging on the wall for other reasons. Intrigued, I left the blind drawn and released the handle from my grip. As the door closed, the sliver of light scrambled over the cluttered wares, tumbling from the Earnshaw to the foot of a grandfather, before gathering itself and leaping from a station to a carriage. It scaled the sheer face of the counter and began a final, desperate dash across the glass, but when the latch on the door clicked shut and the bell tinkled, the shard skidded to a halt, stunned to immobility upon the polished surface.

I moved to the business side of my counter, where I lit a match and with it a paraffin lamp. When I extinguished the match with a sharp blow of air, the shard of light disappeared at the very moment the flame did, leaving only black where it had been and the dingy glow of the lamp. It was as though I had blown out the very sun. I considered the wizened black match with suspicion before looking towards the dead source of the light. My breath had not doused the sunlight. Nothing had. Rather it had been eclipsed by the dilated pupil of an eye that stared at me through the tear in the blind.

The door opened and the bell tolled. The light was ignited again and thrown back onto the Earnshaw, but this time I ignored its progress. My attention was occupied by the large, besuited man lumbering towards me. Before the door closed behind him, I caught a glimpse of another man, waiting outside. He was wearing a dark uniform – a coachman, perhaps; but I saw no coach and did not have time to consider him further. The man before me narrowed his eyes to see through the gloom as he heaved his broad and powerful frame onwards. He came to an uncomfortable stand-still and leaned on the counter in front of me.

The only element of his dress to mark him out, I now saw, was the grubby but exotic neckscarf he wore beneath his shirt instead of a tie, as some do. It was of formerly brilliant colours, the reds faded to orange, the oranges to dirty yellow, and had been tied so tightly around his throat that his fleshy neck bulged over it.

I welcomed him to my shop. He responded in an impatient and unintelligible Scots brogue that left him breathless. Rather than press him further for his views on the uncommonly clement morning we had been enjoying, I decided instead to wait for him to state his business.

Other than his neckwear and conspicuous size, it was what he did not possess that made him striking. His eyes seemed to have no whites to them at all, nor discernible irises – as though they were constituted entirely of pupil. He also had no lips that I could see. Pallid and slightly damp-looking skin spread fully to the line of his mouth without any alteration in pigment. Under his hat, which he did not remove, I could detect no sign of any lurking hair. He did not wear sideburns, nor were there any eyebrows marking his deep and permanent frown.

He shifted his weight from one arm to the other, and as he did so he released the spot of light, which, unhindered, found its way onto the glass between us. I noticed that his pale skin was criss-crossed by a network of visible veins; that those eyes jerked about with fear and anger. It was not a face whose body you would expect to find squeezed into the clothes of a Holborn businessman or lawyer. They were plainly stifling him. Not only was his meaty flesh bulging over the scarf and collar, but the lungs beneath his mighty breast were labouring for every breath. He was like an ageing circus bear whipped into evening attire, humiliated and embittered by the experience. To a distant audience member he would have appeared civilised, domesticated; but to one beside him in the ring, it was perfectly clear that he was not a creature to be taunted. I stood quite still, until his hand, hairless and veined like his face, removed a watch from an inner pocket and pushed it across the counter into the patch of sunlight. I had intended to wait for him to request my opinion, but before me was a watch of such singular oddity that I could not stop myself from forgetting its owner's bearing and, instinctively placing my loupe to my eye, I lifted the object from the glass for inspection.

It was the most remarkable and bizarre piece I had ever encountered. Its casing, made of both a dark wood and an unidentifiable matte metal, was a hefty three-quarter inch in thickness and a full three in diameter. To look at it from the front, it was neither circular nor oval, but somewhere between, and on its stiffly hinged cover was a map of the Indian subcontinent, its outline inlaid with the metal, making it smooth to the touch. Smooth, that is, but for its most prominent feature. Towards its northern borders was clasped an almond-shaped stone, black and with an eye carved into it, like that of a cat or a snake. The eye stared into mine as it twinkled in the beam of light.

When I opened the watch, its cover creaked with lack of use. The clockface inside was numberless, but I could tell that the piece was running very slowly, the minute hand scarcely moving, even though the watch was fully wound. It was surely for this that the gentleman had visited my shop.

I closed the watch as I spoke.

'It's rather slow,' I said to him. 'A very strange piece. I shall enjoy inspecting it further. May I ask where you found such a watch, sir?' I had never before seen one so odd and unusable, and certainly it kept time so poorly that its function could be little more than decorative.

His response was as effusive as I had come to expect in our brief acquaintance, his manner as courteous.

'No time,' he blurted. 'Writing.'

His words confused me, and I was about to tell him as much when he snatched the piece from me and threw it face down on the counter. There was more decoration on its rear, this time rather pretty and abstract. I looked up at him.

He was short of breath and looked set to explode, but he managed to speak.

'Writing,' he repeated. 'You know watches.'

Quite suddenly he seized hold of my shoulders in his powerful fists.

'What does it say?' he gasped.

He released me and tapped the watch violently with his finger.

'Where does it come from?' he heaved. 'The writing, man. The writing. Tell me! Tell . . . me . . . !'

Still I could not understand what he was talking about. He seemed awfully concerned, upset in fact, but he was talking in riddles. Then, all at once, he gave a lengthy wheeze, and my loupe fell to the full extent of its cord as my eyes stretched open in surprise.

This sorry beast, propped against my counter, was quite motionless. His chin rested on that substantial chest and those black eyes stared at the magnifier dangling around my neck. I leaned towards him, my words drying in my throat. He was quite dead.

I had no idea what protocol calls for under such circumstances, so I put my hand to his arm in a futile attempt to revive him. In doing so I shifted him. Starting very gradually, but gaining in speed with every inch, he slumped onto the counter, where his damp and bloodless face hit the glass with a resolute slap. His eye, ringed by the spot of light, looked up at me. His bowler fell to the floor and rolled to a standstill.

Though it was soon to become my constant companion, I had never seen death before that moment, and I do not know for how long I stared at his lifeless form. It was as though there were only the corpse and I in that shop, as though all the time-tellers around us evaporated, disappeared until I was brought from my reverie by the tinkling of the bell and the arrival of a uniformed constable.

*

I removed my jacket and gave my statement to Ruggage, the Inspector whom the constable had summoned. I told him the deceased had come in on account of a watch but that the poor wretch did not have the chance to make clear his enquiry before keeling over. I did not tell of the man's aggressive behaviour towards me – it doesn't do to talk ill of the dead, and besides, I preferred not to reveal the fear he had aroused in me. He looked such a pitiful figure, lying there on the shop floor, and when Ruggage asked if there was anything more I could tell him, pride dictated that I say no. The Inspector said a few words more, but I confess I was not really listening, and he did not press. He could well see I was in a daze, I imagine, and once the body had been removed, I closed the shop early and found my way home.

It was not until the arrival of the next morning's newspaper that the real reason for the Inspector's lack of interest in the case came to light. I went from the kitchen to the post box and into the living room where the fire I had already lit was cutting through the morning chill. I unfolded the paper as I went, keen to see if the journalists of Fleet Street were as disinterested as the police. They were not. I sat in my armchair and read their description of my shop and the events that had occurred in it.

The dead man's name was McNaughton and I was not wrong to have thought him an unpleasant character. I had read of him in the previous day's paper. If you recall, there had been a story concerning the killing of an English academic in Cairo. McNaughton was his murderer. He had been captured by local forces acting on a tip-off; though it seemed to me that locating the blood-soaked white man the paper described as 'towering over the locals as he raged' could not have been much of a challenge, even if the souks of the Egyptian capital were the epic warrens I imagined them to be. The killing had not been a freak offence in a lifetime of rectitude, either – it was the latest and worst in one dedicated to the violation of the law. I was right. McNaughton had been as unsuited to the attire he died in as the grizzly is to domestication and a dinner jacket.

His lawyer and counsel in the trial of Regina vs. Douglas McNaughton was one Jonathan Trout, whose chambers were located in the Gray's Inn. Despite his client being a vagrant known for everything from petty theft and travelling without a permit to desertion and the murder for which he had been on trial, this

Trout had managed to secure a two-hour escorted release for McNaughton in exchange for a plea of guilty and a full confession. The paper thought it odd that McNaughton should choose to visit a musty old watchshop during his final hours of freedom, and promised to pass on the details of his last moments of life just as soon as they located the proprietor. Trout was quoted as admitting that had McNaughton not died in the shop, he was certain to have done so at the end of a rope – a rope that would have wrung a neck which bore a scar from one side to the other, left by the blade of an unsuccessful assailant in years past. The journalist generously thought to describe this feature in great detail and I found myself grateful that, whatever his character, McNaughton had concealed the wound with his arresting neckerchief. The piece concluded, with evident disappointment, that the criminal's death had been a natural one, caused by the failure of a weak and overworked heart.

I closed the paper and stoked my fire, then lit my pipe and stared into the glowing embers. What a terrible and fascinating thing McNaughton had done: to have killed a man for no apparent reason. His victim had been one Professor Forrester, described as a small man, and certainly no match for a bull like McNaughton, in good health or otherwise. What is more, Forrester had been an historian, an ethnographer and bookworm, an expert on ancient civilisations, their rituals and languages. McNaughton had thrown him into a courtyard and beaten him to death with his bare hands. A passer-by had heard the killer shouting 'Tell me!' over and over again as his blows rained down on his helpless victim. Nobody knew what had made McNaughton so angry and it seemed that nobody ever would, since he had not made his confession before he entered my shop. The Professor had only lately arrived in Cairo, en route from India, where he was said to have made a great discovery. What that was, the paper lamented, we should never know. How unfortunate that he should have had the bad luck to encounter a madman, I reflected; and how lucky *I* was that McNaughton had not had the opportunity to unleash his temper on me!

The whole thing confused me, but most of all why on earth McNaughton had chosen my shop to die in. Had he entered in error? And why had he been so concerned about some writing? The only reasonable explanation, I decided, was that in the throes of death, he had mistaken me for another.

It took me until the next day to happen upon a clue to the whole affair. I returned to Chancery Lane, hoping that the interest in my shop would by then have dissipated in the shadow of some other story, but was disappointed to see a knot of journalists already waiting outside the door. To avoid them, I slipped into the alleyway at the end of the block and made my way to the rear entrance. I had no intention of opening the shop to the public, but thought I ought to remove any takings from the till. As I was about to depart, I saw my pinstripe jacket hanging from the chair where I had placed it before giving my statement to the Inspector. I had been so bowled over by McNaughton's death that I had quite forgotten to re-don it the day before, and must have returned home in only my waistcoat and collar, quite oblivious to its absence. I picked the jacket up and put it on. As I did so I felt something in the pocket. It was McNaughton's watch. In my shock, I must have automatically placed it there when I tried to revive the dead man. When the police arrived, I clean forgot what I had done. I had not thought of it since I realised its owner was dead. Now here it was in my hands.

Without a moment's thought, I went to the police station on High Holborn and asked for the investigating officer. When Inspector Ruggage came down to see me, I apologised and explained to him what had happened.

'Don't worry, sir. I quite understand. Easiest thing in the world,' he said. 'But the case is done with, really. The man's dead and good riddance to him. You've read who he was, I take it? A rotten apple. We've more important things to be getting along with around here. Too many innocent living people to waste time on a dead, bad one.'

He looked about us and lowered his voice.

'I'll tell you what,' he continued. 'You're interested in time, aren't you? Well, why don't you hang on to the watch? You keep it and enjoy it. It'll just make trouble for me, and I've enough already. Though I can't say I understand it, tinkering with clocks and the like. But then I suppose police work's as much a foreign language to you, eh?'

I was shocked to hear a police inspector suggesting such a thing, but before I could protest what he said, he closed my hand around the watch and was gone. Befuddled, I walked towards the exit. I did not take long to recover, however. When I opened the door and a freezing pelt of London wind and rain welcomed me, I realised that in so acting, Inspector Ruggage had given me not only a clue to the mystery, but also an opportunity.

The Letters of
Sir Paul Lindley-Small

From a quayside tavern in Dwarka, India

16TH SEPTEMBER 1908

Cyril, old man,

The boat is about to leave, but I use my final moments ashore to write to you. It has been some time since last I did so, I know, but fear not – I am quite alive. That which has embroiled me these months past has recently taken a curious turn, however; and it now seems I am continuing a hunt that we began together many years ago. The *Valkyrie* is to sail west, so in that direction must lie my destination, but that is as much as I can currently tell you. I cannot know where on this route the man I am chasing will choose to disembark from his ship, so I cannot say where, exactly, what he possesses shall move from his hands to mine. That it shall do so is all I can say with certainty of the future. The past is a different matter, of course, and an account of what has brought me here will follow at a later date when more time is to hand.

Meanwhile, the *Valkyrie*'s foghorn is beckoning, as I hope are my co-passengers – a bevy of oriental beauties I spotted some moments ago, scampering up the gangplank. The adventure is under way – and here's to it, lad.

Your friend,

Lindley-Small

THE NOTEBOOKS OF CYRIL KING

1893

Two Old Soldiers

'Squiggles, Cyril,' Hector said, looking at the watch. 'Nothing but orderly squiggles.'

I had arrived at my uncle Hector's house in time for a late lunch. It was now late afternoon – tea time, or in the company of Hector, milk time – and over a mug of the white stuff he was dashing my hopes with this single, oblivious statement. No doubt he was already moving on to a topic he considered more pressing than one of his nephew's watches. He was a distracted man, you see.

He had retired from the Army six months previously and on returning to the motherland had bought a cottage near a quiet Cotswolds village. At the end of a life spent on the battlefields of the Empire, he thought that seeing out the rest of his days in the peace of the English countryside would be just the job. He was mistaken. Despite being of the right age, he had, in fact, retired from the forces too early. Sitting in his parlour, drinking the milk from a cow named after his Gunnery Sergeant, Carnahan, Hector was the picture of wiry good health. He missed his old life terribly and, though he made the best of his new existence and was

certainly not one to complain, Gloucestershire was a poor substi-
tute for the subcontinent. His life of action had made him
incapable of appreciating the tranquillity of his new surroundings
and he did everything he could to disrupt it. As we strode around
his orchard, he spoke of his latest campaign, to do with subvert-
ing the local huntsmen.

'You see, Cyril? Hmm? Do you? It means that if they come galloping across my pristine lawn, I'm perfectly within my rights to
take a pop at them. It means that if any squire shoots a pheasant,
and it happens to get strung up in the branches of one of my
Discoveries, it's thank you very much, into the pot and a game
supper for old King!'

It was his boredom that had driven him to distraction. Since
there was nothing more substantial to get his teeth into, he had
become preoccupied with insignificant issues, to such a degree that
it was a struggle to get him to concentrate on something of genuine interest, such as I believed McNaughton's watch to be. Finally,
once he had manhandled the distinctly feminine-looking
Carnahan and we had returned to the parlour, I placed the watch
on the table between us as he carefully measured out the milk he
had so laboriously procured for us.

When he had finished, he sat down, picked up the watch and
scrutinised it indifferently as he drank.

'Look at the back,' I said, a quiver of excitement in my voice.

The source of this quiver was the stream of illuminating
thoughts that had taken me from the threshold of the Holborn
police station to Paddington, where I boarded the first train to
Kemble and turned up, unannounced, on Hector's doorstep just
outside Bibury. The idea of seeking my uncle's advice came not so
much from the cold London rain as from the words of the mildly
disreputable Inspector Ruggage. They constituted the final cog of
the mental device, but the biting weather was the vital element
that had cranked the suddenly completed machinery into action.

Inspector Ruggage had said that the inner workings of a timepiece, and the desire to understand them, were quite alien to him,
as though a foreign language. In the shop, before he died,

McNaughton had asked me what the writing meant. I had no idea what he was referring to at the time, but in the chill of the London morning, I suddenly understood. What he had pointed at was not random decoration, as I had thought, but words. Words forming a strange and unrecognisable language. McNaughton's victim, Forrester, had studied ancient languages. The witness in Cairo had heard McNaughton crying, 'Tell me!' as he beat Forrester to death, just as he had demanded of me moments before his own demise. Suppose McNaughton believed that Forrester understood what was written on the watch, but was for some reason keeping it from him. I had no way of knowing why Forrester had not told him; but the fact that he had not, that he would rather die than reveal, spoke volumes. What was a man like Forrester, a bookish academic, willing to die for? Indeed, what could be so vital to a man that he was willing to kill for it? What could obsess two men so much that it could bring one to tear the other limb from limb? Fantastic replies fast forming in my head, I determined to establish precisely what the writing meant, before my imagination ran riot with the possibilities.

The ornate script had the appearance of exotic origins, and I thought it reasonable that the watch's maker would single out his own land for decoration over any other. As I have described, a carved stone had been placed over the map of the Indian subcontinent that was etched into the watch. Uncle Hector had been stationed in Kerala. I hoped he would be able to translate the words.

He gulped down his milk as he looked at them, frowned and then spoke those fatal words.

'Yes. Squiggles,' he repeated. 'As good as the doodling of a child.'

He put the watch down, picked up the jug and poured himself the last drops.

'Good juice old Carnahan gives, eh?' he said.

I did not respond. Until that moment I had thought myself to be on the verge of an adventure, an escapade fit for an explorer. Hector's announcement was a devastating blow.

He put his mug down with a sharp thump.

'Of course,' he said. 'Leopold Sprockett'll be able to tell you.'

He had no idea of the extremes he was pushing me to, of the emotional somersaults my heart was performing. To Uncle Hector, we were just passing the time, off-duty in the mess.

'He never stopped poring over those local languages. Wherever he went. Could never see the point of all that stuff myself. The natives were meant to be learning from us, not the other way around. Still no idea why the Army thought they needed a lawyer in India. Never fought a day in his life, Sprockett. Still, a goodish egg. Sure to help.'

I resisted the temptation to leap up and hug the mad old man. It would have shocked him.

'Strange old fruit, though,' he was saying. 'Wonder if he knows anything about hunting rights.'

*

I left Hector constructing a mantrap beneath a pear tree. In my breast pocket was the piece of paper on which he had scribbled Leopold Sprockett's address. He lived in Raven's Court, and from the outside his house looked much like all the others on the West London street. When I knocked, a rotund little man eventually opened the door and scowled at me with suspicion over his half-moon spectacles. He wore a grubby and ill-fitting three-piece suit, with what I imagined was a permanent shadow of dark stubble and oily black hair that stuck to his scalp. When I explained who I was, his expression softened and his face became friendlier. In hesitant words he confirmed himself to be Leopold Sprockett.

'Come in, come in. Of course. Pleased to meet you. Very pleased,' he said.

He ushered me into a house with no discernible walls. That is not to say, however, that the place was spacious and airy, for quite the opposite was true. Every room I entered, whether it was the parlour, cloakroom or stair landing, was filled from floor to ceiling with books. Over doors and under stairs, encasing dead plants and housing a territorial cat, books – stacked, shelved, thrown and lain – hid every conceivable patch of wall from my eyes.

I followed Sprockett upstairs and waded into a room where we found a small clearing between an armchair and a warming fireplace.

'Won't you sit down?' he said, pointing at the armchair with one hand and pushing a pile of books off a stool with the other. I sat and he set the stool in front of me before lowering himself and awkwardly perching on it.

He stared at me, eager that I reveal the purpose of my visit. I explained the situation and showed him the watch. Like Hector, Sprockett frowned at it too, but unlike my uncle, this man's expression was one full of curiosity.

'Very pleased to help,' he said as he turned it over in his hands. 'Very.'

When he arrived at the back of the watch he removed his spectacles and held them close to the writing, magnifying it for his weak eyes.

'Oh, yes,' he said and hooked the spectacles onto the end of his nose again. 'You're right about the region. Clever of you to spot. Don't recognise it, though.'

His broadening smile suggested that he thought this was a good thing.

'It's a curious stone, too,' he added, standing and returning the watch to me.

He reached over my shoulder and heaved a great ledger from a desk that was drowning in similarly giant tomes. He opened it and began to pace slowly around his stool as he leafed through the pages, a frown of concentration forming on his brow. He seemed to arrive where he wanted to, both in the book and the small area, and ceased all movement. His eyes narrowed and he ran a single finger down the page, before tapping it and muttering 'Yes, of course' under his breath. Then he began to say 'Johnson ninety-eight' over and over again as he leafed through the book some more and started to pace again.

'Johnson ninety-eight, Johnson ninety-eight, Johnson ninety-eight,' he whispered to himself.

When he settled on a new page, the process started all over again. When he tapped, the name and number changed.

'Roxton two three seven, Roxton two three seven.'

He gained momentum as he went. Every cycle of this strange ritual, and there were many, was faster than the last, his hand flicking the paper with ever greater speed, the 'shhht' of his finger sliding down the page louder and briefer, the temporary mantra of name and number chanted with more and more urgency and less and less intelligibility. 'Hass toothliate, Hass toothliate.' Shhht! 'Billier, wonfersev, Billier wonfersev.'

I became quite hypnotised by it all and was taken by surprise when all at once he stopped his circling and slammed the book shut, dropped it on the floor and said, 'Of course. Simcott. I should have known. Follow me.'

I did so, out of the room, up some more stairs and into another sea of books in an attic. I stood aside as Sprockett dived in. He looked at every book he picked up and then tossed them over his shoulder until he kept hold of one and stood up. Straightening his spectacles and flattening his hair to his scalp again, he pushed a beaten red leather edition under my nose.

'You see?' he said. 'Simcott. Should have known.' He grinned and shook his head and I followed him back downstairs.

He cleared one edge of the desk by pushing some books into the space we had previously occupied, dug a notebook out of a drawer and said, 'Now, let's see. If I could . . . ?'

He held out his hand. I extracted the watch from my pocket and gave it to him. Craning over his shoulder as he leaned on the desk, I watched him compare what was etched into the wood of the watch with the samples of weird and wonderful patterns that filled Simcott's pages.

As the minutes passed, Sprockett emitted a few satisfied hums and some frustrated tuts, and once said, 'Ah yes. Sheener,' but despite my stretching I could not see what he was writing down.

My impatience and excitement mounted.

In a matter of moments I would discover what it was that had driven McNaughton mad, the information Forrester had died for.

Perhaps the words Sprockett was scribbling would lead to the goal I could not prevent myself from imagining.

Finally he straightened, tore out the page and handed it to me.

On it he had written:

'Ghalat Taqdir, Watchmaker of Gilgit.'

I was stunned.

'I thought it would be Gilgit,' he said. 'Not many places they speak Shina. Even fewer write it, you know? Don't think I've ever come across it, actually. Ghalat Taqdir must be the chap's name.'

'Are you sure that's what it says?' I stuttered. 'The maker's mark? You can't have made a mistake?'

'Well, it's been known,' he replied. 'But not of Simcott. No, no. What you have there is an accurate translation. Comes as a bit of a surprise, does it?' His face creased sympathetically. 'It is a watch, remember. I wager you wouldn't dream of selling one of yours without your name on it somewhere.'

It was disappointment that stunned me. Disappointment and pity. McNaughton must have been mistaken. In this correct translation there was nothing one could consider worth killing for. Already a figure to be pitied, he now became a tragic one, a man driven to murder by a false promise. It had sucked me in, too. The unknown had excited me and appealed to my fanciful side. I had given meaning to things that meant nothing, just as he had done.

'There's always the stone, you know,' Sprockett continued, rousing me out of the quagmire of shattered dreams I was sinking into. 'It looks like jet, I should say. Perhaps even a black sapphire, if you're lucky. It could be valuable, you know.'

He was right. I straightened my sagging body and looked on the bright side. My soul was still my own, and maybe the stone *was* of some value. Not the heaps of gold and trays full of jewels I had allowed myself to envisage lying at the mystery's end, but perhaps some little compensation for my disappointment.

'Not only that, it's a very interesting one, too,' he continued. 'I've never seen its like before. Carved into some form of cat's eye, or a . . .'

The truth was unfortunate, certainly, but I remained alive, ready to hit upon an adventure that would not disappoint. That was something to be grateful for. This one had been the death of others.

I took a deep, musty breath. Sprockett was still talking.

'No, it couldn't be. I'm letting my imagination run away with me. It's the right area, but . . . No, young Cyril, ignore me. Just a fanciful old soldier, a bit like your uncle. He was a terrible bully, you know?'

I had no idea what he was rambling about and made no attempt to find out. I had decided that I was happy to be alive. I would return home, wait for the journalists to lose interest and then reopen the shop. The watch would take its place next to the Earnshaw as a curio for passing trade. At some point, just for the fun of it, I might even have the stone evaluated.

Apparently my change of heart had not yet illumined my face, however, for as I turned to leave, looking forward to filling my lungs with fresh air, Sprockett tried again to raise my spirits.

'You should be pleased, you know? They say Gilgit is an intriguing place. And if you find this Taqdir chap, you'll have an intelligent guide to the area. Yes, if he's able to write the language, he must be quite the learned fellow. But of course he would be – being a watchmaker and all.'

I stopped in my tracks and looked at him. He was grinning again. His thoughts on the stone were not the same as mine.

'You see, Cyril?' he went on. 'If anyone can, it's this Taqdir chap who'll be able to tell you where the thing came from. You're a lucky chap. India really is a thrilling country. The jewel in the crown, they call it. Well, make no mistake, the jewel itself is full of jewels – just like this one and better. This could be just the tip of the iceberg, if you get my meaning. I'd come with you myself if the years were on my side. Oh, yes, India served up many an adventure for your uncle and me.'

He proceeded to relate a series of misadventures he had shared with Hector. Though to all appearances I was listening contentedly to his words, in fact I did not dwell on the details of his stories at all.

Since learning the mundane truth of the writing on the watch, I had resigned myself to returning to my rooms to continue my life as before, with only the addition of a timepiece to show for the remarkable happenings of the past few days. Now, however, quite in passing, this timid man had made a suggestion which, if acted upon, would alter the very fabric of my life. To Sprockett, it apparently went without saying that I would travel to this place, Gilgit. To me, there in his study, engulfed by his books, the idea seemed absurd. Wherever it was, Gilgit sounded an awfully long way away. How would one travel to such a place? Who would tend the shop? When I hoped for a mystery to solve I had envisaged some detection and investigation to take place in and around London. A voyage to India, to whichever part Gilgit would be found, would be to conduct a goose chase for unknown, possibly non-existent, reasons. And all based on the hope that I would find more eyes? Which might be jet? Lunacy.

I returned to Amwell Street, ate my supper and retired. In bed, swallowed by the darkness, I turned the day's events over in my head. As I did so, what had escaped me in the light of day crashed into my mind with such a ferocious clarity that it made me sit bolt upright.

Quite suddenly, it all made sense. Sprockett had been right. The way to find the source of the stone was by asking Ghalat Taqdir. This was not something that had interested me, until I realised that that must have been precisely what McNaughton had wanted to do. Despite its apparent banality, the watchmaker's mark *did* hold information for which McNaughton could have been willing to kill. Sprockett had implied that the stone could be a mere pebble from a mountain of riches. It seemed a long shot to me; but what if McNaughton had thought otherwise? That shortened the probability significantly. And the Scot must have believed it, for what other explanation could there have been for his murderous behaviour? Why he believed it, I could not say. But what if Forrester thought so, too? Was that why he would not tell his assailant what he wanted to know? The piece of the puzzle McNaughton was missing was knowing where to start; who to talk to, and where to look for the pile. But I knew.

This was no goose chase, after all. The watch divulged everything, down to the narrowest detail, if only one understood how to interpret it – the stone, the continent from which it came, the town to seek, and once there, the man to ask. Without my even examining its mechanics, it was revealing a chain of secrets more complicated than any assembly of cogs, mainsprings, jewels, crowns and hands. As for India; to be plunged into the heat waist-deep in a mysterious adventure – why, that was precisely what I had been waiting for!

The watchmaker of my day-to-day existence had briefly got the better of me, but the explorer was roused just in time to cosh him over the head. Before the timesmith fell unconscious, however, he succeeded in demanding of the explorer that he confirm his suspicions before setting out on a dangerous adventure; and so, when at last morning arrived, I leapt from my bed, threw on my clothes and without pause for breakfast, made my way to Goldsmith's Jewellers on High Holborn. Mr Randle's thoroughness is renowned amongst the staff of Goldsmith's, and beyond, and he spent agonising minutes removing the stone from its clasps, pincering it with his tweezers, holding it up to the light, inspecting it through his loupe, then again from another angle, and again from another. He then painstakingly replaced it on the watch and carefully bent each clasp back into position, before removing his loupe and facing me.

He nodded grimly and slid the watch across his counter towards me.

'Black sapphire,' he announced. 'A most uncommon colouring . . .'

Before my legs gave way beneath me, before he could relay its approximate value even, I grabbed the thing, fled from the shop and, frantic with excitement, ran all the way to mine. That Sprockett had been correct was information enough.

The face of the Earnshaw was hinged, but secured by a lock. I located the small key on my chain and swung the face aside. In one piece, I removed the clock's mechanism. Behind it there was a hole that Fallon had dug into the wall long before my arrival as his apprentice. After five years of service, he had deemed me responsible enough to know of this depository's existence and revealed it to me as though it was one of the world's great unsolved mysteries. I had concealed my collection of antique timepieces in it ever since. I sank my arm into the darkness, shoulder deep, and pulled out a twill sack. It jangled as I put it into my Gladstone, a sound I feared others would hear all the way to the premises of Crannick, the Bloomsbury dealer, to whom I headed after returning the Earnshaw to its former, inactive glory.

I was going to him in order to sell a collection of rare and beautiful watches so that I could follow the trail left by another, valued so far only by death. It felt marvellous. Crannick and I were friendly and he gave me a good price, for a portion of which he agreed to check on the shop from time to time. I left him greedily inspecting my finest McCabe and hurried on to Ludgate Circus. I was acting on the nervous energy with which the conclusions of the previous evening and the sleepless night that followed had imbued me. It was a state that would only last for so long, and the explorer knew that if the watchmaker in me was allowed to consider the whole affair with his precise, logical mind, he would decide that my actions were foolhardy and not the thing to do at all. That was why I made my way to the offices of Thomas Cook and impatiently demanded passage to Gilgit.

The counter clerk looked at me blankly, and I do not blame him. I imagine I was quite a sight so early in the day, desperately proffering a grubby wad, probably sweating, my clothes dishevelled, demanding passage to a place of which he had never heard. When I managed to tell him that any ticket to India would do, and the sooner it left the better, he looked pleased to be able to tell me that there was a boat bound for Karachi in two days' time. I counted out my notes in a fluster and he handed me a stamped ticket. I took it from him with both hands and grasped it to my chest. I sighed with relief, and relaxed. There was no choice now. My passage to India was secured. Finally the explorer, who had languished in my mind for so long, would venture into the real world.

4

The Letters of
Sir Paul Lindley-Small

From the Valkyrie XII *steam vessel*
Suez, Egypt

5TH OCTOBER 1908

Cyril,

Dancers, my friend, are a supple bunch; their pliability is their profession. Imagine my glee when I discovered that this was the trade of the fillies I saw embarking in Dwarka as I took a final landbound dram. And Siamese to boot. Yet, once more, I am writing to you. You have heard of temple dancers, I am sure – a tragic breed whose dextrous femininity is wasted on unappreciative deities. Such a situation calls my gallantry into action – and so, if my powers of persuasion do not succeed, nor my charm, for the good of these poor maidens, I may well have to unveil my own divinity. As this revelation will need to be carefully timed – after cocktails, but before supper – I find myself presently unoccupied; and with the urge to tell you more of what has pulled me over the sparkling waters of the Arabian Ocean, round the Horn of Africa, up past the ancient civilisations of the Red Sea, and sees me now arriving at the manmade cranny of Suez.

If you cut a person open, somewhere between his belly and his heart you will find an old-fashioned set of two-pan weighing scales. Value gets put in one pan, effort in the other. Each man's is calibrated differently – by blood, experience, and, I find, The Glenlivet can have a certain amount of say. But common to all is that when effort turns to weighty risk, value must stack upward in order to tip the balance. Once or twice in a lifetime, however, the value of an item is such that what one must place in the effort tray is any and all means necessary, and that is the situation in which I currently find myself. Gold- and gem-encrusted treasures might warrant it. Lost scrolls and holy relics can likewise fetch a pretty price, to the devout or the desperate. A cure for consumption might tempt some, the true secret of alchemy others. But what I seek is none of these. What I seek is a living creature.

How can a mere animal be so precious? I hear you ask.

Well, the King Cobra is a rare enough creature. Indeed, while I have come across discarded skins in the jungles of Mysore and the rainforests of the Western Ghats, I confess I have never encountered one in its wild habitat. I did once know a boy of seven who danced a tranced waltz with one such in the market squares of Madras for the entertainment and the rupees of others; they are popular amongst the natives, so a decent example can fetch a good few pounds from the right buyer. They are awesome, intelligent beasts, and can grow to twenty feet in length when left unrestricted by man's baskets. But they are also violently unfriendly, capable of lifting their bodies high enough off the ground to look even the tallest of men directly in the eyes before attacking him with fangs as long and as broad as your finger and sharper than a physician's needle, which in a single bite can administer enough poison to kill an entire village. Not only that, they can see heat and growl like tigers, too. So in their case risk heavily outweighs potential worth, and I would certainly not set out across the seven seas in chase of one.

But if I am after a priceless creature, you will enquire, why ever am I enriching your life with this thrilling information concerning the only moderately valuable King Cobra, when it has nothing at all to do with my hunt? Ah, but you see, my boy – it does. Just not in its usual form; and therein lies the animal's value.

There is, amongst the many legends that surround the King Cobra, one that tells of the bird-god Garuda most deviously tricking a Naga, a breed of divine cobra, into carnal coiling with a common cat. The result was a creature – part-serpent, part-feline – rejected by all, dangerous, angry and vengeful. Although the offspring resembled cat more than snake, it did, however, retain the reptile's hood, its fangs and venom, its flicking forked tongue, the long tail, and that symbol of infinity upon the rear of its head, bestowed upon its forebear by the Buddha himself for providing shade from the sun. Legend speaks of this lithe and velvety form prowling the country by night and sinking its fangs deep into the flesh of those it found, just as its Naga ancestors did. Their limbs blackened by the venom, its victims were rendered paralysed, incapable of moving or communicating, but still quite horrifyingly alive, aware of all that went on in the world they had so nearly departed, forced to observe it, to hear it and smell it, to feel it if it touched them – and for all time, never to die, never to reincarnate.

After forty-four of our generations, this half-breed was banished by Vishnu to die in the desert. What became of it in the sands of Rajasthan is not known, for it was never seen again, but certainly it did not expire before being joined by a feline with whom it mated and started a line.

Ridiculous, the apostles of Darwin have told me. Obscene, others have said. Satanic, the Christians cry; blasphemous, the Moslems; idiocy, unknowing Hindus. But they were not in Ishkuman with us, my boy, and do not know the truth of such twisted, illegitimate demigods. They would not believe, as I know you will, that it is that mythical creature's descendent that sits upon my scales, pinning the pan marked value to the ground.

But the clock strikes. It is finally time for cocktails aboard this craft, and desire as I may to write more, the delicious company that awaits me in the dining room would deem it most ungodly of me to keep them waiting.

I remain, as ever, your loyal friend,

Lindley-Small

5

THE NOTEBOOKS OF
CYRIL KING

1893

At Sea

My tasks were not complete, but the last of them could be conducted without such feverish urgency. The following morning I made my way to the British Library and in its grandiose foyer I told the clerk that, as a watchmaker, I was there to research rare timepieces. It took me some time to convince him of my credentials, but after some persuasion he admitted me. Though in a way I *was* there to research a watch, more precisely it was my aim to learn as much as I could about my destination.

In all their many miles of books the only interesting titbits I could unearth were these: Gilgit was the main settlement of what was once Dardistan, in the northwestern corner of India. Squeezed among the foothills of the Karakoram mountains, in the shadow of a giant peak called Rakaposhi, where the Indus and Gilgit rivers meet, it was a wild place few Englishmen had visited. Indeed, it had only lately been leased by the British from the Maharajah of Jammu and Kashmir. To its east was Baltistan, to the west the Afghans, and to the north, China. According to one author, the temperament of the people thereabouts varied with

which side of a valley they lived on – those on the shadowed side
being distinctly more morose and serious in disposition than those
in the sun. All were treacherous to a degree that would appear
incredible to a casual observer of their happy and genial manners.
The natives were constantly warring; battling over land, religion,
virtue and loyalty, and capable of a barbarism akin to butchery,
whether Hindu, Sikh or Mussulman.

A Chinese traveller named Hsuan Tsang long ago described the
place thus: *'Perilous were the roads and dark the gorges. Sometimes the
pilgrim had to pass by loose cords, sometimes by light stretched iron
chains. Here there were ledges hanging midair; there flying bridges across
abysses; elsewhere paths cut with the chisel or footings to climb by.'* A
final dusty old tome informed me that Gilgit lay in country rich
with exotic minerals; ore and stones found only in the earth's highest reaches – a fact that boded well for my theories.

I could ascertain no more. The little that I had, and the maps of
which I traced copies, told me quite enough, however. The rest I
would have to discover on arrival.

On my return to Amwell Street I removed my Gladstone from
the wardrobe and placed in it the following items: a lightweight
linen suit; my sturdiest pair of brown leather boots; six shirts, vests
and undergarments; a portable shaving kit and a bar of soap. I was
certain of the inadequacy of this collection, but how could I predict
what a trip such as this one would require? Following a fitful night's
sleep I rose to my alarm clock at five. Before departing I took my
pipe and tobacco from the mantelpiece and paused to look at the
rooms which had housed a watchmaker, wondering what more of
his possessions might prove useful. My eye was caught by a spyglass
I had once acquired from a naval gentleman in part payment for a
repair. I took it from the windowsill and departed that loyal home,
reaching Waterloo in time to board the 6.50 South. I settled with
my pipe in an empty second-class compartment, and the modest
beauties of Southern England passed my window unheeded. The
first step of my long journey was under way.

*

We pulled into Southampton in what seemed like minutes, and there, for the first time in my life, I stepped from the safety of my home shores, and boarded the peeling decks of a steamer called the *Zephyr*. I hung from the railings, waving at anybody whose eye I caught, and threw kisses to young ladies, whether they saw me or not. I was no longer a watchmaker and did not have to behave like one. I was off, and I was free.

The crowds cheered us as we weighed anchor and slipped away from the dock, but soon enough all that could be heard was the chopping of waves and the occasional bellow from the foghorn; and all that could be seen were the diminishing cliffs of the coastline and the seagulls plummeting into our wake. Presently, even they disappeared.

The sea voyage that followed did not bode well for what lay ahead. It was more difficult to buck the watchmaker than I had imagined, I am afraid. In books and tales such journeys are enlivened with sea monsters, pirates and romance. The majority of mine was spent in my tiny cabin nursing a face the wrong side of green. There, all I fought was the increasingly strong urge to abandon this folly and disembark before we left European waters. A *soupçon* of romance was all that equated this part of my trip with the thrill of those fictional voyages – but an unwelcome one, I hasten to add. It came in the form of a woman, herself something of a sea monster, who deemed the allure of cosmetics and perfume preferable to the cleansing powers of soap and water. I ignored her advances as best I could and instead concentrated my reddening cheeks on the rummy I was playing with her husband. He was the distant closest I came to a pirate, since he told me he owned a parrot and took me for nearly five shillings before my knee was seized beneath the table and I leapt to my feet, called the game to a close and ran to my cabin, pursued by a trio of fears – of the woman, of her husband and of the imminent reappearance of the buttery halibut we had enjoyed at supper.

*

The five weeks I spent at sea were gruelling. I failed to locate any sign of sea legs about my person and our vessel arrived in the sweltering port of Karachi not a moment too soon. March was ending by the time the ship rumbled to dock and, as the spray settled, the gangplank was lowered. I made my way towards it gratefully, through the hollering crew, and paused at the top. From the deck, I had an elevated view that would soon be lost. Before I put foot to land, my hungry eyes wanted to absorb the sight, for here before me was a new world.

The wide thoroughfare between the water and an endless row of bursting warehouses was a heaving mass of people, an ocean of colour and noise churning around the docked ships, baskets and crates of cargo floating on its surface, horses and their carts wading through it.

Suddenly I was shoved onto the gangplank by another passenger and made my way down. Once I was on firm ground, I saw that it was the overly familiar woman who had administered the push, though now she ignored me and stepped into the throng, swinging a parasol from side to side to clear her path. I heard her emit a shrill gasp of horror when a member of the crowd touched her, and her husband, tipping his panama to me, skipped after her to attend to the situation.

As the remaining passengers disembarked, I stood to one side, close to the slippery quayside and the muddy waters below. Despite the heat and the discomfort of perspiration oozing through my grubby suit, I grinned with all the inanity of a fascinated foreigner.

All I could see was a blur of bodies, of saris and turbans, rushing to and fro. None of them paid me the least attention. All at once, a loneliness pervaded my excitement. It presented itself only fleetingly, but to feel so alone in the company of so many was an odd sensation indeed. To find myself entirely unconnected to any other being was not unpleasant, only new; a feeling I attributed to my sudden freedom from responsibility. That moment, the only duty I had was to myself, and that duty entailed making my way to Gilgit, so I moved forward to enter the fray. I could find no crack in its liquid shell, however, and I was buffeted by the stream of people. I tried a second time, and a third and fourth, before standing back to reconsider my course of attack. I crouched. I could crawl in, I thought, through the legs. But then I would be crushed by the stampede. Perhaps diving was a better option. I stood and looked behind me. There was no room for a run-up, and besides, gymnastics was not my sporting forte. Cricket was more my game and no use here. I put my hands on my hips and frowned at this conundrum. Before I could come to a solution, the throbbing mass spat forth a short man, who landed before me and just about found his balance. His dark grey clothes, like the man himself, were worn, torn and filthy, but seemed once to have formed a uniform, for there was a scruffy stripe on his left shoulder. Still swaying, he swung a hand wildly to his forehead.

'Captain Spicer, at your service, sir.'

His face was brown, creased and stubbled beneath the dirt, the whites of his hazel eyes bloodshot. He shook my hand enthusiastically and leaned towards me.

'You look like you could do with a hand. New arrival, eh?'

His breath was strong with drink.

'Well, don't you worry. Captain Spicer's here to help you. Take you wherever you want to go. Come on.'

He swooped his hand in the air and pointed onwards as if leading a military assault, then threw himself at the writhing sea of people and melted into it. I had no idea who he was, but he had opened a fissure, so I leapt in after him. In the confusion of the whirly-gig, I briefly caught sight of him as he slithered out of view. He had changed completely in these new surroundings. Gone was the teetering drunkard, replaced by an eel, slipping around the people effortlessly, sliding left and right among the sailors, peddlers and passengers as though they were so much water. In a moment I had lost the strange fellow entirely. I was swept up by the current and thrown wherever it pleased, powerless, without a clue where I was moving. Grinning faces, shouting mouths, brilliant oranges and yellows spun before my eyes. I could not see the *Zephyr*; I had no idea which way was which, or where I wanted to go. I was sinking, about to drown in this bright blaring whirlpool of colour and sweat. In a desperate attempt to keep myself afloat, I leapt up into the air. There, towering over the waving bodies, above their heads, higher even than the bobbing luggage, was the face of Captain Spicer, quite suddenly and unnervingly a Goliath sizing up a populace of Davids. A small, drunken god, he decided that today was not my day, and stretched forth a hand. With a final lunge, I threw myself towards him and caught hold of his wrist. He dragged me onto the bench of a cart that was standing in the shadow of a warehouse. Half leaping and half falling from the wheel on which he had been perched, he took his place at my side, picked up the reins and geed his horse. I gasped my gratitude for his intervention, and set about recapturing my breath.

Most of the people before us instinctively made way for the beast and its burden. Spicer shouted at those who did not, and let them feel his boot if he could reach.

'Now then, young sir,' he said, turning to me and allowing his horse to navigate its own way through the people. 'Where can Spicer take you?'

'I'm heading for Gilgit,' I said. 'In the north—'

'*Geddaht the way!*' he shouted at a pedestrian. Then he wiped sweat from his brow with his cuff and smiled apologetically. 'Are you now?' he said more calmly, as though I had made a joke, even. 'Good for you, lad. Good for you.'

He turned to the horse and flicked the reins in encouragement. 'Gilgit! Very well. To the station with us, then.'

As he guided the horse through the crowds, Spicer gave me a commentary on what was being traded and by whom. Spices, sugars, cloth and livestock were everywhere I looked along the quayside, and traders, buyers and legmen communicated as one throbbing cauldron of noise and gesticulation.

Soon enough, we made our way into the city, where the roads were as busy as the docks, but dissected by a swerving stream of traffic, until we turned and entered yet another area bustling with people, carriages and wagons.

'The terminus,' Spicer announced. 'Pandemonium; but if you're going north, you'll have to put up with it, for it's the only place you'll find passage.'

He led me into the station building where, knowing the local tongue, he bought me a ticket with money I gave him; then to the platform where he pushed me into a carriage, already so crowded that men were hanging on like monkeys on a tree. I leaned from a window and proffered my hand in thanks. He shook it.

'To Peshawar, then out,' he said, over the chaos and commotion. 'From there hire a man to take you by cart to your destination. Pay him well but not too well. You don't want to look like a rich bugger.'

'Thank you, Captain.'

'Don't thank me, lad. It's been a pleasure. But you listen to old Spicer, now. He's been here a long time – knows the country, knows the people. They don't do things quite the same as we do. Up where you're going it's even less civilised than here. And where it's uncivilised they appreciate the fundamentals. Put it this way: if you're ever tempted to steal from 'em, whether it's a horse, food, water, gold or a woman, don't – be they Dard, Dogra or Sikh, they'll have your head off before you know it. Not that a gentleman such as yourself would ever think of doing such a thing.'

He smiled. Then, as if remembering something, his expression became serious and, my hand still clasped in his, he pulled me down towards him so I was bent double over the window. The breath of his whisper condensed in my ear. 'More than that, if you ever see any of them folk fighting, don't step in. Even if it's a lovers' tiff and you fear for the damsel. Even if a friend's in need, don't get involved. Take old Spicer's advice. Just leave. Move on to the next town. It's the only way I've survived so long, and it's the only way you will.'

The locomotive's whistle sounded and he released me, smiled again and slapped my shoulder jovially.

'Off with you now. And good luck,' he said, raising his hand to wave and guffawing, 'I'm afraid you'll need it!'

With a cry from the engine, the train lurched into action and his laughing figure was swallowed by the steam.

I had not discovered the nature of his captaincy, or indeed if he was a captain at all and not just a soak in a captain's clothes. But then enough captains have been soaks, and soaks captains; and whatever the truth, the wisdom he had vouchsafed to me smacked of the adventure and intrigue I had travelled so far to find.

I pushed my way into the carriage in search of a place to sit.

I could not see the carriage for men, let alone seats. Spicer had bought me third-class passage, promising me that doing so would make me a less desirable target for thieves. I think I might have shouldered that risk as fair exchange for comfort, for when finally I managed to locate a perch, it was more wedged between the window and the man next to me than on the seat.

The shuffling iron snake edged its way along the banks of the serene and holy River Indus. The city gave way to open land and we travelled with yellow dryness to our left and irrigated green to our right until we reached Hyderabad. There, the mighty river guided us westwards, and we moved from Sindh into Balochistan, winding between the Thar Desert and the Kirthar range.

Spicer had been right – I was quite safe. My fellow passengers were fascinated and excited that an Englishman would be travelling in their company. In varying versions of English, but each as keen as the other, they explained to me all that we encountered, from the several religions of the populace, to the clothes they wore, to the food I bought from vendors, to simple examples of language. I could not sleep for people pointing out something new to be seen on the road beside the railway, a coarse path of dust defined by years of use, busy with walkers and mules making their way along the edge of the broad waterway. From time to time, both train and caravan drew to an unexpected halt, for a call to prayer or an immovable herd of livestock, but more often for no discernible reason at all. On these occasions, I was surprised that nobody became unduly heated, since unwillingly stationary gentlemen were frequently reduced to common thuggery on English trains. Rather, we were all pleased to stop; and ate, or alighted from the train and grazed and talked or bathed away the day's heat in the river with the pedestrians.

We passed into Bahawalpur and from there into the Punjab. At Multan we parted ways with the river and made our way to Lahore. Through all these places, whose appearances did nothing to dilute the exotic and wondrous images their names bred in my mind, the roads and trains continued to be used by all and sundry, a procession moving perpetually over the country which in seven days' time would deliver me to the invigorating filth of Peshawar.

6

THE LETTERS OF
SIR PAUL LINDLEY-SMALL

From the Valkyrie XII *steam vessel*
Cadiz, Spain

1ST NOVEMBER 1908

And so to Spain, my boy, the native country of the gentleman I seek; but still not a hair of him, I'm afraid. We shall sail northwards then, into the chillier climes of the country of my birth. I hope he has not disembarked there. I have not returned for many a year, as you well know, and I have no desire to do so now. My knighthood may buy me entry into London society and its clubs; but there is still a chance I might run afoul of the General and his minions as they slowly decompose in the Chesterfield chairs of Pall Mall. They might not recognise the name, but I'll wager they'd not forget the face. Therefore I choose to conduct the relationship which maintains the good name I earned at a distance. As ever, I shall not be presenting the fruits of my labours to the curator of the British Museum's Cabinet of Curiosities in person. In fact, I shall not be presenting anything to that august institution this time around. The Princes of the Raj have more lucre than they know what to do with, and when the animal is mine, I shall employ it not for the bolstering of respectability or reputation, but for the feverish bidding of the Maharajahs. Such is the wonder of India. The blighters love to compete with one another. I only feel for the poor beggars left to rot in Siam, where a dancer's devotion to all things holy is as rigid as her body is bendy.

Enough! I write to take my mind off such things and concentrate it on the matter in hand, though it must be said, the beginning of this journey had its roots in my enjoying the carnal hospitality of the Maharajah of Bharatpur's wife – that is until her husband turned against me. It is a pity that I am no longer a welcome guest in that ruler's territory, for Bharatpur is a place much to my liking, as indeed was the man himself, at first.

The city is one full of life, intrigue and possibilities, and to start with we got on famously, wagering heavily on bull races together, enjoying private performances by the city's more nature-defying entertainers and playing for high stakes at the card tables with other likeminded fellows long into the night. We would bet on how long a Sadhu could lie on his bed of nails, whether or not a chap would successfully levitate from the ground, how long someone could keep their head in a cauldron of boiling oil, how far another could walk over hot coals. We would wince when a man put a hook into his flesh, but speculate how much weight the hook could bear before it tore from his skin. In other words, the kind of activities any men of leisure and means enjoy together in these parts.

The Maharajah did not mind losing to such as I, and I have won more than money at the card table in his mighty palace. However, our relationship went from civil to quite the reverse when he discovered that his sceptre, a piece of loud golden beauty topped by an impressive sapphire, was missing. I was staying with him and his gaggle of wives and children at the time, and their hospitality was quite to my liking, as I say. However, when he burst into my luxurious state rooms and accused me of pilfering his sceptre, my liking for him instantly soured. I can quite understand his displeasure at seeing the head of his most beautiful wife popping out from under the covers of my bed when she should have been with the others in his harem's compound – I did not win *her* favours, after all – but really, one cannot forgive his raging that I had never ceased stealing from him since the day we met. Whether or not I took the thing is quite beside the point. I sent him from my rooms and took my leave of his wife with little, but some, further ado.

Here, I thought, was a man in need of a lesson. The opportunity to teach him that lesson came in the form of Sadirah, whom I met in a cave not far out of Jaisalmer. Guided there by a young lad in exchange for a handful of rupees, I took refuge in the cavern because I needed shelter from the wrath of a businessman and his associates, following the chap's investment in a mine some way to the south.

At first, I did not realise that I was not alone, but when I struck a match with which to light my pipe, I saw that I was standing next to a man who sat cross-legged meditating on the ground, his hands on his knees. He wore a red *dhoti*, a nose ring and bangles, and crimson flowers were woven into his knotted hair. Pale, dry mud covered his face, apart from his forehead, where a vermilion blot of paint was located – a *tilak*. He was, I knew immediately, a fakir, a breed of holy man who through strength of mind alone can achieve unlikely feats. I had watched such displays on many occasions with the Maharajah. Doing my very best not to disturb him, I smoked my pipe and waited for the hue and cry to settle down. However, the sweet fragrance of Balkan tobacco is enough to distract even the most devout of men, and after only a minute or two, the fakir came spluttering to life.

'My good man, I'm awfully sorry to intrude,' I said in genuine apology, for these chaps take their meditation very seriously.

It took him some seconds to focus his eyes upon me, but when he finally spoke, he demanded, 'What are you doing in my cave?'

I explained my plight and his expression softened.

'I am sorry,' he said. 'I have been meditating now for twelve days. One is quite disorientated when one comes to.'

When he said twelve days, he did not mean that he had been meditating for the sunlight hours of twelve days, sleeping at night and breaking for food, but that he had been in that same position for *twelve whole days*, dead to the world but alive to his god. He would not have consumed a thing in all those days, so I pulled some bread from my knapsack and offered it to him. He nibbled at it as I took a draught from my flask.

'I say,' said I. 'How do you know it was for twelve days that you were asleep? It's dark in here.' And indeed, very little sunlight did filter into the place.

'I was not asleep, I was meditating,' he corrected me. 'And while I was meditating I was told that even though I was hoping to do so for forty days, I would be awoken after twelve. It is not what I desired, but how can I complain?'

Of course, I have always been sceptical as to the authenticity of the holy men's accomplishments, but enjoyed the shows nonetheless. A man swallowing a worm and making it crawl from his eye-socket is impressive, be it genuine or illusory. However, I had never before encountered a man who could place himself into a state of dormant meditation for forty days; this was truly incredible.

'Have you done this before?' I asked.

'Oh, yes,' he said proudly. 'I once did it for six months. Very easy.'

Six months, Cyril! He was claiming that he had done nothing but sit unmoving for a full half-year. Remarkable.

'My dear man,' I said, the cogs of my brain turning with renewed vigour, 'perhaps I can arrange for you to see your full forty days through without interruption. I would dearly like to aid you after so thoughtlessly bursting in on you today.'

'My new friend,' he beamed, for we were getting on famously, 'it was not your doing. It was not even an interruption, and quite beyond our powers to prevent it.'

'Well, then, at least let me show you my good intentions by aiding you in your solitude,' I requested, for I was not now to be put off. 'We shall stage a demonstration of your talents.'

'Oh sir, I cannot show you how this is done,' he replied, sorry to disappoint me.

'You needn't *show* me, dear man. You need only to *do* it, and, though I am sure it will not interest a sage such as yourself, there will be great remuneration involved.'

My lightning imagination had, you see, already hatched a plan.

'That is very good, sir,' he said, smiling broadly. 'My name is Sadirah.'

'And mine is Lindley-Small,' I cried back at him as our hands joined. 'And it is to Bharatpur with us!'

Though it is against the chosen life of a fakir to do anything in luxury, I insisted that we travel first class on the train between Jaisalmer and Bharatpur, and I must say that, as we planned the exploits that would take place in the Maharajah's palace, I was surprised how easily Sadirah settled into the life afforded us by the mining businessman's investment. By the time we arrived at our destination, I was astonished but very pleased that he had even chosen to join me in regular snifters of the golden ambrosia without which, as you very well know, I travel nowhere. His indulging, however, was not to last.

When we approached the Maharajah's palace, I was unsurprised to find the gleaming tips of twelve spears held to my Adam's apple. At the other end were twelve of the Maharajah's personal guards, each snarling at the sight of me, their impressive red-feathered crests a-quiver. Sadirah was clearly shaken by this welcome, but I calmed his nerves by pushing the blades down, and with a smile requested that one of these chaps fetch their master. The blades quickly returned to my throat, but one guard did disappear, and shortly the rotund ruler appeared, grinning with glee.

'You are foolish to have returned, Lindley-Small. Or are you desirous of becoming a eunuch?' he cackled from the elaborate battlements before descending to the courtyard where we were held.

'Don't be a fool, your highness,' I said, visibly confusing him with a deft mix of superiority and supplication. 'I have come back of my own volition.'

'And why were you stupid enough to do that, pray?' he spat.

'If truth be told, your highness,' I said, 'I have travelled far and wide, and neither before nor since have I met someone so much to my liking as you. My friend, we are two of a kind, you and I. In short, I missed you.'

'We are certainly not two of a kind. You are a liar and a thief!'
he shouted, puffing his chest out, though he was certainly pleased
to hear that he had been on my mind.

'Maharajah, if it is your wife you—'

'A wife?' he yelled. 'Of those I have many; but there is only one
Jalman Sceptre – and thanks very much to you, I no longer have
it!'

'My friend, we certainly *are* two of a kind,' I laughed. 'From
where did you first get that sceptre?'

If possible, his chest inflated even more, and he began to strut
like a peacock in front of his hen guardsmen, who were now standing to attention in a row.

'I cut the throat of the Rajah of Jalman Palace and took the
crown from his dead head and the sceptre from his dead hand. It
is mine. You will return it or you shall be castrated and fed to the
hounds.' With this he stopped and stared at Sadirah. 'Who is this
fellow?'

'I am so glad you asked,' said I, smooth as ever. 'Do you believe
a man can live with neither food nor water for forty days?'

'What rubbish do you speak?' the Maharajah scoffed.

'My friend, I have a proposition for you, one I know you will
relish.'

And so I put it to him that we would bury Sadirah in the ground
for forty days and forty nights. If, after those forty nights, Sadirah
was dead, I would return the sceptre to the Maharajah and he
could do with me what he pleased. I was certain he would release
me, for he greatly appreciated the sporting nature that we shared,
and would sorely miss me, were I fed to his dogs as proposed. On
the other hand, I said, if Sadirah were alive and well, I would keep
the sceptre and in addition gain its attendant crown.

At first, he seemed in two minds about the wager, rightly wondering what, if I possessed the sceptre, was to stop him from
torturing me into giving it back to him. I reminded him that I was
a veteran of the British Army and that I could therefore withstand
any amount of pain lain upon me. If he were to torture me, I told
him, he was certain never to see his beloved sceptre again. The

Maharajah finally agreed to my terms, and the date of the interment was set for seven days hence.

And now, my boy, I must sign off, for tonight I am to dine at the
Captain's table.

Your friend,

Lindley-Small

7

THE NOTEBOOKS OF CYRIL KING

1893

The Watchmaker of Gilgit

The station in Peshawar was as the one in Karachi, but perhaps a degree cooler, and kites and buzzards circled in the clear sky as I disembarked. What they awaited, I did not know.

Finding a man to take me further was another ordeal of making my way through tightly packed bodies, inspecting all those offering carriage, but eventually I happened upon a man with a kindly face. When I announced that I wanted to be taken to Gilgit, he glanced at his horse, a tired-looking beast whose ribs protruded uncomfortably through stretched skin. It looked more used to taking people around the town than up into the mountains, and so I told him I would go elsewhere.

'No, no, sahib!' He slapped the horse's haunches, which barely registered the impact. 'We go. Easy. I am Saandh Ali.'

As though by announcing his identity he had obliterated doubts possessing both our minds, he wrenched the Gladstone from my hand and secreted it under the tarpaulin covering his cart. He seemed friendly, and looked as though he might be handy in a scrape, and since he agreed what I thought was a reasonable price,

I climbed up and took my place on the bench by his side. Before us was the tired, dust-covered horse. Beyond it was the road along which the animal was miraculously to bear us. Saandh Ali saw the disbelief in my eyes as I contemplated the rear end of his mare.

'Very strong. She never stop. We go?' he asked.

I nodded and swallowed hard, trying to wet my throat with saliva that had quite suddenly disappeared. Saandh Ali smiled and flicked the reins. The mare broke into a slow walk. A course for the north had been set, by driver or horse I could not tell. The only certainty was that, at the end of the road, Ghalat Taqdir unknowingly awaited me.

*

To start with we headed east towards the Indus, following the railway back along the way I had come. The first night I insisted on staying in a guesthouse, not sharing Saandh Ali's preference for sleeping beside his cart. However, following a narrow escape from a group of gentlemen whose initial charm belied their uncongenial motives, I decided thereafter to join my reassuringly solid driver outside. There, safety was to be found in numbers with like-minded travellers, whom he proudly told of our epic journey. It was not long before we bade our new friends a fond farewell, however, and cut from the road, heading north into the hills and across the Kabul river.

From there we passed through Mardan and then Malakand, where Saandh Ali advised in his broken English that I conceal my race as much as I was able, for there the attention that I had attracted in other places was likely to be less amicable. In Swat we entered a world of high mountains, green meadows and clear waters. In Besham Qala we found the Indus once again and followed it into Kohistan, where the Hindukush, Karakoram and Himalayas meet, its waters gushing with a power that had sliced passage through the monumental rock of the mountains. By its winding route eventually we passed into Jammu, where the trails proved as inhospitable and empty as the roads of the south were teeming.

We struggled along paths little wider than our wagon, and some perilously narrower. The mountains stretched higher and steeper and shrank the sky until it was no more than a strip of blue above us. Settlements grew smaller and sparser, the green of vegetation rarer, eclipsed by the brown, grey and black of rock and the white and blue of glacier and snow. Up here the sun's rays possessed an intensity quite different from the sultry heat of the lower country. They beat upon me just as fiercely, yet the pure crisp air I took into my lungs was as cool and fresh as water. A most bizarre thing! Looking up at the furthest peaks, I was grateful that I had not yet travelled high enough to enter the realm of real extremes, where snow and ice form regardless of the burning sun's demands that they should not.

The few people we came across were guarded and suspicious. They watched us from their campfires as we passed, wondering what could bring two such strangers to the very upper limits of the earth. When night fell, we were occasionally obliged to share their shelter, for the passes seldom offered cover, and as I drifted I watched the rambunctious Saandh Ali melt their reserve and call them into dancing around the fire with him. When the flames had died and the people slept, I listened as the mountains spoke in their rumbling tones of rock falls and distant avalanches.

In the damp and misty mornings, before the sun had evaporated the clouds that gathered in the valleys under cover of darkness, we continued, alone again, around the remains of rock falls, through the shadow of the mighty Nanga Parbat, past glaciers to the heavens and crevices to the hells. Further and further into the mountains we wound, higher and higher, each turn narrower and more precarious than the last, until finally, one morning, after twenty-one days' travel, the green of cultivated soil greeted our bleary eyes. There before us, beyond rows of fruit trees, nestled in the generous nape of the peaks, overlooking a dramatic confluence of rivers and enveloped in a cloud of dust churned by channels of wind rushing down the valleys, was our destination. Gilgit.

Saandh Ali drew the cart to a stop at the end of an antiquated wooden bridge that passed high over the rivers where they joined.

Moisture rising from the violently clashing water below made it wet and slippery, and in the wind it creaked most alarmingly, but it led directly into the hive of dust that called itself Gilgit. There was not another person in sight.

'I go no further,' Saandh Ali said. 'It is not safe.'

He gestured at the bridge, but the fear in his eyes was directed over the gorge towards the town. I would have to continue without him. I paid him the sum we had agreed, adding as much as I could afford from my store of rupees, retrieved my Gladstone from the cart, and we shook hands. I had grown to like this man who had valiantly brought me so far from his home, and it seemed an inadequate way of showing my gratitude, but there was nothing more to be done, so I turned and and stepped onto the bridge. Making my way in a slow zigzag of careful footsteps, I reached the other side and stopped before the brown maelstrom cloaking the town. I turned and watched Saandh Ali's cart disappearing into the mountains. Though I was quite alone, the racket of the water and the wind made the place seem as claustrophobic as the docks in Karachi. They grew louder and louder in my ears as I stared at the shrinking figures of the driver and his horse. They were returning to civilisation.

I took a deep, dusty breath, covered my mouth with the sleeve of my shirt and stepped into the cloud.

I could see almost nothing. The dust blasted my eyes and they filled with tears, blurring any pockets of clarity before these too were obliterated. I managed to discern the outline of a street, but the storm thickened with every foot it travelled, picking up every loose particle it touched. Briefly, I saw a row of crude structures with canvas walls. One billowed up like a sail in a squall and momentarily exposed a collection of startled figures before swallowing them once more. I squeezed my eyes tightly shut and tried to push on, but it was hopeless. There could have been a chasm one pace in front of me and I would not have known. If I was going to die, I wanted my end to come in the pursuit of the treasures Ghalat Taqdir would direct me towards, not because I was too stubborn to take refuge from hideous weather.

I moved to the edge of the road, towards the flapping I could hear. Only when my outstretched hands touched the material did I dare to open my eyes. I looked up and vaguely saw a wooden sign that bore a painting of a teacup before locating a split in the canvas and pushing my way through.

The place I found myself standing in was so dark that, despite the storm outside, a dazzling pulse of light followed me in, as though a photographer had ignited his magnesium. In the flash, before the darkness enveloped them once more, I saw several figures instinctively covering their eyes, looking to see who was foolish enough to expose their teashop to the weather. I stood motionless at the entrance until my eyes adjusted to the lowest of lights, illuminating a stark interior of low wooden tables on earthen ground. In the far and darkest end of the establishment, I spotted a man tending a stove and headed towards him.

Threatening stares were skewered my way and the shadowy figures lining the place fell silent as I approached. Their eyes followed me as they concealed the rest of their faces with their headscarves and retreated from the stove's revealing glow.

'One cup of tea, please,' I said in as deep and sure a voice as I could muster.

The man stirring eyed me through the gloom before reaching behind him and retrieving a small porcelain cup. To rid it of dust, he banged the cup on the box he sat on and then ladled it full of tea. As I paid him, I noticed that the box was in fact a chest, a crate clearly labelled 'The Glenlivet'. What's more, it had sounded full. I did not stop to wonder what a crate of Scotland's finest was doing in a place as remote as this. This was an opportunity too good to be ignored.

'Could I?' I asked, indicating the chest.

I proffered what I hoped was a generous number of rupees and lit my face with what I hoped was a winning smile. Alas, one was too much and the other not enough.

'You are not the sahib. This belongs to small sahib. It is not for you,' was his response.

He took sufficient rupees for the tea and returned his attention to his neighbours. I walked away with my cup and their whispers recommenced. Only when I seated myself in one of the tenebrous corners did I see his companions lower their scarves from their faces, laughing mockingly with one another.

My failure to hit it off with such men came as no surprise. I was nonetheless disappointed, not to mention slightly unsettled, to discover that an Englishman could attract so little regard. With my confidence knocked, I found myself smiling nervously whenever I failed to avoid contact with the faceless staring eyes. To busy myself I lit my pipe and concentrated on my tea as I tried to ruminate on what a small sahib, which I took to mean a child, could want with a crate of finest twelve-year-old single malt whisky.

The answer did not come to me then and by the time I had drained the diminutive cup, I had regained enough pluck to return to the proprietor and his chums, though this time it was not whisky I wanted from them.

'I say,' I began firmly. 'Could you tell me where I might find the premises of a watchmaker hereabouts? I'm looking for a man by the name of Ghalat Taqdir.'

I had got his attention this time.

'You want to meet Ghalat Taqdir?'

'That's right,' I answered. 'The watchmaker.'

'It will cost you,' he shrugged with indifference.

'Very well,' I said and took out some money. 'How much?'

'This will be enough,' he said, taking the handful from me. 'And why do you want to meet him?'

'I don't see that it's any business of yours,' I said. 'I've paid you, now give me what I've paid you for.'

My authority was being tested again. Feeling the stares penetrate my back, I knew that this time it was a test I needed to pass if I were to get anywhere in these parts.

'All that happens here is my business. Unless you tell me, you will not find out. Not so many people here are speaking English. Come.' He cupped a hand around his ear and glanced towards his friends.

'I don't like your tone,' I answered with irritation. I was stuck, though. I would have to compromise, but I absolutely would not bend and whisper in his ear. 'If you must know, I am also a watchmaker and want to discuss one of his pieces with him. Now, if you please,' I concluded curtly.

I was feeling quite heated and I think he realised it.

'Very well,' he said. 'The premises of Ghalat Taqdir are to the north, on the very edge of the town. You will find it, but to do so you will pass time.'

He burst into laughter and his companions joined him. The reason for their sudden jocosity did not interest me.

'And how do I find it,' I interrupted, 'in all this infernal dust?'

'Sahib, you have not been here long I think. Go now and you will find it.'

I left them chuckling and made my way to the exit. I paused at the canvas curtain and tied a handkerchief around my nose and mouth before pushing my way out.

It was remarkable.

Brilliant sunshine greeted me and fresh air filled my lungs, as though the dust storm had never been. I pulled the handkerchief from my face. I was rooted to the spot. I saw neither trees nor grass, only dried earth, buildings of wood, stone and canvas, a mighty fort towering above them and over that, the great mountains. But wherever I looked, this previously barren place was now alive with people, giddily alive in a way I had never before encountered, not in Karachi, nor in London. Where all this life had hidden during the storm was a mystery, as was the speed with which it had reactivated. Even where there seemed to be none, in darkened tents and shacks, there was the promise of life.

Between the structures were narrow alleys, secretive ways in and out of which tradesmen, merchants and vagrants slipped, hissing words at one another and laughing carefully. The vibrancy of the street itself struck me yet more. A great train of mules was being loaded with grain, bread and dried fruits that their owner had obtained from the various vendors selling foodstuffs. A fruit-seller was eagerly counting the money he was receiving from the leader of the train. He pulled a great purse from a pocket located next to the dagger that hung from a waistband holding his richly embroidered britches aloft and dropped the coins into it. As he replaced his money pouch, he was distracted by a gang of children speeding from hut to hut. One grabbed a small sack of dried mulberries that split and spilt onto the dusty ground. Drawing his blade, the merchant chased the children for a few strides before hurling curses at them, only to be taunted from a safe distance. The children capered and the trader swelled, but not until they were out of sight did he realise that, while he raged at the decoy band, another child had pilfered enough to feed each urchin for a week.

The town's unique geography, slotted in at a crossroads in the peaks, gave it its frantic energy. This very thoroughfare was the mercantile hub for all the mountain communities around it, the last port of call for anyone travelling to the fabled Shangri-La of Hunza at the foot of Rakaposhi, further into the Karakoram up to China. Here, even lepers, amputees, madmen, those born unfortunate and those made so in punishment for their crimes could scrape a living. One of them, a blind, malnourished beggar, held out a hand from his pitch beside a shrine. I threw a couple of coins into his bowl before stepping out onto the street and heading towards the northern perimeter of the town.

As I walked, the voices I heard were in languages so foreign to my ears they sounded like music. The animals I saw were different from those I knew: poultry, reptiles and unnameable beasts in cages; yet more uncaged, tethered to their masters by twine or charm. The scent of spiced stews came from pots heated by fires fuelled by a sweet, alien wood. Even the dust, picked up by the odd stray gust, smelled new and somehow unexplored.

This paradise of sensation was brought to an abrupt halt by the sound of gunfire.

I could not see from whom nor tell the direction from which it had come, but as the volley rang out, the voices around me stopped chattering and the animals fell silent. A man next to me fell to his knees, as though hit. Then others did the same, and as the ringing faded from my ears it was replaced by the strange song

of the muezzin, emanating from a minaret at the very far end of
the street. These people had been struck not by bullets, but by religious devotion. They were facing west, praying in unison. Among
those still on their feet, I spied a small group of men on the road
some way towards the mosque. They were not praying, for they
were not Mussulmen. These men wore the carefully wrapped turbans of the Sikhs, and their long khaki jackets and puttees, as well
as the rifles they were pointing in my direction, were those of soldiers in the service of the Army. A white man in the uniform of a
British officer was running up behind the riflemen, shouting at the
top of his voice as he drew his pistol.

'Fire, you bloody fools,' he yelled. 'Fire before he gets away!'

The man at whom they were levelling their weapons, and who
was indeed getting away, was between the riflemen and me. His
native clothing and partially covered face were caked head to toe
in dust. At a time when the muezzin's call had slowed everything
else to a fraction of its normal pace, when even the pockets of
breeze had become indolent and the dust they carried still, this
man was an anomalous flurry of movement. He was frantically
spurring the heavily laden horse he sat upon and skilfully steering
the beast through the worshippers around him, while they, despite
their fear of being trampled, concentrated their minds on the slow
mechanics of prayer. It was as though his mysterious motion had
temporarily frozen the fizzing lifeforce of the town and was giving
him the opportunity to make good his escape. That the rider was
using the call to prayer to save his skin – for which he would no
doubt go to hell, if these people allowed for such a thing – apparently troubled no one around him but the British soldier. While he
was puce with anger, his shouting and the heat, the townsfolk
clearly thought it the rider's decision to make, and *he* seemed to
think the price for living to fight another day a fair one.

His rearing, leaping waltz was bringing him directly towards
me. His movements, the dust thrown up by his horse and the
rising and falling of the supplicants made it near impossible for the
riflemen to find their target. But the officer seemed more confident of his aim. He was now standing by his troops, silent, one eye

closed, his pistol steady. I was very much in the line of fire, but quite incapable of moving. I was rooted to the spot by what was, until then, quite simply the most arresting image I had ever encountered. The minaret gleaming in the sunlight, the riflemen as frozen as I, the officer calmly awaiting his moment and this witchdoctor of a rider, shimmying his way around us all. Finally, when the horseman was but ten feet from me, our eyes met fleetingly. I am sure he smiled as he passed, his white teeth gleaming, his eyes sparkling with devilry, but I cannot say for certain, since as soon as our gazes locked, I was consumed by the cloud of dust kicked up by his horse's hooves, the percussion to the muezzin's sonorous wail. Then the officer saw his chance and with a crack, a bullet whistled through the air devilish close to my head, and rather too late I dived to the ground.

By the time the dust settled, the rider had vanished, leaving only the townsfolk praying, the dumbfounded alien lying amongst them and the soldiers making their way towards me in a fury of shouts. I stood, and brushed myself down. As I did so, the singing ceased and the riflemen sprinted past me, creating another dust cloud. I coughed and then out of the dust came a voice.

'Bloody fools! He's long gone. Hope I didn't scare you there.' The officer appeared before me and stuck out his hand as the town sprang to life again. He was slim and sharp-featured. He pushed his helmet back and wiped an expansive brow with his sleeve. 'Major Flack, how do you do? Been a while since I've seen any civilians in these parts. God knows why you'd come here. Not that the Maharajah and his Wazir are bad chaps. What did you say your name was?'

'King, Cyril King,' I replied.

'Ah, well, King. If you do decide to stay in this godforsaken place, then make yourself known at the fort. It's the only place you'll find any company around here, and the lads'll spot you a decent round of cards. They call it a Mess, and it is, if you take my meaning. A bloody mess. Wazir still doesn't know where to put who, so they're all in there, from major to sergeant. Even a couple of corporals. Suppose it means there's enough for the table, though. I'd introduce you myself if duty didn't call, but I'd better be off to see what those buggers are up to, eh? Tricky business, hunting down quarry of this sort. You've seen the fort, I assume? Walk east, can't miss it. Just head for the Jack waving at you like a sultry maiden over the door in the east corner. If you can make it out in this bloody dust, of course.'

He strode after the riflemen, readjusting his helmet.

What a curious interlude, I thought, doubting very much that the soldiers would ever catch their prey, on foot or in the saddle, for by now the horseman would surely have fled into the mountains.

*

I made my way north towards the watchshop somewhat dazed. The horseman's stare had unnerved me, but I was certain the cause of my discomfort was not the smile I thought I had seen, nor any lingering fear I had that he might have desired to harm me. The chap had been somehow familiar, yet not in the sense that he was an acquaintance. Despite his clothes and situation, there was something about him I recognised, where all else in this new world was fresh and exciting. Perhaps I had seen him before, but only my memory had registered the fact, and not my conscious mind.

I eventually identified the watchmaker's shop by a piece of wood, at least six feet wide, laid on the ground outside it, on which a clockface was painted. It was a relief to see that below it were written the very words I had first seen inscribed on the watch. The teahouse proprietor had been right, and I now understood why he and his friends had laughed so. I would indeed have to pass time to meet Ghalat Taqdir.

I pushed my way through the canvas and entered the estab- lishment. As I made my way through the folds, I was welcomed by a familiar chorus of ticking. The shop was much like the teashop, that is to say constructed of canvas and wood. However, there the similarities ended. Where the teahouse was bare, Ghalat Taqdir's shop was decorated with great swathes of gold and red material, woven with beads and glass. A small oil lamp hung from a central beam, its thick light barely sufficient to illuminate the watches and clocks suspended around it like a forest of time gently swaying and twisting in an undetectable breeze. Mirrors dangled from hooks among them and rotated slowly. They reflected the dim light in new directions with every degree of their movement, threw it onto unseen walls and droops in the ceiling. It was an unnavigable place.

I inspected the watches and clocks in front of me. Though they all ran accurately, the appearance of every one of them was strikingly eccentric, and no two were the same. None clasped a stone to its cover, however.

On the other side of the shop, beyond the twisting timepieces, I spied a man sitting cross-legged on a cushion, tinkering with a watch on the ground before him. Its cogs, hands and coils were strewn in no discernible order on a cloth, but his long nimble fingers assembled the piece with authority. Finally he closed its cover and rose effortlessly to a proud six feet or more. He negotiated the forest in a single, gliding stride as he approached. His face was one of sombre straight lines and hollow shadows and his hooded, alert eyes considered me with cautious curiosity.

I had found the man I had come so far to see.

'My name is Cyril King,' I said. 'Do you speak English?'

'Of course,' he replied. 'Time is of great importance to the Englishman. My watches are strong – good for your posting here.' He looked down at my grubby suit and smiled. It was a mocking expression, but not an unkind one. 'But I think you are not a soldier, sahib, so tell me – what shall you require of your timepiece?'

'I am afraid I am not here to buy,' I answered. 'I already have a watch, you see. In fact, I have come all the way from London to discuss it with you.'

This disclosure caused him to raise an eyebrow, nothing more, and he looked down at the watch as I extracted it from my pocket and opened it for his inspection.

There was a glimmer of something else in his eyes before he shook his head and spoke. 'This watch is very old, sahib. It no longer keeps time. Come.'

I followed him to his seat where he found another cushion amongst the swathes of material. I lowered myself onto it as he folded himself onto his. Also out of the material came a wooden case which he opened to reveal a collection of his wares.

I lifted a hand to forestall him.

'I really have not come for a replacement,' I insisted. 'Rather I want to learn of the one I have. It was made here, I believe. This is your mark, yes?' I pointed at the rear of the watch, at the writing.

He lowered the case and took the watch from me. He held it with the tips of his fingers, and considered both it and me with a combination of disappointment and disdain.

'You are mistaken, sahib,' he said, passing the watch back to me. 'This is not of my construction.'

Fear rose in me. I thrust the watch back towards him, pointing at the writing.

'Does this not say "Ghalat Taqdir, Watchmaker of Gilgit"?' I asked him. 'Why – it is the very writing you have outside this shop! Surely I cannot be mistaken!'

All trace of humour drained from his face.

'I do not lie,' he said coolly. 'This timepiece *was* made here, and this *is* the mark of Ghalat Taqdir, master watchmaker, but I am not he. So it is as I say, English – not made by my hands.'

'Then who are you?' I gasped. 'Where is Ghalat Taqdir?'

'I am Multah Taqdir, son of Ghalat,' he replied.

As he touched his chest, chin, and then forehead, I wrapped my hand around the watch and closed my eyes, dreading what his answer to my next question would be.

'And your father?' I breathed. 'Is he here?'

'Alas, sahib,' he said. 'My father is dead.'

8

The Letters of
Sir Paul Lindley-Small

From the Valkyrie XII *steam vessel*
Cadiz, Spain

2ND NOVEMBER 1908

Morning, lad.

I dined at his table all right, but there was no sign of the
Captain. Never leaves the bridge, said the Senior Officer who took
his place, and that was about all he said, or all that I heard, at any
rate. Whoever heard of a dry sailor, I ask you? Upon this whole
craft, I believe it is only Ralf the barman with whom I see eye to
eye. He does not set up shop for another hour, however; so I take
up my pen where last night I put it down, and ask you to return
with me to Bharatpur and that remarkable fellow, Sadirah the
fakir.

In preparation for his interment, over the next five days Sadirah
ate nothing but yoghurt and drank nothing but milk. For the final
two days prior to his burial, he fasted entirely. When the day of
his entombment arrived, he went through a somewhat repulsive
ritual of inner cleansing, which included clearing his innards by

swallowing a thin strip of linen yarn thirty yards in length, only to regurgitate it. The sight was abhorrent, the odour pungent, but he assured me it was strictly necessary. To his cleansed stomach he then fed a minute but carefully measured amount of liquid from a vial he kept in the folds of his garments.

In seconds he was in his meditative state, and try as I might, I could detect no pulse on his neck or wrist. Indeed, of all his body, only his head remained warm to the touch. His animation was quite suspended.

I wrapped him in linen as he had requested and called in the Maharajah and his guards. Content that this was the man I had presented to him, the Maharajah ordered his men to place Sadirah in a great wooden chest that had been constructed for the demonstration. The lid was slammed shut, padlocked and sealed with the Maharajah's royal seal. Four of the guardsmen carried the chest to the hole in the courtyard that had been dug in preparation. The soil was thrown upon the chest and grass seed sown within it. And there the Maharajah and I left Sadirah on the first of forty days, each of us confident that, come the fortieth, we would be the winner of the wager.

I admit that over the following weeks I took the Maharajah at his word that he was not concerned by the conduct of his many wives, and enjoyed a month in the lap of Bharatpurian luxury – though this time I did not touch his treasured jewellery.

Before I tell you of the result of the wager, it would be wise to let you know that, prior to our arrival there, Sadirah and I had established a plan of action to be followed when he was revived from his entombment. He would be too frail to flee, but I knew that when the Maharajah saw that the fakir was alive and well, he would be greatly angered and unwilling to give up the crown that was due me. So do not think less of me when I tell you that, once the undisturbed shoots had been dug up, the soil shovelled aside, the padlock unlocked, the Maharajah's seal broken and Sadirah, found in the very same position, had been lifted out and successfully revived . . . I grabbed the crown from the Maharajah's head and ran for my life.

Yes, Cyril, I sped up the stairs to the battlements, then down the marble corridors, from room to room, window to window and balcony to balcony – always, as I had predicted, pursued by irate guardsmen. But do not fear, for I had planned my route carefully. The sceptre already in my satchel, the crown now joining it, I sprinted into the compound of the ruler's harem, a place that his guards were forbidden to enter. In the ensuing confusion – and in my haste unforgivably ignoring the ladies who had made my stay so pleasurable – I managed to escape onto a perimeter wall through a window and from there disappear into the streets of the bustling town.

And what of poor Sadirah? I hear you cry. You need have no concern. He told me of his escape, conducted precisely as we had planned, when we met in the marketplace an hour later and I fed him a malt-flavoured restorative.

My grabbing of the crown from the revered ruler's head had caused an enormous furore and, as I hoped, this act had provoked a greater anger in the Maharajah than any had ever seen before. He ordered every one of his men to chase me down, while he followed, fuming, some distance behind. In his fury, he completely forgot about the fakir, and thus Sadirah was able to saunter out of the palace at his own pace. The only concern we had had in planning his escape were the inevitable guards at the gate; but so befuddled, amazed and downright scared by his achievement were they that they meekly stood aside and let him pass.

It is unlikely that I shall ever be able to return to Bharatpur, but I do not believe the Maharajah will pursue me beyond his borders. He is a proud man, and would not want his equals to know how easily he was tricked. For my part, I shall tell nobody but you, for that is the code of the gentleman people think me these days, though I must say, I was most satisfied by the way our plan played itself out. Sadirah, I should think, will remain equally mute – if word were to get out that he was in the business of duping Maharajahs, his fakir status would be called into question, and no other court would invite him to perform.

The crown was a fine and gaudy thing, its gold frame liberally decorated with precious stones of every kind. It was certainly the more valuable of the two pieces, though what was equally certain was that it was the more difficult to carry concealed. It was too large to put under my headgear, and too bulky for my bag. I was keen to take the two items to pieces, melt the gold into balls of equal size and divide the stones. Certainly they would be less valuable, but easier to carry and conceal. However, Sadirah was adamant. It was one thing to trick a Maharajah out of his possessions, he said, but quite another to destroy them. In his happy innocence, Sadirah told me that it was only fair for me to have the crown and he the sceptre, for the whole thing had been my plan – no matter that *he* had been the one buried as though dead for forty days while I had lived in constant self-gratification. Very well, I thought, I would prise the majority of the jewels from the crown and send what remained of it to the staff of the British Museum to earn my keep. However, Sadirah added as he passed me the crown that next time, when we executed *his* plan, *he* would get the better of the booty. This seemed reasonable to me, though I had no idea that he had already thought up a scheme that would require another man of extravagant means and the cat of an acquaintance of his.

Cat and owner were located in Calcutta. The owner was a *sapera*, a member of the caste of snake charmers and sellers. He had been ostracised by his people, however, for he had not, for some time now, entertained the crowds with a dancing serpent, but with the uniqueness of his feline charge.

'It is really a remarkable beast,' Sadirah said, looking from the sceptre in his hand to the crown in mine. 'It has all the features of a cat, but more besides that are akin to that of a cobra. It has a long tail, great fangs and is quite poisonous. But most strangely of all, when my friend charms it from its basket, the skin of its chest will flare into a hood. It is quite fearsome. He tells me it is the toast of the marketplace. Perhaps you have heard of it?'

I had not, though I instantly recognised the description, as of course will you. Not even I, in all my years of researching the beast, had ever heard of one that was alive. To be told that one such beast was performing tricks in the market forum of a place so accessible as Calcutta was, quite simply, miraculous. At long last, I was within grasping reach of the King Cobra Cat. No mere coincidence could have put Sadirah and his information in my path. I confess I was beginning to believe in fate.

Naturally, in an exhibition of good and brotherly faith, I insisted that Sadirah take the crown and I the sceptre. I then told him that we would certainly go to Calcutta, but that first I had some business to attend to in Delhi. So I left him in Bharatpur and headed directly for Calcutta, for the marketplace and his friend – both of which, feigning casual interest, I had him describe in the utmost detail prior to our parting of ways.

As you know, markets in this country are noisier, dirtier, more varied and far, far bigger than those of English towns. So though I quickly found the one in which Sadirah had told me Ashvin Landa performed with his feline, it took me another two hours to locate the man himself. The occupied expanse was so enormous, so filled with people, beasts and produce that I was never at any moment in all my hunting hours out of physical contact with at least three others. When I asked some of them where a man such as Ashvin Landa might be found, they were eager to help, but unfortunately each one pointed in a different direction.

It was, then, purely by my own inestimable instincts that I finally succeeded in sniffing the fellow out. 'Sniffing' is the apt word, for Landa had positioned himself at the mouth of the most obscure and stinking of alleyways. The stench, in fact, made my eyes water, my flesh creep, my brow sweat and my stomach turn – and all at the same time. I could not tell what caused it, for behind Ashvin Landa the alley fast descended into complete darkness. Believe it or not, at the time, the overpowering reek was not the most arresting element of the scene that confronted me. The sight before me took that honour, though certainly I covered my mouth and nose with my handkerchief as I gawped at it.

I stood amongst a group of people, all of whom were slumped on the ground, nodding their draped heads towards Ashvin Landa and mumbling unintelligibly. Their supplicatory positions and the constant bobbing were not the only things they had in common. Each and every one of them wore a grimy bandage over a nasty-looking injury. Some had lost fingers, some toes, some whole feet and some whole hands. One chap had lost both his legs in their entirety. Fortunately, the supplicants were so engrossed that I was able to gaze at my leisure upon the recipient of their veneration. Ashvin Landa was as distressing a sight as his followers, though for very different reasons.

This man, piratical in appearance, with long hair, a crudely wrapped turban, necklaces made from shells and glass beads, and bulbous gold earrings, was as immobile and silent as Sadirah had been when first I saw him in that cave. This was perplexing enough for a man whose trade involved coaxing a beast from a basket with the gourd-like flute that lay by his side. That there was not a basket in sight was the cause of my greatest anxiety, however – for if there was no basket, where could the beast be that resided within it?

A united gasp rose from the gathering as I picked my way through them and stepped onto Ashvin Landa's rug. My intention was to revive him from whatever he was in the process of doing, so I crouched next to him and spoke his name, but there was no reaction. I took his arm, an act that was greeted with an even greater rustle of disapproval from the people behind me. I shook him and spoke his name with greater vehemence, but still there was no response from the snake charmer. When he then toppled from his position to lie on his rug, his legs still bent as if frozen, it was apparently the final straw for one of his party.

'Ashvin Landa should not be touched,' a voice said from behind me.

I did not turn to face the speaker immediately, for upon the calf of Ashvin Landa's left leg I had spotted two circular holes oozing infected blood. Can you imagine my excitement when I saw that, around them, the brown skin had become black, an unnatural colour that stretched down to his toes and up to his knee? Higher on his leg I could not see, for clothes covered his skin, but it did not matter, for the flesh beneath the blackened skin was unquestionably wizening. Thinking it unwise to delve into the trousers of one so devoutly worshipped, I turned to see the eyes of the ill-fated assembly trained upon me. I leapt to my feet, for it was then that I recognised a final shared trait amongst them. Their faces were liberally decorated with blisters and lumps, the skin dry and cracked. The source of their misfortune came crashing into my consciousness. *They were lepers, every one.*

I am not one to run from the maladies of my fellow men, as you know, but leprosy breeds terror in me like no other disease. This reaction harks back to news of an acquaintance of mine being tricked into the arms of one of its victims and himself then suffering most awfully until his longwinded, much-wished-for demise. The fact that I was acting against the wishes of these people and that they were gradually shuffling towards me with the intention of ceasing my activity merely served to increase my panic. I don't mind telling you that, had I had the option, I would have run from the spot the moment I saw them, but as before me there was a sea of disease and behind me a dead end, I stood rooted to the spot, hoping what elevation my legs provided me with would keep me from the bacteria.

'I did not mean to . . .' I stuttered.

'He must not be touched. He lies in state,' the same man said as they continued to edge towards me. I looked around for some form of defence – a stick, a chair, anything – but could see nothing that might help me in fending them off. Instead, I turned to words to keep them away, but in my fear only the harsh expletives of our native tongue came to mind.

'Ashvin Landa has been bitten,' hissed the man, his bandaged hand reaching the mat I stood on. 'Bitten by the sacred beast.'

'But where *is* the beast?' I spluttered.

'Taken. Taken, along with everything else, by his brother, Dadri Landa of Dwarka. And now we pray for his revival so he can tell us what we must do to calm the spirit of the sacred beast.' The man stumbled onto the rug and then reached out his arms to protect the charmer from further abuse. 'He must not be touched before his revival.'

It was an awkward situation, as you can well imagine. There I was, my back to that alley, a sea of contagion approaching. As much as I did not want to offend them, I had no great desire to walk amongst them either. They had unknowingly greatly aided me, and though it was distressing to hear that the animal had been moved to the rather distant Dwarka, it was no fault of theirs. Indeed, though I was sure to have eventually established who had eloped with the beast and to where, they had assisted my efforts no end, and I had much to be grateful to them for. Normally one would slap a chap on the back, treat him to a meal and a drink, but as neither time nor inclination allowed for this, I had to think of some other plan with which to appease and thank them. I offered to put Ashvin Landa back to his original position, but they sharply declined as they moved ever closer. I even offered them the rest of the bottle I had in my satchel, thinking it could be used as a cleanser if not a drink, but they hissed at me.

My final route from rug to marketplace was not in the end the gallant one I wished it to be, but with every overture thrown back in my face, and the blighted getting ever closer to my virgin skin, I was left with little option. Instead of the magnanimous gesture that I genuinely wished it to be, my last resort was to point in one direction and, amazement in my eyes, exclaim, 'The beast has returned!' Then, as they followed my finger, with my breath held and my eyes shut, I scuttled through them and away. By the time they looked back, all the angrier, I was lost in the crowd, bolting my way back to the station where I could sit in the cool of the first-class waiting room and partake liberally of the medicinal contents of my flask.

In Dwarka it was not a difficult task to learn of the whereabouts of Dadri Landa. Following the lengthy and picturesque journey from Calcutta, I entered a dockside tavern where I encountered a man who wore a silver turban and a curved blade hanging from his belt. For a meal and a pouch of coins, he told me of the establishment on the shores of the lake with the pink and blue birds. There I found Dadri Landa in his hut from where he sold trinkets, jewellery, elaborate pipes, emblems, sculptures, statues and, he informed me, the odd remarkable beast to eccentric sailors. Informing me that a Spaniard with a curious circular beard on the end of his chin had beaten me to the creature by a mere matter of hours, Landa pointed to the sea, and there, heading for the horizon, was the good ship *Syren*, carrying the blighter and my beast off into the sunset.

In hot pursuit, I am, as ever, your loyal friend,

Lindley-Small

9

THE NOTEBOOKS OF CYRIL KING

1893

Bad Omens

'Dead? What do you mean dead?' I demanded, although it was a ridiculous question, of course. The man before me was in his middle years. If he was Multah Taqdir, son of Ghalat, as he claimed, it should have come as no surprise that his father had passed away. At the time, however, this was a logic beyond my capabilities.

'It cannot be,' I continued, scrambling to my feet. 'He is the very reason I'm here. He's to answer my questions concerning this watch.'

'This is the truth. My father expired three months ago,' Multah Taqdir said. 'I told you I do not lie, English. But if you choose not to believe me, it is of no concern to me.'

He had also risen as he spoke, and now stretched his arm towards the exit, but I did not move.

I had travelled more than five thousand miles for nothing. How had I failed to allow for this possibility? Excitement – and, if I was honest, greed – had deafened my ears too well to the voice of reason. The watch could be decades old, after all, yet I had not stopped to consider that its maker could be dead, what secrets it held long lost. What a fool I had been!

'Is there nothing you can tell me?' I persisted.

He considered me with something amounting to disdain.

'There is nothing *to* tell, English. My father built this watch some years ago. A man brought the stone and asked my father to set it in the case. There was nothing of note about him. He was a native like any other. I did not hear his name. He had but one hand, I remember – but then, that is not uncommon in my country.'

'Then what of the stone itself? Do you know where it came from?'

He shrugged. 'The stone is a good luck charm. Nothing more.'

'A good luck charm?' I protested. 'But this is a black sapphire!'

'Perhaps. But it is also a talisman for the superstitious. Once there were many such. It is the eye of a beast half cat and half serpent, which legend calls the protector of Adam-Khor.'

'Adam Core? Who was he?' I asked.

'Adam-Khor. In your tongue, it means The Man-eater.'

My puzzlement must have been plain, for he continued.

'Many hundreds of years ago, before the teachings of the Prophet had arrived, this region was ruled by a king named Sri Badat. He lived in great splendour and worshipped many idols, this creature among them; until the day when a true believer arrived from the west and wed his daughter and deposed him.

'Some say that Sri Badat was a wise and benevolent ruler, and there are those who honour him to this day. Others say that he became a monster, who killed and tortured for pleasure, and drank the blood of children and ate their flesh. Thus he grew into a figure of myth and legend: Adam-Khor.

'One such tells that he did not die when he was overthrown, but fled north into the mountains, taking with him his loyal palace guard and as much of his gold and jewels as they could carry.'

'Gold and jewels?' I echoed.

Multah Taqdir smiled a mocking smile.

'No one believes the legends,' he said. 'Only fools and Englishmen.'

'What do you mean?' I asked, affronted.

'If there were riches, they have been scattered far and wide long since,' he replied. 'Sri Badat was real enough, but Adam-Khor is a legend only, as is the guardian beast, although people still carve its eye as a symbol of warning and protection. We are not like your people, English. Those of us who live in these mountains would not risk death or madness in search of treasure from children's stories. But you, you are never content with what you have, always wanting more, be it land or money. Just like the other who came, asking questions about this watch and this stone.'

'What other?' I exclaimed, alarmed and intrigued in equal measure.

'A small man,' said Multah Taqdir. 'One year ago. A reader of books—'

'Forrester?'

'Yes,' he said. 'Forrester. That was he.'

'He was here?'

I could scarcely contain my elation. Forrester had made it to Gilgit. I was following in his footsteps. But what had happened after he had come here, and what had he discovered?

'Multah,' I said in as steady and low a voice as I could muster. 'You must tell me, where was Forrester headed? Where did he go when he left your watchshop?'

He tutted, already turning away from me, as though he considered our conversation closed. 'I know only that he went into the mountains; and that the mountains turned him mad, as they will you. It was the soldiers from the fort who found him, half dead and raving'

*

The hour was approaching lunchtime. Just as the Major had promised I would, I saw our flag fluttering at the end of its pole above the east corner of the fort that towered over all the other buildings. The great wooden gate was manned by a handful of turbaned guards, of whom I requested directions to the mess. One of them pointed across a dusty courtyard filled with more native soldiers to a doorless threshold located at what was certainly the less grandiose end of the compound. The Maharajah and his Wazir appeared to be still very much in charge here, I thought, as I ducked inside.

The room was dark and filled with tobacco smoke. Its only source of illumination was the sun that streamed through small, high windows and the doorway I stood in. It was also notably cooler than anywhere else I had been in the town. However, this did not prevent the brows of the half dozen men I saw lazing in chairs and on carpets from glistening with perspiration. One was flicking cards into a hat, another was sliding matches around on a table. Another was failing to tune a fiddle. They looked a listless bunch in their yellowing shirtsleeves and unbuttoned uniform jackets.

'I say,' I said. 'Is there a Major Flack here?' for I could not see which was he.

In unison, they all turned their heads towards me.

'There are no mountain goats in here,' said one.

'Now then,' a second said, rising to his feet from a table bathed in one of the few rays that made its way into the room. 'We've a guest, lads. The Major's out chasing a rabbit, sir, but perhaps we can be of assistance. I'm Lieutenant Fowler.'

He stuck out a hand as he approached me, which I took. He was a small, pudgy man who had the look of an overweight ten-year-old – features he would surely never grow out of, for certainly he had long left boyhood behind him. Breaking our moist handshake, he turned and pointed at a man sitting on a carpet on the floor. He was in shadow but I could see him idly leafing through a small pile of books at his side. Plumes of heavy smoke rolled into the room from his direction.

'That's our good Captain Petts,' Lieutenant Fowler was saying. 'Then we have Corporals Finch and Crampers' – he pointed to the card flicker and the match slider – 'the Sarge,' – the fiddler – 'and of course, how could I forget, our very own major – Pound,' he concluded with mild derision, for the last man he pointed at, though barely discernable, was sitting in a corner, snoring gently.

'We are what constitutes the Indian Colonial Army in this merry little town. In his wisdom, the General has sent the rest of us into the further corners of this country to experience the excitement and adventure every soldier craves, leaving us to guard and protect this most vital of outposts from the marauding hordes hereabouts. Which is to say, while others have dispersed to stave off the impending Russian invasion, he has left us here at Mr Partab's to twiddle our metaphorical thumbs until they clean drop off. So a guest is a welcome interruption, sir. And whom, may I ask, are we welcoming to our table?'

'My name is King, Cyril King. I ran into Major Flack this morning. What do you mean by a Russian invasion?' I asked, somewhat concerned by the news.

'Well, now,' he said. 'Do you not know? Someone in Calcutta's got a bee in his bonnet. Thinks they might come in from the north. Can you not smell the Cossacks on the air? We've to make sure they don't. They won't, though. The passes are too high over here. It's over towards the Afghans they've got to watch.' He laughed suddenly. 'But don't you worry. Even if they do come down here, you'll be quite safe. We'd never be so lucky. All we have to contend with here are the Wazir and his Dards and Dogras, and they're not the cruel savages they were before our lot got here. Now then; the Major, you were saying?'

I was relieved to have my mind put at rest and related the circumstances under which I had met the Major, an account that occasioned considerable and mean-spirited amusement from the shadows, which had not been my intention.

'He will chase his rabbits,' Lieutenant Fowler said, leading me to the table. 'Now then,' he said as we sat. 'Who's for a round of hands, then? There's nothing like new blood to bring spice to a game.'

Quite suddenly, as the Lieutenant sat and was lit by the sun, something occurred to me. This Fowler was small and resembled a child, and who else in the vicinity would require fine Scotch whisky more than these bored, marooned soldiers?

'How right you are,' I said hopefully. 'There's nothing like a game and a tipple.'

'Eh? Ah, yes,' Fowler said. He had caught my gist admirably. 'Fetch him a beaker, Crampers, and fill it up.'

Crampers dropped his match and did as he was ordered. Finally, I was to get that drink.

Crampers returned with an earthenware beaker and joined us at the table. Under his watchful gaze, I raised the cup and toasted to the very good health of my hosts. Then I took a healthy draught.

The liquid was strong. I swallowed part of the mouthful, but it so seared my gullet that quite involuntarily I spat the rest out across the table. This was no whisky.

Laughter bellowed through the room.

'Ah,' the man the Lieutenant had referred to as the Sarge said through his moustache as he leaned his fiddle against the wall, rose and carried his seat towards us. 'The joys of mulberries! Who would have thought so sweet a berry could be turned so vile and pungent and marvellous, eh?' He sat down next to me and gave my back a firm slap. He was a broad, ebullient sort of man whose friendly gesture felt more like a sound shove.

'N-not whisky!' I spluttered.

'Ha,' the Sarge continued. 'You're right there. But do not fear. You'll learn to appreciate the value of mulberries soon enough!'

I wiped my chin of residual liquor and Fowler began to deal.

The whisky in the teahouse had not belonged to them, or perhaps they reserved it for special occasions. Whatever the explanation, whisky was not why I was there, and the shock of the mulberry brandy had brought the purpose of my visit back to the forefront of my mind.

'Actually,' I said, taking a rather more tentative sip from the beaker. 'The reason I'm here is to ask you chaps some questions, if you wouldn't mind. About a man who was picked up hereabouts.'

'Well, ask away, lad, ask away,' the Sarge said as he picked up his cards. Finch also took his place at the table and picked up his, as did the other corporal, Crampers. These two were young, no more than twenty, and acted more as audience members to their superiors' show than as active participants in it, remaining silent and laughing only when it was called for. The Captain and Major Pound stayed in the darkness on their carpets, one smoking his pipe, the other continuing his audible snooze.

'It was some time ago,' I continued. 'A man by the name of Forrester disappeared into the mountains and was recovered some-time later by your soldiers. When he was found he was raving, I understand.'

A sharp hack of a cough and a faster plume came into the light. I looked at my cards and asked the room: 'Can you help me?'

'Can't say I remember anything of the sort,' said Fowler. 'But then I only got here in October. The game is rummy, gentlemen. How about you, Sarge? You've been around.'

The Sarge was scrutinising his hand, but then he turned to look into the shadows where Captain Petts was located. Another puff of smoke crept out of the darkness as the Captain placed his book on the pile. It was followed by a sinister hiss of a voice.

'Yes, Sarge. You must remember something of that incident. As Fowler says, you've been around.'

The Sarge turned back to his cards, as though he had been chided.

'I've only been *here* since 'ninety-one,' was his answer.

'But this was only a year ago,' I said. 'Perhaps you can recall. He had one of Taqdir's rather curious watches—'

'Can't say that I do, sir,' he interrupted. 'Nope. Can't say that I do.'

As the Sarge took a card from the stack and put one down, the Captain stood up and approached the table. His face, lit now for the first time, was thin, its muscles and sinews traceable under the skin. He was perhaps forty-five, of a similar age to the man he was addressing, with dark hair, swept back from his face, and that distinct complexion which, regardless of what it is exposed to, never loses its pallor. He tapped out his pipe on the table next to the Sarge.

'Now, now, Sarge,' he said. 'I don't think that's entirely true, is it?'

Lieutenant Fowler frowned at his captain, perplexed. The corporals did not look up from their cards and first one then the other picked up a card and put one down, as the Sarge had done, busying themselves with the game. On a sixpence the atmosphere had turned from amicable to tense, and what had altered it was the opening of Captain Petts' mouth.

'No, it's not true at all, Sarge,' Petts continued.

'Now, sir, I'm not sure I understand you.'

'Of course you do, Sarge. You were there, remember? Just as I was, and I remember it perfectly clearly. Blow for blow, you might say.'

The Captain was circling the table. The Sarge, having been a large, imposing figure, was shrinking before my very eyes, his moustache drooping. Automatically, I played my turn in the game, transfixed by what was going on here.

'Now, sir,' the Sarge was saying. 'Don't let's allow the boredom to get to us, sir. You know what can happen, sir. The less we speak of that man the better. Let's just get on and enjoy the game.'

This was not just the verbal sparring of two soldiers. I could tell from the silence and the averted eyes and the cowering of the Sarge that there was more to it than that. Quite apart from those unmistakable signs, the mere sound of Captain Petts' voice would have been sufficient to tell me that his intentions were cruel. This was an ambush, and I suppose I was the impromptu bait, for the Sarge was very certainly the prey. I did not like being used as the hunter's lure at all. The Captain, with his posturing and prodding and poisonous tone, was threatening the Sarge, taunting him with something both men knew. I was shocked that a member of the British Army should behave in such a manner, an officer and an Englishman to boot.

'I'm sorry I brought it up, gentlemen. Please forget I ever did. I'm quite happy to talk to Major Flack about it,' I said.

No sooner had the Major's name fallen from my mouth than I realised that I had said the wrong thing, for the Sarge shrank another size or two and a slit of a smile cut its way across the Captain's face. It was the smile of a viper.

'Oh, I don't think we'd want that, now, would we, Sarge?' the Captain rasped. 'Oh, no, Mr King. That wouldn't do at all. I'll tell you what. Why don't we do just as Sarge says, and play on? But why not make it interesting, hmm? Let's see.'

He put his hand on the Sarge's shoulder and bent to talk in his ear. As he did so he looked at me. All the other soldiers stared at their cards, for I believe they were as scared as the Sarge – scared that if they spoke a word, Captain Petts might release the Sarge and turn his venom on them.

'If you win, Sarge, you get the pot, the same for Crampers, Finch and Fowler. But if King here wins, you spill the beans, Sarge. And you spill them properly, d'you hear?' He pointed his pipe at Fowler. 'That's how you spice up a game, Lieutenant.'

This turn of events did not please me at all. While I wanted whatever information they might have had, I was not in the least prepared for the way I was going to have to win it. And how would I get them to talk if I did not win? I was a decent card player, but I very much doubted whether I would turn out to be stronger than these men, who had little to do but perfect their games and taunt one another. This was not the way to get what I wanted. Instead, I decided, I would stick up for the underdog. I would pull the prey from the viper's mouth, and with any luck the Sarge would be so grateful that, despite the anguish the episode clearly caused him, he would reveal all he could about Forrester.

'Now really,' I said, getting to my feet. 'There's no call for this. I did not mean to touch an open wound, gentlemen. Plainly I have, and I apologise. And you, Captain, should be ashamed of yourself. I've got a good mind to wake Major Pound here and report you.'

Petts spat his laughter onto the table between us.

'Ha! An apologist! Well, there he is, my man,' he said, pointing at the source of the snores. 'Do as you will, but first let me warn you: if you succeed in waking him – which for the amount of the Sarge's beloved mulberries he drinks daily I very much doubt – but should you succeed, I can assure you he will react to your doing so only with anger. And should I desire it, he will order these two corporals to imprison you, which these lads will dutifully do. They may not like it, and they may not like me, but you, sir, are merely a transient stranger, whereas they will have me to contend with for the rest of their service. I have been in this hideous place for years, and have risen from Second Lieutenant, so believe me when I tell you – the power of rank, duty and orders is all we have out here, *Mister* King. It's all that holds this flimsy Empire together, that divides us from the barbarians on the other side of that wall. Without it I don't doubt that we should be just the same as they. Now, it just so happens that you have stumbled into the little corner of the Empire that is, with the blessings of both the Major and the Maharajah, entirely under my control. So take my word for it, my boy, in my portion of the Empire I do as I please, and when you are in it, I strongly advise you to do as you are told. And now, what I please is that you play.'

He had been pointing at me with his pipe as he spoke. Now he repacked it and replaced it in his mouth. I looked to the men around me for assistance in my rebellion, but clearly they had long been broken and would not meet my gaze. I could tell from the expressions on the corporals' faces that what Petts had said was true. Though I had committed no crime, if their captain ordered it they would place me in shackles without question. I sat down once more. It seemed I was to play for the information, after all.

'So let's get to it, shall we?' Petts said with cheerful cruelty, puffing smoke once more and pulling a chair to the table, gathering the cards from our hands and shuffling them. 'I shall deal. The game is gin and there's all to play for.'

It seemed I had to throw all my moral concerns to the wind if this adventure was to progress. I knew that by doing so I was making myself the despicable Petts' accomplice, but my first duty was to unfurl the mystery that had brought me there in the first place. I closed my mind to its own duplicity and instead set it to playing the gin hand of my life.

It was a sticky, uncomfortable game, punctuated by gleeful hisses from Petts and the squirming of his inferiors, and all but the

Captain were happy when it ended. Even the Sarge looked relieved when, either by the machinations of blind luck or by the merciless hand of Petts, I laid down my cards.

'Gin,' I whispered.

THE LETTERS OF
SIR PAUL LINDLEY-SMALL

From the Hotel Ernst
Kristiansand, Norway

5TH DECEMBER 1908

My dear Cyril,

I am a landlubber again.

And of all the places on the planet where I could have fetched up, it is the curious Norse world that welcomes me. This is a fateful occurrence indeed, since of all the women I have known, one in particular holds a special place in my heart. If there was a reason for me to have remained in Europe all those years ago, it was Else. And now I have even more to thank her for than ever I had thought. It is due only to the times we took our sport on the Shetlands that I can now be sure that the man I trail has alighted here in this smooth-stoned port called Kristiansand. You see, amongst other valuable lessons, Else taught me the rudiments of Norwegian. So when I addressed the dockhand heaving to the *Valkyrie*, my pidgin did me proud.

You will be pleased to hear that my willpower got the better of

my carnal appetite, for when he duly informed me that he had
indeed seen a man with a curiously circular beard, wandering into
town carrying an alarmingly boisterous gunnysack, despite the
imminent collapse of Siamese fortitude aboard the ship, I turned
my back on the gangplank and sought further information. I had
not travelled so far, and to Scandinavia, only to sample the deli-
cacies of Siam, after all. My task was afoot, I was mere days
behind, and looking back only to blow the gals a kiss from the
quay, I made my way into a land whose native blonde beauties
wholly deserve their reputation for a brazen, strong and honest
kinship with nature.

Mystery, the promise of adventure, the potential for fresh
conquests and the possibility of significant remuneration – these are
the ingredients of that willpower. Indeed, these are the ingredients
that have made my whole life such a spiced and varied stew, and
there at the quayside in Kristiansand they saw me handsomely
pay a lad to seek out my luggage. I would await its delivery in
the tavern my eagle eyes had spotted even before the *Valkyrie*
had found its berth at the docks. There, as I waited, I would skilfully
wheedle information out of its patrons and barkeeper as to where
my beast and that damned Spaniard had got to.

The tavern was called Den Gamle Oksen, which is to say The
Old Bull, and even from the outside it was a seedy, chipped old
place, leaning against a giant boulder smoothed by the Arctic wind
of ages. Inside, it was much as I had expected. The air was stagnant
and the bare wood of the floor was thickly layered with dust. As
I passed the few who drank there, a cloud rose in my wake and
danced in the shards of light that illuminated the place enough
only to guide me to the fellow behind the bar, from whom I
ordered a measure of whisky.

Of the three men whom I could see in the gloom, two were
apparently asleep and the third was busy telling himself a tale
which was meeting with such an angry response that I felt disinclined to interrupt. I learned from the pasty young lad who handed
me my drink that the *Syren*'s journey had ended here in
Kristiansand, but further than that he had not heard or seen

anything of help, so I decided not to dally with my tipple, but to drink up and move on, to make my enquiries elsewhere. However, this was a decision fast reversed, since the liquid I raised to my mouth smelled like quite the rummest stuff in my experience. Lowering the glass, I took a seat at a table beneath one of the filthy windows and set about considering the best way of tackling this curious beverage.

I saw that there were particles floating in it, but whether these came from the glass or the whisky itself I could not say. Whatever their origin, I thought it best they should remain suspended where they were for the time being, rather than allow them to enter my system. As I sat speculating upon their likely composition, a sudden rasp of a voice emanated from my right and gave me the answer to this very quandary. I ignored it at first, but then, accompanied by the screeching of a heavily encumbered chair across the bare boards, it came again.

'Rust,' it said, and as the whine of the unhappy chair ceased, I saw a ball of hair growing profusely from the neck of a dirty burgundy shirt edge into the light by my side. I kept my wits about me.

'From the pipes, no doubt,' I replied politely.

Apparently this was the wrong thing to say, since the dark curly hair parted briefly and pushed to the fore a single bubble of a blue eye, glistening, bloodshot and angry. As quickly as it had appeared and bulged, it retreated into its lair.

'Not the pipes,' he said. 'The people.' This time the other eye fleetingly ogled me – equally blue, bloodshot and moist – but this one seemed more amused than angered as it inspected my reaction.

'I see,' said I, seeing nothing of the sort, and in the half-darkness trying to distinguish where it could be his eyes retreated to. 'How morbidly fascinating. Adds to the taste, no doubt,' I proffered as I forced a sip.

At this he emitted a sudden hack of a laugh, though there was no parting in the matted locks where one might expect to find a mouth. I leaned in to inspect him more closely, thinking that this remarkable creature would make a fine partner piece for the feline which I was hoping to wrest from its latest owner's withering arms. I caught a glint of enamel beneath the tangle as he addressed me again.

'Just in, no doubt. Which vessel, now?' Then quite abruptly there was a discernible ruffle in the tight curls just above the spot where the eyes intermittently appeared and disappeared. 'What date is it?' he demanded.

I informed him that it was the fifth day in December.

'By God! Three weeks!' he exclaimed, thumping the table, causing the dust to leap into the air, and hacking his laughter again. 'Three weeks! Is it possible for a man to sleep that long?' he cried, his left eye goggling me in disbelief.

I was about to tell him of a man I once knew who had passed six months entirely oblivious to the outside world, when I decided instead to ask him if he had heard of my man and the creature he carried, before sleep enveloped him once more.

'I know nothing of roundheads and their cargoes,' he replied. 'But if it's a sailor's story you're after, then you're in luck, sir.'

I sighed with disappointment as his left eye stretched from its hirsute socket, the orb expanding to popping point. Then, relaxing, it swivelled some ninety degrees and rested on the distance.

'But why would a gentleman – and a well-heeled one at that,' (here he tugged at my lambs' wool Crawford suit with calloused fingers, hairy to the nail) 'why would such as you want to hear the tale of a drunken sailor?' The blue eye slowly retreated into its haven. 'I would take your leave of me, good sir. Take your leave of me and this destitute tavern. It shall be more than tales and whisky taken by eve, and I shall not be here to protect you, as I'd wish. My life's task takes me yonder.' He turned his face to the window and nodded at the sea beyond the filth, where the last of the *Valkyrie XII*'s passengers were disembarking.

I am not, as you know, averse to a tale, particularly over a glass or two, but that moment I was keen for my own to commence. However, he was such a sorry beast that I could not bring myself to tell him this, so out of the goodness of my heart I informed him that I would be pleased to hear his tale.

He turned to me, excitement written in both his eyes, which I was privileged enough to see together this single time. The glint became palpable and the phosphorescent glow of teeth never cleaned radiated through the hair like the beam of a lighthouse through black fog.

I had made this poor brute grin.

'Call young Ole for the bottle,' he told me. 'You may be after this Spaniard you speak of, but what I'll tell you is a tale rarely told, for it is one known only to me – and the telling of it shall bring thirst upon you and its bearer.'

Preparing myself for a session of the kind only delved into lightly by sailors and Dubliners, I did as he suggested. My feline and the fate of the Iberian could wait. The sun was setting, after all, and besides, my luggage was yet to arrive. It would be pointless to undertake the rest of this journey without it, and how else could I pass my time in such a place?

When the pasty Ole arrived with the bottle, my tablemate shook it and displaced the crimson particles that had gathered like dregs at its bottom. Then four times he poured full his glass, raised it to that place where I had seen the glow of his teeth and drained it, poured a fifth and me a second, fixed a staring eye upon me and proceeded to relate The Legend of the Curse of the *Valkyries*.

His name was Roald Agnar Johansen. He came from a fishing village in the north called Hundsund and was the only son of Roald Petter, a seaman who had risen to skipper, and Gunhild, a seamstress.

This hulking man recalled his father with surprising tenderness, and related vague memories of the pair sailing when the father was home from sea. They had done so in the fourteen-foot boat they had named *Loki*. Father and son were painting it a wonderful deep blue at the bottom of their garden by the water, when Roald Agnar had asked why they should name it after Loki, the mischievous, troublemaking god, rather than Odin, their wise king. This had been his father's response: 'There's only ever one Ruler, my boy, and it's never a bairn. And when bairn becomes man, he'll likely be the Ruled, not the Ruler. But the Mischievous, well now, he is never ruled, is he? And let none rule *you*. So we'll name this rig *Loki*.'

Thinking his father must know best and hoping to one day understand the words he spoke so solemnly, Roald Agnar had agreed to the naming. To the day of our meeting, this scene was the only specific memory of his father remaining in his alcohol-addled head.

Roald Petter's vessel, the *Valkyrie*, sank in Roald Agnar's twelfth year. However, when Finn Stein, the ship's First Mate and sole sur-vivor, arrived on Gunhild's doorstep and told her that young Roald Agnar's father had not been lost to the seas, but to the Kraken, that he had battled for seven hours trying to save his skipper but had finally and tragically failed . . . through his tears the young lad that moment made a promise to the memory of his father. He would seek this Kraken out and, whatever the cost, force battle until either he or the beast was dead.

The moment this thirsty chap spoke of the Kraken, I knew I was dealing with one of my favourite kinds of tale. A fearsome, squid-like creature, the Kraken has jaws the size of a house and tentacles the length of a rugby field. When boats are inexplicably swallowed by the ocean, more often than not the Kraken gets the blame. No man has lived to confirm that it actually exists, though, and the beast grows larger with every retelling of its legend, more terri-ble with each unexplained wreck. So when he mentioned this mythical monster, I knew the man before me was nothing less than a teller of tall and exaggerated stories, and one who would gladly tell them in exchange for another drink. But then something struck me.

Although every moment this man spoke, the Spaniard and my quarry were doubtless disappearing further into this land of jagged peaks and secretive fjords, I suddenly grew more interested in Roald Agnar's tale, for what if this Finn Stein character, the First

Mate and only survivor of the first *Valkyrie*, really had caught some glimpse of the Kraken, and thus could offer proof of its existence? You can imagine my excitement. If the beast existed, I was the man to locate and capture it, I decided. However, despite my beseeching that he tell me where I might find this Finn Stein, Roald Agnar would not be swayed from his narrative. Instead, he refilled his glass and continued as he saw fit.

Naturally enough, Finn Stein enjoyed the well-earned status of celebrity in his community following his miraculous survival. Indeed, I am surprised news of his unique position as the sole living viewer of such an infamous creature did not travel further afield. However, that is neither here nor there. When Roald Petter's widow Gunhild took up with her deceased husband's First Mate, the young Roald Agnar was pleased that his mother would have some company when he was off seeking the Kraken for a suicidal battle to the death; at the time he was even quite proud to be the new son of a man so renowned and revered for his bravery. He was even better pleased when his stepfather decided that it was about time the lad went to sea, for that would give him the experience and the opportunity to seek the beast that had torn his father from him.

For fear of it being seen as foolhardy, Roald Agnar had taken his oath in silence, so his mother did not grasp that going to sea was an ardently held ambition of her son's. In fact, she felt quite guilty for sending him off at such an early age, and in her eagerness to explain it to him, she allowed the boy to depart with these disreputable words echoing in his ears – on that day in Den Gamle Oksen, twenty-seven years later, words spat through the carpet of hair as though branded on his brain: 'Finn Stein must have a room to smoke in and deliberate things. You understand, don't you, love? So he can look after your dear old mum the way your dear departed dad once did, but never can again. A way a boy can't care for his mum, but one day will do for a lucky young lass.'

Roald Agnar paused as he poured another measure of whisky into his beard and waited for it to douse these unexplained flames of anger.

He did not return to the subject of his mother for another half-bottle, but told me instead of the following four years he spent on the water, four years that found him maturing, growing immeasurably in size and producing the most remarkably unfettered head of hair I have yet seen on a man.

He departed Hundsund dragging his boat *Loki* behind him and boarded the whaling vessel on which Finn Stein had secured him the position of cabin boy. The dinghy was to remind him of his duty to the memory of his father, and though an odd and sizeable cargo for one so lowly as a cabin boy, the ship's Captain was unwilling to cause difficulties with the new son of the miraculous Finn Stein.

Large as Roald Agnar became over those four years, when finally the opportunity arose to battle the Kraken at the age of sixteen, he was still but a human being, armed with only a man's natural defences, and a whaling harpoon in addition.

Roald Agnar learned of the Kraken's whereabouts when his ship was docked in a port called Harstad, located at the foot of the island archipelago of Lofoten. On leave, he moved from island to island, hoping for news of the beast. *Loki* was now a boat as suited to him as it was to the great harpoon he lashed to its bow, and it sat low in the water as he moored at the village of Ballstad. He had intended to pause long enough only to sate his great appetite, but came upon a loud commotion as he squeezed into an eatery. Barging, with ease I expect, to the front of the ruckus, he ordered boiled fish from the establishment's proprietor, a man who took little notice of him. He was far too involved in the conversation he was conducting with his fellow ageing villagers to pay a customer any heed.

'I don't believe it either,' the proprietor was saying. 'How long has it been? Years, I'll bet!'

'Eight years, Hårvard. Eight years at least,' one of his friends informed him. 'But there's no question. It's started again. And you know what that means . . .'

'Bah!' said another, wearing spectacles, a thoughtful beard and great, protruding eyebrows. 'Poppycock. It's a whirlpool, that's all – a celestial whirlpool. The work of God. There's nothing more to it than that.' He raised his chin high above the collar of his shirt and sniffed the air.

But apparently, the divine manipulation that this man spoke of was not enough for some.

'It's *not* merely a whirlpool, Henrik. It is the Mælstrøm,' the informative chap argued. 'I know you are not from these parts, but even for one as learned as you, such disbelief is remarkable. Do you not recall the man who survived to see the beast? Do you not, Henrik?'

'I recall him,' Henrik said darkly from beneath his eyebrows. 'And he convinced you that the Kraken exists, did he? He convinced you that it has returned to its lair? That the Mælstrøm is born of its snores and thrashing tentacles as it dreams nightmares of the terror it has wrought?' Shaking his head, he laughed mirthlessly. 'I cannot help you people,' he said, donning his hat and turning to leave.

Forgetting his hunger, Roald Agnar followed this disbelieving gentleman into the refreshing June air. He confronted him as the man paused in his stride to put on his gloves.

'You do not believe in the Kraken?' Roald Agnar demanded breathlessly.

This chap Henrik narrowed his eyes and frowned at the boy he found towering over him.

'Son,' he said finally, 'what I believe is of no consequence to you. What you must do is find out for yourself. Nothing I nor any other man can say is going to restrain you from doing so. But if it does not exist, what then?'

He paused to allow Roald Agnar to rein in his confusion.

'Go now,' he continued. 'You will find the Charybdis of the north between Lofotodden and the island of Værøy, southwest of the main chain in the archipelago. Head for that small island and as surely as you do, you will be given the answers to your questions.' With that, he left.

If it does not exist, what then? Roald Agnar did not want to consider the question this strange man had posed and knew the best

way of avoiding it was with the labour of sailing, so without further ado he returned to the water's edge and launched *Loki* onto
the sea once more. However, his intentions were frustrated. There
was not a whisper of breeze in the blue skies. He would have to
row. Such was his determination to avenge his father and his desire
not to consider the ramifications of the Kraken being a myth, that
the burly lad fair sped over the water. There was so little movement in the sea that never once did it slop into the hull and never
once could Roald Agnar raise the sail. In fact, it was only after
another hour, when he was in the middle of the ocean, that anything distracted him from his steadfast strokes.

He was refreshing himself from a flask when he thought he
heard a deep rumbling from beneath him. The sea around him
was still, and he imagined the noise to be his anger welling within
him, so he corked his bottle and continued rowing, keen to avoid
the thought that could so easily lead to fear, which in its turn could
lead to cowardice and the abandoning of the realisation of his
young life's task. As his strokes took him further and further from
land, the rumbling amplified and he knew then that it could not
be coming from his body, but certainly it was travelling all the way
through it. It was the most fearsome sound he had ever heard, and
as he splashed on through the serene waters, it reached such levels
that he could no longer bring himself to row. Pulling the oars into
the boat, he covered his ears, closed his eyes and yelled to the heavens for deliverance.

When he opened his eyes once more he realised that even
though he was no longer rowing, even though there was still not
a breath of wind in the air, *Loki* was being carried onwards, and
with ever greater speed. He looked ahead and saw a great void in
the water before him and beyond it a tiny mass of land, two jagged
fingers of hills cursing all who approached. This was the
Mælstrøm, sucking him towards its vortex, and Værøy beyond.

Leaping to his feet, Roald Agnar grasped hold of the harpoon
with all his great might just as *Loki* entered the incline of a whirlpool
miles in diameter. The boat was swept around its rim as its skipper
looked into the churning, lightless jaws of death leagues below.

Round and round Roald Agnar went, roaring his madness to the killer of his father, faster and faster, each revolution shorter and quicker than the last. Water, flotsam and long dead fish were thrown at his face as he circled deeper and deeper into the rushing fury, and the bright and brilliant sun was eclipsed by the towering wall of water swallowing him to its depths. *Loki* buckled under the speed and pressure, her splintering blue wood disappearing into the liquid inferno, the water wrapping itself around the harpoon, ceaselessly trying to wrench it from Roald Agnar's grip. Then finally, after minutes that seemed like hours of battle, at the furious depths of the murderous whirligig's epicentre, Roald Agnar, through his fear and the great sheets of water that sliced into his face, saw two enormous pink, claw-like jaws part and a great, fleshy, razor-toothed orifice of a mouth open before him. Giving a terrible scream, he shot the harpoon's bolt forth. The barb and its rope whistled into the soft flesh between the foul fangs of teeth, the sharp metal and burning twine slithering into the great beast's soft body.

Then, quite suddenly, the rope had run its length and Roald Agnar was pulled towards the sea monster's mouth with such speed and power that he did not even have time to loosen his grasp before all went black, and he believed himself dead.

And now I must depart this hotel for the station in order to follow a lead. I will take up my pen again very soon, I promise you. I only hope that even though I must cut off this narrative so abruptly, you will continue to consider me

Your good friend,

Lindley-Small

THE NOTEBOOKS OF CYRIL KING

1893

Tolliver's Travels

Petts clapped and rubbed his hands together.

'Now then, lads, take your money back,' he smiled. 'No one's a loser here. And now Sarge, it was just beyond Gahkuch, if you remember.'

'I remember, sir.' The Sarge turned to me. He was a miserable sight. He did not look at me with hatred, though, despite the fact I was the one who had brought this scene about. His expression was both pleading and apologetic, full of a meaning I could not instantly identify.

'This Forrester, sir,' he said. 'He came rolling out of the hills. Practically under our hooves. He's injured, so we picks him up and bring him back here to the Captain. He was stark raving, as you said, sir.'

'That's right, Sarge,' said Petts. 'And we knew this chap already, didn't we? Rather well.'

'We did, sir,' the Sarge responded, shaking his head and looking at the table. 'He was a card player, sir. Played many a hand with us.'

'And lost many a hand, eh, Sarge?'

'That's right, sir. And he owed us plenty, sir. Plenty.'

'Then he ran off, didn't he, Sarge? Welshed on his debts. And we didn't like that, did we? And what did you do about it, Sarge, on his miraculous return?'

'I asked him for our money, sir.'

'But he didn't have it, did he, Sarge? Not a penny to his name.'

'No, sir.'

'So what did you do, Sarge?'

The Sarge suddenly looked up at me. There was fear in his eyes. When he looked down into the palms of his hands, I realised that it was not a fear of the Captain.

'I beat him, sir.'

'That's right, Sarge.' Petts turned to me. 'This ox of a man before you beat that ageing mouse of a man to within an inch of his life. It was a thing to see, I can tell you, lads. Right here in this very room. Wasn't it, Sarge?'

The fear was gone from the Sarge's eyes. Now he was looking at Petts with nothing short of loathing. The Captain seemed indifferent to his Staff Sergeant's reaction, though, for his face was still illuminated by that insidious smile.

'But you're not a violent man by nature, are you, Sarge? A good soldier, good at maintaining morale, but blood and guts aren't really your thing, are they? Not a born frontliner – that's why *I* got you.' Petts rose to his feet and started to pace back and forth behind his victim. 'And then Forrester got away, didn't he, Sarge? Escaped that very night. Still something of a mystery, eh, Sarge? But then, these civilians are slippery characters.' He turned his smile on me. 'Now, tell the man, Sarge. Why did you beat this poor wretch so, hmm?'

The Sarge looked at me.

'Because it was an order, sir,' he whispered.

'That's right. An order. And from whom did the order come, Sarge?'

I could barely hear the Sarge's voice when he said, 'You, sir.'

'That's right,' Petts said triumphantly. He jabbed a thumb at his own chest. 'Me, sir.'

I had thrown myself into the middle of something here, a nasty affair, with a foul character. Indeed, I was partly to blame for its inception, but so far it had nothing whatever to do with the information I was keen to obtain.

'Now, listen,' I said. 'What goes on here – well, a soldier's life is a soldier's life. I don't like what I hear, but what's done is done.'

Captain Petts was not listening.

'And why do we follow our superiors' orders?' he was saying as he strode. 'Because that is how we maintain discipline. And discipline is what divides the English from the rest of the world. So when our superior burdens us with an order, it is our duty to carry it out, no matter how unsavoury it may sound, no matter how deranged you may think it or its giver. A soldier's life is necessarily brutal, isn't that so, Corporal?'

He rounded on the corporal called Crampers, and waited for an answer. Crampers nodded meekly to his captain.

'Look,' I tried to continue. 'I'm not here to learn of your activities. All I wanted to ask you was where in the mountains Forrester had come from, when you found him, I mean.'

'Ah, but first, King, I must demand something of you … Corporal! Even if I order you to leap from a cliff, you must trust in my logic and do as I say, mustn't you? For the greater good. And if I order you to beat a man senseless, you shall do it, though it may only be for my enjoyment.' Petts spun round to look at me. 'Or perhaps the need for such an order can be avoided.' He held my eyes with his for a second, then turned again to Crampers. 'If you do not, Corporal—'

'Leave now, man.' It was the Sarge, whispering beneath the words of his hated captain. 'Leave now, or you may not at all. Your man came from the north, I know not from where.'

'—there shall be a court martial,' Petts was saying.

The Sarge's eyes were in earnest. He meant what he said. He spoke hurriedly. 'All your man could say was "Oliver's command", over and over, as though it were a peace offering. Nothing more than gibberish. Now leave, before you get the same treatment.'

If I correctly understood what the Sarge was saying, I was in danger of receiving a thrashing at the hands of Corporal Crampers, to satisfy the perverted pride of the lunatic Captain Petts. In exchange, the sum total of what I had learned was that Forrester was babbling nonsense when they found him. I rose unsteadily to my feet and edged away from the table. The Army compound, this station in Gilgit, established to advance British civility and law, was not the hub of sanity and safety I had thought it would be.

'"Oliver's command"?' I repeated. 'Who on earth is—'

Before I could move or say more, Petts caught me by the arm and twisted it behind my back.

'That's what the other one kept saying,' he whispered. 'Tut-tut. A man should learn when to keep his mouth shut. You leave me no option. Come on, now, laddy, Crampers needs the practice.'

Crampers was wilting in his chair. I felt Petts' voice in my ear.

'Make no mistake, before I have finished with you, you will reveal precisely where—'

'Tolliver's,' someone said. But the interruption did not come from Crampers. Nor from Finch, Fowler, or the Sarge. It did not even emanate from the Major, for I could still hear his snores. Not from Major Pound, at any rate.

Petts swung us round to face the entrance and stiffened instantly.

Major Flack had removed his helmet and was brushing it free of dust with his gloves. 'Not Oliver. Tolliver. Before your time, boys,' he said, then looked up at Petts and walked towards us purposefully. 'Now, Captain.'

'Major,' sneered Petts. 'You've returned empty-handed once more, it would appear. Did your rabbit elude you again? They are tricky customers, aren't they?'

'That they are, Captain. That they are.'

Major Flack stepped past us, glancing at me as he went, and said, in a perfectly pleasant tone, 'But it's only a matter of time 'til I bag him.'

At the table, with his back to us, he started to turn cards face up from the deck.

'Now, why don't we unhand that civilian, eh, Petts? Unless, of course, he's committed some crime in the few hours since I last saw him.' He turned his head slightly and I saw him smile with a lethal kindness. 'And that is an order, Captain.'

Petts loosened his grip.

'Wait for me outside – King, wasn't it?'

'It was – it is,' I stuttered.

'Very good. I'll be with you directly. I have a couple of matters to address here first.'

Without another word, I left the darkened room.

What a strange world I found myself in. I had not been surprised to learn that it was one capable of sending a man like Forrester round the bend. But that it could also turn upstanding, trained soldiers into bored and bloodthirsty madmen, well that was a revelation I should do well to keep in mind. I had not learned what Petts had wanted from me. Probably he had merely wanted to see me beaten, but thanks to Major Flack's timely arrival I would not have to find out.

I heard raised voices from the mess, but Major Flack joined me in the courtyard a few minutes later and he was still smiling. Here was the reassuring face of the Englishman, the gentleman and soldier famous throughout the world for his chivalry and fair dealing.

'Terribly sorry about that. Not very welcoming. Bit of a loopy sod, our Petts, but essentially a good soldier. Should've known not to've left him under Pound, though.'

'No luck on your hunt?' I queried.

'These things take time, you know. We're on the bugger's trail. Seems the opening of old wounds is the order of the day. What with me on the hunt for that blighter and you asking about Tolliver,' he clarified.

I was pleased that he had brought it up, since I was keen to find out about this Oliver, or Tolliver, and why Forrester should have been mumbling his name. Flack was only too willing to divulge all he knew, and I found myself wishing I had arrived at the compound a good hour later than I had. That way I would have got straight to the chase, instead of stepping into a viper's nest.

'Tolliver was a soldier, one of the first to be sent up to these parts, before we got the Maharajah on side. Spoke the lingo. Supposed to look things over, smooth the path,' the Major said. 'He was a captain, like Petts. Eccentric like Petts, too – in a different way. Spent a lot of time with the natives. Knew their customs, even passed as one when called for. Useful chap in the beginning, before he went all the way to outright bloody mad, of course. His entire outfit was taken captive, up towards the Wakhan. Tortured, they say. Only two of them made it back alive, Tolliver and his *jemadar*. Tolliver'd had a hand lopped off. Bloody miracle he made it back at all, really. Gone entirely native by the time he got back to Gilgit. Invalided out of the service; but when they tried to send him home, he headed back up to Hunza, where he'd been stationed. They say it was there that the madness overtook him. Ended up a bloody mess . . . Small by massacre standards, but infamous amongst the locals.' He paused to frown at the sky and rubbed his chin. 'And all because of a ruddy game.'

'Game?' I prompted, bewildered.

'Polo. Local matches, and taken jolly seriously they are, too. Up here they call it the game of kings. They invented the sport, apparently – it's quite something, the way they play it. You should watch a game if you get the chance. These chaps used to fight amongst themselves even more than they do now, if you can believe it. Valley against valley, village against village. These days they're as likely to do battle with mallet and ball on the pitches as they are with swords and daggers in the mountains. There's a field up Hunza way. Hundreds crowd back and forth along the trails to see the games. Used to send a company along to show willing with the Maharajah. Tolliver was with them. Lost his head without any warning whatsoever – started shooting at the natives with his pistol. Bad place for panic, up there. The path's only wide enough for a wagon, then sheer cliffs, up on one side, down on the other. Whole thing ended pretty badly. Natives shot, trampled, fell down the cliff. Nothing we could do to stop it once the panic set in.' Flack shook his head disbelievingly.

'Our lot weren't too popular after that, as you can imagine. The natives wanted blood, and they would've got it if Tolliver had been found, but the fact is, he disappeared back into the mountains. The man he made it back from the Wakhan with, his *jemadar* adjutant, headed up a team to bring him in. Searched for weeks. Found his body in the end – looked as though the natives got their vengeance after all. Hacked to death and left there for the buzzards – only recognisable because of his missing hand.

'What's your interest in all this, anyway?' Flack asked suddenly. 'We've got other things to worry about in those mountains. Russians and all that.'

'Well, I don't know that I have any, really. It's Forrester I'm interested in. He's what brought me here.'

'To the fort, you mean? Or Gilgit?'

'Both, really,' I answered. 'I was told the Army picked him up last year. He owed them money, and couldn't pay.'

'Forrester, yes, I remember,' he said. 'He was hell-bent on heading off further into the mountains. Had some idea about the people up there. Migration of man or some such nonsense. Spent his evenings in the Mess, telling us how it would make his name if he could prove it, trying to persuade us to escort him. If that's your notion, you're as cracked as he was.

'I warned him not to try it alone. Told him what happened to Tolliver. Thought it might frighten him off, but it didn't work. If anything it spurred him on, because off he went – just like that.' Flack clicked his fingers. 'Mind you, dangerous though it is up there, it's here, stuck in these settlements, that would send me dotty. It's not in the nature of a soldier. When a fellow like Petts is on the move, he's a different man altogether. Forrester had him to thank for his rescue, you know – Petts. He's been idle too long, that's all.'

The Major looked out over the fort's walls and up towards the peaks.

'Our boys gave the Ishkumanis a good hiding after Tolliver made it back from the Wakhan,' he said. 'That kind of savagery can't be tolerated. Had to get rid of the troublemakers. Not much left up there now. A nasty business.'

'Ishkumanis? Who are they?' I interrupted.

'Ishkuman – that's where Tolliver and his men were taken,' he answered. 'It's a valley to the northwest of here. Your chum Forrester was picked up in Gahkuch, though. I can show you, actually. Follow me.'

He led me to the stables, where he delved into the bags of a saddle that was hanging over a beam next to a horse. The place was musty and cool.

The Major unfolded a map and held it against the animal's ribcage.

'Steady,' he said, as the horse shifted its weight. 'Now then, King. We are here, yes?' He pointed to Gilgit on the map. Then he drew his finger northwest, along the Gilgit river. 'That there is the Ghezar valley. And there's Gahkuch, where Forrester was found.'

I peered over his shoulder. Beyond Gahkuch the map showed neither trails, towns nor villages. Nothing but a wilderness of sharply shaded peaks.

'God knows what he thought he was doing, a man like that' Flack was saying. 'Any villages north of that are a bloody long way apart. Days and days of tough mountain terrain before you get to the nearest. We've not mapped it properly yet. Impossible to find your way about without a guide.'

He refolded the map and regarded me sternly for a moment.

'I must advise you to go home, King,' he said. 'Forrester's long gone, and never found his proof. He was lucky to get out alive. There's nothing up there but bandits.'

'I understand your concern, Major,' I began, 'but I've come too far—'

'Well,' he cut me off, his expression brightening 'if you must go, I'm taking a detail out that way myself tomorrow. Escort duty. Leaving soon after daybreak. Be here at first light and you can ride along with us as far as Gahkuch. After that you're on your own. Don't expect Her Majesty's forces to rescue you if you find yourself in trouble. We've got other fish to fry. But in Gahkuch you can hire yourself a guide and a couple of horses. 'Til we get there, we'll kit you out with one of our remounts here.'

I could scarcely believe my luck. 'That's very generous of you,' I said.

'Not generous at all,' he replied as we made our way to the gate. 'Never really believed I'd be able to dissuade you, but I was duty bound to try. It's a long ride, so be here on time. Oh, and there's a decent rest house not a minute's walk up that road. I'm assuming you'd rather that than bunk here?'

Major Flack was quite correct. I did not want to pass a night inside the fort with the likes of Captain Petts. Besides, the sun was still well up in the sky. Beyond the town, a bare and rocky hillside rose up steeply to a gap between two peaks, so I resolved to climb it, in the belief that solitude and mountain air would clear my mind and allow me some time to reflect on my discoveries.

I had much to think about.

12

THE LETTERS OF
SIR PAUL LINDLEY-SMALL

Awaiting The Wings of the North *locomotive*
Kristiansand, Norway

6TH DECEMBER 1908

My friend,

I must fast conclude what I began, and get it sent off before my train arrives and takes me north to further developments. So, onwards with Roald Agnar's tale.

You will remember that he thought himself dead, but of course he was not, for here he was finishing off a bottle at my side in Den Gamle Oksen and calling the pallid Ole for another. No, all went black, but he came to lying prostrate, clasping something to his chest. Hauling himself onto his palms, he propped his broken body against a rock and looked down at his hands. In them, he held all that was left of *Loki* – a blue plank bearing the boat's name. The rest was gone. The harpoon, the mast, the sails. All memories of his father, gone and lost. To his right a jagged hill rose above him, to his left the same. He was far from the water's edge.

The water, good God! He was far from the water where the Mælstrøm still raged. Where the damnable Kraken still lived.

He had failed.

Bellowing a curse on the beast with all the power his water-logged lungs could muster, he gave up when his voice turned to gurgling. Hearing a quiet chortle from behind him, he scrambled around to see the familiar form of Henrik.

'You . . . You . . .' gasped Roald Agnar. 'You said it didn't exist. You said you didn't believe in the Kraken.'

'I *don't* believe in the Kraken. It is not a question of belief. It exists, and I know it as well as you now do. In fact, I know it better than any man.'

He paused and waited for this news to filter through Roald Agnar's hairy and now waterlogged ears.

'You see, I am the world's foremost expert on this beast,' Henrik went on. 'Of course, there's only one other who possesses cate-gorical knowledge of its existence – you. But still I like to think I know a good amount about it. What is missing from my ency-clopaedic knowledge is why a lad who did not yet know it existed sought the beast so desperately, and sought to do it harm, at that.'

Roald Agnar's heaving lungs were calming and between breaths he managed to say, 'I will kill it. Kill it for taking the life of Captain Roald Petter, my father.'

'That's a common enough ambition. But not one ever achieved,' Henrik said gently. 'And it's usually one that dilutes with time – a process I hope I speed up by spreading word that the Kraken is a mythical beast. Why *you* should be so sure that it really exists where others are so easy to convince otherwise is what I don't under-stand.'

Roald Agnar took several deep breaths and composed his mind as best he could before speaking again.

'You said that I am now only the second living man to know of its existence; to have seen it. You are wrong, old man. I am the third.'

'You speak of that First Mate, I assume, who some years back claimed to have survived the Kraken's attack. His entire ship, the wood of its masts, its crew, even his Captain, they were all consumed, and he alone escaped. Is that what you refer to? Do you think it possible to survive the Kraken's attack?'

'*I* have survived it,' Roald Agnar responded, reasonably enough.

'You were not attacked. No, no. You merely approached the beast as it slept in its lair. You are fortunate not to have experienced the power of a full assault in all its glorious fury today. There is nothing on this earth or in God's blue seas that could survive such a force. It's a thing of great and terrible beauty, one that I have been lucky enough to observe on occasion.'

'And you survived?'

'Enough talk of me. You are only the second living observer of the Kraken, you can take my educated word for it, and as such, you must keep your knowledge of its existence to yourself and stop seeking to destroy it. Continuing to do so would only bring about your death and yet more hatred for this magnificent creature and more hunters for its scalp. It may have killed your father, lad, and I'm sorry for that, but cease your hopeless task. Cease it now.'

Roald Agnar's hairy brow was ruffled. He was thinking with an intensity of which Socrates himself would have been proud. Henrik awaited a reply to his pleas. The one he received surprised him.

'Are you sure Finn Stein did not see the Kraken? Absolutely sure?'

'If Finn Stein is the survivor of that boat, I can assure you – there is no possibility that he laid eyes upon the beast. No possibility at all. Because it was not the Kraken that took his boat.'

Henrik had approached Roald Agnar and now put a consoling hand on his shoulder. In response, Roald Agnar grabbed him by the collars of his surprisingly urbane suit with all his remaining might.

'But can you prove it, man?' he roared.

'I do not answer questions under threat. Unhand me.'

Roald Agnar did so and slumped back against his rock.

'Of course I can prove it. Tell me why it concerns you so and I shall do so directly.'

'My father, Roald Petter, was Captain on that very ship, and the day I learned he had been taken by the Kraken I swore an oath: I would hunt the creature to its death or mine. And here you say that it was not the Kraken who took him. If not, then what? Who? Now speak, man, and speak clearly.'

'Wherever the Kraken goes, I go,' Henrik said wearily, sitting down. 'Over seas, oceans, fjords, lochs and lakes, wherever its desire takes it, I must follow. Whenever it feeds, I must watch; whenever it sleeps, I must work to protect it. I am a man of the ocean rarely in company of my fellow men or women, feeding only from the remains of the beast's hunt, drinking only what the seas can offer. Though the Kraken dives deep, I know its course. Though it swims fast, I do not struggle to keep abreast of it. Do not ask how this came about, for I will not tell you, but it is my pleasure and my curse. That is why you can believe my words. It returned to its lair here only two weeks ago after an eight-year journey around the waters of the globe. Four years ago, when it was said by his fortunate First Mate to have consumed the entirety of your father's ship off the coast of Spain, the Kraken was in fact enveloped in a month-long amorous entanglement not a mile from Messina. I watched the curious courtship from a mountain on the Sicilian coast.'

He looked at Roald Agnar, who was furious and confused.

'So it is not the Kraken you seek, I am afraid, lad,' Henrik said solemnly. 'And I fear you must ask yourself why a man would claim it to be so.'

This was a question Roald Agnar had already asked, and already answered. The confusion was gone, leaving only his rage.

As you know, it had taken very little time for Finn Stein to move into both the house and the place of Roald Petter. It took substantially longer for him to grow tired of his new surroundings and of Gunhild, who saw to his every need every moment they were together. But bored he became, and after three years he left the seamstress in their home and set out on a new voyage, this time as Skipper of the newly built *Valkyrie II*. It was in search of this boat that Roald Agnar departed the island of Værøy. He left the strange and urbane Henrik at the port of Å, swearing to a new oath – that he would never again speak of what he had seen at the eye of the Mælstrøm.

It was on returning to their mothering port of Kristiansand that the deck hands of the *Valkyrie II* spotted a body in the water clinging to a deep blue piece of flotsam. With a glee that glowed through his matted locks, the drunken and hairy character at my table in Den Gamle Oksen told me that the ship's log would reveal as much, if only I could locate it at the bottom of the sea many leagues southwest of the town. For not long after they had taken him aboard, the ship began to sink due to a breach in its hull. So quickly did it go down, that none survived. None, that is, but the ship's Captain, the remarkable Finn Stein. He made his way ashore, cursed the Kraken that hunted him, blessed his fallen crew and soon enough became Skipper upon the newly built *Valkyrie III*.

The new boat was stronger and bigger, capable of carrying more goods and more stores than its unfortunate sisters. It sailed the world, delivering spices, sugars, woods and peoples. It ferried goods far and wide, from Iceland to Australia, India to Brazil. For those months the crew toiled against the seven seas, and for each that passed more keenly did they await a return to wives and children, sweethearts and parents, the rocky shores of home and the green and snow. Alas for these men, they were never to see anyone again but their Maker and His blue oceans below.

Only after a full year at sea did she fall, just as her sister had done, in fair weather and soon after the crew had hauled aboard a stranded sailor clinging to the deep blue remains of his craft, though this time it was in the Pacific two days' sail from San Francisco. Just as with the second *Valkyrie*, the sole survivor of the shipwreck was Finn Stein, its Captain, and the cause he gave for its wrecking, the cursed Kraken.

A fourth *Valkyrie* was built, and again Finn Stein was given captaincy.

Now, the sailors of this world are a superstitious breed and only the most desperate, brave or foolhardy could be persuaded to man this latest vessel. Finn Stein, a sailor like any other, was also a man of superstitions, and his grew to revolve around his own mortality, or lack thereof. He began to believe that when on a *Valkyrie* he was immortal, a God of the Seas. Neptune as Man. And the more times he could convince people he was blessed to survive the attacks of the Kraken, the greater his fame grew and the greater his opinion of himself. Without regard for the disreputable crew he managed to amass, Finn Stein sailed the world with never a return to home waters for five full years. On returning from the Americas in May of the fifth year, the *Valkyrie* sank some distance from the Azores and again, of registered crew, he alone survived, and again, when he returned to the fanfare reserved for a national hero, he blamed the Kraken and their sacred feud for the deaths of his men.

However, on his return to Norway, following this fourth consecutive miraculous survival, opinions began to divide over Finn Stein. To some, to the very dullest and most impressionable of sailors, he became the god that he himself saw in the looking-glass. To these men, he was a sailor the likes of whom the world had never seen, a man so extraordinary that he was to be followed to its very ends. When he skippered a *Valkyrie*, it would ride the worst weathers but never come to any harm. Only when fate deemed it must meet the Kraken would there be any semblance of danger, but many were willing to take that risk for the privilege of sailing under a legend, in the belief that they too could survive the Kraken's wrath, as well as getting the chance to glimpse the beast feared by the entire world.

To others, the many good and simple sailors of the seas for whom self-preservation was ultimate, Finn Stein was not a man to be followed, but one to be feared, a skipper whose cursed *Valkyries* were to be avoided at all costs. Fate had fingered him to survive the hexed family of ships and their attacker, but, it seemed, at the expense of all others on board. To these men, starvation at home was preferable to years of hardship on the oceans, followed with devilish certainty by a watery end.

To the remaining few who knew him, Finn Stein became an object of suspicion. How had he survived? Was it the sea's madness? Or was it the bartering of a man who had sold his soul to the devil? They could not say, but logic dictated that no man could live as Finn Stein had without some supernatural dealings. The whisperings of conspiracy were upon this remarkable fellow.

However, what nobody – not the dullest, not the simplest, nor the most intelligent – had considered was that Finn Stein was himself cursed, not by any deity or higher or lower power, but by a man, once a boy wronged.

Even though port and shipping governors themselves suspected him of being an unfit skipper, Finn Stein's reputation among the public was such that to every boy in a boat he was a hero, the only man in the world the Kraken could not kill, linked in fate to the Valkyries, both the vessels and the mythical carriers of the dead. The Norse legends tell of Odin's twelve handmaidens marking warriors to be slain in battle. Upon each of the ships they had chosen all to ride with them into the afterlife, but each time Finn Stein had fought the beast more bravely than the rest and was spared to fight it again and again and again. 'He is quite mad, though, child,' mothers would tell their sons, and the authorities would echo them. But as long as there were sailors foolish enough to sail under him, they could do nothing to stop him. Even the company that built the *Valkyries*, men of business whom one would expect to disregard legend and superstition in the light of such severe financial losses, were persuaded by his name to continue building the ships for him to man.

When he had first returned to Hundsund with tales of the Kraken, Finn Stein had been a very fit man, one quite capable of swimming to shore. Each ship, from the fifth to the eleventh *Valkyrie*, lost its way in water further and further from land. However, though each time the icy waters consumed the ever-reducing crew, Finn Stein successfully swam ashore. In the freezing waters of the world there is only so much physical fitness can do for you – no matter how trim you may be, the cold will finish you off. That is, of course, if you are sane. Luckily for him, it seems that Finn Stein's mania was precisely the type required to survive so many wrecks. Were he as sound in mind as he was in body, I daresay he would have died years ago. That he lives to this day I am certain is due to his mental decline and his belief in his own indestructibility.

You may recall that I arrived in this country on the twelfth of the ships and landed quite safely on mainland Norway, without so much as a hint of wreckage. I put this to my new acquaintance, Roald Agnar Johansen, and he roared with laughter, before slamming his glass onto the table with such force that the two men I had seen sleeping on my arrival at the tavern jerked to attention, only to subside into mumbling slumber once more. His laughter came again and I split what remained of the second bottle of whisky between us.

'It was twenty-seven years ago that I looked into the jaws of that beast,' he said. 'Twenty-seven years since I learned of that man's skulduggery. Learned that he killed my father in order to take his place in my mother's bed. Twenty-seven years and ten *Valkyries* I've sunk, and *still* he's not dead.' He drained his glass in a single tangled gulp.

'Why don't you just buy yourself a good machete and have his head off?' I asked, for I had become quite taken up by the whole affair.

'He must die as my father did,' was the sombre reply. 'And so I must go yonder.'

He looked out towards the *Valkyrie XII*.

Enthralled as I was by Roald Agnar's story, he had not provided me with any evidence of the beast's existence. His story, I concluded, was nothing more than a custom-tailored tale, of the sort often told by a sailor in need of a drink. As I sipped pensively at mine, it occurred to me that it was his way, in a very roundabout fashion, of asking my aid. His next words confirmed my suspicions.

'Perhaps, sir,' he said, turning back from the window to face me, 'perhaps *you* can help me get aboard. I'd do anything required on the vessel. He shall not escape this time – nor, I wager, shall I. It is the destiny of both who have lived by each other's actions for so long to perish together.'

Gone was the rage from his left eye and the amusement from his right. All that was left was solemnity and a lifetime of damage. This, after all, had been the humble purpose of his storytelling: there in the tavern he was doing nothing more than looking for work, as a thousand, thousand sailors had before him. I decided that doing my bit to secure him honest labour was the very least I could do in exchange for such a fine tale, and since Ralf, the *Valkyrie XII*'s barman, had become rather an acquaintance of mine, I gave Roald Agnar a letter of introduction, requesting that Ralf give this down-trodden brute any position there might be on the rig.

In grateful response, Roald Agnar suggested I approach the har-bour-master for news of the *Syren* and my Spaniard, and it was then that the lad I awaited arrived with my luggage. I told Roald Agnar that I would follow his advice, and wished him luck upon his quest. I left him the rest of my glass and took my leave of the tavern and a cab to my evening's lodgings.

The following morning, as I made my way back to the harbour, the urchin who had procured my luggage the day before stopped me in midstep and pushed a handwritten note into my palm. It was from Roald Agnar. In a near-illegible scrawl, he thanked me profusely and told me that he had secured registered employment as an engine hand upon the *Valkyrie XII*. I was pleased to have helped the poor fellow on his fantastical way and moved briskly on to the office of the harbour-master, my hotel and the train I have now boarded.

I shall hand this letter to the conductor to post before we depart, but prior to that I must inform you that I am now burdened by a deep concern. I fear I might have cost this strange fellow Roald Agnar his life, not to mention any passengers aboard the *Valkyrie XII* and the rest of its crew. It is a pity so many could have met their watery end, especially Ralf the barman, for he served a fine tipple, and a teller of such tales as Roald Agnar is perhaps also a loss, but to lose those dancers . . . well now, that would be nothing short of a tragedy. Those dear girls had much to offer, and so little time to give it.

I am now sitting in my train awaiting the commencement of the next leg of my journey. In our compartment, the superficially prudish, but, I am convinced, fundamentally smouldering lady seated beside me translates the newspaper stories for me as I write and as she builds to flames. There was nothing in the paper relating to what I seek, though I must say that I was quite distracted by the alluring way in which she passed her tongue over her teeth at the close of each sentence. That is, until she read the one which told of the sinking of the *Valkyrie XII* and of its sole, unnamed survivor.

Fearing that I am perhaps the unknowing perpetrator of this disaster, I nonetheless hope you will still consider me,

Your good friend,

Lindley-Small

13

THE NOTEBOOKS OF CYRIL KING

1893

Epiphanies

As I climbed, I reflected on what I had discovered. Multah had told me what the stone signified, and of the legend of Adam-Khor. He had told the same story to Forrester. That was crucial, to learn that Forrester had been here; surely that meant that I had been right to come to Gilgit, and I was on the right trail. Major Flack had said that Forrester had come to these parts to seek out an ancient people. That could have been a blind, of course, but then Forrester was an historian, after all. Whatever the truth, I believed I understood why Forrester had bolted all alone into the mountains. There was something other than people out there, something worth risking his life for, and it had to do with the renegade soldier, Tolliver. Until Flack had told him about Tolliver, he had been content to kick his heels in the fort and lose money at cards while he tried to persuade the Army to give him an escort. All of a sudden he no longer wanted their company; whatever he had got wind of, he wanted to keep to himself. What else could that be but the treasure of Adam-Khor?

He must have made the same connection that I had made, for

I now knew, or thought I knew, who had set the stone into the watch. Multah had said it had been a one-handed native. Tolliver had lost a hand, and Major Flack had said he could pass as a native, even among the tribes. Tolliver had been sent up here to explore the mountains – what better position from which to have found whatever secrets they held. Was that why he was so keen to get back up to Hunza when the Army removed him from active service? And after the massacre on the Hunza trail, he had disappeared into the mountains. Before his death, had he been trying to get back to the treasure he had found?

I had learned from the soldiers, however, that Forrester had come back empty-handed. If he had had precious stones on him he would surely have used them to pay his debts and save himself a beating. That meant either that he hadn't found any, or that he had and he meant to come back for them later. But if that was the case, escaping Petts, why had he fled all the way to Cairo? He had been en route to London, I remembered from the newspaper – perhaps he had meant to raise enough funds to mount an expedition.

Forrester had been picked up near Gahkuch, but Gahkuch had not been his destination, I was certain. Mulling over what Flack had told me, I had a sudden flash of inspiration. Forrester *had* tried to bargain for his safety, with information he thought Petts and co. might value; only because he was insensible and raving, they had not understood him. What he had been saying was not 'Tolliver's command' at all, but 'Tolliver, Ishkuman'. By Jove! I thought. That was the final piece of my puzzle. I knew where it was that Forrester had been trying to get to, and where I must go from Gahkuch, and where Tolliver had got the black sapphire stone. The same place he had narrowly escaped with his life. *Ishkuman*.

*

It took me some time to reach the top of the gap between the peaks, despite the fact that the height to which I climbed paled beside those that grew steadily upwards on either side. When finally I did so, owing to both strenuous physical and mental activity, I was short of breath. Pausing and looking back, the town appeared small and weak in the palm of the mountains. To my right, a stream ran from the higher peaks and disappeared ahead of me. I followed it along the flat area I had come to, beyond a gigantic boulder to a point where the water abruptly plunged off a cliff, forming a deep pool more than a hundred yards below. From there, a river meandered along the foot of an uninhabited valley, before snaking out of sight.

After the effort of the climb, the sudden drop before me made my knees wobble, so I retreated a little way and sat leaning against the boulder, facing the new valley. In places dry, coarse thyme was growing through the rock and lent the air a pleasing scent as I basked in the sunlight. I pulled my pipe and tobacco pouch from my pocket, packed and lit up, exhilarated by the way things were taking shape.

As I put match to bowl, I chanced to look through the rising smoke and a movement caught my eye. From a gulley between two mountains, a faint blur was travelling towards the waterway. The spinning air had picked up the dust on the mountainside and was leading it downwards. At the mountain's foot, it paused momentarily, as though choosing a direction. Selecting to come my way, it proceeded to dance from left to right over the valley floor, a dust devil trapped, it seemed, in the great cage formed by the mountains.

I narrowed my eyes. The movement of the dust was odd, I thought, almost as if it had a sense of purpose. I reached for my Gladstone and groped within for my spyglass. As I did so, I heard the crack of gunfire, for the second time that day. Fumbling for speed, I extracted the spyglass, flicked it to its full length and frantically scanned the landscape.

At once I saw why the whirlwind had seemed so anomalous. The dust was raised neither by wind nor mountain but by a lone rider and the hooves of his horse. At the river they burst from the cloud, dashing across the waterway, a spume of spray around them, galloping at a pace of which an Ascot Gold Cup winner could be proud.

The only weapon the rider held was the length of rein with which he was relentlessly lashing his animal. Dropping the glass from my eye, I saw whence the sound of gunfire must have come. Following the route of the first, a second, far greater whirlwind had appeared. Through my glass, I saw more horsemen, eight of them, garbed in the beige coats and puttees of native uniform. They were Major Flack's men, chasing down their quarry. Those who had fired their rifles were labouring to reload at speed, while others struggled even to level theirs, let alone fire.

But fire they did, and as the single rider worked his way towards me, he was zigzagging wildly, dodging the bullets, his grey horse, dripping with water and sweat combined, digging its hooves at every turn into the sand of the riverbank. His pursuers, travelling in a more direct line, were gaining on him by yards every second. They slung their rifles over their shoulders and drew their pistols, closing in for repeat fire, close enough now for me to see the blasts from the outstretched barrels and the puffs of rock and splashes of water pinging around the rider with every shot.

As the valley narrowed below me and the desperate beggar approached the unscalable cliff face that led up to the peak I sat upon, he reared his beast to a standstill and turned it to face oncoming death. He drew his own long-barrelled pistol and levelled it. I watched as he shot all six rounds from his revolver in the time it took each of Flack's men to discharge one. He found a target with four, throwing the riders from their saddles.

Then, as quickly as he had turned to face them, he violently pulled his reins again and whipped and kicked his horse into a renewed frenzy, galloping onto the slope of the mountain to my left. The horse's hooves plunged into the scree, slipping backwards almost as fast as they climbed. Their progress was painfully slow, but they were moving onwards, for then I lost sight of them under the lip of the cliff.

Flack's remaining men, still within view, brought their horses to a halt at the foot of the mountain and calmly took aim. Despite my knowledge that these men were in the Queen's service, I found myself rooting for their enemy. He was making yet another valiant effort at a getaway, and in the same dashing style he had exhibited earlier that day in town. Besides, there still remained the niggling question of his familiarity, and I should be sorry if I never had an opportunity to resolve it.

I knew it was dangerous, for the excitement of this scene had only added to the unsteadiness of my knees, but I made my way to the lip of the cliff as quickly as I was able, hoping that I would not see his summary execution.

In the seconds it took me to get there, all firing ceased, and I was sure that the poor villain had been shot down.

I crawled to the very edge of the crag and at its foot saw the four remaining horsemen, each shouting incomprehensibly to the skies. I edged forward to see the cause of their apparent celebration, but there was neither bloodied corpse nor grey horse to be seen.

I scanned the entire mountainside for sign of them, but there was not a trace. Those were not celebrations being conducted below me, as the soldiers retreated to gather their injured comrades, but yells of anger, frustration and disappointment. It seemed the lone horseman had vanished just as whirlwinds do when the swirling air dies down. Both man and horse had been swallowed by the earth.

I withdrew to the safety of my seat among the rocks and gazed into the sky. Over and beyond the peaks to my left, dust was rising into the air.

*

Pleased that this chap had apparently avoided such a nasty end and sure that he would in time be picked up and arrested in the correct fashion, I repacked my pipe and reflected on how I might imitate his actions if circumstance called for it once I parted ways with Major Flack in Gahkuch.

I must have been considering it for some time, for when I was abruptly roused from my reverie, the sun had lowered and, ignoring the rules of physics, was balancing on one of the peaks to the west.

The sound that brought me to was the scuff of hoof on rock and came from the slope behind me. A man on foot came over the hillside, leading a horse, and eclipsed the sun, leaving only the solid black silhouettes of man and beast for me to make out.

'Salaam aleikum,' he said when he saw me, as unsurprised that I should be on this barren spot as I was surprised to be happened upon.

I narrowed my eyes to see whom I was addressing. 'Aleikum salaam,' I responded, touching my chest, lips and forehead as he had done.

He was tallish, six foot I should say, and thicker set than me by half. Indeed, this bull-like figure did not fit anybody I had encountered thus far except the Sarge, and he was a shorter man. Besides, this man was a native – I could see the outline of his turban, the scarf that covered much of his face, and his *chapan* cinched in at the waist by a belt. He could have been a shepherd but for his lack of sheep, or a traveller perhaps, though the route he was taking was not one that struck me as common, leading as it did to mountains inhabited by no one but soldiers and their prey.

'Can I help you, sir?' I asked.

But he did not get the chance to respond, for meanwhile another two men had silently joined us. These two I could make out, for they were slightly to the right of the other and partially illuminated by the orange sun. Their dress was also native, but torn and dirty, their horses bony, their faces hungry and desperate. One was perhaps sixty; the other was young, not yet twenty. Straps held ammunition to their breasts and swinging from their waists were swords and daggers. The elder cupped the butt of a pistol stuffed into his belt. They were unquestionably bandits. I had not had to travel into the mountains to encounter them, after all. The three of them formed a gang, I thought, and I readied myself to fight tooth and nail to the very end, determined to leave this world as an explorer rather than a watchmaker. I then realised that the two latecomers were not yet looking at me at all, but at the man I could not make out. He was, I suspected, their leader.

The silhouette followed my line of vision and turned to look at them. The old bandit drew his pistol from his belt, pointed it at his shadowy countryman and spoke with some aggression. His tone suggested that they were not of one mind. The silhouette did not seem to register this, however. At the very least, he did not care, for he laughed and said something in return.

The two exchanged more words and the old bandit grew more civil. He lowered his firearm and I felt distinctly uneasy when the silhouette casually gestured in my direction.

'Hmm? Hmm?' he said to the old bandit, and rubbed his fingers together in the universal symbol for money.

Smiling now, the old bandit led his horse towards me and reached out a hand with which he stroked my clothes and tugged at my Gladstone. I began to back away from him. It seemed now that they were not a team, but were deciding to whom the booty would go, and that booty was me. I was unarmed, and edging towards a drop of one hundred yards. I could do nothing more. The silhouette and the youngster would seize me if I ran. Onwards the old one came, moving with the awkward precision of a mountain goat, grinning through an armoury of yellow teeth. Behind me I heard the sound of pebbles falling. I was at the cliff's edge; but on he came, nearer, closer, until I could feel his fetid breath on my cheek. I readied myself to grab hold of his bandolier. If I were to die, I would not be the only one.

And that was when I saw it.

The bandit did not realise it at first, for the hand holding the knife moved slowly and utterly steadily, the stalking feline to the old man's goat. Indeed, he was still grinning as I watched the hand make its way around his neck. The poor beggar must have thought my eyes were widening in fear of him, for he laughed. It was this movement that made the silhouetted one's arm brush the ageing bandit's whiskers, and then there was a lightning flurry of movement. With one hand the bandit grabbed his assailant's wrist, while he clawed at the face behind him with the other. But the blade already pressed against his throat. The old man panicked and began to flail his arms and shout. He seized hold of my shirt collar and pulled me towards him and I saw his own eyes widen with fear and the knowledge of imminent mortality. And as they pleaded, I heard words whispered into his ear.

'Send my regards to Allah!'

Then the knife cut his throat from one side to the other and the pounding blood of terror sprayed across my face.

I was speechless. Never before had I seen such brutality, and it went straight to my stomach. I fell to my knees as my gut wrenched, and the killer dropped the bandit at my feet. The dying man's eyes were open still and I watched life drain from them as his blood pumped from his throat.

Had I thought of it at the time, I would have considered it odd that the younger of the bandits had not prevented this murder from occurring. The reason he did not, however, was evident when I looked up to see the killer walking away from me, wiping his blade clean on some thyme he had torn from the ground. He sheathed it and removed his rifle from his saddle. The young lad, younger than I, had fled in terror. As I rose to my feet, I saw him on his horse, galloping down the mountainside towards the town. He was not even halfway yet, and I saw that he would never make it alive, for the killer had lain on the ground and was resting the muzzle of his firearm on his steady palm. He was taking aim at the boy. Not only had he secured the booty, he was also eliminating the competition. So cold a killer could hardly miss at that range.

I do not know why, or even how, but my sense of justice rose above my fear and nausea and I found myself sprinting towards him, bounding over the rock. Just as he squeezed the trigger, I succeeded in kicking the gun off aim. The shot echoed, and the bullet whizzed into the loose stones twenty yards distant. There was no time for a second shot, for moments later the youth was lost from sight.

Suddenly my legs went from under me and I fell to the ground. I landed face to face with the man whose murderous spree I had interrupted. His eyes were a blue inferno of anger. He clenched my shirt collars in one powerful fist and shook me violently.

'Good God, man! What do you think you're doing? They're sure to find me now, you imbecile!'

The meaning of his words, though significant, did not filter into my brain. There was another aspect to them that was busy striking me. Had I not been so mesmerised by his repellent behaviour and the fear that had filled the old bandit's eyes, I should have noticed it when he had whispered those taunting words in his victim's ear. They were not uttered in the musical language of the locals. On the contrary, I had understood them. It was English, but not the awkward English spoken by the teahouse proprietor and Multah Taqdir. This was the English of an Englishman.

I reached out my hand and pulled away his headscarf. Under dust, tan and beard was the white skin of an Englishman, and a pair of familiar, crystalline blue eyes. I had seen this man twice already that day and on both occasions he had made a miraculous escape. It was the one the soldiers had called the rabbit, who had galloped through the praying crowd in Gilgit, the very man I had seen escaping from the soldiers in the valley below. He was vile, uncouth and criminal just as I had expected he would be, but that he was a vile, uncouth and criminal Englishman was not something I had bargained for, and that altered the stakes considerably.

14

THE LETTERS OF
SIR PAUL LINDLEY-SMALL

From a butcher's hut in
Kautokeino, Norway

19TH DECEMBER 1908

My dear Cyril,

This Norway I find myself in is a land which covers an area half again as big as the rock which you call home, but with a twelfth the number of people living upon it. The population lives predominantly in the warmer southern parts or else in the coastal towns, although here in the north these are more akin to settlements than cities. It is, therefore, a kingdom bottom-heavy in both shape and demography, leaving the northern tundra virtually deserted, but by no means entirely. The land here is not divided among farmers as are the pastures of England, but left to those who dare test themselves against it.

As my travels take me further northwards, it seems as though I am once more told of fantastic and even criminal goings-on at every turn. It is possible these are just stories. Perhaps such geographical seclusion makes people more imaginative with their tales, come the long winter nights. Then again, you know as well as I that isolated regions can give rise to all manner of bizarre human behaviour, so perhaps these accounts are not mere constructs of the imagination. I am tempted to think that the mountainous landscape has had an effect on the minds of the people who so sparsely inhabit it, and news that fundamental alterations can occur in the brains of some of the isolated few comes as no surprise. This, it would seem, has brought forth results both kind and good, as well as terrible and warped – a sobering but thrilling notion, my friend; and it is thus that I explain the actions of the Bakklands, whose story I will now relay to you from the warmth of a giant's hut before I set out into the blizzard.

The harbour-master at Kristiansand was an officious and nosy sort of fellow, all sharp features and pince-nez. However, standing in the pleasant shelter of his office, I managed to give little information away while gaining much. I thought it unwise to fully explain what I am in his country to obtain, for I was sure that if he learned how valuable the feline is to me, he would demand unreasonable remuneration for any aid he may pass me. Such is the mentality of small men. Therefore, in the guise of a struggling writer, I asked him first if he had news of a man with remarkable chin growth disembarking from the *Syren*. Irritatingly, he did not, and so I further enquired if he had heard of any stories that might interest a writer, hoping that one of them might suggest the feline was afoot.

Thinking them good material, he began to inform me of all manner of dull experiences that had occurred during what can only be described as a drab life. Within seconds, my mind began to wander. As I leaned forward in my seat to inform him of my immediate departure from his company, I happened to look upon his orderly desk. Beneath his cup of coffee was his morning paper, from which the word *kat* leapt out like a jaguar from jungle foliage. Ignoring his coffee, I grabbed the man's paper, but when, following a perfunctory scan, I saw that *kat* was the only word I could comprehend in the entire article, I turned to him and demanded that he translate.

The story he related in stuttering English, nursing his scalding hand, sent a pleasurable tingle running around my extremities, for it told of a remarkable feline to be found in a northerly region called Finnmark.

Leaving the bore searching for a word, I dashed to the station, bought a ticket for the next train and, as I waited for it and my luggage, I wrote you that last letter.

The train journey proved that that temptress of a newspaper reader was indeed smouldering under the surface, but unfortunately the flames I ignited proved to be of anger rather than passion, so it was a long journey, only made bearable by my faithful liquid companion. When I was awoken in my new compartment by the conductor bashing on the door to inform me that we had reached the end of the line, it was the cream of Scotland that kept me thawed for the endless cart trawl to my final destination: this isolated tundra town of Kautokeino.

Once arrived, I went directly to the butcher's shop, for he, I had learned from rudimentary investigation, was the man to speak to.

Roar was a giant of a man, whose magnificent name was, I soon found, at odds with his languorous nature. Seeing his breath condense and freeze on the windows of his oddly meatless shop, I immediately produced a bottle and got down to business. I had not travelled so far for niceties, and niceties were not what I got.

Mrs Bakkland was, it seems, something of a repulsive woman to look at. Once she had been comely enough to attract the attentions of the dashing and proper Mr Bakkland, but those days were sadly long past. Now a middle-aged woman, she was squat, rotund and ugly. The warts and sores on her face twisted each of its features into caricature obscenities, and the constant scratching of each and every part of her body sent Mr Bakkland quite demented. Her scratching was in part the reason why he saw fit to kill his wife one winter's day and bury her in snow until summer and softer ground would allow for her more permanent disposal.

The cause of the itching and scratching was fleas. There were fleas everywhere. In his house and in his workshed. In his bed and in his drawers. Down his aquiline nose he watched with disgust as they jumped from his wife's hair to her ears, from her chin to her bosom. He saw them burrowing down to her scalp and making their way up her skirt. Had it not been for the fleas, Mr Bakkland might have considered keeping her. She had been a fine cook in the early days of their union and had even outdone his mother in the bothersome realm of darning. Yet fleas there were and die she had to. It is, however, unfair to wholly blame the fleas for the robust whack that the back of Mrs Bakkland's head failed to endure, for fleas require a vessel to travel upon, and it was the woman's love for these vessels that made her refuse to rid them of their passengers. This led to the uncontrollable scratching and finally the spade with which said head was whacked. The vessels were cats, and very particular ones at that.

After they had married at an early age, Mr Bakkland's job as an officer in the Navy had taken him the world over. He knew that a life alone on the remote tundra of their native north would be a lonely one for his wife and that his naval existence would rarely allow him to return to the inland home his parents had imparted to them on their wedding day. Considering, also, that he had failed to make his young bride pregnant, he decided to buy her two cats for company. One had been male and one had been female and they had both shared the genetic oddity of polydactyly, an anomaly resulting in additional digits. I once downed a leopard that wore this wonderfully strange condition upon its rear paws, but it is one not monopolised by the animal kingdom. It has been known to give people as many as eight fingers on each hand, in addition to the requisite thumb. Some have utilised what others thought a disability to become exceptionally accomplished pianists, I hear.

Upon domestic cats – upon the two given as gifts of company by an amorous young officer to his swooning young bride at least – polydactyly had resulted not only in the felines having an extra fifth finger upon each forepaw, but also in a greater pronouncement of the dewclaw, that claw where a human would have a thumb. The polydactyl cat, the husband told his wife as he presented them to her on the day of his departure, is said by sailors to bring you good luck. With that, a kiss and his promise of return, he took his leave and went off to sea.

The young Mrs Bakkland, alone on the plateau, took very closely to these cats and to the offspring they spawned. To her they were each a symbol of the love that her husband would bestow upon her, did he not consider his duty to his country to be of greater import than that to his wife. Though dashing in appearance – he sported a carefully groomed pencil moustache upon his upper lip – it was nonetheless a staid, austere man the young woman had married, but she was prepared to be an obedient wife and await his return patiently. Meanwhile, she took to rearing the kittens as the symbols she believed them to be. Each newborn was a child her husband failed to bless her with prior to his departure and upon his subsequent but increasingly infrequent returns. She watched over each birth and the feeding of each kitten until it was weaned. Thence, she would take great interest and apply great effort to their training in all manner of disciplines. As the lonely years passed, the practices became tragically closer to those a young mother would teach her own young.

As she moved from youth to adult, her desperation for a child of her own grew steadily, but her husband was never to grant her dearest wish. In fact, so great was her want and physical need for a child that, startlingly, she commenced to produce the milk that every mammal mother does for her progeny. At first confused and worried by her situation, alone on the tundra, she soon adjusted and saw fit to put her new talent to use. She and the mother, whichever of the now numerous cats it happened to be, would sit side by side, mother cat in a blanket-lined box, mother human in her rocking chair, and feed the kittens simultaneously, dripping the benefit of their nutrition into the baby mouths, drop by drop.

Of the thirty-four years that Mr Bakkland claimed to largely enjoy with the Navy, he spent only seven in his native and secluded

Finnmark with his steadily declining wife. To start with, he had returned whenever he was given leave and would wrench the increasingly disinterested woman from her cats and force his unwanted attentions upon her, keen as he was to prove that he, too, could supply her with children. In their eighth year of marriage, however, he returned one day to encounter his wife feeding a kitten from her breast. She had gone beyond merely considering the cats her foster children, he realised. Her belief that she was mother of all was absolute, and though he was deeply worried by the implications of her activities upon his own physical capabilities and, more particularly, how society might look upon them, his cowardice did not allow him to interfere with his poor wife's new existence. Quite the reverse. His disbelief and shame led him to leave her for periods as long as he could manage. When he did return, he spent most of his time at the hut of newly established neighbours, one kilometre away over the snow, ice and brush. His wife, he was relieved to hear every time he stepped out, refused to accompany him, due to the fact that the really very nice Mr and Mrs Strandli kept three large Riesenschnauzer dogs, and the odour of such hounds upon her would upset the cats most fearfully. Mr Bakkland would fast agree, then leave her for respectable company, pleased they would not encounter what he called his 'eccentric wife'.

What turned Mrs Bakkland from the relatively comely young maiden to the rotund, facially mutated ball that Mr Bakkland with difficulty packed in snow, was a change of diet. Considering the fact that, by the time she reached twenty-nine, her feline family had happily reached the number of one hundred, and that, being capable of producing more milk than any one cat, she was feeding more kittens than ever, it seemed sensible that she take on the diet of the cats as well as the wet-nurse duties. Travelling on skis and pulling a sled for over thirty kilometres for her stock of food was terribly wearisome, and there was still the occasional delivery of post to keep her in contact with the outside world. On the other hand, so good a customer had she become of that which others would not buy from the butcher – the offal and offcuts that she fed her cats – that the supplier was only too willing to deliver it in quantity to her door on the tundra. It could be kept exposed to the cold, chilled in metal buckets, for indefinite periods. Sharing the diet of her family, she decided, allowed her to concentrate all the more on their welfare and education, as well as providing the very young with nutrients in her milk identical to those the biological mothers supplied.

By her fiftieth year, Mrs Bakkland's cats numbered over five hundred, and they were difficult to keep, particularly in the dark winter months when they rarely thought it sensible to venture outside into the cold. She had long ago given up trying to control the epidemic of fleas in the small hut, and indeed, considered them part of her children, just as one might consider pustules upon the visage of a seventeen-year-old son – regrettable, but nothing to warrant extreme measures. Much of the furniture that had been bought by her husband when they first moved in had been banished to the tundra. She and her cats all slept and fed on the carpet together, fighting for room between feline bodies, dirt and fleas. The only piece of furniture that remained in the hut was a bookcase, filled from top to bottom with exercise books. Whilst she continued to use the outhouse, though she had trained and educated her family in many human rituals, its use was not one of them. You can only attempt, if you must, to imagine the odour!

Upon retirement, a now gaunt and frustrated Mr Bakkland was determined to demand from his wife and neighbours the respect of which a near promotionless career had been devoid. The resulting accentuation of his pompous demeanour, which he was certain perfectly mimicked that of his superiors, really disguised a desperate, destructive and wholly vain need to be served with the esteem his pride called for and downright deserved. So when he returned for the first time in seven years to find a wife portlier, uglier and filthier than he had imagined possible, he took badly to the situation. His house was entirely occupied by felines and their entomological passengers. The floor, the single bookcase, the windowsills and even the roof sported perching cats and leaping fleas. His workshed, where the once modest young man had dreamed of retiring to woodwork, was now filled with cat-food buckets, both empty and full. The interior of each of the buildings emanated such a stench, that, despite the plunging temperatures, he was forced to construct a bed of heather thirty feet from them and demand that his meals, which his wife dutifully prepared on a fire, be served at an equal distance. When Mrs Bakkland brought his platter she would be followed by a legion of greedy cats and he would have to hold his plate high until his wife departed with them. Alas, it was not only the scavenging felines that had to depart, but also his wife.

At first, Mrs Bakkland had made an effort to return to civilised ways. She would close all the cats in the hut and dine with her husband upon his bed. However, the cats were so great in number it seemed she had always forgotten one, though she promised she had not. She would be pleasantly surprised at their appearance and proud that they had managed to escape, rather than apologetic for her failure to control them – the reaction her sour husband expected. When they then approached and she fed them from her plate and even allowed them to take food directly from her mouth, Mr Bakkland caused such a fuss that she quickly returned to the hut to dine in the way to which she had become accustomed. The despicable Mr Bakkland was grateful he no longer had to eat in the presence of his revolting wife, and encouraged her return to feeding on all-fours.

It was whilst spying upon his wife one day as she prepared his dinner that the last straw was presented to Mr Bakkland. His wife, having not seen fit to have food for human consumption on the tundra for many years now, had been serving her husband a stew consisting of the offal that she and her family ate, disguised by a thick, brown gravy. Though he had happily eaten it for the three weeks that he had been back, he now took to secreting his platterfuls in the snow some way from his bed, and in his ensuing hunger quickly formulated a plan that he was sure would not only result in his leading a normal life, but also, he felt, be suitable punishment for a wife who played such a disgusting trick upon her husband. He, in short, would show her.

And so it was that one night, as his wife slept, Mr Bakkland, util-
ising the spade that would later play an even more dastardly role,
plucked a cat from the roof of his workshed, wrung its neck and
hid it under his pillow until the execution of his plan the next day.
He hardly slept a wink that night, due in part to the excitement his
plan imbued him with and in part to the discomfort caused by har-
bouring the corpse of a cat under his pillow.

When finally daylight came, he entered the hut and, holding his
breath as best he could, told his wife that she had done so well with
her readjusting that he insisted, simply insisted, upon cooking her
a special lunch. She protested, knowing that the only food in the
house was cat meat, but her husband eased her fears by telling her
that he had already asked the really very nice Strandlis to pick
something up for him. On hearing this news, Mrs Bakkland agreed
that she had indeed been trying ever so hard and that it would be
very nice if her husband would cook her lunch, and further
requested, as an exhibition of good will, that they eat it within the
cat- and flea- and stench-infested hut. To this Mr Bakkland reluc-
tantly agreed.

Come lunchtime, as the sun dipped behind the horizon, from
where it would not peek again for another twenty hours, Mrs
Bakkland was dining from the fine silverware the couple had been
given thirty-one years before on their wedding day and which Mr
Bakkland had polished that morning. From it, she ate such a richly-
flavoured stew that she assumed it must be game.

'But what sort of game might it be?' she asked between
scratches, and spooned in mouthfuls that dripped down her
chin.

'That is a surprise,' her husband replied, smiling mysteriously.

'Oh, my dear,' the emotional Mrs Bakkland said with tears of
joy. 'You have not surprised me since first you left me here, and did
so with Adam and Eve.' For these were the names of the first two
polydactylic cats. 'And what a wonderful surprise that was!'

'For that I am sorry, Ida.'

'Do not be sorry, my love. It makes little difference now. We are
together again. Truly together again. Oh, how I have missed you.

Longed for you to be here with me. With me and our beautiful children,' wept Mrs Bakkland.

'How I too have yearned for it,' Mr Bakkland convinced her. 'But do not cry, my dear. Eat.'

'And why do you not eat with me?' asked Mrs Bakkland, taking another large, brown spoonful. 'It is so delicious.'

'I am not so hungry as you, my dear,' answered her husband. 'Perhaps I will join you in pudding.'

'Oh Lord – pudding! You spoil me so! It is true. My dear, loving husband really has returned!'

As she wept and ate with joy, Mr Bakkland briefly took his leave of her and went to his workshed for the fetching of the pudding.

'What could it be?' Mrs Bakkland asked herself and the cats as she licked her tongue across her plate. 'Plum crumble and custard? Perhaps my husband has even remembered my favourite pudding!' Her excitement mounting, she closed her eyes in anticipation of the glorious, sweet, sticky pudding.

Mr Bakkland returned with a platter even bigger than the one that had carried the stew, covered by an ornate silver dome. He placed it ceremoniously in front of his wife, who rubbed her hands together in girlish greed.

With an evil grin, the retired officer addressed his wife.

'And now, my dear wife, you asked me what game it was you ate with such gluttonous relish. In response I ask you what game it was you played as you fed me that foul cat meat. And what repulsive game you play in taking these odious felines to your bosom!'

At that he whipped the silver dome away to reveal the empty tabby fur of the cat she had just consumed lying flatly upon the bottom of the platter.

'This is the game you have eaten, and the game I have played on you,' he cried, pointing in her face with glee. His wife gasped in terror and shock. Mr Bakkland giggled at his audacity.

'How do you expect me to lead the respectable life a retired Naval Lieutenant deserves if he harbours such an animal as you for a wife? How could someone like me be expected to be joined in union with so revolting a crone as *you*?'

In response, all his poor, heartbroken wife could whisper was, 'My baby!'

It was then that the fatal blow was administered with the spade that Mr Bakkland had acquired at the same time as the pudding and had propped against the door behind his wife.

Let me assure you here, Cyril, that the packing in ice of this wretched woman's corpse is not the end of the tale. For what use would such a story be, other than to depress the spirits of its reader, with no justice for the despicable Mr Bakkland? No, my dear chap, there is more, and if you will believe, more fantastical even than that which has already gone.

Once Mr Bakkland had temporarily dispensed with his wife in a drift of snow behind his hut, he promptly went about clearing the structure of all that had to do with her family. At first he attempted to do so with the spade, but quickly found that chasing the cats over the tundra, tool in hand, was both tiresome and ineffective. Wheezing in the cold, he struck upon the idea of borrowing the three Riesenschnauzer hounds from the very nice Strandlis. The latter were happy to give them to him, being told that it was for a hike of some distance. The exercise, they said, would do the dogs good. And so Mr Bakkland returned to his hut and, the cats carefully herded into the warmth of the building, he opened the door and fed the huge dogs through before closing it behind them. From his bed on the tundra and a soothing pipe, he heard the screaming turmoil of violent and bloody murder.

Some hours later, he returned to the structure and, on opening the door, the three shaggy black canines burst from it in excitement. Looking inside, he considered the bloody sight with military dispassion. Gathering the corpses in sacks and doing his best not to slip on the abundant blood, he searched the single room for any sign of life. Gratifyingly, there was none. He then searched the roof and the workshed. Not a single cat left. What a stroke of genius those dogs had been, he thought to himself.

Had he continued with the spade, such an operation could have taken weeks!

Placing the many filled and sodden sacks outside, he locked the door to the hut. After returning the tiring dogs to the Strandlis, he retired to his bed of heather on the tundra, hoping for a good night's sleep, for tomorrow would be a heavy day of swabbing the hut and burning the sacks. The reasons for which it was to be a testing one were quite unforeseen, however.

When Mr Bakkland awoke, he gathered a bucket of water and a mop and entered the hut. On the floor, gradually soaking up what blood had not yet dried or frozen was an exercise book from the bookcase. It was open and upon the page was written a single line in a spidery, ageing hand that shared great similarities with that of his late wife. The colour drained from the face of Mr Bakkland as he read it: *I know what you are guilty of.*

How Mr Bakkland came to be hanging from the hut on the tundra over his wife and the really very nice, but awfully dead Mr and Mrs Strandli and their three late Riesenschnauzer hounds was something of a mystery to the police. The supplier of food, who first came upon the mess, was not a man to be mystified, however. Upon this pile of carcasses, having lived off their flesh through the winter, he found a single cat of great size and orange pigment. Its forepaws were of such a pronounced size that to all appearances it seemed to be wearing a pair of sparring mitts.

You will recall, my friend, what I told you of the curious condition that is polydactyly and its effects upon felines. Well, imagine if you can what would occur if one bred generation upon generation of such cats, inward and inward, polydactyl with polydactyl. In addition, imagine now what an obsessive, cranially tweaked woman, alone with them on the tundra for much of her life, could make of the resulting physical pronouncements. It is amazing to behold, to be sure even more amazing to believe, but before me as I write is the very exercise book that the sole survivor of the tundral slaughters wrote upon and in such a way as to take Mr Bakkland to the very edge of sanity and back to his spade and the door of the really very nice, but awfully interfering Strandlis. For his panicking mind drew the only reasonable conclusion it could: the Strandlis had observed his dreadful deeds and were punishing him for them. He utilised the same spade and then their very own hounds to drag the bodies to the drift, and having packed them, Mr Bakkland lived for some days in anxious tranquillity. The consequent lugubrious howling of the canines was the only disturbance, until again he found the open exercise book upon the floor of the hut on the tundra.

And now the hounds, or the whole world will know your crimes, the new writing read.

Shocked, upset and quite mad, and with the Strandlis now awaiting the summer thaw, Mr Bakkland had no inkling by whom the writing could be composed and came to believe that it was the gods or devils punishing him for his murderous ways.

So the howling ceased and great silence came to the tundra. Breaking the whistling of the wind, there was only the supplicatory mumbling of Mr Bakkland's lowered tones and the scratching of pencil on paper as he attempted to communicate with the unseen powers. Alas, it seems the mystery power chose not to pass word for some time, for Mr Bakkland filled twenty-three pages with increasingly desperate and incomprehensible pleas before the spidery hand shows again in the exercise book.

A rope from heaven will show you the way. From over our beloved shall you come to us, it reads.

Soon afterwards, Mr Bakkland discovered a noose tied from the mainbeam of the hut, which projected beyond the eaves and over the disturbed drift, and it was thus that the now far from staid and austere man ended his life, gibbering, relieved and terrified.

Come the thaw, the deliverer of cat food arrived and saw the sight. Three people and three hounds piled under a condemned man whose bootless feet had been eaten to the skeleton, and a cat besides, an open book under its paw, the writing therein spidery.

Homicide, uxoricide, infanticide.
I am guilty of these three sins,

And now my neck hangs, long and thin.
Take this cat and feed him well,
For he is the toller of my bell.

And so Roar assures me that he does, for it was from his shop that
poor Ida Bakkland bought that which others would not, and for
that privilege he is the new master of that singular feline which
was so tragically trained by the ill-fated Mrs Bakkland.

He insisted that I accompany him to his hut outside the town on
the tundra to behold the feline and attest that its talents are not
mere myth. I did so and here I am, awaiting transport for the next
leg of my journey. His beast is not the one I seek, but it is certainly
remarkable, and perhaps as valuable as the one that awaits me
yet further north in this continually surprising land. It was outside
feeding on Roar's finest produce as the man himself proudly presented to me an exercise book. The opening pages are preoccupied
by the alphabet and the following with such words as *purr* and
miaow, and at its end that chilling rhyme.

How can I be sure that I must travel further north, I hear your
finely-tuned mind ask of me. Well, it seems the man I am after, this
Spaniard with the beard, is a chap after my own heart, for he was
here, making an offer for Roar's cat, little more than a fortnight ago.
I too was about to ask Roar's price, but when he told me, as he had
told the other, that he would not part with his closest friend for love
nor money, and would tear any man who tried to part them limb
from limb, I took the giant at his word and instead pressed him for
information.

The man I am after is a Spaniard and a sailor – this we knew –
but also a collector, it appears, and one who knows his way around
this land better than I, for he travels faster. That is of little matter,
though, for it seems he has come to a standstill three days north
over the tundra from here, in a place called Honningsvåg, situated
at the very tip of the country. In that place, these weeks past, a
series of mysterious disappearances have occurred.

I would tell you more, but my coach has arrived to take me
there.

Though cold, and thus far empty-handed, I remain excited, expectant and, of course, your good friend,

Sir Paul Lindley-Small

15

THE NOTEBOOKS OF CYRIL KING

1893

A Killer and His Clock

'You damned fool, man! Of course I'm a bloody Englishman. Thanks to you I might not be for very much longer, though. Did you not see me down there? Those brigands are after my head, and you've just supplied them with a silver platter to lay it upon!'

This cold-hearted murderer did not strangle me, however, nor did he slit my throat, stab me through my heart or shoot me point blank with his firearm. Rather he released me from his iron grip and got to his feet, disgust filling his eyes. I did not move from the rocks. I was still in shock that he should be a fellow countryman, and feared what fresh act of violence any movement would result in. Instead I watched as his thickset form made its way to his horse and wondered what manner of savagery could turn an Englishman to such barbarism.

He reloaded from a pouch on his belt, slid the rifle back into its sheath and pulled his turban down around his neck. His years were difficult to guess. He could have been less than forty, but looked nearer fifty. On his head was a thatch of dark hair, stiff and flattened with sweat and dirt. Inhabiting his cheeks and chin was an

overgrown beard and thick whiskers. This mass of hair was interrupted by a weather-beaten forehead, a twisted, broken nose and
a thick scar that travelled from the darkness of the growth under
his jaw, up past the corner of his mouth, all the way to the tear
duct of his left eye. It was as though tears had eroded the hair, as
though acid spilled from that one eye, and burned its way down his
face, but I knew the truth behind such a wound would be less
romantic, and certainly more brutal. They observed me now, those
eyes, assessed me. It was a broad, ravaged face that they belonged
to, one that had been broken and healed several times over, and
looked to have lived more lives than most. So tanned was his skin
that he could have been a native but for the blue of his gaze, and
it was by looking into those sky-coloured orbs that I saw he was
not the savage that I had judged him. Yet, I thought, I had more to
fear from a civilised killer than one who knows no better; for the
savage may be outwitted, where the civilised killer may not.

Nonetheless, there is, of course, an unspoken code between
Englishmen, especially when abroad, and I knew that, if this man
could still be classed as English, and more doubtful still, a gentleman, I could be certain that I was safe. In the wake of his actions,
however, I could not be sure that he was either.

He was shaking his head as he pulled something from a saddlebag.

'Here. Clean yourself up,' he said.

He threw a piece of material at me. I had quite forgotten that
I was coated in the blood which had sprayed from the corpse lying
but ten yards from me, and remembering, I began to wipe my face
ferociously. The man, quite composed now, looked down at the
town.

'You've really stepped up the pace now, lad. I'd say we've twenty
minutes. Perhaps twenty-five, and we'll be able to see their direction from up here, of course. Not that we'll have much choice in
ours.' He looked back and down into the valley he had been
chased along. 'Damn pity, really. I was looking forward to a nice
leisurely introduction.'

He turned to me again.

'It's awfully ungrateful of you, if you don't mind me saying.'

I did mind. 'I beg your pardon?'

'Saved you, after all, didn't I? That old bird wasn't here for jollies, you know.'

This sudden accusation cleared my mind of fear in an instant, and replaced it with indignation. I sat up and threw the rag aside.

'It rather looked to me as though they were interested in you until you managed to turn their attention,' I retorted.

'Men like those are not known for their fussiness, lad. Mine was a vital diversionary tactic that saved both our lives. You can be sure that he wouldn't've been able to resist checking if you really had a heart of gold, as I told him you possessed, so if I'd not acted as I did I'm afraid you'd now be heartless and I branded a liar.' Suddenly his eyes widened and sparkled as a smile stretched his scar. 'Unthinkable!'

'Anyway,' I said. 'Even if you were justified in killing the old one, there was no excuse in trying to shoot the young one in the back. None at all.'

'Try telling the General that,' he said pensively, his cheer dissolving as he spoke. 'Lad, you may think so, and I can well see how you might, but you'd be wrong. About now, that boy – who was waiting to see you gutted like a fish for your shiny organ – will be arriving in the fort down there and heading straight to the Mess with vengeance and cash on his mind. With any luck, the delightful soldiers he'll meet there will be bored enough to beat him about for a while. Maybe five minutes. Five more will be taken up trying to understand his words, and another five to discern if he's telling the truth. When they're convinced, there will be the bargaining for the reward. Then, when they've paid him or merely beaten him into revealing our location – it rather depends on their mood – the soldiers'll saddle up and make their way towards us. They may find one of us waiting for them here. The second will be long gone. They've made their intentions for me quite clear, I think, don't you? But that's a good twenty minutes away, as I say, so . . .'

He started to dig once more in the saddlebags hanging from his horse.

'I really must advise you to give yourself up to Major Flack,' I said as I wiped the last of the blood from my cheek with the back of my hand. 'He seems like a reasonable man to me.'

'Oh, yes, they looked it down there, didn't they?' he said with a derisory laugh. 'Quite ready to negotiate. And what of earlier, in the town? If good old Allah hadn't intervened, I wouldn't be around to conduct the civilised chat we're both so enjoying. A shallow grave and decent pickings for the buzzards is the best I could've hoped for.'

He paused with his arm elbow deep in the saddlebag and furrowed his thick eyebrows into a frown.

'I don't suppose you know why they call a rabbit a rabbit, do you?'

I shook my head.

'And why would you? It's quite simple, though. A rabbit is a rabbit because he runs. And that is precisely what I intend to continue doing. There'll be no handing over and no attempts at negotiation. There are things to be done elsewhere.'

'Why did you come back here, then? If they're so keen to finish you off, surely you should have taken to the mountains.'

'Well, why don't you put that down to my charitable heart, hmm?' he said. As he continued to speak, he started to rummage again. 'Perhaps you wondered how I chanced upon you so precisely? Perhaps not, but allow me to enlighten you nonetheless. As you know, I was making my way down the mountain yonder,' he nodded his head over his shoulder towards the slope where I had first caught sight of his dust. 'And as I was, I chanced to look up in the direction of Gilgit and saw what could only be smoke from a pipe. As you say, the sensible course of action for one in circumstances such as mine would have been to turn left and disappear into the mountains. But I said to Bucephalus here, "We'll turn right", and why? Because show me a man settling for a soothing bowl, and I'll show you one in need of an accompanying tipple. And more besides, show me one so foolish as to advertise himself to bandits in so provocative a manner, and I'll show you a foreigner in need of aid, and no doubt it's the Englishman who gawked at me in the street as guns were levelled. So here I headed, and lucky for you that I did, or else the bandits would've found you alone and doubtless had away with that precious heart of yours. You've a lot to learn, lad, but you've taken your first lesson well and earned a draught.'

I did not quite know what to say. I was grateful not to be dead, of course. However, this murderer was telling me that he had saved me rather than led the bandits to my perch as I had initially believed, and that was distinctly less easy to digest.

'You're safe now, though,' he continued. 'And I will be, too, if you'll return the favour and prove you aren't loose-tongued with your friends the soldiers.'

'All I said was that Flack seems like a good enough man,' I protested. 'And he is, as I imagined they all would be. But that's not the case, I don't mind telling you.' I was thinking of the detestable Petts. 'They are certainly not my friends down there, and if you know them, I must say that I resent your implication.'

He grinned. 'That's the spirit, lad. That's the spirit. I don't know them, not these ones. I just know the Army. Anyway, I should never have doubted you – after all, you'll not be wanting to miss out on my supply in this dry country, eh?'

With a grunt, he pulled something new from deep within his bags and threw it over the horse to me. I reacted only just in time, fumbled with it and then held it securely to my breast. It was a glass and pewter flask, three-quarters full with a translucent amber liquid.

'How long has it been since you felt the warming shiver of Scotland's finest, hmm? And never fear, there's plenty more where that came from, though I think I lost a couple of bottles down there.'

He pushed the horse round and as it moved, I saw that it bore a most curious piece of tack. Made of well-worn leather, attached behind the saddle flap on both sides of the beast, it resembled a bandolier whose slots were large enough to hold heavy artillery shells, rather than mere bullets. Munitions had been entirely rejected, however, for in each pocket but one was a glass bottle, and all were filled with the same golden liquid that occupied the flask I held. There were eight in total, and I now saw a ninth, in front of the saddle where one would expect a canteen of water to hang. There was no pine box to be seen, but from where else but the teahouse could it have come?

'I could have lost more, those damned savages,' he concluded as though speaking of companions fallen in battle, picking broken glass from the empty slot.

I opened the flask. First I inhaled the fumes and then sipped the ambrosia, and as its owner had promised, it made me shiver with pleasure as its malty smoothness eased its way down my throat and into my belly.

He finished checking his supply and made his way towards me. I followed his approach with diminishing nerves. Instead of his knife, in his hand was a pipe. He lowered himself beside me and watched as I took a second draught. When he had lit up, I handed him the flask.

'Now, that is a flavour I had been looking forward to,' I said.

'Ah, my good man,' he said, taking it from me. 'We shall be friends after all, despite your ingratitude. You're young, but soon enough you'll realise that there are only so many bases on which to judge character. An appreciation of whisky is not the least of them, let me tell you, and in my experience The Glenlivet is the best brew on which to form a friendship. Always keep a supply and you will never be found wanting.'

He raised the flask into the air before putting it to his lips.

'And you,' I said, 'have a very loyal friend in a teahouse down there.'

'Ah. You have met Abdul-Khaliq,' he said. 'Yes. Of course. He mentioned somebody interested in my whisky. You caused quite a stir, I understand.'

The proprietor of the teahouse had said that the whisky was for the small sahib. I had thought the idea absurd that it could belong to a child, but for the life of me I could not see what was small about the bull of a man next to me. The drink's owner did not give me time to fully consider this question, however. He was sitting on the rocks as though in a club on Pall Mall – as if settling before a roaring fire with time in hand and reminiscences in mind. I was curious to discover what nature of affairs had driven him to kill so casually. He did not appear mad with the greed that had made McNaughton a murderer, nor filled with the cruelty displayed by Captain Petts. I sat mute, and listened to him talk in the hope that he would unravel this little mystery.

'My friend,' he said sucking on his pipe. 'I have loyal friends on the streets and, as you have seen, vicious enemies in the forces. I have had lovers in palaces and bordellos, and don't doubt that sundry children bear these blue eyes. I have plied most trades at one time or another, from soldier to sailor, bawd to gigolo, thief to custodian, gravedigger to grave robber, but never have I found my true calling in this world. Instead, I have roamed her fruitful lands these past years, and she has been a hard mistress, my young friend. But, in a mistress, one looks for a certain hardness, don't you agree? And without doubt she retains all the characteristics you would hope for. She is most contrary, but most beautiful, and when you think you can stand no more, she reveals a hitherto unsuspected talent and draws you helpless back into her boudoir, your face all a smile at the wondrous possibilities. As with any mistress worth her salt, the pleasure is immeasurable, outdoing all past successes tenfold, until the next time you have had enough of her and she unveils yet another secret.'

He turned from the landscape, leaned forward and looked me in the eye with some intensity.

'I have been away from these parts for some time, but have been coaxed back, and when I re-entered from the west, I found a reason to stay. It was in that wild country just beyond the Afghan border that I happened upon the information I now carry – information concerning a very interesting piece. A very interesting piece, indeed.'

He paused for a dramatic swig from the flask and sighed with satisfaction before continuing.

'It is sought by characters the world over. Governments, religious leaders, secret societies. Collectors and glory-seeking adventurers all hunt for it. And I now find myself in the unique, no doubt risk-laden position of knowing its whereabouts. And it is my intention to get my hands on it. It lies in the very south of this land, where the air is wet, the jungles thick and the maidens delightful. And here's the map that'll take us there.'

He drank again and returned the flask to my grateful hands as he removed a collection of papers and pieces of hide from his shirt. He took one from the stack with his other hand, returned the rest deep into the folds of his *chapan* and proceeded to delicately unfold that which he had kept with thick, nimble fingers.

'This map is four hundred years old, my boy, and before me had only ever been viewed by two and twenty members of a single bloodline. Descendants of its maker, they claimed, but more likely custodians of stolen property, I should say. After all, why live in a simple village in the north, when a thing of such value languishes hidden and unseen in the south? They blamed the curse, of course, and bless their simple minds and ways for such beliefs. We've only their superstitions to thank for making me the twenty-third in the line, and now you the twenty-fourth. Now I may not be blood, and you don't have the look of an Afghan about you, but I'm sure we'll appreciate it nonetheless.'

This all sounded rather tall to me, but there was no doubting the basic map he presented. It was adorned with indecipherable writings, rough illustrations of a city, camels and other beasts, strange triangular shapes which I took to be mountains and a thick cross marking the location of something. And it looked, smelled and felt the age he claimed for it, too.

'Of course, it's this that's to blame for the bullets raining down on me, but that's a small price to pay, lad. A small price to pay. Even if I have to run all the way to the south, it'll have been worth it. As my old friend Melancovic used to say, there's nothing quite like the chase, after all, is there? If you don't enjoy the chase, what good can the booty be? And if the booty's not up to scratch, what hope can you have for the hunt, eh? These blackguards have been hunting me ever since I left that village, and all because of that young beauty. Innocent, they said. Well, if that's innocence, the sinners must be something to behold. Never since my days in the steaming Amazonian jungles have I heard of such depravity in one so young. They lock her away and expect that I'll not be curious, that I'll not take on the challenge. They deprive her of the glories of life and lust and expect her mind to be filled with purity, and not crazed by thoughts of the very joys she has been without – joys I was fortunate enough to unleash and sample before any other man. Strange ways they have, some of these natives – but how pleased I am to experience them first hand. Pity the missionaries who try to make the folk hereabouts shady reflections of the English Christian, eh? They don't know what they're missing.'

He shook his head again, this time in disbelief.

'Do you know what it is, lad, to be adored by a young, beautiful, nubile virgin? No? Well, it is, I have found, a most irresistible set of affairs, even for my iron will, made all the more temptatious by its taboo. She was a girl of rare beauty, this one, quite simply one of the ripest I've seen in all my years. It was, unfortunately, a union disapproved of by the rest of her village, though. It was her mother that found us, and her husband-to-be and his brothers and cousins who saw me off. Apparently it'll save the girl's chastity if I'm slain. No doubt they'd fillet and serve me up on her wedding day to boot, the fiends! Then the Army entered the fray. Heard of the map and want it for themselves, I shouldn't wonder. Savage or soldier, there's not much difference between them when they've got a blood lust on, and one or the other has been after me ever since. Ah, but the mountains protect.' He patted the rock beneath him and grinned.

I certainly did not approve of his conduct, and I was pleased that my shop on Chancery Lane had never been the setting for so spicy and disgraceful a drama. He told the tale with such gusto, however, that I could not help but marvel at his daring, and even found myself envying him.

'That doesn't explain why the map is to blame for anything, though,' I said.

'No, you're right. That's true. The map is to blame because the purpose of the mother's visit to my hut was to accuse me of stealing the thing. Quite absurd, of course, but had she never thought to accuse one so innocent as I, very possibly I should still be in the embrace of that remarkable she-devil instead of conducting our delightful chat. But then you would be lying here without your golden heart, and that wouldn't do at all, now, would it? Well,' he said, refolding the map and tucking it safely to his breast once more. As he did so, he leaned towards me and his face grew serious. His voice lowered to a growl. 'Unfortunately, there's one thing missing from the whole affair, one thing I absolutely cannot do without before I get to the place shown on this map.'

I confess that his words intrigued me, and I struggle to describe my reaction to those that followed. Suffice to say that the wind was snatched from my lungs.

'This piece, you see – it's a timepiece,' he said. 'And a very remarkable one, at that. However, if I'm to succeed in getting my hands on it, and reap its not inconsiderable rewards, I shall require the service of somebody who has an intricate understanding of such things, for in all my experience I have never learned the mechanics of time. You see, my young friend, this map shows the location of the Faddhuan Clock!'

He finished his sentence with a flourish of his hands and the overwrought triumph that apparently befitted this mighty treasure. I write 'apparently', for I must admit that never before in all my years as a student of my trade had I heard of this Faddhuan Clock. However, I did not want to disappoint him, so I chose not to disclose this information. To have happened upon precisely what he was looking for in such an unlikely backwater was a remarkable coincidence, the fragile singularity of which I was unwilling to puncture with my own ignorance. Besides, although I considered myself at that moment no longer a watchmaker, I had my professional pride. For my sins, I responded thus:

'Really! That I cannot believe! The actual Faddhuan Timepiece?'

'You know of it?' he asked, incredulous.

'Know of it?' I said, feigning affront. 'Allow me to introduce myself, sir. I am Cyril King, formerly watchmaker of Chancery Lane!'

'Well, the sweet bairn of that unfortunate virgin!' he cried. 'This *is* a coincidence!'

'A twist of fate, I should say.'

'Well, young fella-melad, I am Paul Small. Just Small to those I allow to call me friend. And may I welcome you to that exclusive company, and to an adventure of the very highest order!'

He stretched out an arm and spread his burly paw in front of me. I took it, for whether it was the warmth of his whisky, that of his ebullience or merely the effects of so unlikely a meeting, I found myself enjoying the society of this man. He was still an Englishman, of that there was no doubt, and if not entirely of the gentlemanly persuasion, then all the better company for it. His tales were amusing and thrilling in equal parts, his manner carefree and gregarious. His character was questionable, of course, and he was the enemy of Her Majesty's forces, and so of the Crown, it is true. But with the exception of Major Flack, I had learned that even British soldiers were not all I had expected. I thought it likely that I too would do my best to avoid them, were I unfortunate enough to be pursued as Small had been, for nothing more than a map.

He prodded my shoulder.

'What do you say, old man? We'll have a ball. I've got cases of this stuff deposited all over the country. We'll lie low in the mountains for a couple of days, those blackguards down there will lose my scent and then we'll be off, free as birds to enjoy this country as it should be enjoyed. Adventure, the thrill of a hunt and, now you're with me, there's no need to be entirely sober ever again. What could be better?'

He made his offer sound highly tempting, there is no doubt. Indeed, his description met my desires to a tee. With him I could combine the life of the explorer as I had set it out in my head with the knowledge that my training had bestowed upon me. We would be a team, he and I, a leader and an expert. But my own adventure was not yet concluded. It was, in fact, only just beginning, and I had my purpose just as he had his.

'Small,' I began. 'I'm indebted to you for your aid here today. I'd dearly like to repay you for it and come along to search for the Faddhuan Clock. But the fact of the matter is that I'm afraid I can't go south. I'm in these parts for my own reasons, you see, and those reasons demand that I head out tomorrow.'

I saw at once that Small was disappointed. His face dropped, a slight frown formed on his brow and his lips parted.

'I'm awfully sorry,' I said sincerely, but it did not help.

He grabbed the flask roughly from my hand, jumped to his feet and marched to his horse.

'I really am,' I persisted as I rose. 'You see, I'm after something, too. I think. Hope. It's not a clock, although it was a watch that brought me here.'

I pulled the rags from my pocket and unwrapped Taqdir's strange timepiece. Small turned back to me immediately. The watch lay face down in my palm and the name of Ghalat Taqdir stared up at him.

'This curious piece quite fell into my hands in London. Initially, it brought me here, but tomorrow I must head towards Ishkuman – or part way, at least; west first, to a place called Gahkuch. Then north. That's where it leads, you see – to Ishkuman. I've come so far, Small. Found so much out. I simply can't turn my back on it now. I'd feel terrible, just terrible if I did. It would completely defeat the point of coming here at all.'

Small looked from the watch to me, and continued to stare my way for some moments, as though deliberating a particularly spiky dilemma. He inspected the watch as it lay in my hand.

'Yes, it is odd, isn't it? But it's just wood and lead, King,' he said, looking up at me quizzically. 'What possible interest could such a thing hold? I hate to disappoint you, old chap, but it's quite worthless. I suppose the stone might pick up a shilling or two in England, if it's jet or apache tears.' He lifted the watch from its rags and turned it over to consider the eye-shaped jewel. 'It might even be a black sapphire if you're lucky. But then you had the stone when you were in London, didn't you? Why come here with it, where it won't fetch a penny?'

'It's not the value of the watch that interests me, Small,' I responded. I liked the chap, was warming to him, as I have said, but I was not prepared to tell him all I expected to find at the trail's end. He was a murderer, after all. 'It's the mystery. Men have killed for this watch, and others have died to protect its secrets. I want to find out why, what those secrets are. Curiosity, if you want. If it were riches I was after, you can take my word for it: I'd be off with you this instant. But, tell me, Small, how did you know of the stone?'

It was an odd thing, indeed, that had just occurred to me. He had spoken of the stone before he had set eyes upon it.

'Ah, you forget that I have friends in this town, lad. Do not fear, it's not another coincidence. It was Abdul-Khaliq, you remember my whisky guard? He described it to me. I should have guessed you a watchmaker, I suppose, but I must say, little did I suspect then of the value we could be to one another. I have the whisky, the map and the adventure and you have the knowledge that can get us the Faddhuan Clock. We'll split it sixty–forty. If it's just curiosity that brought you here, take my word for it this time – Ishkuman is not the place to head. Whether you go there out of a professional interest in this trinket, or curiosity in a mystery as you say, forget it, lad, you'll not last a day alone. I've always found that intrigue comes from loot, ladies or both, and if there was the promise of either it'd be a different affair; but no, there'll be both of those in the south, I can promise you that, and none of these Karakoram to cross. Rid yourself of your intentions and come with me to Marwar. It's madness not to, I tell you.'

'You've been there – to Ishkuman?' I asked hopefully, ignoring his pleas.

'No, no,' he said, giving the watch a final ogle before replacing it in my hand. 'But I know the mountains thereabouts. High, cold and nasty. Killers, and you'll be lucky if you find anything as recognisable as booty or beauties. You'll see 'em of course – they say a man always sees what he most wants before the mountains take him. Now don't be a damned fool, lad.'

I wrapped the watch in its rags again and dropped it into my pocket.

'Well,' said Small, and turned dramatically away from me. He tightened his girths somewhat violently and checked the bindings that held his precious whisky. He set his eyes upon me once more and shook his head.

'I'm sorry my adventure isn't interesting enough for you,' he sniffed and, placing his foot in the stirrup, he heaved himself into the saddle. Before my very eyes and in a mere moment he had gone from worldly, amoral adventurer to upset child. His theatrical sulk and offended cheek-baring were a sight to see, and I must admit to being almost touched. But there was something else nipping at the periphery of my mind; and besides, he had his Faddhuan Clock to think of.

'That's not it at all, Small. Really not at all. I feel awful for letting you down like this, after all your help, but it doesn't look as though there's a thing to be done about it. I can't come with you and you must go.'

'As you say, boy, I must go. I don't have time to listen to your snivelling. Thanks to you, that bandit got through and now they're on their way.'

He pulled the reins and pointed behind me, down towards Gilgit. I followed his finger and saw, moving away from the fort and through the low buildings of the town, a familiar cloud of dust being raised by galloping hooves.

'If you'll excuse me, I've got a firing squad to avoid. Here,' he said and threw something at me.

It was a fresh, unopened bottle of Glenlivet.

'You'll be needing it in these mountains. I'm just sorry I can't stop to persuade you of what you're missing and what you're going into. Good luck to you, sir.'

And with that he swung his horse's head to face the slopes, dug his spurs into that long-suffering beast and set off in the direction from which he had come.

What a remarkable fellow he was, I thought, as I made my way to the dead bandit's horse, which had wandered a little way off, back down the slope towards the town. I really was sorry to see him go, for I should have liked to have had so useful a companion at my side. A coincidence such as had occurred there in the crook between two mountains was not something to be brushed off lightly, and nor was the valour of one who heads into the very jaws of his enemy for no other reason than to rescue an absolute stranger. Nonetheless, brush it off is precisely what I attempted to do. Small was gone, as was his Faddhuan Clock. As I had told him, I had other matters to address.

I met the colourfully saddled creature and while I was gathering its reins I saw the mounted soldiers reach the foot of the mountain. I hoped Flack was leading them, for I would have to explain the death of the bandit and the blood that stained my shirt. Flack would take my word over that of the bandit youth and believe me when I told him that *I* had put paid to the attacker in a straight case of him or me.

The incline of the mountain made the troop slow. From the flurry, I could make out some eight horses and the points of rifles rising out of the dust. I had begun to amble back towards the nape between the mountains, where I could more comfortably await their arrival and work out the precise mechanics of the lie I was about to unveil. But when I turned to check their progress, surprise, fast followed by terror, froze me to the spot. I pulled out my spyglass once again, and my worst fears were confirmed. I was looking at the crazed face of Captain Petts. He was pointing his sabre forth and spurring his horse furiously, shouting his men on as though charging into battle. Behind him were Fowler, Finch, Crampers and four natives. Major Flack was nowhere to be seen.

Although they were sliding on the scree, what had previously looked slow now took on the appearance of a decent speed. The five hundred or so yards between us would be swallowed in less than a minute, I realised, and then I would have to face Petts and whatever treatment he deemed fit. Another glance at his face was enough to convince me that he would care less about capturing Small than humiliating one he surely felt had humiliated him – one he could now claim had aided a villain in his escape.

At four hundred yards, all of them dropped their reins and

brought the stocks of their rifles to their shoulders. Finch and Crampers were thrown to and fro in their saddles, unable to steady their hands. Fowler too struggled, as did two of the natives. The two remaining, however, did not. Their rifles were still and their faces calm as they took aim. I tried to move, but I was hypnotised by the rumble of the hooves and the face of their leader, contorted by hatred and excitement.

At three hundred yards I heard the whiz of a ricochet and saw rock bursting into shingle some fifty yards in front of me. I looked up to see smoke rising from the steadied rifle of the native soldier who had fired, and only then did I hear the delayed crack of the shot. He was testing his range. A renewed burst of fear thawed my limbs. I rammed the spyglass into my pocket and scrambled with the horse back towards the top of the mountain.

Small had been right. There would be no negotiation. This was to be an execution. Petts had brought a squad that included crack marksmen, and if possible the job would be done at distance. Had it been Flack, to be safe I would only have had to make him aware that I was not Small. He would have called his men off in an instant. Petts, on the other hand, would not give a damn who it was. Indeed, of the two, doubtless he would rather find me up there, accuse me of murder and see that Crampers completed the job he had not managed to start in the mess. With the dead man's horse, I hurried back towards the boulder that lay only feet from his inanimate body and the great drop into the valley beyond. They would have to kill me face to face.

The blood-curdling glee of Petts' shrieking chilled my very soul. So this was the sound of death, I thought to myself.

They were only two hundred yards distant when I flung myself to the ground behind that rock, pulled the horse to safety with me and drew my knees to my chin. More gunfire, louder and closer, but they had no chance of hitting me. They were firing merely to frighten me. I looked down into the valley, determined that my final seconds on earth would be spent in contemplating its wondrous vistas rather than looking into the face of Captain Petts, surely one of our Maker's greater mistakes.

The valley was lifeless as soon I would be. Even the river seemed not to run.

Death was approaching as surely as horses could carry men up a mountain, and I must confess that under such circumstances the explorer in me dived for cover and I felt the quivering watchmaker take his place. I could possibly have flung myself onto the horse and attempted a dash uphill, but I knew so inexperienced a rider as I could not outrun them. All desire to escape slipped away, flowing out of me just as the blood had flowed from the bandit.

The soldiers must have been travelling faster than I had guessed, for almost at once there was the scuff of a hoof next to me. I stifled my instinct to look at its source. My killers would have to shoot me where I sat. No matter what they said, no matter what I heard, I would not move.

There was more shuffling next to me, and then a grunt. A scattering of small rocks fell over the cliff's edge, resonating off their fellows as they went. Then the body of the bandit joined them; and as he disappeared I heard a voice whisper close to my ear, just as he had moments before his throat was slit.

Gradually, words penetrated my consciousness and with them hope, fear and panic flooded my being once more.

'King!' they said. 'King, old man. I had a thought.'

16

THE LETTERS OF
SIR PAUL LINDLEY-SMALL

From a fur-lined cabin in
Honningsvåg, Norway

24TH DECEMBER 1908

Cyril, old boy

I am on top of the world, at the edge of the map, or at the very least at the northernmost tip of continental Europe. There has been a recent and continuing spate of infantile disappearances here, you see. One by one, a total of twelve children have vanished in the night. However, as folk hereabouts are known for their love of storytelling, and since there was no actual evidence to support their story, their claims had gone unheeded, the case ignored.

The twelfth child to have gone missing was a twelve-year-old lad named Bjørn. Though sparsely populated, it seems news finds its way across the tundra and Roar, with a few questions put to the good people of Kautokeino, was not only able to tell me the name of the boy's guardian, Frukern Galstad, his sister, but also to aid me in getting a letter to her. So it was that I sent word to the help-less lass not to fear. I was on my way, coming to solve the mystery of Bjørn's disappearance, for only this dastardly Spaniard and the beast he carries could be responsible.

The lad being of twelve years and the sister being his guardian, I thought she could be of no more than twenty in years and sent the letter with great paternal tidings and even greater personal hopes.

Well, old friend, once again my luck has served me royally, for though the journey was long, arduous and very cold, and though I was to learn the girl was twenty-two when finally I met her, I was greeted as a hero, and heaped upon me were all the niceties a hero deserves.

'Hailed a hero by a lass who did not even know you!' I hear you exclaim. 'How so?' you will rightly demand.

And I shall tell you, for certainly if you thought the words of Roald Agnar and Roar the Giant amazing, those from the far more delectable lips of Miss Galstad will surely take you to even greater heights, as they have me, and will again when I cease to write.

I travelled to Honningsvåg on a wooden cart pulled by a stiff old nag, and only regular snifters from my flask kept me on the right side of frozen until I found a miserable seller of furs and animal skins. The old woman, whose palm I crossed amply with silver, assured me that reindeer hide was the garment of choice of the Sami for as many generations as could be traced and, albeit lacking in the Crawfordian elegance to which I am accustomed, it does its job admirably. Crawford himself can be happy in the knowledge that the cashmere double-breasted sat thawed beneath the reindeer coat until I encountered the recipient of my letter.

The town that has grown up around the questionable fame of being the northernmost pinnacle of Europe is a strange one – barren, quiet and closed, even at this most festive and joyous time of the year. Rare is the sound of chatter, even rarer still the warming tones of laughter. The death cries of slaughtered deer and the weeping of women in their snowbound huts, on the other hand, are all too frequent. Even with my added fleece and a dram upon a snifter, a chill ran down my spine as I, Honningsvåg's sole visitor that day, headed from the lady whose mournful eyes were too cold to cry, to my hotel, the only one in this hamlet – a single storey of blackened wood decorated with antlers and skulls, the former owners of coats such as mine. It was here, upon opening the door to a cosily timbered room warmed by a roaring fire that occupied much of the east wall, that I discovered a silent quartet playing a rule of cards that even my well-travelled purse had not yet dipped into. Without a word muttered, every one of the eight eyes observed me as I dropped my luggage and rid myself of my coat, and necks craned to follow my progress to the fire. Before the licking flames, I first warmed my front. When I turned to do the same service for my numb and frozen rump, I encountered unbroken stares.

'Please do not allow my presence to interrupt you,' I requested, most civilly.

There was a brief pause during which the two men and two women appeared oblivious to my words. There was terror and misery in every eye, men and females alike. When finally my words penetrated their distraction, they looked away, picked up their cards and partook of their brews, all in thick silence. Being an eternal student of the human condition, it was clear to me that these people had been affected by the disappearances. I would need all the information they could supply me with if I were to locate the Spaniard and my creature, but it would not be as straightforward as simply asking them outright. This was an operation to be undertaken tactically. They were afraid of a stranger, and in no frame of communal mind to initiate the conversation that would establish my disposition, so I manoeuvred that yoke onto my own substantial shoulders, and leaving the fireside to approach them, I politely enquired after their pursuits.

'It's not a game I've seen before,' I told them. 'If I am to play, I am afraid you shall have to teach me.'

Still they were not forthcoming, but played on, and taking a seat and watching their activity, I succeeded in establishing that the game was a twisted sort of Ram Sutch, only with Queens and Knaves taking on a murderous slant, and the Two and Four of Hearts becoming bizarre elixirs of health for the clearly under-threat monarchs. I insisted on sitting in on a round of hands, and soon enough whispers, then voices, began to circulate.

In a short glass, I was served a thick black liquid that tasted of various, mainly inedible herbs. Despite its flavour, it further thawed me, and as I warmed, so did my humour, to such a degree, in fact, that I returned to my luggage and unsheathed a fresh bottle from its snug hay blanket. I proceeded to disperse the whisky among the people I sat with, something that would usually be against my better judgement due to the natural limits set upon a man with only a boxful. That evening, however, I was willing to ignore these constraints if doing so would reveal the secrets hinted at in their uniformly pained and strained eyes and faces.

I allowed them to clear me of change, for a card winner is a better talker than a loser, and as we played and spoke of the game, though still reserved, they began to relax in my presence. When the bottle held only four fingers more, I slowed the pouring and to get things going asked after the young lady to whom I had sent the letter.

'Ooh, Mari,' said one man, shaking his head so the great sagging moustache that hung from his upper lip waved hither and thither to such a degree that I do not mind telling you I flinched as if under attack. 'She's the lucky one. And now she's got a visitor.'

I was pleased but unsurprised to learn that they saw my visiting her as such a privilege. Keen to prove her luck, I enquired after her whereabouts. She already sounded rather more a bundle of joy than this bunch constituted.

I was, however, entirely ignored.

'Very lucky, that Mari. Just in time she was. Not for Sara, though. Poor dear, she lost hers,' said a large and ruddy middle-aged woman, as she drained her glass and looked from it to me, hope flooding her wet eyes. As she did, the second woman at the table, frail, pale and of a similar age, suddenly burst into tears and let out a wail that filled the room. The man with the moustache wrapped her in an arm and did his best to calm her.

'What about Evi then, eh, Birgit?' said the second man to the ruddy-faced woman as he wiped a drip from his long, straight nose the very moment before it dropped onto his cards. 'She lost two, she did. Can you imagine?' he said to me.

I said that I absolutely could not.

Each of them now held an empty glass and they all looked at me with the same hopeful expression that the ruddy-faced woman had thrown my way. Seeing in their desperation my chance to get from them what they knew, I poured myself another two fingers and took a slow slip. Their eyes widened as they looked on. After a sigh of satisfaction, I held the bottle out and let it hover in mid-air.

'I cannot imagine because I do not know of what you speak. She is lucky for the visit, of course, but how can you call a girl who is wretched enough to lose both her parents and her brother lucky?' I raised my eyebrows and swung the bottle from its neck, as if a carrot for a donkey.

It was the man with the still dripping nose who was first to break.

'Oh no, sir. He's back. The boy's back. But all the rest . . .' His voice trailed away and he shook his head as I poured him a dram, which he swallowed greedily.

Next was the ruddy-faced woman. She licked her chops as she saw the liquid gold disappear into her neighbour's gullet.

'It was too late for all the rest. Too late. Thems were killed and . . .'

Her glass partially filled, she murmured to a halt and took it up with both hands. Finally the chap with the aggressive moustache caved in to finest Scotch persuasion.

'Bones, sir. Bones! Only bones left! Ooh, I'm sorry, dear,' he said as the woman he still had an arm around let out another piercing wail. 'Grete here's granddaughter was one taken. Horrible it was, sir. Horrible. Here, drink this, dear,' he said, passing the glass I had filled for him to the wailing woman. So touched was I by this gesture that I filled her glass for him to drink from, and in so doing emptied the bottle.

'He is back, then, this boy?' I said, my dextrous mind quickly establishing the consequences of this fact. 'That is most curious. It means the mystery has been solved.'

'Oh, yes. And young Mari solved it herself. Single-handed,' said the man through his handkerchief. 'Just for that she deserves the boy back,' he added, more to the wailing woman than to me, before trumpeting a noseblow into his well-used rag.

'And what was its solution?' I demanded, rabid for answers. But it was not from them that I was to learn of the mystery's resolution, for their glasses were drained and they turned back to the thick black liquid and paid me little further mind, saying stoic things to one another, such as, 'Life goes on, Grete,' and, 'It could happen to anybody. That's the way you've got to see it, dear.'

Their increasing drowsiness was to offer neither further information, nor the chance to win back my money, so I called out the proprietor from a cubbyhole and as he fetched my key, I enquired as to where Frukern Galstad resided. On learning this, I mounted the stairs with my luggage and in the sanctuary of my spartan room, bolstered my constitution with a swig from a fresh bottle, pocketed it, donned my furs and then headed back down, past the snoozing card players and out into the cold.

I fought against the blizzard that met me outside, and gradually made my way along what was apparently once a road, now little more than another strip of snow. The town, if one can call a collection of two dozen buildings such a thing, was not a sight to be encountered without a bottle at one's side. The buildings, all on one side hidden by snowdrifts reaching to the tips of their roofs, were rundown and in need of painting. More than one front door had lost its steps to the weather and not a single window emitted even a glow of light. In fact, the only signs of life anywhere in the place were the mournful wails of women occasionally heard over the whistling winds, and the smoke drifting from chimneys. Indeed, in the blue light of the night's moon, there were more signs of death than of life. Skulls and antlers adorned the walls of every building, the white snow sticking to their white bone, transforming them into fearsome mutants that watched from hollow eyes as I tramped through the swirl. Hidden between the bleak mountains and the churning Arctic waters to the north, this, I thought, pausing for a nip from my bottle, was a lost place, left to exist at Nature's bidding, forgotten by the world. But not by me. And if one outsider alone remembers, it can be neither lost nor forgotten.

I found this to be the most cheerful way in which to consider the singularly cheerless place, so rather than returning to the deep depression the town otherwise suffered from, I instead took to thinking of my reason for being there.

There are very few large indigenous predators in Norway. There is the lynx and there are wolves. There is also the wolverine, but it is unheard of for any of these beasts, as lone hunter or as a pack, to succeed in taking twelve sleeping children from their beds. Had they been responsible for such acts, though, was it not even more unlikely that only eleven of those taken would be consumed? These are bestial carnivores with an insatiable hunger for meat. Their instincts would not allow for the preservation of food for harder times to come. On the other hand, a beast as astounding as the one I seek could be capable of precisely anything. After all, once filled, a serpent does not feed again for weeks, sometimes months.

Whatever the answer to that, I could see no actual reason, or way, for the King Cobra Cat to have travelled of its own volition from the densely populated lowlands to the sparsely inhabited snowlands – which was akin to going from an abattoir to a swami's pantry for your joint of beef. I therefore concluded that the Spaniard had brought our creature north, but then had somehow lost control of it. Having contained it for such a great distance, that it was now ridding Honningsvåg of its weakest was surely a sign that he would not be involved in the final stand-off. This did not displease me, for a stand-off with Mari, who I assumed now held the creature, or the secret to its location at any rate, would form a preferable finale by far to this search than wrestling down a Spanish seaman, curious circular beard or none!

So it was that the cold, but also excitement that I might be in the proximity of my prize, brought me shivering to the small plain hut on the other side of the village that the hotel proprietor had told me was the home of Frukern Galstad. As I looked up and gratefully saw woodsmoke billowing from a small chimney, I knocked upon its heavy door. My fur coat was encrusted with a great layer of snow and I was glad to see a rampant fire when the door opened. Between it and me, however, stood quite the most beautiful young woman I have seen since I arrived, and the elated smile that shone from her face warmed me more than any fire or amount of whisky could hope to, though I was certain the tally of all three would be the preferable combination.

It is growing late, it would be rude to write more, and while most of all I now hope to discover that my certainty was well-founded, I hope too that you will still consider me,

Your good friend,

Lindley-Small

17

THE NOTEBOOKS OF CYRIL KING

1893

Countdown to Death

I had no opportunity to discover the precise nature of the thought that had struck Small – for it was, of course, his voice that had crept into my ear. Once again, he had arrived in the nick of time. Briefly, I allowed myself to hope that the resourceful fellow had another wheeze to rid us of this latest peril, and one that could be acted upon that very instant. Even as that hope reanimated me, however, the reality of our position became clear.

For the moment we were sheltered by the boulder. Before us was the sheer drop. Behind us, the murderous Petts. To our left and right were rising mountains. If we took to them on the Gilgit side, the soldiers were close enough now to shoot us down like fairground targets. If we tried the other side, even if we made it unscathed through the open, Petts and company would reach the cliff edge, where they could dismount and pick us off at leisure. To stay and fight would be futile. To run would be suicide.

I glanced over the rock. All the soldiers were firing now, except for Petts. Surrounded by the flashing muzzles of his men's firearms, he was swinging his sabre as though striking down invisible foes.

They would be upon us in seconds.

When rock shattered only inches from my face, I ducked and turned to face Small.

'You damned fool, man,' I whispered. 'Now we're both for it!'

His face was set in stone, but those eyes were sparkling more than ever. Surely he could not be enjoying this countdown to death?

In a lightning move he seized the collar of my shirt and threw me roughly across the back of the dead bandit's horse. As I struggled into the saddle he thrust my Gladstone at me. I bent low over the horse's neck in order to remain under the rock's protection, and grabbed a handful of mane. In front of me, Small mounted Bucephalus.

'Hold on, now, boy,' he growled as he took hold of my reins. 'There's only one way out of this.'

Small kicked Bucephalus and she skittered sideways from cover. A bullet glanced off her saddlebags, and I heard the shattering of glass. The shot had missed the horse, but Small swore nonetheless as he pulled me towards the stream. I should not have been surprised to feel an extreme heat on my arm as the lead of a bullet grazed it, but I was, very. The soldiers' aim was growing more accurate. With a shot or two more, I was certain they would squarely hit their prey. I squeezed my eyes tight shut.

I heard the splash of water beneath the horses' hooves and Small's voice again.

'Here goes nothing!' he whispered to himself, and then he yelled at Bucephalus. 'Hah!' he cried. 'Get your meat down there, girl. Hah! Hah!'

I lurched forwards.

The sound of our pursuers and their bullets disappeared instantly. It was replaced by the panicked whinnying of our horses. But I could not hear their hooves impacting with rock, nor sinking into the scree and throwing it noisily about us. Instead I heard the sound of hooves screeching along smooth, slippery stone. In a moment that too was lost – drowned out by the air rushing past my face. It felt as though we were moving downwards, headlong, virtually vertically. Certainly our velocity was increasing with every yard we travelled. We couldn't be . . . Was he quite mad?

I forced my eyelids apart, battling against the rushing air.

He must have been. Only a madman would attempt such a thing.

Small had thrown us down the cliff, into the wet of the waterfall. I had not been wrong. We *were* moving vertically. Only thrown is the wrong word, for our brave horses were doing their damnedest to take the fall under control.

I saw Small and Bucephalus by my side now. The beast was practically sitting, her rear legs entirely bent, her forelegs quite straight, backtracking as hard as she could, trying to slow her descent, but with both the wet and gravity against her, she was failing. The whites of her eyes were bulging beyond their sockets.

Small too was showing white, but not in his eyes. They were practically closed in the blast of wet air. He was leaning back in the saddle as far as was possible, grinning, and his smile only broadened as the rocks and river at the foot of the cliff grew closer with every second.

I was controlling nothing. I could not hope to. More worryingly, nor was Small. We were entirely at the mercy of gravity. Yet we were fortunate. Where it was dry, the cliff was rough and craggy. Had we been flung down there, we'd have tumbled as soon as we got going. Instead we had gone off where the stream and the falling water had eroded the rock flat. There was a price to be paid for the smoothness of our path, however – a slickness that accelerated our descent into a freefall no less terrifying, only perhaps more elegant. On the wet rock, as on an ice-rink, the friction was minimal. Any guiding of our horses was impossible. If either hit the merest obstruction or crack in the rock face it would be the end of us. So, when all at once an enormous split in the cliff came into view ahead of us, growing at an horrific pace, I knew we were done for. The horses' forelegs would sink straight into it, their bones would snap like dried twigs and beasts and riders would go head over heels to their deaths.

The grin vanished from Small's face. He looked left and right.
With yards to go before we met our end, he tugged first on one rein
and then on the other with all his might. He grunted and yelled.
Alas, poor Bucephalus could not obey her master's orders. Our
speed was too great. The rock face too wet. At least Petts would not
get us, I thought. And then a gut-wrenching lurch near took me
from my saddle and my eyes locked themselves shut in fear.

So this was it. Not death as I had expected it, but death nonetheless.

So fast and so painless.

I had not even been aware of falling to the foot of the cliff, let
alone of having my body smashed against the rocks. I had heard
it said, and now it seemed that instant death really was a blessing.

I opened my eyes. It was as though we were flying, I on my horse
following Small on his. Perhaps I had lost consciousness before
the fatal impact, and now we were sweeping through the air to the
heavens on wingless Pegasi, up to meet our Maker—

I returned to earth with an almighty splash. I was thrown clean
from my saddle and deep water swallowed me. I sank through it
until my head and one shoulder collided with rocks in the river,
jagged stones tearing at my side. Panic ran through my body,
eliminating the pain. I only realised I was floating upwards when
I felt air on my floundering arms. My head broke the surface, and
I looked up to see Bucephalus, Small on her back, swimming
towards me. My own horse had already reached the bank. Small
grabbed my outstretched arm and dragged me to the water's edge.
He looked down at me and grinned. Behind him, the cliff towered
above us. Our scored tracks on the rock face ceased just above the
crevice. Five feet from certain death, the horses themselves had
done the only thing they could to save us all. They had jumped,
and by plan or miracle the leap had landed us in the deepest part
of the pool formed by the waterfall.

I traced those tramlines with my eyes – a straight line of terror
all the way up. They were beginning to fade, to be erased by the
falling water. There would be no record of our derring-do, no proof
that man and his brave beast had defied the might of Nature.

When my eyes reached the cliff top, such colourful fancies vanished like the white lines into the wet black face of the rock. There, at the lip, I saw distant silhouettes gathering.

Small leapt from his saddle and pulled me to my feet. I was dazed. My head was throbbing. When I rubbed it my hand returned wet and red.

'Come on!' Small said. 'It's not over!'

I looked up again and saw the outlines of men and puffs of smoke from the barrels of their weapons. Then the cracking of rifle shots came to my ears once more and I heaved my aching body into the saddle. As Small led us on at a canter along the valley, I held my head with one hand and my horse's mane with the other.

On the level ground we galloped away from the gunfire. Then we turned and went up again and the shots and their ringing were cut out by a great wall of rock. Down again we went, and along, and down again and up. By the time we turned to face the final rays of setting sunlight in the west, the juddering of the ride, the gash in my head and the evening's amber glare overcame me and no more sounds nor sights entered my rattling brain. Small would say that the mountains had protected us. It seemed to me we had overcome them, but whatever the truth, it was not a question I dwelt upon. Rather, I promptly passed out in my saddle.

*

When I came to, there were stars twinkling above me and below. I had made it to heaven after all, I thought. Into the skies where the gods reside. But my head still throbbed. When I put my hand to it I felt a damp rag, and despite the blanket strewn over me, I was cold. In this heaven, there were no celestial horns, only the heavy breathing of horses; and though our escape had been nothing short of miraculous, the bearded man I saw sitting some yards away carefully inspecting something in the moonlight was certainly not the host I hoped would welcome me to the afterlife.

I tried to lift myself to my feet, but fell back before I made it half way. Small turned his face to me.

'Hope it's worth the trouble, lad,' he said solemnly. He got to his feet and dropped the watch into my hands. 'But I couldn't leave without putting it to you. Why don't we combine forces, after all? You wouldn't make it a mile alone. Wouldn't've made it another yard, in fact. So here it is, old man. I'll take you to Ishkuman. You'll find out whatever it is you want, and afterwards you'll follow me south to Marwar and to the Faddhuan Clock. What do you say?'

I touched my head again. Certainly I would have been dead had he not returned. It was a bargain I could not turn down. I nodded.

'But where . . .' Speaking hurt and I did not finish my sentence.

'Here,' he said, handing me his flask. 'That should take the edge off.' He gestured towards the stars below us. 'That down there is the Hunza valley, lad. You said this man Flack was heading west, so I've taken us north. We'll head into that village at sun-up and buy some mules and supplies to see us through to Ishkuman.'

I nodded again.

'My bag?'

'Lost in the river, I'm afraid. Nothing in it, was there?'

I had not known what I would need on this adventure, and still did not. I shook my head and shivered.

'So we're a needless bag the lighter,' he said cheerfully. 'There's a chill in the air, I know, but it would be unwise to light a fire under the circumstances. I must say, that chap leading those soldiers seemed to have quite a steam on. Have you encountered him before? I've not seen that sort of reaction from Her Majesty's finest since . . .'

His voice petered out and I nodded again.

'In the Mess,' I stuttered.

'Ah,' he responded. 'But he didn't quite take to you as I have, eh? Well, that's the Army for you, lad. Animals not to be trusted. Now get some sleep. You'll need it – tomorrow will be a long day.'

And so it was. It began at sun-up when we descended on a precipitous mountain trail into the village below. The peaks of Hunza were the highest and steepest I had yet seen – jagged monsters reaching into the skies, crowned by the shining wall of Rakaposhi. When we reached the settlement, we bought two mules from an uninterested trader. We then loaded the animals with as much cured meat, dried fruit and grain as they could carry. We bought furs to fight the cold, tarpaulins for shelter and some bundles of wood for kindling. Water, Small told me, we would get from rivers and by melting snow. Then, our beasts fully burdened, on foot we headed up the mountain once more. At its pinnacle Small handed me his pistol to carry for protection. Then we drank to our journey and set a course for the northwest.

The rest of the day was occupied making our way down into the next valley and only part way up the other side. Small decided that crossing the mountains at night was too dangerous and so we pitched chilly camp beneath our tarpaulins, and tried to sleep.

Progress was slow and over the next two days we made it across only two more valleys. On the third night, Small proclaimed that we were far enough from civilisation so lit a fire and changed my bandages. The gash on my head was deep, he told me, and looked to be infected.

'We'll have to cauterise it, boy, or the gangrene'll settle, and then amputation's the only course,' he grinned.

He built up the fire and placed his knife in the embers until it glowed. Despite the stick he placed between my teeth, the scream I emitted when he placed the heated blade on the side of my head would be, I thought, enough to rouse the interest of any man for miles around. When the next morning we woke undisturbed, I was in no doubt that we were quite, quite alone.

The going on the snow and ice was slow and tiring, even when riding. But on the fourth day, the brilliant, dazzling white of the snow gave way to a deep valley where naked brown rock broke through on the lower slopes, and so we altered our direction northeastwards to ease the animals' burden. Between the spires, snaking their way from snow to river in a magnificent array of browns, were enormous piles of rubble, dust and sand, landslides creating miniature mountain ranges on each face. They were like a network of enormous, bulging veins creeping down the widening bodies of the hills, supplied by pumping hearts hidden high under the ice. Lower down, the brown was replaced by brilliant green where grass still grew, nourished by the precious water the summer months briefly offered, which, in its turn, fed our animals and saved us grain. We drank from the river water and at night, Small caught fish for us to eat.

At the end of day seven we came to the river's source – a mighty glacier edging down from the peaks which took us an entire day to climb. There the greenery ended, and we entered the true Karakoram – snow, ice, rock and little more. The occasional creature was to be seen scraping a life there, and on the lower slopes we gave our animals time to take advantage of any shrub or twig they could find on which to graze. Small tried and failed to shoot ibex on two occasions, but when his second attempt brought an avalanche of snow tumbling down the mountain opposite, he desisted. We even caught a fleeting glimpse of what looked like a great white spotted cat on one morning, but come our ninth day of travelling, we had risen to such an altitude that even birds did not risk passage. Only man would be foolish enough to try.

To begin with, we talked as we went. Small regaled me with visions of the Faddhuan Clock, and boosted both our spirits with marching songs, and come evening he would tell tales of his past that reached heights even greater than those at which we travelled. The wound on my head was healing well, and Small had removed the bandage. 'You'll bear the scar always,' he told me, 'but fear not, you'll depart this world intact.'

We tackled sudden crevices, dealt with sinking chest-deep into the snow and overcame the extremes of cold and the burning sun with our heads held high. However, on the eleventh day, my horse and I slipped into deep snow. Small, leading our rope-linked train, managed to drag me to safety as I sank, but there was no hope of rescue for the horse. We were forced to cut the rope linking it to the mules behind and Bucephalus in front, or they too would have been pulled in. The poor creature fell into a deep fissure in the ice, taking valuable food and Small's pistol with it. The distressed whinnying from below compelled Small to chance avalanche and fire his rifle into the hole until it was silenced rather than leave the valiant animal to suffer.

This turn of events meant that by the fourteenth day, our rations were fast depleting. On day seventeen Small judged that one of our mules was excess to requirements. It consumed grain that could keep its partner and Bucephalus alive, and it held meat that could sustain us. I turned away as Small approached the animal, but my ears could not escape the squeals of slaughter, nor the grunts that followed as Small hacked at its flesh. We trekked on. Meat from the carcass filled our bellies, but morale was seeping from us as surely as the mule's blood had soaked into the snow. As our spirits waned, so too did our loquacity, and without conversation or song to distract me I took a turn for the worse; whether from the altitude, exhaustion or the after-effects of my head wound, I could not tell.

I began to feel that the mountains themselves were against us; that they were the guardians of Adam-Khor, determined to keep his secrets from us, leading us deeper into their icy fastness, and always astray. What hope had two such insignificant figures against these giants? They gazed down on us, implacable, indifferent, waiting for us to die.

Other times I was convinced that Sri Badat had never existed at all, that Adam-Khor was nothing more than a legend, his treasure a myth. Why had I allowed myself to be seduced by fantasies, first of adventure and then of riches? The watch was cursed. McNaughton had been crazed with greed and the impulse to violence, and had died in my shop. Forrester had attempted the search alone, and been driven back, only to be savagely murdered in Cairo. Tolliver had lost hand, head and then life in these very mountains. Everyone who had held the watch was dead, and all had gone mad. And now I was losing my reason, and my life was ebbing from me.

Amidst my delirium, Small judged that the second mule must also be sacrificed. What grain remained Bucephalus required. It was slaughtered on the twenty-sixth day, the last I counted, and we carried as much of the fresh meat with us as we could, but it was hopeless. Before long, we would have to eat it raw. Lower down, we had gathered scraps of shrub and root for firewood, but we were above the treeline, and many days had passed when we found none. I was gibbering insensibly about Tolliver, Small tells me, and Small himself had grown weary and exhausted. He refused to kill his faithful Bucephalus, whose remaining grain we eked out in ever diminishing portions, when to do so would only extend our sorry lives for additional days of torture.

We had been wandering for weeks, months it felt. We both wore frozen beards, and furs caked in ice. We had seen no sign of life since we mounted that glacier so long ago. We had changed direction to head up that valley, and now we were lost and dying.

★

We pitched camp, lit a fire with the last of our kindling and prepared to drink what whisky remained before cold, exhaustion or drunkenness took us to unconsciousness. The only good to come from the hopelessness of our position was that, as I came to terms with my inevitable death, my delirium subsided, leaving only a feeling that this was a lonely, inauspicious way to die. I had not even reached Ishkuman.

Our supper was a muted affair. Though they were to be our last hours on earth, neither of us could muster much jollity to rouse the other.

'It's been a fine adventure,' Small said finally. 'I don't mind telling you that. And when some unfortunate bugger comes across us, they'll find my map. Only one who dares to cross the Karakoram as we have will ever know its secrets, and that is a warming thought. Only one who succeeds where we have failed – and so they'll deserve it.'

'Small,' I said, 'I'm sorry. If it weren't for me you'd be warm in the south, sharing your whisky with beautiful women. Not freezing on the mountainside with a watchmaker.'

'It's conceivable, lad, but don't dwell on it. The choice was mine to make and I made it, so if anyone's the fool here, it's me. Here,' he said, passing the bottle.

The whisky warmed me to the core, obliterating the cold that the dying fire was letting in.

'And do you know what's the worst of it, Small?' I asked after a long draught from the bottle. 'The worst of it is that I've not even been honest with you.'

'Well, now. Don't you worry too much about that. Honesty is an over-rated virtue in my experience. If we were all honest all of the time, what a dull world we would live in.'

'But now that we're to die here, Small, I feel compelled to tell you what I've kept from you,' I continued. 'To get it off my chest.'

'Something of a confession, eh?' he said. 'Well, I'm no priest, lad, and can't guarantee you'll pass over comfortably, but if you feel *compelled* . . .'

'The reason I was heading to Ishkuman – it wasn't curiosity. Well, it was, but not quite of the sort I told you. You see, this stone on the watch. It is valuable. A sapphire. And there might be more. I was after the lost treasure of a king, Small. Adam-Khor. This eye – I believe it came from a statue of his protector. I thought so, anyway. Now . . . now I don't know.'

'Well, if that's all you've got, I'd not fear the oncoming eternity. If you'd have told me that, I'd have followed you even more certainly. So we could both have been kings, eh? And now we're lost. It's of no matter. As I said, it's been quite an adventure.'

'Well, I'm glad I told you, nonetheless. I wouldn't like it to end knowing I'd deceived you.'

'We've become good friends, you and I,' he said. 'And you're right, good friends shouldn't deceive one another.'

I noticed that Small looked older than he had in Gilgit. The skin around his eyes was sagging and his beard was long. There was silver hair amongst the brown where before there had been none.

He showed his teeth briefly in one of his broad grins. 'I've not been honest with you, lad, either, and since you've begun the confessional trend, I might as well confess myself. I let you believe that the Army was after me for the map. That's not entirely the truth. In actual fact, it's not the truth at all. They don't know of the map, but they know of me. Paul Small, you see, is sought for the crime of desertion.'

He took the whisky from me, drank and smiled.

'Oh, yes. I told you I was once a soldier, didn't I? And so I was until my thirtieth year. I had to get to Egypt, you see. After my parents were killed, I lived sheltered by the school of Harrow half the time and under the wing of a gloriously disreputable man called Melancovic the other half. He was a Slavic cripple, a criminal from the east, moved to London to escape his past. Not a thing you can escape, though – the past. But, before old Melancovic was hanged, he passed on to me his greatest secret – a map he said would lead me to the greatest pile man has ever seen. Riches fit for Pharaohs, hidden in the sands of Egypt, just waiting to be plundered by the likes of me. With no legs, he couldn't go – it was a sure bet he'd never make it – so on his way to the gallows, he threw me the map and told me to head for Egypt. Now, all the money left to me by my dear parents, that blighter of a lawyer Shankle thought best spent on my education, so when I came to leave at the age of seventeen, there was none left to get me to Africa. So I joined up. It took me thirteen years to get posted to the Sudan, but when I got there, it was cheerio lads, and off to Egypt with me. I found the stash, but the Army found me, and I had to be off again before I could get my hands on much. I hid what I took in the sand and made an additional mark on the map, and got this decoration into the bargain.'

He traced a finger down his scar.

'You know the punishment for desertion, lad. Firing squad no matter who you are – if they know who you are. Gives them no greater pleasure than to punish one of their own. Now, not only did I manage to hide what little I took, but I also disguised the entrance to the stash, and it's still there, under the sand. A find like that would be on the front pages of all the newspapers in the world, so I know it's still there waiting for me. All of it.'

He had drained the bottle and threw it over his shoulder, shaking his head resignedly. I got to my feet and went to retrieve another bottle from the saddle lying next to Bucephalus.

So Small was a deserter. A crime tantamount to murder. Worse even. It was treasonous. But what did it matter now?

'Not many left,' I said, throwing him one of the four remaining bottles.

I looked out over the moonlit valley, my eyes feasting upon their final vista. Dawn was coming. Above the ridge that faced us, a smudged grey line was angled across the deep blue sky, bisecting the paling moon.

'And then, lad,' Small was saying as he tore the cork from the bottle. 'There's worse to come.'

I scarcely heard him. Whether he was talking about the end of the whisky or about his confession, I could not say. I narrowed my eyes, to be certain that my vision was not playing tricks.

'I've been—'

Small did not complete his sentence, for I interrupted him.

'Look, Small! Look!' I cried, pulling him to his feet, pointing like a disciple on the third day and turning him to face the moon.

Then, as though speaking too loudly would chase what he saw on the horizon back into the mountains, he whispered.

'Smoke!'

18

THE LETTERS OF
SIR PAUL LINDLEY-SMALL

From the same cabin
Honningsvåg, Norway

25TH DECEMBER 1908

Well, lad,

It is morning, and while that marvellous lass prepares me a
hero's breakfast, I take up my pen once more.

There is only one room to the house I arrived at, and in it is a
crude kitchen stove fed on wood. Beside it is a small table to eat at,
and two chairs. Before the open fire sit two armchairs and there is
a bed in one corner, large enough to occupy a full third of the
floorspace. The fire and a single lantern amply light the place with
an inviting warmth. The floor, all the chairs, the bed and much of
the walls are covered in furs, the two small windows hidden by
them. It is a furry and bestial haven of conviviality, and I liked it at
once.

At the threshold, I announced myself, whereupon the girl
immediately threw herself into my arms with abandon, wound
her own arms around my neck and showered my face with kisses.

Her brother Bjørn was returned to her, she told me in a charming broken English, and I was the lad's saviour. I hadn't the foggiest how, of course, but nor did I have the heart to suggest that her worship might be unfounded. Such disappointment would have crushed her. As she worked to leave not a spot on my face and neck untouched by her hungry lips, I spotted that one of the few furless items in the hut was the chubby young lad sitting at the kitchen table watching us as he ate from a bone.

'This is Bjørn,' the now breathless haven-keeper told me. 'And my name is Mari. Please, you will eat?'

I had not eaten since I had arrived in the town, and was ravenous. I said I would be delighted to join them. She shooed the lad from his chair, and he resettled with his platter on the bed, from where he eyed me in silent suspicion. Mari sat me down and then served me up a great bone of my own, drenched in a thick brown sauce of unknown origin. Sitting opposite, without food for herself, she stared at me, her sharp elbows on the table and her chin in her hands. I looked around for cutlery, but seeing in her face a concern that I might be dissatisfied, and not wanting to upset her, I took my cue from the boy, who was holding his bone with both hands, and tucked in.

Mari herself was a feast for the eyes. She wore a simple blue dress of a rough material and seemed content to watch as I tore meat from the bone like her Viking ancestors. Her almond-shaped eyes were blue and dark-rimmed and somewhat slanted towards her nose, which, though slight, possessed the angle of a break. Her high and perfectly symmetrical cheekbones served to emphasise this, the only, but rather wonderful fault on such a beautiful face. Her skin was pale, but rosy where one wanted it to be and her hair was a golden-blonde; her lips were thin enough to make it an effort for her to close her mouth, but where this can be an unattractive trait in some females, suggesting bucked or oversized teeth, here it enforced a constant and licentious wetting of the lips that I challenge any man to find unappetising.

When I had taken my fill, she led me to the seats before the fire, then shoved the boy from the bed, pushed a pouch of coins into his hand and took his place on the furs. He accepted the money and left, harrumphing as he donned a coat, for in the minuscule town I had seen nowhere a lad of twelve could spend a coin, let alone an entire pouch. Forgetting him the moment he departed the hut, however, I poured the girl and myself a dram each, determining that it was time to get down to the business her hero had come to elicit from her.

Mari well remembered everything that had occurred on the day Bjørn had been taken. Since the disappearances had commenced, all children in the vicinity had been schooled in their homes, and Mari herself had taught Bjørn. That day, they read through a chapter of Snorre's history of the country's Viking monarchs. Brother and sister then practised woodchopping, simple arithmetic and handwriting in the form of a seasonal list of gift requests that they sent to St Nicholas from the post-office at lunchtime. They then went for a ski around the town and dipped into the hotel for a warming toddy. In the afternoon, the boy continued to read from the book of legends as his sister prepared their evening meal. Once their appetites were sated, young Bjørn fell to slumber in the bed the pair share, and Mari left the cabin to gather sufficient firewood for the night from their store at the back of the hut. When she returned, Bjørn was gone.

Despite her panic, Mari had the presence of mind to investigate the scene of the crime for clues, and was able to deduce the following and inescapable facts: the box in which kindling was stored was lying upturned in front of a window, where before it had sat by the hearth; the window was placed low in the wall; the fur that had covered the window when she left to fetch wood no longer did so when she returned – it was pushed aside and one corner was pulled from the nail that had held it in place; outside, fast being swallowed by falling snow, her hunter's eyes spotted the remnants of footprints. They were unclear, but busy – and small. She was not able to judge just how large the abductor had been, nor, now she thought of it, how many legs it possessed. All in the village had assumed it was an adult human taking these infants, but considering these facts, Mari concluded that the abductor could only have been a child, or a child-sized beast. But what breed of child would kidnap a dozen of his fellows? What manner of miniature monster would kill and leave only the bones of eleven? My prize had to be the guilty party, and I smiled knowingly as Mari spoke, but she was telling me the story with such an earnest exhilaration, which was pleasingly evolving into a state of high and bouncing excitement, that I felt disinclined to interrupt.

She found it too appalling to believe that it could be another child committing the abductions, she was saying. Besides, all the children that were left in the town were being carefully watched over by worried parents, and she personally knew all of them. Nonetheless, she could not deny the facts that she had discovered and so decided to keep an eye on the remaining infants, at least until another clue arose.

It was, of course, a fruitless task, for with news of this latest disappearance, the children were kept even more firmly by the side of their parents, who swore never to let them out of sight before the mystery had been solved and the twelve safely returned. Certainly they would not be so foolish as to leave their children alone when fetching firewood, they whispered behind the wondrous contours of Mari's back. These all too audible mutterings caused her guilt to increase, for when their parents had died in an accident involving a herd of reindeer and an unruly sleigh, she had persuaded her uncles and aunts to let her care for Bjørn and swore she would never let anything happen to the child, then only six years old. But as her guilt grew, so did her determination to rescue her brother. She watched the children and their parents for days on end, but alas, nothing came of these observations, and soon enough she began to lose all hope of ever seeing Bjørn again.

The mothers of all the missing children had each become a wailing mourner since their loss, and Mari seemed destined to join their hopeless ranks, though she swore not to wail, but hunt for her brother until her dying breath. It was this oath that saw her take to skiing endlessly in the mountains, calling his name and searching and fruitlessly searching. This she continued until she was told that a letter awaited her collection at the post-office.

Surprised by any correspondence, she was hopeful that this could pertain to the lost Bjørn, so the contents of my letter proved a disappointment to her. But only initially, she assured me, scrambling up onto her knees and stretching out her long-fingered hands in apology for her foolishness. It had been the letter that held the key. Were it not for my valiant desire to aid a stranger in need, Bjørn would never have been found at all.

I raised my arm and let her pull me to her side on the soft warmth of the bed. As fur enveloped us, she explained that, in her dismay, she had been on the verge of throwing the letter into the fire, but on the moment immediately preceding release from her hand she noticed smudged fingerprints upon the envelope. On closer inspection, she saw that in addition to the fingermarks, there was a slight and weak palm print. Together, they formed the impression of a small hand. Ignoring the plain fact that the letter had travelled from Kautokeino, that the mark could have been printed at any point between there and here, in her torment Mari leapt upon a coincidence tragically turned by desperation into a connection.

There must be a link between the impression, the box and the size of the window, she convinced herself, and in Honningsvåg there were very few to whom the grubby hand could belong. Conceivably a wicked child, but even if the incredible were true and a minor was guilty of the crimes, she could see no reason why they should desire to intercept her post. The abductor had left the mark on the envelope in passing, she decided, by pure accident, which meant the criminal dealt with mail as a matter of course. This conclusion left only the postbag collector and the post-office proprietor as remaining possible small-handed felons. Either was possible. She had never even seen the postbag collector, and the post-office proprietor was never to be found enjoying a drink in the hotel. He kept himself to himself, a reclusive chap one only ever saw manning his post. But then, that was not so surprising. The post-office sent their own representatives out and they resided in the post-office buildings. Someone who accepted as lonely and desolate a posting as Honningsvåg was hardly likely to be a socialite. On her rare visits to the post-office, however, Mari had thought the proprietor a civil enough man, and more importantly, now she thought of it, of normal stature.

However, since he was always at his post, and the postbag collector only came to town on irregular occasions, Mari decided that whilst awaiting the other man's arrival, she would first eliminate the post-office proprietor from her investigations. Thereafter, she made many trips to the post-office and sent many letters to people who existed and some who did not. Though she explained herself by saying that they were letters conveying news of her loss, the envelopes contained nothing but pleasantries.

The post-office is, she told me, a cabin much the same as hers from the outside. Customers enter and find themselves in a room occupying half the building. It is lined with ledges where one can write addresses and stick stamps on letters. In the wooden wall that divides the cabin, located at head height, there is a small window. Behind it is a man, the proprietor. It is cold in the post-office and he always wears a hat. One receives and pays for stamps through a small slot just below the window. The customer, address written and stamps stuck, hands the letter through this slot and it is retrieved by the proprietor, who places it in a sack for collection.

On all her visits to his place of employment, Mari saw that, though his head was perhaps slightly smaller than is the norm, and though he took her letters without revealing so much as a finger through the hole in the wall, the post-office proprietor could not have been of a hither before unseen pint-size. If the diminutive hand that left its print on my letter had been his, and the rest of him was in scale with the paw, he would have had to bend quite over to take money and letters from the slot below the window. The expressionless man behind the glass barely moved at all when doing so. Then there was the height of the window. Mari looked straight into it, and though she could not see down towards his body, he was some inches taller than her. Still, it was conceivable that he was possessed of freakish, disproportionately small hands, but if that were the case, he could never have fitted through the window out of which Bjørn had been taken. More besides, the prints Mari had seen disappearing under the snow suggested that the abductor's feet were as small as his hands. If this were true of the post-office proprietor, he would have struggled to stand, even without the burden of a child. This was not her man, Mari concluded, so she moved on to the only remaining possibly small-handed culprit, the postbag collector.

She was told, after a one-sided casual chat with the man behind the window, who had a rather high-pitched voice he was reluctant to use, that the collector came weekly, either very early in the morning or very late at night. However, the postbag collector was obviously a topic that incensed the post-office proprietor, and as his voice reached new heights of volume and pitch, his hot breath condensed on the cold glass and interrupted Mari's view of him. Calming himself, he explained that the source of his ill temper was the fact that the day on which the post was collected was bound to vary and that his sleep was consistently interrupted in the dead of night. Thus every night Mari took her place in the darkness of a lean-to not forty feet from the post-office to await the arrival of the collector.

On the night he came, the third, the moon was shining, but was dissipated by a dense mist. Over the blustery wind, Mari heard the dull thud of hooves on compacted snow well before she saw a creaking cart, pulled by a single carthorse, crawl from the fog into the dim light. The man, as yet unseen under multiple warming layers, swore profusely as he prepared to expose himself to the cold. Slowly, he stood in the cart and, silhouetted in the fog illuminated by the high and full moon, Mari saw him throw the furs from his shoulders to reveal a tiny, lithe, long-armed man. He leapt from the cart into the snow, still cursing to himself with every movement. As he disappeared behind the post-office to collect the bag from the no doubt equally foul-mouthed proprietor, Mari was convinced that this man – short, slim and no doubt small of hand – was surely her young brother's abductor.

Being the thorough girl that she is, however, she knew that evidence was required, so she crept to the wall of the post-office and hid in a shadow, positioning herself to see the collector's hands on his return.

Shivering, for on leaving the lean-to she had forsaken her reindeer furs for the sake of mobility, Mari bit down on her lip to stop
her teeth from chattering as the collector, now swearing dissatis-
faction with the complaining post-office proprietor, returned to his
cart with the postbag.

Mari held her breath in case he saw it steam in the night light
and watched as he heaved the bag onto the cart and himself back
into his seat.

It was as he threw furs over himself that she saw his hands lit by
the moon. They were freakishly large, the fingers of both long and
spindly, near blue with cold. Forgetting herself, from the shadows
Mari let out a sigh of disappointment, to which the collector
reacted immediately. Though he looked straight at her, she dared
not move, for then he would certainly see her. He squinted into
the darkness and Mari held her breath again as he craned his neck.
He moved slightly, as though he was once more preparing to rid
himself of his skins, but as quickly as he had done so, he tightly
covered himself again and geed up his freezing horse.

'Damnable rats!' Mari thought she heard him mutter as he
rounded the cart and departed. 'How they can take this cold, I'll
never know.'

This time Mari could sigh freely and she returned to the lean-
to glad she had not been spotted, but upset that the collector had
not been the small-handed chap she was after. She re-donned her
skins, tied them tightly around her waist, threw the bag in which
she kept food and a warming brew for her vigil over her shoulder
and stepped out onto the snow. As it crunched under her foot, she
froze. She could hear voices. Bickering voices. Not far away. The
tone was clear, but she could not make out the words. She closed
her eyes and strained to discern from precisely where they came.
She reopened her eyes at the slamming of a door. The volume and
emotion of the arguing increased, but more importantly, the feroc-
ity of the door closing made snow cascade from the roof of the
post-office.

Wondering who on earth could be entering or leaving the post-
office at such an hour, and who its proprietor's visitor could be, she

was struck dumb when she saw three children walk around the corner and take to the snow on the hill that led away from the town. Try as she might, shock would not allow Mari to move, and there she stood, illuminated by the moon, a dark blot in a universe of white mist and snow. But the children did not see her, for their quarrelling quite occupied them and they were walking in the opposite direction.

Despite their disagreement, they moved quickly and were soon mere blurs to Mari's straining eyes. Gathering herself as a hunter must after the initial excitement of sighting her prey, Mari followed the children more by the indistinct sound of their continuing argument and their diminutive footprints than by her ability to see them, for they carried no torch in the fog, yet appeared quite definite in their direction. She sank into the snow and pushed against the strong winds, and managed to follow them to the peak of the mountain and down the other side. She fell on the slope and feared the tumbling snow would alert them, but she need not have feared, for the children paid heed to nothing but each other. There was not a moment's respite from their arguing. Even when the trail they left entered a cave so low that Mari had to crawl along it and could not help but make all manner of clatterings, it never ceased. In fact, their high voices did not let up until they had exited the cave and walked in Nature's snowy elements for further miles. Their voices finally ceased to squawk when they reached a large mound of snow at the foot of a sheer mountainside, as though their infant gods had thrown down a ten-foot snowball.

Mari watched them inspect it. They moved around it, looked up to the mountain, began to feel it with their small gloved hands, and then suddenly one drove a hand into the snow, elbow deep, as though in silence his anger had brimmed over. He punched his fist into the snow several times more before, with a final thrust, he left it embedded. Or rather it was stuck, because his fellow travellers grabbed him, their disagreement forgotten. 'One, two, three,' they counted and then heaved and they were all thrown over. The snow had given way, but not to reveal more snow, or even a great boulder, but light, in the rectangular form of a doorway, gushing forth, illuminating the children and the ground around them.

Fearing that they would see her, Mari dug herself yet deeper into the snow, but again she need not have worried, for as soon as they had picked themselves up, the infants continued their argument, entered the doorway and slammed the door shut.

In darkness again, Mari clambered to her feet and cautiously approached. As she neared, she could see in the moonlight that both the door and its frame were of wood. In silence, she searched it from top to bottom for a keyhole to spy through, but found none. The door fitted tightly into its frame and there was not a single crack of light to be seen. Instead she placed a frosty ear to the wood, and tried to listen. As before, she could not ascertain precisely what the children spoke of, but they were no longer arguing. They were toadying in deference to the far deeper voice that had joined their ranks. This voice Mari could make out perfectly as the winds died and the snowflakes ceased to fall.

'Do not worry, my little ones,' it told them. 'We shall all have our share. The fire is built, so let us get along and light it.'

The children cheered and whooped and over them Mari heard the deep voice again. 'Patience, patience,' it said. 'This cannot be rushed, as you know.'

Then came a great grinding sound and the voices died away.

Alas, I must say goodbye – to you for now, to Mari perhaps forever. I am to depart tomorrow, and cannot show my gratitude to a lady with pen in hand.

L-S

19

The Notebooks of Cyril King

1893

Paradise Found

'Get moving, boy. It'll be full daylight soon and there's no guarantee they'll stick around after sun-up.' Small grabbed his knapsack and slung it over his shoulder. 'We don't have much choice but to accept them as our salvation, whoever they are. Bandits or soldiers, I'd say. Either's a damnable way to answer our prayers.'

We led Bucephalus as fast as we could in the direction of the smoke, stumbling and wading through deep snow in our haste. More than once we lost sight of it, and prayed that it would be visible when we reached the crest. What, in our wildest dreams, we never would have thought to pray for was what met our eyes as we clambered onto the ridge.

Below us, suddenly bathed in the brilliant golden light of the sun rising behind us, was a valley. Snow and ice covered its upper slopes. But unlike the barren landscape that had led us to the glacier, here there was no bare rock beneath the white. Further down, beyond the snow line, what lay before our disbelieving eyes was the lush green of life. Trees, bushes, shrubs, all fed by a glittering river. In the midst of this frozen desert we had stumbled upon a miraculous oasis. We were both speechless. I was stunned into inactivity, for I feared it was a mirage that would vanish before we could reach it. Small, on the other hand, had removed the spyglass from my pocket and was scanning the mountainside.

'There!' he said after some moments and handed me the instrument. I put it to my eye and aimed it at the spot to which he pointed.

'On the other side, lad. Whoever they are, I'll bet you three to one they're cooking breakfast!'

I saw it. Smoke rising above green branches halfway up the other side of the valley.

I pushed the spyglass shut. Small had already mounted Bucephalus and was proffering a hand. I took it and, despite his weakened state, he hauled me bodily onto the horse behind him. He kicked the mare, and then we were descending towards life and the hope of sustenance.

We dashed and slid down the snow until we reached the woodland. Beneath the darkness of the canopy it was hard to make out our path. Turning this way and that, we wove our way in and out of the trees, but always down. Thorns tore at Bucephalus's shins, but never once did she falter, as aware as we were, it seemed, that at the end of this headlong rush would be food and fresh, delicious water. The foliage grew thicker, the trunks broader. If it were not such a glorious place, I should have said it was like descending into hell; but there in that strange mountain world, I had discovered that hell was up high and heaven below. The place was alive. Small deer fled from our path. Wild flowers sprouted from the forest floor. I stretched my hand up into the leaves and grabbed at white dots that caught my eye.

I licked my fingers. The sweet flavour of mulberries torched my mouth. 'Fruit, Small!' I cried. 'We're saved!'

Water splashed beneath us. We had reached the river. Small tugged on the reins and Bucephalus stopped. Immediately she dropped her head and began to drink. I reached up into the overhanging branches, pulled down great bunches of berries and stuffed them into my mouth. Small did the same, before looking up to where we had seen the smoke.

'Dismount, lad,' he said, doing so himself. 'We're on foot from here.'

I wanted to head up the mountain towards the fire at once, but Small insisted that first we must let Bucephalus take her fill. She cropped the thick, wet grass at the river's bank, and Small loosened her girths. As we waited for her to sate her appetite, we stared up through the trees and filled our bellies with more fruit.

'Lad,' Small said, wiping his mouth with his hand. 'We don't know who we'll find up there – whether they'll be friend or foe. Anyone to be found in such a place as this, so far from anywhere else – as I said, my guess is bandits or—'

'Soldiers,' I said, completing his sentence, in just as solemn a tone, for I had realised the implications of such a possibility.

'Small,' I said. 'You have accompanied me through this ordeal. You saved me twice in Gilgit. Though in my delirium I have been a burden, you have stuck by my side. Here I am presented with an opportunity to repay you in some little way. I alone will approach the fire. For you to do so is too much of a risk to take.'

Small nodded sagely.

'I don't it like, lad, not one bit, but I fear you're right. I'll do my best to cover you with my rifle, but in this dense forest it'll be a difficult task. We need to head above them, so I can look down on you. We'll get me up in a tree for the best view possible. Now, we have to move slowly,' he said, gathering up the reins and starting into the rushing river. 'And keep quiet.'

I took hold of a stirrup, and we waded into the water. Though it was shallow enough for a man to walk, my feet were instantly numbed. However, Bucephalus, her strength renewed by feeding and watering, led me to the other side without mishap. We started up the mountainside, stamping feeling back into our legs and walking directly up from where we had emerged from the river. Shards of light penetrated the canopy, illuminating our way through the forest's shadows. When we gained ground that was suitably higher than the smoke, we turned right, to the north, through the undergrowth.

The sound of distant laughter came to our ears. I felt suddenly uneasy. If Gilgit had turned upstanding soldiers into the likes of Petts, imagine what monstrosities these mountains could produce. My pace slowed, and before I knew it I had lost sight of Bucephalus. I heard Small hiss from some distance ahead.

'King! Get up here, man!'

I found him standing before a wall. It was made of stone hewn into blocks, and it was curved. This was a building, or at least the remnants of one. It looked hundreds of years old and appeared to have been abandoned, for vegetation had taken over where once man had dominated.

'This will be perfect,' whispered Small. 'It must've been a fort once. We'll find a way in, and I'll perch myself up high.'

He removed a satchel from his saddle and the rifle from its sheath, tied Bucephalus's reins to a tree and we began to make our way round the dilapidated structure. As we did so, I had the uncomfortable feeling that we were being watched. I scanned the shadows, but saw nothing. This secrecy, this creeping about, was making me jittery.

As we moved, I saw that various grand trees had grown into the structure of the building. Indeed, its stability now looked to rely upon these living buttresses, but nowhere had their intrusion created a hole through which Small could fit, even though his frame was substantially depleted. We edged further around the perimeter.

'Look,' Small whispered.

I looked over his shoulder and there before us was the reason the builders had chosen this spot on which to construct their fort.

It perched, somewhat precariously, on the very edge of a sudden cleft in the mountain, one so narrow that from the river we could not have seen it. Forty feet below, the ravine ended in a narrow path. From this vantage point one could see north and south along the valley, east to the mountains on the other side and west through this tight pass.

Small turned and pointed to the wall behind me.

'In we go, lad.'

At ground level there was a gap through which we could squeeze. Small went first, and I followed. I shuffled through as silently as possible. As I inched my way into the single, circular chamber, I twisted my head to face Small, and was surprised to find that I was not looking at his feet, but at his chest. The ground here on the inside was a good four or five feet lower than outside. Other than fallen leaves and stones that were strewn all over this sunken floor and branches growing through the walls above us, the place was quite empty.

I edged my way through and lowered myself from the ledge. The gap had been created by a stone, once embedded in the wall and pointing inward to form a step, which had slipped from its perch. Others spiralled up the curved walls above us, clearly the ruins of what had been a staircase; but most were stumps at best, many no longer there at all, lying instead in rubble at my feet, leaving windows that were never meant to be.

'There's my spot,' Small said.

He pointed upwards and I saw sunlight shining through a hole in the wall some twenty feet above us, made larger by the branch of an adjacent tree growing through the masonry, pushing stones aside.

'I can get a clear shot from there.'

He was already clambering up towards the branch, scrambling from ledge to ledge with an agility surprising for a man of his dimensions. When he had reached it, he sat with his feet dangling, checking his rifle, and looked out through the hole.

'I can see the fire from here. In a clearing, two hundred yards straight down. Looks to be about a dozen of them. Now, stay aware of where you are in relation to me. Try to keep anyone you come across between us. If you're between them and me, the only way I'll be able to get to them is through you. And stay in the clearing, whatever you do. I can't see through trees.' He took my spyglass from his pocket and pointed it through the hole in the wall. 'Hello,' he said.

'What?' I said staring up at him.

'One of them's wearing an Army issue turban. A Sikh's. Could be Army; could be bandits who've run across the Army. You be careful down there. Take Bucephalus – but be a sport and leave a bottle for me out there, will you? If there's trouble, let the old girl get you out of it. She's seen more action than either one of us. She'll get you away. Then take a long route back to me and when you approach make plenty of noise. Creeping trespassers are liable to be shot.'

I nodded.

'Right,' I said and took a deep breath, trying to rid myself of the fear rising in my belly. Quite what I had let myself in for, I did not know. I made my way back to the ledge and, as I was lifting myself to the hole, I heard Small's whisper again.

'And King – don't forget my food. This snipering lark's hungry sport, and unless my nose deceives me, there's meat being roasted down there.'

I left him taking position on his belly and poking the rifle through the gap in the wall.

*

I rounded the wall and found Bucephalus. I removed a bottle of whisky from the saddle, as per request, took a fortifying swig, set it down and continued until I could see the barrel of Small's rifle above my head. A hand appeared and waved me on. I turned and led Bucephalus towards the glow flickering between the trunks and branches. I could barely see the fire. I was being guided more by the sound of voices than anything, until suddenly they fell silent.

I stopped dead in my tracks.

Surely they had heard me.

I held my breath until my blood pounded in my ears.

Just when I thought my veins would burst, the voices started again. I sighed with relief, and as the last of my breath left my lungs I felt something prod my back. I spun round and found myself staring into a pair of eyes. The face was all but covered by a black headscarf. I looked down. His hand held a long, curved blade. I looked beyond him, up to where I hoped Small was taking aim, but saw only the dark green of the canopy. I lifted my hands into the air. I was being taken prisoner by bandits.

He took the reins from me with his free hand and gestured with the blade that I turn about. Keeping my hands high, I did so. When he prodded my back again, I started slowly towards the fire. There he and his friends would ask of me how I, an interloper, had come upon their lair. Doubtless the heat of the fire would be used to demand of me what had brought me to such an isolated place. Perhaps it would be employed for their amusement, and nothing I could say would make them stop. I would be tortured and killed. Indeed, as we approached, I smelled the burning flesh that Small had mistaken for roasting meat. That such it was, I was certain; but not the meat of a sheep or goat – more likely their previous victim. I looked left and right, trying to discern the best direction in which to bolt. But I was weak, and did not know the terrain. They would be on me in a second. I could have called for Small, but my belly would have been opened long before he got to me.

In the shadows of the forest, my eye was caught by a rapid, flitting movement among the trunks. I squinted, trying to make out what it was and in doing so eclipse all thought of what awaited me, but it was gone. We had come at length to the clearing, and there the odour of burning flesh was stronger, even over the sharper scent of smoke. More figures staring out of headscarves stood within it; I counted nine of the dozen Small had seen. No one spoke. There was no sound but for the crackling of the bonfire and the sizzling of the carcass that was roasting on a spit. I was relieved to see that the blackening skin and crisping flesh were clearly those of an animal; most probably, I judged from its size, a deer.

Then, as though from out of the very flames, a man rose to his feet. He stepped forward and inspected me with brown eyes that looked out from a dark and heavily bearded face. His turban was unlike those of the other men, being tautly wrapped where theirs were loose, and striped where theirs were plain. This was the Sikh that Small had pointed out. He was dressed in black and his posture was ramrod-straight.

Not knowing what else to do, I extended my hand. His men flinched as though mine had been an act of aggression.

'How do you do?' I said in as authoritative a tone as I could muster.

He did not reply, and nor did he take my proffered hand, but instead he indicated that I should be seated. To refuse would have excited their suspicion, and I did not want to antagonise them more than I could help, so with some trepidation, I complied. The rest of the group edged in to surround us, and lowered themselves to the ground. No shot had rung out from the fort, and no man had slumped lifeless in the clearing. Now we were all in a huddle around the bonfire, with none of them a clear target. Small, I suspected, had missed his chance.

I stared into the flames, not daring to look at any one of them. When a piece of bark on which lay strips of steaming, juicy venison was placed before me, I glanced up in surprise. The man at my side lifted fingers to his mouth, gesturing that I should eat. I did not want to disappoint him, and besides, I was ravenous. I threw the meat into my mouth. When the men around me laughed, I froze, a portion halfway to my lips, fearing what the venison might be laced with. But when I saw the Sikh himself was partaking of the meat, I gladly wolfed down all that they had given me. The rest of the men settled into a reverent silence as they too took from the carcass and ate while they waited for the Sikh to announce my fate.

In sitting down to eat, they had each removed their headscarves from their faces, and as I stole glances at them to see what manner of men they were, I realised they were hardly more than boys. I saw, too, that their skin was lighter by several shades than the Sikh's, and the eyes of the nearest were hazel, where his were brown. I had learned as I travelled northwards from Karachi that those in the south of the country were darker in the main than those in the north, and in Gilgit I had seen men who were lighter than Small's weather-beaten tan, and whose hair was brown, not black. But these were paler-complexioned still than any I had seen. Perhaps, I thought, it had to do with the constant snow and ice in these high valleys. The Sikh, on the other hand, was clearly not a native of these mountains.

One of them passed me a cup made of a twisted leaf in which

was a clear brown liquid. Not wishing to offend him, but fearful of what strange brew it might contain, I took it from him and drank. The liquid was hot, sweet tea. I swallowed that first blissful mouthful, and several others in rapid succession until the cup was drained. So far, they had offered me no further violence, and I felt my dread beginning to subside.

Finally, once we had eaten and drunk, the Sikh spoke, in English. 'I am Manraj Singh,' he said. 'Your name?'

It was as though all the youths had been waiting for him to break the silence, for suddenly a torrent of speech erupted from their mouths. They were excited, interrogative voices, asking what no doubt were questions, which alas, I could not understand.

Then, as I was about to reply, my gaze was distracted by a sudden movement in the forest; the same, I thought, that I had glimpsed before. The Sikh turned his head to see what had caught my attention. Trotting fleetingly out of the shadows and retreating as if they were woodland spirits were two sleek ponies, healthy and strong, the colour of bark, each carrying a fellow dressed as the youths were, each rider weaving his mount in and out between the trunks of the trees. Momentarily, I was transfixed by this strange and incongruous vision.

My captor gestured over his shoulder.

'Our young men like to practise their skills,' he said. 'For polo. You shall watch them play.'

I nodded eagerly, for surely such an invitation would not be extended to one they meant to kill here in the woods. Perhaps, I reasoned, ransom was their game.

'Your name?' Manraj Singh repeated.

'My name is King. Cyril King,' I said. I paused, unsure how much I should reveal. Yet, since they clearly knew these mountains, I would be foolish not to extract what benefit I could from this encounter. 'I travel to Ishkuman,' I continued. 'But now I must confess that I am lost. Tell me, do you know this place, Ishkuman?

Manraj Singh stared into the fire. But eventually he spoke.

'Yes, I know of it,' he said.'

20

The Letters of
Sir Paul Lindley-Small

From an unidentifiable backwater
Norway

31ST DECEMBER 1908

Lad,

Far better methods of celebrating New Year's Eve spring to mind than sitting here, quite alone in the darkness of a station in the middle of I don't know where, writing to my oldest of friends. My devotion to the mission sometimes surprises even myself. Auld lang syne indeed, eh lad?

Thank God for The Glenlivet.

Down the hatch.

Now then – that's enough of that. Let us return to the wonder that is Mari.

You will recall that she was outside this pile of snow with a door, not only extremely cold, but also increasingly frantic, for surely the children she had followed from the post-office had placed their handprint on my letter, and surely, therefore, *they* had abducted Bjørn. Their size explained how they had taken him through the window, their number how they had succeeded (plus all the tracks they had left) – and then there was this strange behaviour and the deep-voiced man.

As I worked this information to fit my own theories, Mari told me that what made her wait only moments before gathering her courage and wrenching open the heavy door was the latter – the deep voice and its owner. She had not recognised it, but be it familiar or not, the fact that somebody was in charge of and instructing the naughty children lent the entire affair the sinister bent that all had suspected from the off, but had prayed was not so.

As she had anticipated, when she threw the door wide, there was not a soul in the cabin, for that is what the mound of snow really was. The light that had previously gleamed from the doorway was no longer apparent, but the moon found its way through the door to help her see. Inside, the walls were white and shiny with ice. Even tins and jars were layered in the stuff, thick dust frozen in place. Icicles hung from the rafters and shelves. Suspended from a metal hook embedded in the roof-beam was a single unlit lantern. When Mari's numb fingers had successfully fumbled matches from her pocket and lit the lamp, she inspected the cabin for more evidence of the children and their master's whereabouts.

A table, three small chairs and a large one sat around a stove in the middle of the room, but the stove was not linked to any chimney and it, too, was white with disuse. There was a bed in one corner, the mean quilt upon it frozen into its ruffled position, the creases solidified. By the wall next to it was a lidless porcelain box, a yard high, like a square bath, but marked *Ice*. The place was the antithesis of Mari's warm and vital home, and yet, though it possessed this cold air of neglect, there was little doubt that it was now occupied. In another corner of the room was a large bowl that held unfrozen water and platters. On the windowsills, which from without were as caked in snow as the door had been, were bones bare of the flesh they had been cooked for. Below one of the windows was a large barrel, three-quarters filled with paraffin for the lanterns.

Wherever she searched, however, Mari could see no other door, so where had those she sought gone? She looked up, thinking there could be a trap door in the roof, but there was none. Then she recalled the grinding sound that she had heard before she had entered. Something heavy had been moved – and though there were various items in the hut, few things could have created such a noise.

First, as quietly as she could, she slid the bed from its position. Beneath it she found only sturdy floorboards nailed securely in place.

Then she dragged the stove from its place upon a block of slate. She could not prevent it from screeching as it passed along the stone, and the noise it emitted was quite different from that which she had heard. Besides, the scratches she had made in the stone were the first, suggesting the stove had never before been moved.

So she turned to the final object that could have made such a noise and potentially reveal an exit, the box marked *Ice* – truly an odd thing to find in a land so awash with the stuff.

First she tried to pull it from the wall, but failed. Then she placed her back against it and pushed, but it would not budge. Finally she sat upon the floor, her back braced against the wall, and put her feet on the side of the porcelain box. She pushed and pushed, and pushed until her face quite flushed, but finally it shifted, and with that very same grinding sound. From within the cabin, the noise was even more ear-splitting, and she was in no doubt that the children and the deep-voiced man would come leaping out towards her from the room in which they hid. However, when she heard nothing and dared to peek into the small gap she had created, she did not see the children, nor any man, nor a room, nor even a wall. Instead, what she saw as she held aloft the lantern was a tunnel, cold and dry.

Pausing for a moment to listen for voices but hearing none, she tentatively ventured forth.

The tunnel rose steeply and curved to left and right. Though there were no voices to be heard, the whistling of the wind reached her, and as she continued further in and higher and higher, the sound grew louder and louder. After some minutes of walking and more of crawling, when the whistling attained a near-unbearable pitch, she reached the end of the tunnel and extinguished the lantern. It was then she realised what was making the screeching of the wind so affecting.

The tunnel had brought her to the top of the mountain at whose foot the cabin lay. However, she had travelled to its other side and into a natural bowl protected from outside eyes on all sides by towering, snow-clad peaks. It was akin to the crater of a volcano, only here, rather than spewing forth molten rock, a glowing bed of snow lay in its throat. To the left of the hole she knelt in was a rough path leading around the bowl, halfway between the snow at the bottom and that on the peaks. Her eyes followed it around until, sheltered by a natural lip in the mountain's face, she saw the three children and a rotund man with a grey beard standing before a fire, over which hung a large cauldron. Behind them was a wooden cage. In it was Bjørn. It was he who screamed in accompaniment to the wind, and at the same time as chilling her to the very marrow, seeing her brother so terrified raised the temperature of Mari's blood to boiling point.

The children were no longer arguing, but warming themselves at the fireside, excitedly watching the bearded man as he added carrots and parsnips to the steaming broth. They were completely engrossed in their activity and apparently quite used to the disturbance of a screaming child. No matter how preoccupied they were, however, Mari knew that now the blizzard had ceased, she would quickly be seen moving in the moonlight, were she to take to the path. No matter how accomplished a hunter she was, she would be no match for the broad and burly man and the knife with which he was cutting a parsnip. But if her suspicions of their revolting intentions were correct, there was not time enough to return to town to raise a posse and overpower the group, for the broth would soon be simmering and ready for more substantial ingredients.

Brave girl that she is, and boiling as her blood was, she decided that the best method of gaining ground on Bjørn would be to head downwards before moving along to the dry indent in the mountain. As she considered the best route, she paused to hope that the whistling of the wind and the wailing of her brother would be sufficient to hide the inevitable sounds of loose rocks and tumbling snow, and then she turned about and lowered herself onto the snowy rocks below.

She went down until she could no longer see the heads of her enemies. Only then did she start to move around the bowl to a position below the flickering glow of the fire. When she reached that spot, very slowly, checking every footstep and handhold before laying weight upon it, she started to ascend. It was just as she reached the lip that the sickeningly high voices of the cannibalistic children came to her.

'What shall I have?' said one familiarly squeaky voice.

'And which part will be mine?' said another.

'It is my turn to choose, Nikolai!' said a third. 'I was left with nothing but gristle and bone last time.'

'Do not worry, my loyal friends,' said the deep voice. 'There will be plenty for all. There is much meat on this one. You chose well when you plucked him from his cot.'

As you can no doubt imagine, old friend, it was rather disconcerting for me to hear all of this from Mari's sweet lips, for here it was confirmed that it was these children, not the King Cobra Cat, who had plucked young Bjørn from his slumber and then delivered him to this man Nikolai. Where, then, could my beast be amongst all of this?

I was about to mention this to her, but quite suddenly she said something diverting. 'They were to eat him, Sir Paul. Eat him! Poor, scrawny little Bjørn.'

I did not like to say that 'scrawny' was not the word I would call upon when describing the lad, but were I to be in the business of abducting, cooking and eating infants, he'd be a very

tempting prospect. Born diplomat that I am, however, I feigned
a gasp at the thought that anybody would consider the boy
worth the broth he was to be cooked in, and allowed her to continue. It had been quite some time since I last heard tell of such
behaviour, after all. Not, in fact, since the Kiunga pygmies
cooked for me the head of our common enemy in an onion
sauce. Besides, as it was looking increasingly as though I had
been misled by the well-intentioned Roar, I thought it best to
have her tale told – and all the more quickly so I could get on
with my pursuit.

You, dear Cyril, will no doubt revel in the continuance of the
history. I, for my part, sat in silent disappointment.

It was as the children began to bicker once again, Mari said,
that she peeked over the lip. She could see the face of none but
the man called Nikolai, for the children were wrestling in anticipation of their meal. Nikolai's dirty grey beard was stained
yellow and brown around his pink sausage-like lips, and hung
long to sit upon a large belly. Between the buttons struggling
to hold closed a grubby and stained collarless shirt were
glimpses of pallid flesh and crawling, greasy body hair. Above
a purple and veined nose, yellow-grey hair grew in all directions from his head, and bloodshot eyes looked greedily into
the cauldron.

'Now, now, boys. I told you – there's plenty for all,' he said to the
fighting children, and grinned wetly as he spoke. 'I know you're
hungry. We all are, but it won't be long now. Put some logs on and
get the heat up, why don't you?'

On the walls around them, Mari saw pieces of paper, scrawled
upon in childlike writing. They were lists of wishes. A velocipede,
a hoop, a magic lantern, a railway set, a pony, a kitten. One was
from Bjørn.

The scrum broke and for the first time Mari saw the faces of the
children. Only, with a gasp of fright, she realised that they were *not*
children; they were dwarves. And not only were they dwarves,
they all shared an identical face – and that face was the face of the
man behind the glass in the post-office.

It was him, after all – only he was not a him, but a they. A team of identical sibling dwarves working as one, two stealing the children as the other provided a face in the window. One sitting and talking to customers through the glass, another passing stamps through the slot below, a third cooking young Grete in a parsnip and carrot broth. A well-oiled machine of villainy.

The wood they collected was stacked next to Bjørn's cage and when they neared it, they each stuck a hand in and pinched his flesh and smacked their lips. Bjørn screamed yet louder and they all laughed as they placed the wood carefully onto the fire.

Mari's blood must have been steam in her veins, for it was then that she chose to strike. I say chose, but she assures me that she had no control over her actions. Rage dictated them entirely.

She sprinted forth as the dwarves bent to place the wood under the cauldron, and before Nikolai could warn them, she first kicked one, then pushed the next and finally threw the third, all into the hungry fire. Immediately their hair and clothes ignited and their screams outdid the wind and Bjørn together.

So insane were they with pain that one threw himself from the fire into the cauldron to douse the flames. His method of extinguishing them was indeed successful, but he had apparently not bargained for the scorching temperature of the broth and resurfaced screaming more loudly than ever, before running straight over the lip and hitting the rocks and snow below, when his howls of pain ceased to be heard.

The second dwarf, the flames burning steadily through his clothes and into his skin, also ran into the snow, but not with such vehemence. More sensibly, he rolled in it, covering himself head to foot in the cooling stuff. He then froze with shock and expired – most interestingly, from both exposure to the cold *and* extreme burns.

The third, equally maddened by the burning of his skin, also

ran, but not into the cauldron and not into the snow. He dashed
around the place entirely at random, shrieking all the while. This
quite exhausting and not awfully constructive remedy served only
to feed oxygen to the flames, which burned with ever greater
intensity. His sprinting, but not the burning, was brought to an
abrupt halt when he ran headlong into the wall of the mountain
and quite opened his skull. His body continued to burn and sizzle
alongside the children's notes to St Nicholas until there was little
left of either.

There was, of course, still the man Nikolai to contend with. The
epicentre of Mari's rage was the safety of Bjørn, however, and as
soon as she had buffeted the dwarves into the flames and they were
each discovering their hopeless remedies to fire's pain, she rushed
to the cage that held her brother captive.

Now, much has been written of a mother's superhuman
increase in strength when her child encounters hazardous circumstances. It has been told that, on seeing a horse collapsed on
top of her child, a mother has lifted the beast quite off the ground
to whisk her presumably rather crushed offspring to safety.
Another mother, I have heard, saw off twelve Rumanian bandits
who had set upon the child for its gold teeth. Mothers have lifted
burning beams, fallen boulders, buffalos, bison, bears and loco-
motives. Thus is the level of instinct motherhood breeds.
Substantially less has been told of the powers of the sister, and it
has been unjustly ignored. For if Mari, regardless of the stout lock
that kept it in place, succeeded in throwing open the door of a cage
to rescue her brother as if blowing a feather, surely there must be
countless other examples going on all over the world every bit as
remarkable as the celebrated mothers. And this Mari did succeed
in doing.

Just as Nikolai launched himself at them, she threw Bjørn to
safety, and Nikolai landed squarely in the cage. Of course, had
she the logical mind of the father and male, she would have
regretted the breaking of the lock, for were it still in working
use, she could have locked Nikolai in place and made a leisurely
escape. However, she did not stop to consider this and instead

rushed after Bjørn, who was already making his way along the path to the tunnel.

As they ran, the bellowing Nikolai was following close behind. It was perhaps foolish of the rotund and unhealthy man to shout so, for had he not, he might have retained more breath for his pursuit and thus not have allowed Mari and his absconded supper to make such headway. As it was, bellow he did and Mari and Bjørn began to gain a lead. Indeed, another element to take into consideration when pursuing and bellowing is the thought that, rather than slow them down, the fear one drives into the hearts of the pursued will increase their desire to escape and so the velocity of their attempts. Certainly, as Nikolai's voice echoed towards them in the tunnel, Mari and Bjørn did not slow and think of giving themselves up, but ignored the cuts, grazes and scratches they endured and threw themselves downwards through the tunnel with ever more vigour.

'I am Nikolai!' the booming voice came. 'Saint to the dwarves, master of the elves. You shall return to my pot! You must be eaten in twelves!'

Mari and Bjørn reached the frozen cabin and the girl immediately took to heaving the enormous porcelain ice container back over the hole to the tunnel. Bjørn meanwhile ran to the door and pushed it open.

'You waste your time, sister,' he cried. 'He moves the box with a simple shove. We must run. Run into the snow!'

However, Bjørn was not savvy to the idea the resourceful Mari had hit upon during their rapid descent. As she pushed, she ordered Bjørn to take the fuel for the lanterns and pour it from the barrel onto the floor of the cabin. He tried to do so immediately, but struggled to tip the heavy barrel on its side. The box finally sliding into place and sealing the hole, his sister joined him and together they emptied the flammable contents onto the ground.

'You will be my supper, boy!' thundered Nikolai as he reached the entrance. 'I will eat the flesh from your arms, from your legs and from your rump. I will savour your liver and your kidneys, and drink of your blood!'

Mari took matches from her pocket, held her breath as she lit one, then threw it down.

A carpet of flames instantly covered the floor – upon which she slammed the door shut and she and Bjørn disappeared into the snow and hills beyond.

Now, Cyril, I am no more an expert on fire than you are, and would have imagined that on entering the cabin, this Nikolai could have about-turned and headed to his cauldron to find an alternative route. Mari, too, was surprised by the outcome of her arson, thinking it no more than a delaying tactic, a method by which they could escape. However, when the raised posse returned to the cabin the following day to reclaim the bones of the eleven eaten children, it was still smouldering. The cabin had turned to ashes and nothing but the box marked *Ice* remained. At its foot was found the charred body of a rather fat man. On closer inspection of the site, the sooty residue of fire was discovered all the way to the top of the tunnel. Somehow, when he had entered, Nikolai had fed the fire all too suddenly, and flames had burst through into his face and beyond. An unimaginably successful ruse by Mari and one which I heartily congratulated her on as she lay next to me and grinned with satisfaction.

The next day, she promised, she would take me to the site of this cannibalism, but I did not give her the opportunity, I am afraid. You see, later that night, the lad returned to the hut with news of interest to me. At first I thought it was a ploy to get rid of me and have his sister all to himself, but with a little investigation, his story proved true.

A man had been arrested some way to the south, accused of a spate of murders. Descriptions of the deaths were unavailable, but rumour suggests they were grisly, and so could be the work of my creature. News travels as slowly as carts in these parts, of course, so I cannot know how fresh this new trail is. The Spaniard was not in Kautokeino, nor in Honningsvåg, so he has more than a month on me now. I can only hope, and remain,

Your errant friend,

Lindley-Small

21

THE NOTEBOOKS OF CYRIL KING

1893

The Willing Prisoner

'If you are to reach Ishkuman, you will need supplies, I think,' said Manraj Singh. And you will need a guide. Without one, you will most certainly die in these mountains. These we can give you. Come.'

He rose and one of the youths leapt to his side and placed a thick felt coat on his shoulders. I now saw that Manraj Singh wore leather riding boots, of the sort issued by the Army, whereas his men's were cut in the native style.

'We go,' he said. 'You shall have meat and fruit and grain for your horse.'

He beckoned me to follow him.

Somehow it seemed I had fallen on my feet. That they were bandits was still the most likely possibility. After all, how else could the man leading me into the undergrowth have obtained his soldier's boots and turban? It was also possible, therefore, that they were taking me to my death; but if that were so, why should they offer me their hospitality? Why had they not killed me on the spot?

I got to my feet and looked over towards Bucephalus. One of the Sikh's men was taking her by the reins.

Manraj Singh must have seen my reluctance to leave her in the hands of strangers.

'They will bring your horse, sahib,' he said. 'They know horses. She will be safe. Come. There is food for you both in our village.'

'Village?' I repeated, turning back towards him in surprise, for who ever heard of a group of bandits living in a village. 'Is it far?'

'Not far,' he said, and off he went into the trees.

More so even than Bucephalus, there was Small to consider, waiting for me to bring food for his growling stomach. Even though Manraj Singh had assured me that the village was not far, it would inevitably be some time until I could return to my companion. But I had little choice in the matter. To turn down their offer of aid would have been to invite suspicion; the same went for revealing I had a man in the fort gazing down at us through his rifle sight. Of course, they did not have to know about the rifle; and since they were clearly not a detachment of British soldiers, I briefly debated the wisdom of telling them that I was not alone, and summoning Small to join us. I swiftly thought better of it, however. If they were bandits, it would be foolish of me to put us both in their power. But if, as the Sikh had said, they could help me to reach Ishkuman, then my journey would not have been wasted. The hunt was back on. I had been given another chance. I could only hope that Small, from his vantage point, could see I was going with these men of my own free will, and for the good of us both; that the confidence which now filled my being, and which had quite evaporated from us both as we sat and waited to die in the snow, was physically apparent. So I squared my shoulders and, leaving Bucephalus to his men, strode northwards after Manraj Singh.

I quickly caught up with him, and very soon after that, we reached the cleft in the mountainside which I had seen from the fort. There at its opening was a patch of land where the trees were dead and broken, and nestled amongst them were what looked to be the remains of buildings; stone foundations – houses, perhaps, of whatever village the fort above us had once served to protect. These stones were blackened, however, as if they had been burned.

'An old battle,' Manraj Singh explained. 'There have been many such in these mountains. Come. This way.'

I glanced up at the fort before moving again, but saw no sign of Small or his rifle, so I followed Manraj Singh westwards along the narrow pass. It was as though a giant axe had been driven into the rock, cutting the cliff face in two, leaving a path just wide enough for a man and his horse to pass along, sheer walls towering on either side. A trail leading from the green of one valley to whatever lay on the other side.

The trail rose steeply as we went, and before long the winding creepers and grasping shrubs of the lower slopes were replaced by familiar, barren rock. As the vanishing plant life suggested, the other side of the mountain, when finally we reached it, was not a lush valley like the one we had left. Indeed it was quite the opposite, and what met my eyes when we emerged from the ravine and gained the head of the pass was singular for its own reasons. The mountains were jagged and tall as snow-tipped cathedrals, their spires like fingers reaching up to heaven. The sun, now beyond its midday height, threw shadows onto the peaks on the western side. From the north, from the sky itself it seemed, flowed a glacier broad as a city, spreading itself over the rock below and into the distance as far as the eye could see.

'My valley,' Manraj Singh announced with pride, sweeping his outstretched arm from south to north. Then he indicated a stony trail that snaked away to our left, directly towards the spire of a monstrous peak. I followed him in silence, since the path was too narrow for us to walk abreast. At times it wound between towers of rock; at other times it would round a bend and reveal a spectacular view. Finally we came to a great arrow of stone that must have tumbled at some point from the mountainside above and blocked our way. From a distance, there did not appear to be any way round it; but then Manraj Singh vanished from view, and as I approached I saw that in fact there was the slimmest of gaps through which a man might pass, and, with some difficulty, a horse.

On the other side of the massive boulder Manraj Singh was waiting. 'Our gods protect us,' he said with a smile, and then he pointed ahead. 'My village. Up here we are safe, but it is not so very good for hunting. And so we hunt on the other side of the pass. There, game is plentiful. But it is not so safe.'

I could not imagine that they had many invaders to fear, but I did not question him, for before me was not the makeshift camp of tents I had envisaged, but an actual village, a settlement hidden from the world, one which surely no man could find if he sought it. Doubtless the Sikh and his companions, who, along with Bucephalus, had now joined us from the trail, had happened upon it by chance as they moved through the mountains, and seen its remote properties as an ideal outpost in which to hide themselves.

A small, half-frozen stream came down from higher up the mountain, running from one side of a jutting peak. At the foot of that sheer face, between two boulders, was a solitary stone-built hut, isolated from the others, which were situated further down the gentle slope and built on either side of the stream as it ran towards a circular area which was free of dwellings. This caught my attention immediately, for it was covered in grass, not snow, and the brilliant green was a vivid splash of colour in this otherwise monochrome landscape. In its centre the water flowed beneath a great stone slab raised up off the ground like a table, on either side of which two curious stone pillars stood, each about five feet tall.

The place seemed deserted but for a few grazing animals: a cow and some goats. There was not a person to be seen, and I was beginning to wonder if Manraj Singh and his band of hunters were the sole inhabitants, when I heard a voice call out from up ahead. It was deep and strong: a man's voice, not a boy's. A figure was striding towards us from the huts. Manraj

Singh lifted a hand to him in greeting, and turned off the path to meet him as he approached. Some twenty feet from me, they spoke rapidly to one another in their own tongue. All I was able to discern was the word Ishkuman, mentioned by both men a number of times. The new arrival initially frowned at what he heard, and glanced towards me as they spoke, but soon enough he appeared to agree with Manraj Singh. He was dressed in a long felt coat much like the Sikh's, but no turban. His shoulders were broad, his skin darker than that of the fair youths, and his hair was black. His beard was closely trimmed, and above his thin mouth his nose was aquiline. I placed his age at thirty-five years.

'And so it is decided,' Manraj Singh said finally, in English, returning to me. 'Rustam Khan shall guide you to Ishkuman. But first, he shall play polo, and you shall watch him.'

'I should be glad to,' I said. 'But I fear I must not.' I was think-ing of Small and how long he had been waiting. I pointed at the sky. 'If we are to get a good start today, surely we should soon be on our way?'

Manraj Singh smiled. 'Why such haste, sahib?' He pointed behind us, to where the young men were already unsaddling Bucephalus, and beginning to rub her down. 'You and your horse are much in need of rest, are you not? And it will take time to gather supplies. Rustam Khan must play, for his team is waiting. Polo is of great importance to my people. No one else will leave the game to guide you. Come, watch, and continue your journey once you have been refreshed.'

Once again, I did not see how I could decline. I was tired, as was Bucephalus. As was Small. And if these people were going to supply me with what I required to continue on to Ishkuman, I could hardly refuse their hospitality. Small would have to sit tight until I returned, and I would have to hope that he did not believe me kidnapped.

I was soon distracted from thoughts of my companion, how-ever, for at that moment, from behind a line of huts came a woman leading a saddled horse. I mean no disservice to womankind, but to call this vision a mere woman would be to do her an injustice. She was quite the most beautiful and statuesque thing I had seen in all my days. Her face possessed faultless caramel skin and a fine, straight nose. Long golden hair of a colour quite unlike any I had seen since I first set foot in India fell in a loose braid over her shoulder to her waist; but it was her eyes that struck me dumb. They were the very glimmering greenest of things, emeralds clasped in ivory, their radiance lighting my very heart with joy at my good fortune to be living in the same universe as such a creation.

Standing there on the mountainside, staring, doubtless with my mouth agape, her serenity enveloped me. And she did not shy from me. Indeed, she seemed entirely unafraid of the white stranger, as she spoke warmly to the man Manraj Singh had called Rustam Khan. As I watched them talking to one another, somewhere in the small part of my brain that was operating as normal, it struck me that they did so quite as equals. Were she typical, the women up here seemed freer and altogether more independent than I had thus far encountered elsewhere on my travels in this country.

Rustam Khan turned to me.

'This is my wife,' he said. 'Fahlhana.' He took the reins of the horse from her. Luckily his voice was enough to shake me from my reverie.

'I'm very pleased to meet you, Fahlhana,' I stuttered. 'You will come to watch the polo, too?'

'She will, sahib,' Manraj Singh answered for her. 'When the game is played, the whole village watches.'

As the four of us climbed the slope, Rustam Khan leading his horse, the sound of galloping hooves came to our ears. The thunder grew until we crested the ridge and there I was greeted by polo in action on the top of the world. Seven men on small ponies were playing on a natural pitch, a flat tableland some two hundred yards across that sat in a nape of the mountains. In one direction stood the jagged peaks of the upper valley, in the other lay the lush green that hid Small. Around the pitch,

seated cross-legged on boulders and shelves of rock, were perhaps sixty spectators. Rustam Khan mounted his horse and
cantered into the midst of the game, the cheers of the crowd
welcoming him.

For some time, quite how long I could not say, I found
myself absorbed by the excitement and the colour of the spectacle. Horses and riders were galloping headlong after the ball,
which was made of stone and bound with hemp, the players
swinging their long mallets in great, sweeping circles. The
riders turned their rearing beasts on a sixpence each time the
ball was hit in a new direction, so that wherever it went, a
flurry of legs and mallets followed it. The instant he joined the
fray, it was clear that Rustam Khan was by some distance
the most skilled player riding that day. His horse was quicker to
accelerate, turned more suddenly, and he himself was capable
of controlling the ball where all the others struggled to follow
its irregular course on the stony ground. Where the other players were tense and straining to best one another, Rustam Khan
was calm and relaxed. He was stronger, more experienced.
Older.

Manraj Singh had led Fahlhana and me to some rocks a little
way from the rest of the villagers. I was sure by now that they
could not be bandits. Other than the knife with which the
youth had first accosted me, I had seen no sign of weapons,
and they had been after all a hunting party. Most of those here
were women and children. And none of the young men I saw
looked older than eighteen, or perhaps twenty, and, far from
regarding me with savagery or avarice, they seemed almost
indifferent to my presence. It did strike me as curious that
there were no adult men to be seen, other than Manraj Singh
and Rustam Khan. Where had they gone? I wondered. But no
sooner had this thought occurred to me than another, which
came rushing forcefully in upon me, quite knocked it from
my mind.

I had turned my attention from the game upon my fellow
spectators, and as I gazed at them gathered together I realised

what had escaped me when I had glanced at them before. I had
remarked on the complexions of the youths in the clearing, but
I had not seen their hair, which had been hidden by their turbans. Up here, where women and children and even some
youths were bareheaded, I saw that every one of them was fair.
When I had first set eyes on Fahlhana, I had thought her a rare
anomaly, standing beside the two darker men with her hair of
deepest gold. And indeed, her beauty was unparalleled, but I
saw now that it was Rustam Khan and Manraj Singh who stood
out amongst these villagers. A few had hair of a chestnut brown,
but almost all were fair, some of a paler shade even than Fahlhana;
and their skin, to a one, was light.

Were these remote valleys their ancestral homeland? Or how
else had they come here? Such idle wonderings did not occupy
me long, however, for what then struck me shook me to the
core. These must be the very people whom Forrester had been
seeking! The reason he had come to Gilgit in the first place. It
had not been a blind, and Major Flack had been wrong to call
him deluded. Poor Forrester, he had not found them; and now
I had.

Fast upon that realisation there came another, more unset-
tling still. What if Forrester had found these people, after all?
That was what the newspaper had referred to as his great discovery, not the treasure. It was not the jewels of long-dead
kings that he had found proof of, and was hotfooting it back
to London to announce to the world – it was these people I
saw before me. Forrester had been an historian and an ethnographer. For one of his profession, I could quite see how such a
discovery, revealed in the hallowed halls of the Royal Geographical
Society, could make his reputation, to say nothing of fame and
fortune. But did that mean that I had been mistaken in following Forrester's trail, and that it had never led towards the treasure
of Adam-Khor? After everything that Small and I had been through
in the mountains, had we been on a wild goose chase from the
beginning?

I tried to calm my racing heart and force myself to think

clearly. The people may be what had brought Forrester up to the Karakoram, but that did not mean that Tolliver and the treasure were any less real. It was not until he had reached Gilgit that Forrester had first heard about Tolliver, as had I, and had learned the provenance of the watch and its stone from Multah Taqdir. I had no reason to suppose that those clues had played me false. Somewhere up here, more than likely Ishkuman, Tolliver had acquired his black sapphire, carved into the likeness of an eye – the eye of the protector of Adam-Khor.

*

I was lost in my reflections, the polo quite forgotten, until Manraj Singh touched my arm.

'Sahib?'

'What?' I said, startled.

'The game – it is over. You have enjoyed it?'

And indeed it was over. My fellow spectators had dispersed. Only Fahlhana, Manraj Singh, I and Rustam Khan remained, and the latter joined us sitting on the rocks. The sky, I suddenly realised, had darkened, the dusk throwing long shadows onto the pitch.

'Very much,' I managed.

'Very good. And now, this night, you rest in the home of Rustam Khan,' Manraj Singh said, getting to his feet. 'Tomorrow he shall guide you to Ishkuman.'

Tomorrow! Small would not be pleased. Even when I had agreed to watch the polo, I had not realised that by the time the game was over, the day would be nearly done. We could not travel in darkness, however, and so there was nothing for it but to stay here in the village and rejoin him as soon as it was light.

Manraj Singh nodded once and walked away into the oncoming night. I was left with the polo player and his wife.

'Our home is this way, sahib,' Rustam Khan said. 'You will be comfortable there.'

I followed man, woman and horse as we made our way among the huts, now glowing with life, until we reached one no different from any other. Rustam Khan ushered me inside and I entered to find a single sparsely furnished room. At the far end of it a fire burned, the smoke from which found its way out of a small hole in the roof. On one side of the room was a bed. Before it was a large mat on the floor, flat cushions on either side. The walls were bare. Fahlhana approached the cauldron hanging over the fire and stirred it. Rustam Khan and I sat on cushions as she ladled a meaty, red stew into earthenware bowls.

'Eat, sahib. Eat,' Rustam Khan said, and I did so. The food was rich and filling.

'Very good,' I said tentatively. 'Thank you.'

'It is our pleasure to welcome you,' Rustam Khan answered. 'Our honour, sahib.'

'You are very generous,' I answered.

'Tell me, sahib,' Rustam Khan continued after some moments of silent eating. 'Why do you come here? Into our mountains. What is it that you seek?'

'I seek Ishkuman,' I answered.

He mulled over my answer for a moment, then said: 'This is not a place a man seeks only to visit, I think. You have travelled far. Why Ishkuman?'

'I am going there because I found something in my country that I believe comes from there. I want to discover if it is so,' I said. 'Is it far from here?'

His expression did not change.

'Not far, sahib. Not far. But I fear your journey is wasted. What is in these mountains does not leave them. Here, Ishkuman, any village. Even that which does not come from them, once it arrives here it does not leave. What is it that you believe to have come from Ishkuman?'

'It was a watch. Well, a stone, really; but, you see, I am a watch-maker by trade, and the stone decorates a timepiece.'

The polo player's smile vanished. His expression was cold.

I looked at his wife. There was fear in her beautiful eyes.

'What manner of watch do you speak of?' he demanded.

'It was made by a man in Gilgit,' I said.

'You have this watch? You must show it to me!'

His sudden change of mood and tone had unnerved me. I did not want him to discover I had kept it from him, so I thought it best to do as he had asked.

'Why, yes, I have it here,' I said, removing the watch from my pocket and holding it out for him to see.

As soon as I did so, he seized it fiercely from my hand, inspected it for a moment, and then suddenly wrapped his fist around it and squeezed. He closed his eyes, lifting both his bunched fists to his forehead. I was astonished by his reaction and did not know what to say. Fahlhana moved closer to her husband, alarmed, and laid a hand on his arm. At that very moment he leapt to his feet, throwing his wife aside.

He grasped me by my shirt and lifted me in one single movement and pushed me against the wall. Try though I might, his strength was the master of me, and I was pinned.

He barked demands at me in his native tongue.

'I don't understand!' I cried. 'I don't understand!'

I had no idea what had happened, what I had done.

He pulled a knife from his belt. The blade was inches from my face. He was going to kill me, I was sure of it. Behind him Fahlhana looked on helpless.

'Rustam Khan. I don't understand,' I begged. 'English, Rustam Khan. English!'

'This watch,' he spat, finally in my own language. 'Where have you found it?'

'In London,' I said, trying to calm my quavering voice. 'In London, Rustam Khan. In London. The watch – it was made in Gilgit. But the stone – it comes from Ishkuman. I am certain. Was certain.'

Confusion edged into the anger that filled his eyes. His grip on my collar loosened very slightly.

'Why are you certain?'

'There was a man, a soldier who was captured in Ishkuman. His men were killed, but he escaped. I believe him to have returned to Gilgit with this stone, that he had it set into this watch. I thought I would find more stones in Ishkuman. That is why I was going there. For the treasure of Adam-Khor.'

'From where does this watch come?' he demanded, utterly ignoring my explanation, moving the knife closer to my eyeball. 'Where is the boy?'

'Boy?' I cried. 'What boy? There was no boy, Rustam Khan! I have told you everything. Everything!'

'How do you come to possess it? Why is it in London?'

'I had it from a man who died in my shop. The man who held it before him died, too.'

'And before that?' His eyes were wild and his body tensed to strike. 'Speak!'

'I don't know,' I cried. 'I don't know. I swear it, Rustam Khan.'

He must have seen my genuine fear, for all at once he dropped me and turned away, his chest heaving for breath.

I slumped to the ground, terrified.

'All I know is what I've told you, Rustam Khan,' I wheezed. 'And that soldier who escaped . . . the Ishkumanis, they – they cut off his hand.'

Rustam Khan grew very still. He took a long, shuddering breath and sheathed his knife. All of a sudden he seemed composed, and all the deadlier for it.

'You speak the truth, sahib. And I have listened. Now you must listen to me. You have arrived at your destination. The green valley you were led from is Ishkuman. But these are not the people of Adam-Khor. They have legends and gods of their own, older even than his. If Adam Khor was ever here, there is no trace of him now, nor of his treasure. Tomorrow, there will be no supplies, and no guide. Tomorrow you shall be killed in cold blood, not for their gods, but only because you have come to this place, and in so doing, you threaten these people's peace. No one leaves here, sahib. It is how they keep themselves hidden from those who wish them harm.'

'But . . . who are these people?' I asked him. 'The Ishkumanis are dead!'

'Not all,' he answered. 'These few are left. All their menfolk, yes. Did you not see how young they are? They were children when their fathers and uncles and brothers were killed. They were concealed here with the women when the British soldiers came to Ishkuman. Do you wonder if they welcome strangers now even less than their fathers did before?'

'Why did they not kill me right away in the green valley? Why bring me here and betray the very existence of this village?'

'To learn from you why you sought Ishkuman, and if any knew you were here or were likely to follow you. They have no fear of bringing you here, knowing that you would not leave alive.' He paused. 'But now you must leave, sahib, and go in peace. Take this and go. It will remind you of the justice you have brought this day. Go, and do not return.'

He threw the watch to me.

I did not understand what he meant about justice. I did not know what to do.

I looked up into his eyes. 'Why are you doing this? Why are you letting me go?'

'Enough!' he said. 'It is better you do not know. Go, now!'

'Yes, go!' Fahlhana said.

I scrambled to my feet, looked at them both once more and then dashed from their hut.

I did not think of horse or food, but ran to the path as fast and as silently as my legs could carry me, past glowing huts and along to the trail and down. I rolled and tumbled more times than I could count, and tore both clothes and skin on jagged rocks. But eventually I succeeded in finding the narrow pass and only when I reached the cover of the green valley did I stop for breath.

If on encountering Manraj Singh and his men I had felt a spinal shiver, it should have been doubled when the devils had taken my horse and lured me into their lair. When Manraj Singh demanded that I watch the polo, it should have quadrupled and when he persuaded me to spend the night in his village, hidden from the sight of men, my fear should have grown eight times as strong. He had been cajoling me into staying until the light had gone, I now realised, gaoling me without my knowing it, and I had been a willing prisoner. Why the watch had aroused such anger in Rustam Khan, I did not know; and what I had said that made him release me, I could not tell. But we had arrived in Ishkuman; of that there was now no doubt.

Reaching the fort, I threw myself at the gap in the wall and struggled through.

Small was nowhere to be seen. He was not on the lowered ground inside the fort, nor on the perch where I had left him.

'Small!' I whispered as loudly as I dared. 'Small!'

His satchel was there, and an empty bottle of whisky amongst the rubble, and on the ground beside them was a hole that had not been dug when I had left.

I stumbled from the ledge and crawled across the leaves to inspect it. It was only six inches in diameter, perhaps the same in depth. At its bottom was damp brown rock. The dirt that had not been cleared drew a bizarre, contorted face upon its surface. As I stared into its muddy eyes quite suddenly Small's voice came to me.

'Up here, man. You're lucky you made such a racket coming in, or I'd've had your head. Where the bloody hell have you been?'

I rolled over onto my back. He had rid himself of his native garb and was climbing down towards me from a ledge above my entry point in shirt and belted waistcoat.

'And where's my food, hmm? More to the point, where's my bloody horse?'

'I – I left her. In the village.'

'Left her? Are you quite mad, man? The whisky's on her. What

possible earth-shattering occurrence could have taken place
that you would even consider such a thing?'

'Small. We're here. We've arrived in Ishkuman!'

He grimaced. For him, that was not reason enough.

'I know,' he said.

22

THE LETTERS OF
SIR PAUL LINDLEY-SMALL

From Dr Holm's Convalescent Hotel
Gjeilo, Norway

2ND JANUARY 1909

Dear Cyril,

Dr Holm's is spartan, white and clinically clean, and there is a whiff of disinfectant about the place, but today these are attributes for which I am most grateful. You see, I am lucky to be alive.

Let me explain.

The man arrested for the spate of murders I had come to investigate had been gaoled in Solheim, a hamlet located in the mountainous heartland of this country, more or less between Bergen and Kristiania.

At the end of a track winding its way into uninhabited territory, I arrived at a small boarding house to find it quite unoccupied by anyone but the proprietor, a wonderfully scarred ruffian called Vegard. I asked after the gaol, but he informed me it would not open for many an hour, since the Constable is responsible for quite a large area and must do his rounds. I briefly considered breaking into the place and demanding the feline from the Spaniard in exchange for his freedom – for if the animal was the killer, then surely the arrested man must be he – but Vegard informed me that the reason such a dangerous chap was being held here of all places was down to the fortress-like strength of the medieval prison, and so I reappraised the situation. If I could not get in, it stood to reason that the Spaniard, and more importantly, my beast, if it was incarcerated in there with him, could not get out.

Vegard had quite the largest forearms I have seen on any man, and as we waited, he fairly beat me eight-nil at arm wrestling – at which, as you know, I consider myself a dab hand. I am glad to report, however, that his card playing was less unbeatable and that, fortunately, he did not revert to the employment of arms and fists when I won the price of four days' feeding from him. Then, before Vegard could suggest a return to arm wrestling, a rush of whistling wind ushered in a chap from the cold.

Vegard lumbered to his desk to greet the fellow, and following a brief and quiet chat, the visitor settled in a seat before me. Physically speaking, he was a short, thickset man, his puce complexion stretching quite up to his trim and fiery orange hair. His eyes were hardly discernible above his bunched ripe cheeks, and his pink neck bulged from a rather yellowing white shirt. His snug and fraying but tastefully speckled three-piece Harris tweed suit assisted in the procurement of the puceness, as did the warming embrace of the hearth. This unkempt appearance suggested him to be a man of little or moderate standing, so imagine my amazement when he stuck forth his right hand and said, 'How d'ye do? Charles Bannister, QC.' And the man was an Old Harrovian, to boot. I didn't recognise the name, but then, thanks to that cutpurse Shankle, my natural boisterousness, and the siren call of the Valley of the Kings, I was not long at that institution. Besides, this man looked several years my junior.

That, my dear Cyril, was the first of a string of amazements delivered at the hands, or rather from the mouth, of this Bannister chap. I thought myself fortunate to have stumbled upon a fellow Englishman in these remote parts and hoped we could enjoy a meal together and a round of travellers' tales before I met the lawman. It was upon the account that I had accrued from Vegard that I insisted on entertaining Bannister, and the arm-wrestler led us to a large and bare dining room.

Vegard's was a ramshackle place, very wooden and musty and rustic, and Bannister and I must have been quite a sight in our bespokes, but as it was otherwise deserted, and Vegard declined to comment, there was nobody to inform us one way or the other. Over an odd repast consisting mainly of cabbage and what Vegard said was lamb, I learned that Bannister was not holidaying as I had assumed, but was on his fifth and, as it had turned out, final trip to the country. You can imagine my shock, but more my profound curiosity, at discovering that Hilary Flootham of the Lower Crimpton Floothams, that highly respectable family, was charged with the cold-blooded murder of six middle-aged men – and not in the Marxist political *coup d'état* in the Central Americas which his Harrow comrades would have hazarded, but here, in the back of beyond. And so it was that Bannister went first in the tale-telling.

Young Hilary's crimes had taken place in a string of quiet farming hamlets, lying in a straight line, south to north, each no bigger than the one I sat in as I poured healthy dashes of Glenlivet into the coffee Vegard brought to our table. In fact, I poured the last of my hip flask for Bannister, so retaken by the horror of his tale was he. Indeed, at a natural pause I even delved into the crate and cracked open a bottle, and invited Vegard to share in it. It was, more so than usual, whisky well spent.

Hilary's father, Hildebrand Flootham, had contacted Bannister. As a fellow Old Harrovian, Bannister was sensitive to the need for keeping too much attention from the case and so from the good Flootham name. He travelled out here and found his old friend Hilary in quite a state and entirely imprisoned. Hilary was skinny and dirty and his hair had grown surprisingly long since being gaoled, as had his beard. The warden tried to encourage him to wash, but the lad refused to remove a single item of clothing from his body or even to shave. This was not what struck cold into

Bannister's soul, however. That was Hilary's eyes. They were as wide and bulging as a lemur's, the pupils so dilated there was barely room enough for iris, and white showed all around. There was nothing of human compassion in them, Bannister saw, indeed nothing left but the bestial instinct for survival. With his wild eyes, his overgrown hair and his torn clothing revealing a far hairier man than Bannister remembered seeing in the rugby baths, Hilary Flootham looked in every respect a lycanthrope midway altered on a full-moon eve. That is, all but his feet, upon which were a pair of well-worn, but highly polished and exquisitely cobbled red-brown leather boots.

Keeping close to the warden, Bannister approached Hilary and addressed him through the bars of his cell.

'What ho, old boy,' Bannister said, suddenly held in the garrulous grip of panic. 'Now you don't have to worry about a thing, Hilly. I know you didn't commit any of these atrocities, and even if you did, I'm here to see that you're taken safely home. I say—'

Bannister's comforting words, which were, he admitted to me, the babblings of a lawyer at a loss for defence, were cut short when Hilary leapt six feet into the air, grasped the top of the bars with all his might and emitted a brain-piercing scream. Apparently, the bars were indestructible, for every vein on Hilary's neck, head and torso bulged with strain, every muscle tensed, and if the metal were breakable, the possessed Flootham would have bent them asunder. Sweat streamed from Hilary's brow. He opened his eyes as the echo of his scream died, and looked at Bannister. The eyes protruded like everything else on his body, but this time there was pain and fear and a plea for help in them, where before there had been merely the animal. Then he spoke. It was a whisper, one that the warden did not hear. Bannister himself only succeeded in doing so by stretching his whole body so his ear was by the mouth of Hilary Flootham.

'The boots,' were the words he said then, and would do so twice more before his painful death.

He fell to the ground unconscious, peaceful at last, the effort of fighting whatever it had been, too much for him.

Bannister considered the words, 'the boots'. The footwear? What was it that made them so brilliant where everything else to do with Hilary was so bedraggled? And what was it about them that so concerned the madman that Hilary Flootham had plainly become?

Thinking that now he was unconscious, the prisoner could be cleaned, Bannister, with the warden, first lashed Hilary's wrists to the bars in case he awoke and then they entered the cell to remove his clothing, wash and shave him. Together they successfully tore his shirt from him and roughly cropped his hair back and shaved his beard with a minimum of nicks. Then they sponged down his upper body.

When they turned to his lower half, naturally they began by trying to remove the boots.

Bannister had never touched such hide! It was as soft as chamois, but as sturdy as buffalo. His fingers sank into its pliability and became one with it. It was quite simply of the highest quality he had ever encountered. And it would be a mistake not to mention the colour of the hide. Never had Bannister seen such a rich, ruby brown, and never a leather whose colour so complemented its texture. They really were quite the most beautiful men's ankle boots Bannister had ever seen. Though wasn't it odd that Hilary should choose to wear such fine footwear without socks, he commented to the oblivious, but good-natured warden.

After trying to share this amazement through a number of charades where words had failed him and noting the cobbler to be one Mr Scratcher of Jermyn Street, London, Bannister went about removing the boots from Hilary's feet. He tried slipping them off, but found that these boots were not to be removed so easily, particularly as, though still certainly breathing, Hilary was as stiff as a corpse. Rethinking the technique, the warden took hold of Hilary's leg as Bannister gripped the shoe and they then attempted to tug one from the other. They pulled and pulled with increasing force, but the boot simply would not budge. They removed the lace entirely, but still the boot would not move. They smudged grease into it to lubricate the foot, but still there was no movement.

Finally they decided to give it a last, gut-wrenching heave before giving up in defeat.

Both put all their weight into the effort, and as each reached new shades of colour, Bannister started to feel a slight shift between foot and boot and heard a moist, tearing sound. It was at this moment that Hilary awoke. He roared and thrust his knee into the warden's face and knocked him clean out, flailing his body like a medieval weapon. Bannister grabbed the warden by the wrists and dragged him to safety outside the cell. He then bolted the gate and cut Hilary free before he could do harm to himself.

Hilary immediately pounced into the darkness of the cell corner and, speaking in tongues, tenderly caressed the boot Bannister had just handled.

What strangeness, Bannister thought as he nursed himself and the warden back to health with a snifter from the bottom drawer and looked through the case history of Hilary Flootham.

The young man had been walking due north through the mountains when he was arrested two weeks earlier. He had no memory of his crimes and when asked where he was going answered simply, 'North.' A photographic picture was taken of him that day. In it, Hilary was skinny, but not emaciated, and his beard was shortish, his hair no more than a knotted, tousled premonition of the wild thatch it so rapidly became. His clothes were dirty and torn, but they were not the ribbons Bannister had seen on him. In fact, the only elements the black-and-white emulsion showed the two Hilarys to share were the eyes and the boots, animal and brilliant.

The pictures of the men Hilary had killed were bloody and gruesome. Bannister was usually a lawyer of finance and apparently not a hunting man, for it took another visit to the warden's bottom drawer to bolster his constitution.

Each victim had been between forty and sixty years of age, each had been overweight and that was as far as the corpses took the investigation, for the body of each man had been submerged in pure lye, which locals use mixed with water to preserve fish. The chemical reaction and immediate erosion of human tissue had been such that the men were unrecognisable as anything more than human. It was family members who had confirmed that, in a strange turn of events, they had also all been crowned with orange hair. Other than these similarities and the fact that all the deceased were Norwegian as one would expect, there was no discernible link between them. They were, it seemed, the victims of a madman's logic, joined only in the horror of their demise.

Having learned all he could, Bannister returned to London an older man and initiated the machinations of Hilary's case and repatriation. The lad was plainly mad, and following a trial, it would be a straightforward if time-consuming transferral to a British asylum, one the Norwegian authorities would welcome, he was sure. The source of poor Hilary's insanity was an investigation for the doctors. Bannister's job was to get him back home. Writing up his findings, he happily dismissed the strange thread of orange hair that ran through the case – albeit admitting that it quite unnerved him, being a wearer of such himself. As he worked, though, another component to the tale tweaked his curiosity: Hilary's only words to him, and the boots to which they referred.

His fascination with the quality of the footwear saw him leave his office early one Wednesday afternoon, cross St James's Park, walk up The Duke of York's Steps and along Lower Regent's Street, where he turned into Jermyn Street. Mr Scratcher's shoeseller was on the left halfway down. The sign was plain gold on deep green enamel, the gold leaf gradually peeling behind the protective glass. It said *Scratcher's est. 1827* and only just managed to squeeze into the narrow width of the premises. The window was filled with fine-looking shoes and boots, all being sold at such a price it was certain only gentlemen of a certain standing would bother to enter. There was, however, no shoe of the startling quality Bannister had encountered in the remote valley in Norway.

He entered and saw shoeboxes stacked to the high ceiling to his right and a row of seats and foot props to his left. Beyond the narrow passage these left between them, was a shelf filled with more boxes, out of which a low arch was carved leading to an old-fashioned till and a dark staircase that doubtless led to yet more boxes. The shop was empty of customers and indeed anyone at all until an ancient, hunched little man came shuffling through the arch.

'Yes, sir. How can I help you?' he asked, looking only at Bannister's feet. 'A nine-and-a-half wide, if I'm not mistaken, sir.'

'You are not,' replied Bannister, 'but I'm afraid I'm not here for shoes, my good man, but rather for help. You must be Mr Scratcher. I am Charles Bannister, QC, and I am working on a case with which I hope you may be able to help me.'

'No, sir – I am Mr Holloway, Mr Scratcher's assistant and salesman,' said the observant little man. 'Perhaps I can still be of assistance?'

Bannister gave Mr Holloway Hilary's name and what I imagine was a very florid description of the shoes. Mr Holloway opened a giant book labelled *Sales* on its spine and flicked through the thick pages. He stopped at one page, removed his glasses and recalled.

'Yes, the Specials. Now I remember Master Flootham, sir. He had spent many years looking for the ideal pair of boots. Made a scientific study of it, you might say. He looked the country over, he said, only to see heels too high or too flat, toes too pointed or too square. And always with too much decoration, and never a hardy enough sole. So difficult to find a quality boot these days with a hardy but elegant sole, he said it was. The country over, he said. Started here in London, on Savile Row. But they were all too dressy, too smart, none of them a boot that could be taken the world over, as he was planning. A similar thing troubled all the Italians he tried. Fine shoes, by all accounts, but just not enough to them, sir. But at the same time, a little too much, if you take my meaning.'

Bannister didn't, but was unwilling to break the old man's flow, so frowned and nodded knowingly.

'And so he moved on, thinking country-style shops were more likely to have the thing. But they just had farming boots – huge metal-toed things with no elegance. He said he once found a pair in Malton, Yorkshire, but that the leather wasn't up to Scratch, if you'll excuse the pun, sir.' Here he gave a game grin and Bannister managed to return it, though he was too rapt to say anything.

'Well, finally he stumbles on old Scratcher's doorstep, looking for a pair of Alders he'd read of. An American shoe, sir, and a good one, I don't mind telling you. But brutish, and really not quite what he was looking for, I'm sure, even though the lad had his heart set on at least seeing them.

'Well, sir, we here at Scratcher's only have Scratcher shoes. It's been that way since 1827 and never a complaint. So even though we couldn't give him the Alders he was after, we were confident there would be something in our stock to please his needs. We supply three hundred and eighty-four different shoes, all told, sir, and strike me down if we didn't go through the whole lot. When we realised that we had what the Spaniards call "an aficionado" on our hands, sir, Mr Scratcher ordered the shop closed, and threw out the two gentlemen waiting. Never seen it before or since, sir. Well, we both worked on Mr Flootham for nearly three straight hours, sir, but it seemed nothing was good enough for the young master. Too hard, too soft. Too high, too low. Too dark, too light. Too heavy, too flimsy. No, nothing was good enough, sir. At least not until Mr Scratcher brings out a new boot he'd been working on, with some special new leather. You should have seen young Master Flootham's face then, sir. We all knew immediately that it was the boot for him. He left wearing them, sir. Left saying, "Super, Scratcher. Absolutely super." And you're right, sir. Never was there a finer boot. Even Mr Scratcher himself says that never has a Scratcher cobbled a finer pair.'

When Bannister had succeeded in absorbing all this fascinating information, he asked Mr Holloway if he might arrange a meeting with Mr Scratcher. Mr Holloway looked doubtful, saying that Mr Scratcher was rarely in the shop these days and preferred spending his time in the factory in Norfolk, but he agreed to ring him on the telephone and disappeared into the darkness once more. Mr Holloway returned from a muffled conversation with the master cobbler, beaming, and said that, considering the fact that Bannister was a man of the law, Mr Scratcher would see him at the factory a day later.

Much pleased with himself, Bannister returned to his desk on the other side of St James's Park with the factory's King's Lynn address and a pair of suede tan-coloured Oxfords that he was sure would be a perfect match for the linen two-piece suit he was to collect the following week.

At his desk, he phoned Hildebrand Flootham and arranged to meet him for luncheon at the Athenaeum, of which they were both members.

Over sherry, Bannister reported the sorry state in which he had found the other man's son. It was sad, the father said, that such a young life should go so awry.

'Is there any hope of recovery, Bannister?' he asked from his armchair.

'I fear not, sir. He seems quite possessed,' the lawyer replied.

'Very sad, Bannister. His mother will be quite distraught. Is there any chance that he may not have committed these . . .' Flootham's voice trailed to a blank stare.

'It seems unlikely, I'm afraid, sir.'

'Oh dear, oh dear, oh dear. What shall I tell Cynthia? Are they all that I am told, these murders?'

'I fear so, Hildebrand.'

'Well,' Flootham Senior said, straightening and looking on the bright side. Floothams, he told himself, had not been sitting on the governing board of Lloyds of London for four generations by looking on the dark side of things. He had other sons. Three out of four, after all, is acceptable. 'Well, we'll just have to get him the very best of care once you bring him home.'

'Yes. Quite,' Bannister said, finishing his sherry in one go. 'Unfortunately, that may be more difficult than it sounds, sir. Or at least take longer than one would hope. These foreigners do things decidedly differently. There's an awful lot of red tape to get through, but I can assure you that I will give this case my full attention.'

'I'm sure you will, Bannister. We can't have Cynthia travelling all the way to Sweden to visit her son, can we?'

'Norway, sir. But we most decidedly cannot, sir,' Bannister said decisively, and signalled their attending waiter for another sherry.

'And it is on that count that I'd like to ask you a couple of questions, to see whether you've observed anything.'

'Like what?' Flootham asked, looking happier now, believing his son to be on his way home already.

'Well, it might sound rather strange, sir, but . . .' Bannister stopped as his sherry was delivered and considered how best to frame his question in such a situation to such a man. '. . . is there anything you might be able to tell me about a pair of boots Hilary had recently acquired? You see, these boots are currently a strong thread in the tapestry of this case.'

Bannister needn't have worried.

'By Gad, those damnable shoes!' Flootham Senior expostulated. 'I thought I'd heard the last of them. We had a towering argument about them. Sent poor Cynthia into floods of tears. Three hundred and fifty pounds for a pair of shoes! Have you ever heard anything so ridiculous? Not even the King of England pays that much. It was *I* who had to pay for them, of course, and I did so just to soothe poor Cynthia's nerves – and so I'd never have to hear of the blessed things again. Three hundred and fifty pounds! I *ask* you! But no, of course not. Young Hilly never did consider his mother's feelings, and went about talking to, mark my words, *talking to* the blasted boots. I couldn't stand it, Bannister. Simply could not stand it. When I broached the possibility of him stopping, he told *me* to stop because I was offending – *offending* – them. He would wander around the house staring at his feet, mumbling away for hours on end. At the supper table, he would ask the damned things if they liked the food, as though he were feeding them. Hardly spoke a word to anyone after he'd found them, and absolutely refused ever to take them off – even when Cynthia asked him. She didn't stop weeping for a fortnight before he left.

'I thought it would be the end of it when he did leave. I should have known better.' The man's rage seemed to ease, his defiant, bloated frame deflate. He let out a long breath and remembered something. 'They were a fine boot, though, Bannister,' he said thoughtfully.

'They were indeed, sir. I've never before seen such a pair, and never such a colour. And to feel them, sir – you'd think they were made of . . . of . . .' Bannister stopped short, not wanting to appear too excitable in front of Flootham. 'Can you recall anything else of note, sir, or anything strange about Hilly, or anything else at all, for that matter?'

Flootham frowned with concentration. 'He was looking rather pale, and Cynthia – well, you know mothers, Bannister – she kept insisting that he shave. But he never did, of course. And his appetite seemed to grow. "Feeding the boys", he said. Great Scott, that boy infuriated me!'

Before Flootham could go too far into nostalgia, which would inevitably lead to anger and so around and around, Bannister paid his condolences, repeated his promise that he would do his very best, and promptly fled to his rooms in Pimlico.

However, what led Hilary from the cobblers of Britain to his murderous heights of Norway will have to wait, as I must now leave this haven of safety and Iberian hospitality. Despite the pause, I sincerely hope you consider me,

Your good friend,

Lindley-Small

23

THE NOTEBOOKS OF CYRIL KING

1893

The Catacombs and Their Creature

'You – you know?' I stammered as he pulled me to my feet. 'How could you know?'

'Where else would a place like this exist, hmm?' was his enigmatic reply.

'What do you mean?'

'I'll show you, lad, in time. First, tell me what's occurred. Are we to expect company? You looked to be in a hurry.'

'I – I don't know,' I whispered, looking about me, suddenly terrified that somebody might be watching us from the branches above, through which the moonlight filtered.

My mind was awash with the fear that Rustam Khan had roused in me. Small's announcement that he knew we had arrived in Ishkuman merely stirred my brain into further confusion. The possibility that we were being watched made me gibber. Small grabbed my shoulders and shook me.

'Pull yourself together, man, and tell me what happened up there, from the moment you left my sight to the second you rolled back in here.' He released me and picked up his satchel. 'And speak fast. If we're to have visitors, we need to prepare.'

I gave a stuttering, disjointed account of what had happened since I left him. Manraj Singh, the polo, the fair-haired villagers, Rustam Khan's inexplicable reaction to the watch, my impending death, my release and my headlong dash to the fort. Small listened without looking at me. Instead he crouched and removed various objects from his knapsack and laid them on a flat patch of leaves at his feet. Two torches, unlit; a bayonet; his flask.

'Adam-Khor did not come here, Small. I was wrong. It's a legend, after all. Forrester came up here to find these people. There's no treasure, Small. No more stones,' I said.

Small stood, grinning, his blue eyes flashing with excitement.

'These bloody natives, lad. No stones, indeed! I suppose he wanted to keep them for himself, the greedy blighter. But I'm afraid he'll have to share. Of course there are stones. Such a reaction only confirms what I already know. Now then. It sounds as though your leaving dear Bucephalus behind might just have saved us. Her hooves would surely have been heard, but we can hope that on foot you left undetected. What that lying polo player does next is a variable we can't predict, so we must still act quickly. You see, lad, it's not a question of if there are stones, as I say, but where they are.'

'What do you mean?' I spluttered for a second time in as many minutes. 'Do you not understand me? Am I not speaking plain English? He said it. Before he released me and saved my life, he told me. Adam-Khor is a myth. *There are no stones!*'

'Well, now, lad. That's more like it,' said Small. 'A bit of blood. Better than a whimper. Use it. There *are* stones, and I have proof. Now's not the time, though. There are other matters to attend to, like finding the cache. I put my time to use, waiting for you here. Unearthed a thing or two, you might say.'

He walked over to his carefully arranged possessions, picked up the bayonet blade and tapped its tip on the leaves.

'The stones, lad. They're beneath you,' he whispered. 'Listen.'

He thumped the ground with his fist. The resulting sound was not the dull thud you would expect on the soil of woodland, nor even that of a building's stone floor. Instead, the sound resonated as though the skin of an enormous drum had been beaten by a giant palm. I stood silently, feeling the reverberations rattle my innards, and stared at Small, wondering from where on earth such a tone could be emanating. In fact, it struck me as a distinctly unearthly sound, as though a gong signifying our entry into the Other World had been rung.

Once the sound had subsided, Small cocked his head to listen for the galloping of hooves. Only when he was satisfied that there were none did he speak.

'It's hollow, lad.' His eyes were blazing with excitement. 'I've been up there the entire night waiting for you to return, resisting the temptation of opening it without you. You're lucky I've the patience of a fly trap. But you're here now, eh?'

He opened his flask and drank, then threw it to me. As I poured a much needed restorative past my lips, he picked up the two torches and put them under his arm. Then he grabbed me by the collars of my shirt and pushed me roughly to the wall.

'Stand here and don't move,' he said, thrusting the torches into my hands. 'Not an inch, do you understand?'

I nodded my answer and he took the flask from me, drank again and replaced it in his satchel, which he threw over his shoulder.

'Really, I should thank you, lad. We both should. Or those lying natives up there. Or perhaps we should just settle and thank the fine Scots from the Livet valley, eh? I should never have discovered a thing had you not deposited me here long enough for a good draught of the finest to take effect. Its consumption blessed me with the entire lack of co-ordination that made me drop the bottle. Then came the sound, then the dropping of the penny, and sobriety close behind. The last is a pity, of course – but trust in The Glenlivet, and ye shall be shown the way.'

He picked up the empty bottle from where it lay among the debris and looked at it with pride before placing it at his side and taking up the bayonet.

'Now,' he said, and without another word, he stabbed the point

of the bayonet through the dead leaves on the floor of the chamber. He pushed it further and further into the earth that must, I
thought, lie beneath them. Deeper and deeper it went until only
two of its ten inches were still visible to us. He worked the blade
back and forth a little, like a saw.

Then it happened. The ground surrounding his knife
descended, as though repelled by the metal of the blade, shrinking
away in order to avoid contact. Moving quickly, Small pulled his
bayonet out of the ground. He backed towards the wall next to me
and put an arm across my chest.

'Now,' he said. 'Hopefully—'

It was as though his initial plunge had caused a chain reaction,
started the sands of an enormous hourglass to flow – an hourglass
in which we were standing.

'If my calculations are correct—'

There was a tearing sound. Both Small and I pushed ourselves
tighter against the stone. The earth and leaves began to disappear
in lines drawn in towards the centre circle, as though the glass had
cracked, the sands now measuring seconds rather than minutes.
There was no time to react. No chance of moving anywhere
before we too were sucked into its blackness.

'Calculations?' I whispered.

'Fine. My guess, then.' Despite the smile he forced, Small's tone
was strained.

The ground itself was opening. It was simply wilting before us,
and would shortly be wilting beneath us.

I could not prevent my eyes from clamping themselves shut in
terror. The sound of falling earth and stone grew louder. I moved
onto my tiptoes, grinding myself into the solid wall behind me,
trying to lift myself off the ground.

Then the sound stopped, but I only dared opened my eyes again
when I felt Small's arm release me.

Below us was a black void of indefinable depth. Around the circular room there was a sheer drop, the walls simply continuing
down where seconds before ground had been. Suddenly panicked,
I looked at my feet. I was standing on the only section of earth left

to give way, but before I could do a thing, it did so, the soil scattering into the darkness. My heart leapt into my throat, and I landed awkwardly on a piece of flat rock measuring a precarious two feet by two, only six inches lower.

What luck to have chosen that spot! What enormous fortune to have been shoved, of all places, to the one position where we would survive. I looked at Small, who was standing on a similar stone a foot or two further down the wall. There were more beyond him spiralling into the darkness. This was a staircase, a steep flight of steps that had once continued upwards as well as downwards, the remnants of which had carried Small to his perch. The false ground Small had destroyed, it must have been constructed to conceal something. Or, I thought with a shiver, to cage something.

Small was inspecting the floor that had peeled from beneath us and now hung down in ragged sections, its edges embedded in the walls of the structure.

'Tanned hide,' he said, and cut a sample from the bulk and threw it to me.

Even through my fright, I could identify it as such. I rubbed it with my fingers. It was stiff with age. Like a boot, it had also once been embroidered, or perhaps repaired, for five holes of varying sizes had been sewn shut. The material had long since melded together, though, the thread decayed to uselessness. A horrifying possibility dawned upon me. Before I could speak, Small confirmed my suspicions.

'It's a face,' he said. 'A human face. Several layers cured and sewn together. Like a giant, morbid drum. Must've been a well, I think. Deep. Fed by the river. Steps could be for gathering water. But then why seal it up?'

I did not like what I held in my hand; it was the remnant of a godless savagery. Nor did I like what I had discovered in the village. But Small had claimed there were stones here, no matter what Rustam Khan had told me. And I could not ignore the fact that this patchwork quilt of human skin was quite in keeping with the Adam-Khor story.

Having come so far, to be put off now by the word of one man would be absurd. Though that man had saved my life, he had reason to misguide me – that unknown source of his anger. I threw the piece of skin into the darkness, and steeled myself to delve into the pit.

'Shall we?' I said in my most worldly of tones and stepped gingerly forwards.

'That's the spirit, lad,' Small responded. 'But before we go further – your thieving savage says there are no stones here. I say it was stones that have brought us here, that led us over the mountains to this strange and green valley, and it's those stones that'll depart with us.'

I followed the finger he pointed over my head, to the wall above, where he had been perched on my return.

'Up there, lad. There's your proof.' The grin had stretched further over his hairy face, and he nodded. 'They're too small to be of much worth, but they'll interest you, I think. Be quick.'

I took hold of a ledge above my head, gripped it with my fingertips and heaved my way up. It was no easy task. The stones of the wall were loose and each time I thought I had a foothold and put my weight on it, the rock gave and sent a shower of stones into the chasm below, into which I would end up falling were I not more careful. I reached the branch where Small had been and, with a final effort, I managed to get a knee onto it. Above me and to my left, I saw something glitter in the moonlight. Cautiously, my excitement rising, I struggled to a precarious standstill.

I was looking into two small reptilian black eyes, their pupils sparkling slits. They belonged to a carving of a creature, roughly twenty inches high. Eroded though the stone was, I could see that its features were of a malproportioned feline, large of head and diminutive of body. Its neck was flared, its tail long and its prominent fangs were bared in a fierce snarl. Flicking from its black mouth was a forked tongue. I paid these details little mind, however, for I was too busy returning the stare of the eyes. Black as night, they were in every way identical to the one that adorned the watch, which I took from my pocket and held up for comparison.

'Small,' I called down to him. 'They're the same. That means—'

'You see now, lad,' he said. 'We're in the right place, and there's no reason whatsoever not to hope there's more to be found down there. There must be. All this must be hiding something.'

As the realisation dawned on me, my foot slipped. I threw myself against the wall and grabbed on to anything I could. Only by my fingernails did I succeed in retaining balance. It was, however, at the cost of the watch. I gasped as I saw it fall, hit the ledge and spin towards the darkness. My heart thrashing against my ribs, I lost balance again and hugged the wall, cursing my idiocy.

'And if the protector's here,' I heard Small say, 'Your Adam-Khor must have been, and I'd give no better than two to one that with him is what we've come for.'

I cranked my head around to see Small considering the watch in his palm. He had caught it.

As I descended towards him, he extracted a length of twine from his knapsack and attached it to the watch. When I got to him, he hung it around my neck.

'Keep it close to your heart, my boy. If you can feel it, you'll know it's safe.'

As we started to make our way down, I proffered one of the torches to Small.

'No light yet, lad. Not for as long as possible,' he said. 'If they do come, we don't want to be fish in a barrel. The moonlight'll have to do us.'

He was probably right about the dangers of using the torches, but he was definitely wrong about the moonlight. I could hardly see a thing and the deeper we went, the worse our vision grew. Each step had to be carefully judged in the dim light, lest a stone was missing. I lost track of the number of spiralling circuits we made, but when Small stopped in his tracks and moved the torches from under my arm into my hands, I looked up at the circle of moonlight from which we had come and it was no larger than a ha'penny piece.

Small lit both torches. 'Well, young fella-melad,' he said. 'We've reached the bottom.'

He rummaged in his satchel for his whisky flask. He tilted it to his lips and then passed it to me, taking one of the torches as he did so.

'Fortify yourself,' he said.

I drank from the all-too-miniature flask. We had indeed met the bottom of the spiral staircase. At my feet the leather face I had discarded into the darkness looked up at me in the flickering of the torchlight. The visage made me shudder.

'Where do we go now?' I asked.

But he was no longer by my side, and his response was echoing and distant.

'This way, lad. Keep up.'

Where Small had been last I looked was now only an opening in the wall illuminated by his retreating torch.

I hurried after him into the tunnel as quickly as my legs would allow. Clearly this was no well, after all. I rounded a corner, unprepared for the horror that confronted me, through which Small appeared to be pawing with gusto.

The hairs rose on the back of my neck. The tunnel was lined with skeletons – dozens, no, hundreds of them, though my swaying torch only illuminated those that lay before my feet. We were in a charnel house. The bones were dry and dark with age, their flesh long since decayed, and their skulls grinned up at Small as he moved the light of his torch over them. He bent and reached out a hand. As he retrieved whatever he had seen, bones scattered about him, their rattle echoing along the tunnel. Small proffered his find, a necklace, for my inspection. He was deaf to the shocking clatter. He was too excited.

'This is pretty poor stuff, King. Hardly worth taking,' he said. 'But still a good sign. If there's no stockpile, then we might at least find some decent jewellery for our efforts.'

I scarcely glanced at his prize. I stared in amazement at the death that surrounded us. Ahead, the stream of bones continued as far as the eye could see, thrown down at random with an utter indifference. This was no respectful graveyard, but a dumping ground. Who knows how many had been disposed of in such a way. Adam-Khor or no, I thought, this inhuman behaviour must have been acted out for longer than anyone could imagine. I could not count the dead even if I had desired to do so. Their bones were too randomly strewn to distinguish one corpse from the next.

Yet as we picked our way over and between their remains, trying to disturb them as little as possible, I could not help but look at them, and gradually I realised that there was not a limb amongst them. Skulls and ribs lay everywhere, but all the long bones were missing. Were they defeated in some great battle? I wondered. But if such were the case, why did they all display identical injuries? Surely there should have been at least some arms and legs undamaged. Perhaps they were criminals, thieves who had suffered some ghastly mutilation, executed in barbaric fashion. Or were they victims of torture, deprived of limbs and left to die a slow and lingering death? No sooner had that last thought occurred to me than it possessed me entirely. What agonies they must have undergone before they died! It seemed to me that the shrieks of the tortured filled my ears, their cries rising in such a crescendo in my mind that I stopped dead where I stood, and could not move. I covered my ears, but still the sound increased in pitch and volume. I only became aware that in my efforts to block them out I had myself joined in their screams when Small shook me from my state and the pleas for mercy died away to silence.

'Quiet, man. And for God's sake, stay close,' he said, now without a trace of mocking or excitement in either his face or voice. He too was unnerved by this turn of events. 'You must keep the noise down, lad. I see it, too. A nasty sight, and no mistake, but we don't want to announce our arrival to whatever occupies these catacombs before absolutely necessary, d'you hear? Here, take this.'

Small pushed his bayonet into my hand.

'Swing it at anything that moves,' he said gravely. 'Except me.'

*

On we went. The air became thicker and more oppressive with every step we took, our breathing shallower. Ahead the tunnel lowered so far as to be impassable.

'Is it just a graveyard, Small?' I asked.

'It can't be. Surely it can't be.' He swung his torch around the wall, searching for a way through. 'What about the cat? Why seal it up?'

'Shame, perhaps,' I said.

'Men who do such things have no shame . . .' he began. He lowered the torch a little. 'What's this?' At the base of the wall was a hole barely two foot square. But above it was another carving of the feline creature. In the torchlight I could see that it had once been painted; the forked tongue was red where the pigment had not yet been consumed by time. Colour was apparent in other places, too. Its body was a patchwork of brown stone and black paint, and just discernible at the top of its head, between its spiked ears, was a figure of eight. It was identical in size and design to the one at the top of the spiral staircase; identical, that is, except in one respect. Where the previous carving had met my gaze with eyes of glinting black sapphire, this one's sockets were empty.

I took the watch from around my neck and held it up to the carving. 'Look, Small,' I said, for he was already crouching, trying to illuminate the hole with his torch. 'The eyes, Small. They're gone. And the stone on the watch would fit those sockets exactly. This must be where it came from. Tolliver was on this very spot!'

'Perhaps,' he said. 'We can't be sure it was he who took it from the cat. But whether he did or not, it looks like it's telling us something,' said Small. 'This way's our only choice.' He slung his rifle over his shoulder and nodded towards the opening. 'In we go, lad,' he whispered. 'Me first, you follow.'

He did not wait for a reply, but dropped to his belly and crawled into the hole, thrusting the torch ahead of him. I was close behind. The tunnel ended after no more than ten feet and opened into an enormous chamber, a cavern dug out of the stone by time, water or the hand of man. There was a heavy, musty smell, as if the air itself was long dead.

In the centre of the chamber sat a stone plinth, perhaps an altar; but what caught our attention was not the plinth itself but the large wooden cage that was standing alongside it. Within it was yet another skeleton, although this one was not human. It was feline, and no larger than that of a domestic cat, although its tail bones stretched to an abnormal length and its ribcage was strangely over-sized. Small put a hand through the bars and lifted the skull. Disproportionate fangs some two inches in length made it resemble a miniature sabretooth. Unmistakably this was the beast whose likeness had been carved in stone up on the wall of the fort and in the tunnel, somehow made real, embodied through witchcraft, surgery or forgotten generations.

'It's the cat,' I said. 'It's real, Small!'

Small pulled the skull towards him and manipulated it through the bars.

'You're right, lad. A fascinating creature. In all my years I've never seen a thing like it,' he said, turning the head over in his hands with more delicacy and interest than he had treated its human counterparts. 'Had no idea such a species actually existed,' he whispered more to himself than to me as he considered the oversized canine teeth. 'They're hollow,' he said, stroking them tenderly with a finger. 'More like the fangs of a snake than the teeth of a cat. The bizarre things this country coughs up, eh?' He placed the skull in his satchel, saying: 'I know a Maharajah or two who'd like one of these. They like to brag of their menageries, and don't mind parting with good money for a strange beast. The things that are neither one thing nor another, that scientists don't quite know how to define, they can win you all manner of friends. One like this, long-dead, won't get us far, so if these bloody—'

I no longer heard him. Exploring the chamber beyond him, my torch had illuminated yet more bodies at the far end of the cavern. I saw at once that these were different from those behind us in the tunnel. They were not scattered randomly as the bones had been, but neither had they been laid out with reverence. They were piled unceremoniously in a heap against the wall of the chamber, heads lolling, arms and legs outflung. As far as I could tell in the torchlight, none of these had been dismembered. And they were clothed.

I forced myself to approach them. These were newer. Not yet reduced to skeletons, their skin was browned and hardened and shrunken over their bones, the flesh desiccated almost to nothing beneath. And the faces – dear God, those faces! They were demonic visions of death. Hair still sprang from what skin still clung to the scalps; their eyes were soulless black cavities; their lips drawn back beyond the teeth, exposing the bone of the jaws, forming a chorus of cackling faces.

'Small,' I called. 'Over here!' He came to join me and, seemingly unaffected, inspected them with a clinical curiosity.

'They're entirely dried out. Mummified, almost,' he said, as he contemplated a hideous, bony hand that hung from the pile.

The hand protruded from a sleeve stained crimson, the crimson of blood. And yet these bodies were anything but fresh. Small stepped back and moved the arm with his raised foot. I saw the shiny buttons on the cuff. The red was not blood but dye. They were uniforms, scarlet uniforms.

These were soldiers.

24

THE LETTERS OF
SIR PAUL LINDLEY-SMALL

From Private Compartment 8c
The locomotive The Flying Norseman
Norway

4TH JANUARY 1909

My friend,

Having been sunk deep in the frosty backwaters of this country,
I now head towards its capital city. I am pleased to say I share this
train with a young woman three compartments up, who displays
all the comeliness I have described to be native to these parts.
However, while she mounts the escape from her dragon of a governess, which we planned together when we met in the corridor,
I will take the opportunity to tell you what I learned in Solheim
and Gjeilo, both of the Spaniard and of Hilary Flootham.

After a night of fitful sleep in his Pimlico quarters, the follow-
ing day brought with its bright sunshine Bannister's meeting with
Mr Scratcher. The lawyer rose early and caught a train from King's
Cross that took two slow hours to reach its destination in King's
Lynn. The Scratcher factory, he discovered, was more a small series

of workrooms than a factory. It was not far from the station and, being early for his meeting, Bannister was able to take a brief look round the ancient facility and observe how sheets of hide would gradually be refined into footwear, a process using tools he guessed had not been replaced since the first Scratcher forged a shoe in 1827.

Eventually, the most recent Mr Scratcher appeared, shook the lawyer's hand energetically and then ushered him into an office at the end of the production line. Mr Scratcher was even older than Mr Holloway, and even more stooped, but slightly less loquacious. He looked harmlessly, even charmingly, unhinged; he wore a pencil behind his ear and, oddly for a man in his line, Bannister thought, a pair of Plimsolls on his feet. When he saw Bannister looking at them, he began to speak in what were to prove characteristically broken sentences.

'On my feet all day. No matter how you make a shoe, rubber's a winner.' He winked at Bannister who, uncomfortable with that level of intimacy, looked away and blushed. The old man took the pencil from behind his ear and started frantically sketching shoes on the pad in front of him, looking up at Bannister intermittently as he spoke.

'Holloway . . . you want to know about the Scratcher Specials . . . Hilary Flootham. Quite a day. Holloway told you everything . . . more than I can.' He tapped his head with his pencil. 'Hull's beginning to leak, you know?' Bannister looked back at him in bafflement; he had no idea why the northern city had been brought up at all, let alone how it might suffer a fissure.

'Holloway's reason I stay here. Can't take talk in shop. Ended up in basement most days.' His pencil continued apace on the pad and Bannister noticed an empty pot of coffee behind the cobbler. 'What I tell you?'

'Well, whatever you can about the boots,' Bannister said, and then as an afterthought, 'They really were the finest pair I've ever seen. If you ever make another pair—'

'Never be another pair of Specials,' Mr Scratcher interrupted. 'Never.'

'Whyever not, Mr Scratcher?' Bannister protested. 'They really are the finest—'

'Know how a cobbler makes a pair of shoes, Mr Bannister?' Mr Scratcher challenged. 'Traditional cobbler like me, not a high street fly-by-night. Trained, professional cobbler?'

'Well . . .' began Bannister, though he needn't have bothered. Mr Scratcher was not after an answer.

'I was taught by my father, Mr Bannister . . . my father by his . . . likewise since eighteen twenty-seven. Long time, Mr Bannister. And every Scratcher made his shoes from leather from the same tannery. Norfolk. Pollier's Tannery. Polliers and Scratchers go back a long way. Godfathered children. Great Uncle George Scratcher married a Pollier. Close-knit families, like. Only not any more, see.' Mr Scratcher looked up from his shoe drawing and stared unblinkingly at Bannister, making him blush again, though this time the lawyer could not avert his eyes. 'And the Specials are to blame.'

The old fellow gave a long, regretful sigh. 'Couple of years ago, never thought of using leather from another tannery, Mr Bannister. But received a delivery from a tannery in Norway, of all places. Hadn't ordered it, letter from tanner, Mr Rød-Larsen . . . heard Scratcher's was the finest cobblers in the world. Honoured if Mr Scratcher would consider using his prime hide. And prime it was. Oh yes. Better than anything I'd ever handled my whole life . . . better than any Scratcher had ever handled. Polliers fine tanners, but nowhere close to the quality of this Norwegian. Felt it yourself. But you never tried the boots, Mr Bannister. Never have you worn such comfort. Didn't walk. Glided . . . boot supporting every slight twist of ankle, every bend of toes. Leather shaped around foot's every movement.' Mr Scratcher suddenly broke eye-contact with Bannister and returned to his scribbling.

'What d'you know about tanning, Mr Bannister? What d'you know about process that makes the leather makes our shoes?'

Bannister, still wondering at the brilliance of the shoes, took a moment to answer.

'Well, I know it's skin. Not much more than that, really. It's a dead animal's skin.'

Mr Scratcher gave a little amused laugh. At the time, Bannister thought it was a response to his lack of knowledge.

'Yes, Bannister. Usual way's skinning dead animal. Cow, for instance. Skin's rubbed down – dung, wood, bark – every tanner has own way. Down in a tanning pit, Mr Bannister, treated with all manner of substances . . . ghastly smell. Whole thing filled in . . . earth, tree branches. Know how long it stays there? Years. Not to mention what goes on after coming up. But doesn't matter. What matters is this Norwegian tanned leather, Mr Bannister. But his leather – there's something wrong with it. It's *alive*.'

Bannister gawped at him.

'Not only is it alive, Mr Bannister,' Mr Scratcher continued, staring again, revelling in the shock that he was writing over his audience's face. 'It feeds.'

'Feeds?' Bannister spluttered.

'Feeds,' Mr Scratcher confirmed impressively, then swung his left leg onto the desk between them and pulled off the canvas shoe, to reveal a rounded stump at the ankle.

'Comfy, Mr Bannister. But hungry.' He emitted a wheezing laugh from the bottom of his lungs and watched as Bannister's understanding of the situation deepened. 'What I got for changing tanner, Mr Bannister. It'll not happen again, I can tell you.' He grinned madly. 'Now you'll be wanting that Rød-Larsen's address, I expect.'

Still in shock, Bannister made it back to the station in King's Lynn just in time for the 2.50 train, and by the time he had alighted at King's Cross, he had come to terms with this horror. An hour later, he telephoned his travel agent, Thomas Cook & Son, from the safety and comfort of his St James's desk.

Hilary, Bannister considered as he mentally formed a case for his defence, had been driven to madness by these boots. Temporarily insane, he had no control over his actions. If only they could remove the boots, perhaps Hilary could be saved the horror of an asylum, and even prison. But the word of an eccentric cobbler would not suffice. Proof would be needed if Bannister were to convince a jury of any nationality that footwear – boots cobbled from living leather that fed upon the feet of their wearer, driving them to madness and murder – were to blame for the crimes. Mr Rød-Larsen was the key to young Flootham's sanity and freedom, and fearing tales of Mrs Flootham's misery, he returned to Norway without further ado and went immediately to the small but inescapable prison in Solheim.

Hilary's condition had visibly worsened. He was thinner, paler and hairier. His eyes, so bestial before, if possible had become more so. He was without shirt, but with trousers and boots, as Bannister had left him. Only there was a difference to the boots. If anything they were even finer, even more brilliant than before. Their colour, previously red-brown, was now closer to pure red, with only a hint of brown. Somehow the leather, with its soft, tough texture, seemed to be bulging.

At first the warden balked at Bannister's request that they tie Hilary down, citing the fact that his charge had become increasingly wild, but they agreed that knocking the prisoner out first was a good idea and the warden seemed to enjoy coshing poor Hilary. They tied him to the bars again and this time the warden sat with all his considerable weight on Hilary's chest while Bannister secured the boots' position by placing his own considerable weight upon Hilary's shins. Then Bannister opened his pocket-knife and cut across the toe of the left boot. Hilary awoke with an even worse scream than upon Bannister's last visit, as though the knife had cut into his own skin, but the combined weight of the two men was sufficient to keep him in place. Blood trickled from the boot's fresh wound.

Bannister went to the lad's other end and grasped poor Hilary's lolling head in his hands.

'I know about the boots, Hilly. I'll do the very best I can,' he said, echoing his hollow promise to the wretch's father, when really he did not know what to do.

The words broke through the bestial in Hilary, and again the human returned to his eyes and he whispered for the second time, 'The boots,' and then passed out.

Leaving the young fellow in the capable hands of the warden,

Bannister set off to see the mysterious Mr Rød-Larsen with a
determination that he did not know he possessed. The tanner's
house and workshop was just outside a town called Gjeilo, not
many miles north of the place where I was hearing this tale. It
perches on the peaks and is the location of Dr Holm's
Convalescence Hotel. Bannister's route from the valley to the
town was winding, and he found himself forever climbing the
mountainous terrain along a narrow road that disappeared around
tight bends and in and out of sheer crevasses. When finally he
passed through the town of Gjeilo and out the other side, he
arrived at the foot of a lane that ascended into the very clouds.
Bracing himself, Bannister strode into the wet fog. Within minutes,
however, he was out of it again and faced sunshine that bore down
onto the flat bed of cloud from which he had emerged. He was on
one of many mountaintop islands that broke out of the sea of
white, and though it was clear and beautiful, in the air there was
the unmistakable odour of flesh in the advanced stages of decay.
Not what Dr Holm promised, he thought as he walked on with his
handkerchief over his mouth and nose, but certainly the foulness
Scratcher had described as inherent to the tannery. The lawyer carried on his way and at the very peak of the mountain saw that Mr
Rød-Larsen's tannery was little more than a wooden cabin flanked
by two wooden sheds.

All sorts of possibilities were running rife in his imagination, so
Bannister decided not to announce his arrival and instead walked
as quietly as he could over to the structures. Looking through the
first window he came to, he saw the tanner's living quarters: the
usual heavy wooden furniture, a fireplace smouldering and a large
collection of bones and antlers mounted upon the wall, not from
the usual reindeer, but somewhat familiar nonetheless.

From that window, Bannister moved to the nearer of the two
sheds and peered in. There upon a table, lying on his back and visible only from his bare chest up, was a slim man of thirty, fast
asleep. Bannister sighed with relief, delighted that the potentially
dangerous Mr Rød-Larsen was resting from his toil, and was not the
mountain of man he had envisaged. He was, however, shaken by

the stained implements he saw around the sleeping man and hanging from hooks in the wall and ceiling. There were all kinds of brutal-looking tools, dull blades and sharp ones, pokers and stretching racks. The tanner's toolbox looked much like a torturer's.

Terrified, yet excited and still keen to obtain a vital clue for this most mysterious of cases, Bannister then turned to the second of the sheds. He was there presented with an image that he assured me would never leave him. It made him gasp with horror and smack his palm across his mouth in fear of alerting the squat, powerful-looking, fiery-haired man whose back faced him. This was surely the real Mr Rød-Larsen. But if that were so, who could the sleeping young man in the first shed be? This was not a question Bannister immediately addressed, however, for on one side of the red-headed man was a knee-high pile of hairless skin. To his right was another, equally high, of bloody bones and flesh, some fresh, some rotten, all attracting the flies that buzzed around the room. From the rafters hung strips of drying skin. The man himself was employing his powerful arms, though in what Bannister could not yet see. Repulsed by the sight, yet as fascinated as I was by its retelling, Bannister adjusted his position to see beyond the immense shoulders. The large face (surprisingly noble as Bannister reported) was covered in a wild red beard and had thick eyebrows, smudged with blood where the brute had swatted a fly. His two enormous hands were both covered in blood to the elbows and worked savagely. One held a knife that looked small in the ham-sized fist. The other securely held a crimson human leg in position, as its skin was parted from its flesh. As the realities of the case came flooding into his brain, Bannister fled before this murderous beast, this curser of souls, this human skinner became aware of his proximity.

It was not until he had reached the famed clean air of Gjeilo, so at odds with its evil twin not a mile away, and paid high above the going rate for a trip to the safety of Hilary's prison, that Bannister had time to truly ruminate upon his discoveries. And it was only then that he came to realise the apparent similarities between Rød-Larsen and the six murdered by wretched Hilary. As he told me of the somersaults this caused his brain to perform, so I in turn soothed his shaken mind with the intractable truth that there is little we can do about the way we are born. Some of us are merely luckier than others. Regardless of the unfortunate physical features with which Bannister himself was endowed, he had solved the mystery of the boots, and had even got to the heart of his case.

The wonderfully frightful conclusions my fellow Harrovian drew were these: Mr Scratcher had quite unknowingly manufactured the Specials from the skin of a person with a vengeful spirit – so vengeful, in fact, that the hide continued to live, and fed from the feet of he who donned the boots, possessing the wearer, just as Bannister had told Flootham Senior his son Hilary had been possessed. And there was purpose to this possession. It drove poor Hilary forever due north, towards the snowier climes inhabited by the hideous Rød-Larsen; it drove him bloodily to murder every man he came across who was unfortunate enough to share both the age and the fiery red hair of the tanner who had turned the skin of the vengeful individual into leather.

Hilary was nothing more than an innocent victim of circumstance and of his love for fine footwear – but would a jury accept a defence that told of murderous tanners, living, feeding boots and a man possessed by them driven to murder? Bannister feared not; and I must admit, that I myself, eleven men short of a jury, would not have believed him had he not presented his proof in the form of twin souvenirs.

They came from his final visit to the pitiful Hilary Flootham, whom Bannister would never have the opportunity to defend. For when he arrived at the prison, the warden came running out, babbling unintelligibly in his native tongue. Bannister rushed to Hilary's cell. He saw the boots lying by the back wall. Hilary was quite fifteen feet from them and, almost in complete darkness, leaned upon the bars of his cell.

'Hilly!' Bannister exclaimed, relieved that the warden's incomprehensible cries had been of joyful surprise. 'You've got them off! The boots are off!'

Hilary didn't respond, but rolled his head towards Bannister, revealing a face even more pallid and drawn than before, but one wholly human, entirely devoid of the animal that Bannister had seen. His eyes, though tear-filled and scared, were certainly the human ones that had defied Harrow masters with Marxist rhetoric, and with such aplomb. Filled with glee, Bannister swung the cell door open and rushed in. He knelt beside the poor weak youth and took him to his breast, so filled with emotion was he.

'Hilly, how did you do it? The boots are off! We will burn them!'

It was at this point, as he felt liquid soak through the knees of his plus-fours, that Bannister began to suspect the horrific truth. The liquid was blood, and as he dragged Hilary further into the light, the lawyer saw that, where before there had been the boots, and where he now had expected to see scarred, perhaps bloodied feet, were only twin stumps of bone, skin and flesh. He dropped Hilary in shock and, looking over to the boots, saw the dying man's feet and ankles still within them. As the last of his lifeblood leaked away, Hilary whispered into Bannister's ear for the third and final time, 'The boots.'

And it was these very boots that Bannister now presented me with in evidence of his tale. An old trick of the experienced story-teller, I hear you saying, and I would have agreed with you, my dear Cyril, had it not been for the very real bone within them and the wizened skin attached to the inner upper, as well as the single bloodstained slice over the toe of the left.

It was then that Bannister informed me of the fact I already suspected: Hilary Flootham had died within the inescapable walls of Solheim Gaol. And he had been the only prisoner to see its bars for six months. There was no Spaniard here. No Spaniard, and no beast.

Needless to say, I was incensed, but rather than take it out on a chap who had just held me in such thrall, I swallowed my anger with the rest of my glass. I then rose to my feet, and as both were falling to slumber before the fire, fared the native and the rotund lawyer well before leaving to vent my spleen in the luxury of Dr Holm's.

After relating this tale to the delightfully ripe young creature with whom I am now sharing my compartment, I am certain she considers me quite a deviant. I am pleased to report that she quite *squirmed* with excitement at the horror of it all! Before I respond to the expectant looks she sends me, however, I must impart to you a postscript, the implications of which could send such innocent youth squirming out of my devious grip and back to the considerable and no doubt comforting breast of her governess. But you, I am sure, can cope.

It was at Dr Holm's that my first suspicions arose. When I arrived there, the sweet Spanish maid Rosella showed me to my room, and as she did so told me that she did not blame me for abandoning Vegard's basic lodge for the unalloyed pleasures offered at Dr Holm's, but that I mustn't think poorly of Vegard's, for what could one expect of a place run by a man who is also the warden of the local gaol? Among other things rather more delightful, she also revealed that she remembered well the shaken Bannister who had come to demand a journey to Solheim. She described him as a thin, miserable man. My grey matter was, of course, doubly pricked, so I dispatched the young delicacy to send a telegram of condolences to Hildebrand Flootham. In it, I mentioned that I did not recall the Bannisters at Harrow. Such are the wonders of the twentieth century, that only hours later he responded with gratitude for the condolences and the challenge that I must remember the Bannisters – a family of lawyers, the latest of whom, prior to his disappearance, had been the Defence Counsel for his dear, departed son. At Harrow, contemporaries had given him the moniker 'Beanpole' Bannister, and he had achieved fame in his schooldays by breaking the Harrow high-jump record, which until then had stood for ninety-eight years.

My dear Cyril, though I did not know it, the killer and tanner of young men's skin, whom Hilary Flootham had sought to kill under the orders of his vengeful boots, and Rød-Larsen's insidious accomplice, the warden, had for an entire meal been eyeing up my leathery hide for a new pair of Specials. Why such characters are disposed to brag upon their exploits with unknowing victims, I cannot say. That they should not do so while partaking of Scotland's finest is without a doubt.

As we hurtle towards Kristiania, I am, by the very skin of my teeth, still,

Your very good friend,

Lindley-Small

25

THE NOTEBOOKS OF CYRIL KING

1893

The Forest of Death

'At least they select their victims wisely,' Small said, looking up from the uniformed arm. 'Whoever in bloody hell they are. This is a strange business, lad, and no mistake. But we mustn't let our minds wander from the task at hand. There's nothing for us here.'

'These must be Tolliver's men,' I said. 'The ones who died when their captain and his adjutant escaped.' I looked at them lying there, slaughtered so far from home. 'Get a move on, lad,' I heard Small say and there was a hand on my shoulder. 'It continues through here.'

He was indicating off to one side of the mound of dead, where his torch lit an opening leading out of the cavern. He coughed and spat. 'If these are newer than those others, maybe through here they'll still be alive,' he said.

I shuddered at the thought, but I moved to follow him into a low tunnel, our torches throwing light only yards ahead, with no inkling of what lay beyond until we emerged into yet another cavern. There, if such a thing were possible, the scene that met our eyes was more gruesome even than those that had gone before.

This cavern was not possessed of a high ceiling like the previous one. In fact I would now hazard to say it stood at no more than seven feet. I could not see it, however, for the decoration that hung suspended from it. If the word decoration calls to mind colourful paper chains or jolly, glittering baubles, I mislead you and apologise. What greeted us here were the very foulest of adornments. The chamber was festooned with severed arms and legs, the dangling feet forever unable to reach the floor, the hands cupped in futile gestures of supplication.

I turned my head away in disgust.

'Come on, lad,' Small said. 'It wouldn't do to give up now. Besides, we're stuck between the two.'

With that, he squared his shoulders and struck forth and in a moment he was consumed by the forest of limbs. I faced them, knowing that I must follow him in, yet unable to force myself to do so.

These grotesque exhibits were not reduced to skeletons like the bodies to which they must once have belonged, those limbless heads and torsos we had met in the first tunnel. Nor were they mummified skin stretched over bone like the wretched soldiers from whom we had just come. These had muscle and sinew still attached, yet all those I could see were black and wizened, the flesh shrunken and hardened, for all the world as though they were ancient joints of meat hanging in a nightmare butcher's shop. How they had been preserved so long I did not dare to guess. In places, moisture from above ran down to the tips of fingers and toes, where it hung in droplets like bulbous, deformed nails. Hands and feet reached for my hair and brushed my face as I bent low to avoid them, took a deep breath as well as I was able and stepped further into the chamber.

The drenching liquid rolled down my face and neck. Both my hair and my clothes were sodden. I swung to move limbs from my path, but they were at once replaced by others, all eager to touch the living, beseeching one so fortunate as I. Fortunate!

My torch hissed and dwindled and I was lost in the thicket of limbs. I could barely make out the glow of Small's torch ahead, but the acrid smell of it singeing the blackened remains led me on.

Suddenly I lost my footing on the slippery stone floor. As I reached out a hand to save myself, my fingers grasped at the leathery skin and pulled loose long-dead sinews and strips of desiccated flesh.

I saw Small ahead, struggling to make his way, violently swinging his torch from side to side as though a broadsword, holding the fear he surely felt at bay with vicious threats. Then his stream of expletives ceased and on my second fall I saw that his torch was no longer moving. As I got to my feet he called out.

'King, get up here, lad. You must see this.'

He no longer sounded distressed, but excited.

I managed to push myself upright and stumble towards him, hoping that what he had found would justify the dreadful approach.

I burst from the limbs into a vaulted open space and found Small standing before a patch of wall a good fifteen feet high. Occupying it was a great, protrusive carving, identical in design but many times the size of the two we had found already. That strange cat towered over us, twelve feet tall at least. Pockmarks covered its body, as though it had withstood a firing squad. This version was not painted, however, nor were there jewels in its eyes. Their sockets were empty hollows that flickered mockingly down at us. The creature was quite naked, made only of stone, except in one or two places where thin strips glittered yellow in the flame. Small approached it and touched it where it shone. His eyes were close to the beast and he moved all around it, inspecting every inch he could reach. He swore beneath his breath.

'What is it, Small?' I whispered.

His eyes raged in the torchlight. 'You see where it shines? That's gold. Used to be covered in the stuff, I don't doubt, and jewels, too. All those holes and indentations, they're where the gems were set. They've been prised out. This is where our treasure lay, all right. This creature. Damn it, lad. We're too late. We've been beaten to it! It's been stripped!'

We stood before the statue and looked at one another.

'Tolliver,' I said under my breath.

'He was here,' growled Small. 'He stripped it.'

'But Tolliver came back with nothing but the one stone,' I said. 'They caught him. Mutilated him. He can't have got away with the rest.'

'Caught with his hand in the kitty, eh? It's not here, though, is it, lad? Maybe the natives shifted it when they found that Tolliver and his men had desecrated their statue. Or it could have been taken years ago, long before Tolliver came here. We'll never know. Either way, it doesn't change the fact that the loot is gone.'

Small was staring at the floor, dispirited. I could not disagree with him, and I did not know what to say, so I was silent.

'Look!' he gasped and fell to his knees. So amazed had we been by the statue that we had not noticed a small pit, a foot square, that had been cut into the ground to one side of the beast.

Small moved his torch over it to reveal another sculpture there in the darkness. It was much smaller than the one that stood over us, and free standing, an idol, but was of the same design, a fierce kitten protected by its mother. And well might it require protection, for it shone with all the glory and effulgence with which only gold can shine.

I leaned my torch against the wall and dropped to my knees beside Small.

'We've made it, Small! It's gold!'

I edged closer and extended my hands. Gingerly, as though it might bite, I delved into the hole in the ground and touched the cold statuette. I grasped it and lifted. A split second later, Small grabbed my arm.

'Wait!' he cried, but it was too late. I was holding the piece, and lifting it closer to the light.

'It's ours, Small,' I whispered in awe. 'Why wait?'

He sighed and shook his head.

'Have you ever handled gold before, lad?'

'Oh yes,' I said and stared at the cat's long fangs and into its eyes. 'But never this much, Small. Never this much!'

Its eyes were carved black stones.

'Small, look. Again, the twins of the one on the watch!'

'Lad, the people who stripped this cave of its valuables – whoever the bloody hell it was – Tolliver, Adam-Khor himself – do you think they'd leave something like this behind?'

I had already thought of that.

'Nobody stripped it, Small,' I said. 'At least, not thieves. They stripped it themselves and condensed the gold into this little wonder. No one else has been in here for centuries, after all. Tolliver must have got his stone from somewhere else.'

'It's very thoughtful of them to leave something so convenient for us,' was his sarcastic response. 'I notice you're holding that thing up and looking into its eyes. It's ten inches tall, lad. Have you any idea how much it would weigh if it were made of gold? Solid gold, I mean, of course.'

He had got my attention, but before I could respond, a faint grinding sound came from the floor. We both looked down. The bottom of the pit from which I had removed the statuette was rising.

Small shook his head.

'Gilded. Though it might as well be fool's gold,' he said. 'For fools.'

The grinding noise suddenly amplified, filling the chamber. It was no longer coming from the pit alone.

Small's eyes became immediately alert. He looked over his shoulder.

'The entrance, lad. It's a trap.'

He grabbed my torch and wedged it into the crack between the wall of the pit and its ascending floor and the rumbling was immediately replaced by a whining, as whatever dastardly mechanism was at work here was stalled in its business.

Small leapt to his feet.

'Come on, boy.'

The rising platform was struggling against the torch, but the wood of the handle was beginning to give way. I threw myself forward on all fours and ducked beneath the hanging limbs as the whining grew suddenly higher in pitch.

I could barely see where I was going as feet and hands slapped my face and poked at my eyes, but I ploughed on, spurred by Small's incessant cries from ahead.

'Get a move on, boy! D'you want to live on this meat for the rest of your sorry days? Move it!'

Then the torch must have given way and fallen to one side, for the piercing whine ceased and was once more replaced by the rumbling.

'Half way, boy. Come on. Another twenty seconds and you'll be shaking these hands for ever!'

I pushed onwards, following the light ahead.

'Ten seconds, lad. I'll not wait for you. Come on!'

The stone floor bruised and tore my knees and palms.

'Five.'

He was only yards ahead of me.

'Four.'

I threw myself forward.

'Three – faster, lad!'

Small came to a stop at the wall as a great slab slid from left to right.

'Two – you'll never make it!'

He placed the torch to brace the remaining six inches of space.

'One!'

The torch splintered and died as I hurled myself the final yard.

My palms slapped against stone.

I had reached the entrance, only now it was a sheer rock wall. Small had lied, I was grateful to see. He had waited for me, and now both of us were trapped.

'For fools,' he muttered and walked past me as I heaved for breath. 'But at least we've food, eh?' he called as he crawled beneath the limbs.

We were trapped, as I say, and that seemed to be the point. The ceiling did not begin to descend upon us, nor did walls collapse, spikes appear or waters flood the cavern. Starvation was the aim for any grave robbers foolish enough to lift that statuette, a slow, degrading and unspectacular death.

I found Small sitting by the great carving of the cat, staring into the flame of my torch. The small golden sculpture sat next to him. The floor around him was level, the pit nowhere to be seen. He held his flask in his hand.

'Well, lad, after all we've been through, this is rather a hum-drum end to things.'

'Is there no way we can open it again?' I asked lamely.

'Lad, if that slab were gold it couldn't weigh more.'

He took a long draught and tapped the torch with the flask.

'This'll last us another ten minutes or so. With any luck it'll take the rest of the air in here with it and hasten our end. Unless, of course, you have any more bright ideas that might get us out of here.'

I slumped down next to him and filled a pipe.

'I'm afraid not, Small.'

'Well, lad. I'm just sorry we were beaten to it. A damnable dis-appointment. And now we're both going to end up joining the ranks here. Perhaps not in a bloody heap like those soldiers, nor with our limbs hanging from the roof, nor our faces adorning a thousand-year-old drum, but dead sure enough.'

'Do you really think they were a thousand years old?'

'I am prone to exaggeration, as you know. But I should say hun-dreds, yes. Melded together like that, set into a building that must've been here since God knows when. And that necklace we found back there. I should say everything dates from at least a hun-dred years ago, except those soldiers.' He paused. 'But if they didn't come in the same way we did, why then . . .'

We had hit a dead end. The entrance through which we had come had not been used for a long, long time. But Tolliver's men had got here somehow, and the statue had been stripped. Small turned his head slowly, looked me in the eye and grinned. My eyes widened as I understood his gist.

'There must be another way out,' we said in unison.

'Quick, lad,' Small said, jumping into action. 'Before the torch dies. A lever, a button. Anything. Pull or push every last thing you see, even those bloody hands and feet. The switch could be any one of them.'

We swept the entire wall, starting with the great carving of the beast, delving into every hole, pushing every feature, leaping to reach its forked tongue, its ears, its nose, its long tail, its flared chest and its fangs, but nothing moved and nothing happened. Then Small turned to the walls on either side, and I to the ground around it. I stamped where before there had been the hole. On my hands and knees I crawled over every inch of the stone floor, sliding dirt and shreds of dried flesh aside, but still nothing. From there we moved to the wall where the tunnel had been and the rough rock around it. But neither of us happened upon anything. The flame of the torch grew low, and in a final desperate attempt we set to the hanging limbs. Methodically we worked our way around them, pulling and pushing, hoping as dead skin and blackened flesh came away in our hands that something would shift, that some other mechanism or fulcrum would release us just as one had imprisoned us, but our efforts were in vain.

Exhausted in both body and mind, we stood before the carving and watched as between us the last flame on the torch grew smaller and smaller.

Small looked up from the flame and into my eyes.

'Well, lad,' he said. 'It's been nice seeing you.'

Seconds before the flame died and we were thrown into darkness, his eyes left mine, and he looked beyond me and frowned, but before I could look round, darkness came, thick, heavy, black darkness.

'What is it, Small? What—'

I did not complete my sentence, for I felt him take hold of my shoulders. He twisted me to face the great cat, but of course I could not see it. I expected to see nothing at all, much less what met me. In fact, I was dazzled.

A sliver of light was streaming into my left eye, a minute sun the size of a pinprick.

Small released my shoulders and moved away, and then the light was eclipsed.

'Come here, King,' he whispered, and I think turned, for once again the light struck me. 'Towards the light, lad. It's a hole. And listen.'

I approached him, held my breath and put my ear to the light.

Coming from beyond the hole through which the light streamed was the definite sound of voices, men's voices, muffled by distance and the stone between us.

'Now don't get excited and call for help, lad. Remember where we are. If those savages find us here, likely we'll end up even more like all the rest in here.'

I *was* excited, but I was not about to shout out. I was holding my breath and straining to hear. There was more than one voice, certainly. One sounded angry, agitated, a second steady and soothing.

'Can you make out the words?' I whispered to Small.

'No, but it's probably some mountain language, anyway. Even if I could, I'd probably not be able to tell you what they were saying. But that doesn't matter. This must be the key, lad. Or rather the keyhole, and we need the key.'

Small stuck his finger into the hole.

'There's nothing there, so far as I can tell. You try. Your fingers are slimmer.'

I poked my finger into the narrow gap, and it slid in to the knuckle, but when I rotated it, all I could feel was stone.

'Nothing,' I whispered.

I heard Small sigh.

'Well, we'll not suffocate, I suppose. Perhaps it's just a ventilation hole to prolong the suffering. It looks as though we'll be feeding on the dead after all.'

'It must be here for more reason than that, Small,' I said, putting my eye to the hole. 'I can't see the source of the light, but there must be a torch—'

As I spoke I saw something that froze my heart. Where the light had shone there was now an eye, looking directly into mine, watching me. I turned my head away in shock. While the voices continued, another character was observing our impotence.

'What's up, lad?' Small asked.

I did not answer him, but composed myself and looked again to check that it was not an illusion.

The eye was still there, watching me through the far end of the hole. I drew away again.

'Small,' I whispered. 'We're being watched.'

'What?' he said, springing to my side. 'Let me see, there.'

I moved aside, and Small put his eye to the stone. Not an air hole, but a spy hole.

'Good God, man. You're right,' he muttered. 'Well, at least we can take one with us, eh?'

I heard him drop his satchel to the floor, and then the sound of a rifle being cocked.

'The bastards! Just watching and waiting for us to die, eh? Well, I'll show them. Move aside, lad.'

I was looking through the hole again.

'Wait, Small.'

I stared into the eye and its owner stared back unflinchingly. I narrowed mine, and he narrowed his. What was this form of torture through mockery?

'Come on, lad! Before he moves!'

Small's mouth was by my ear and his breath blew rock dust into my eye, which instantly filled with liquid. I blinked repeatedly to clear my vision.

'Well,' I said, wiping my eye at the hole. 'At least a gunshot will alert whoever those voices belong to. We'll not die of starvation, anyway.'

I looked once more into the eye, and was about to move so Small could take his shot, when I realised that the eye was watering.

I laughed.

'Small, look again before you shoot,' I said, ushering him to the hole. 'Now, tell me what you see.'

'Eh?' he said in confusion as he put his eye into the light.

'Just describe to me precisely what you see.'

'I see some blighter's eye, soon to be replaced by a speeding bullet, that's what I see.'

'Describe it.'

'Well, all I can see is the eye, a normal eye.'

'How normal?'

'Very.'

'Too normal,' I said. 'Look at its colour.'

'Why!' he said. 'It's blue. It's a bloody European watching us like rats in here. That's it! I've had enough. If I'm to die, I won't be watched by some sadistic, cowardly—'

He moved away and lifted his rifle.

'Why on earth are you laughing, lad?' he said to me, for my joviality had risen in direct proportion to his anger.

'Small,' I gasped. 'Do you not know when you are looking into a mirror? That eye is yours. If you'd not blown that dust into mine, I should never have realised. There's a mirror behind the hole. What other reason could it be there? It must be the key.'

He looked again.

'By Jiminy, lad! You're right.' He laughed and slapped the wall. 'I was about to shoot myself in the head! Ha! Now, then. Mechanics are more your department than mine, so how does this thing work?'

I swallowed my laughter.

'I haven't a clue, Small. Not the tiniest inkling. I should have thought that it was shining on something in here, and that cutting its stream would have some effect, but we've been doing that ever since you discovered it, and nothing has happened.'

I shook my head.

'Well, that's not good enough, lad. Think, man. What does that tell you?'

This conundrum was beyond my realm of watchmaking. I walked up and down, racked my brain and hit my head against the wall, but nothing I did brought a solution swimming to the surface. It took inspiration from Small to spark my mind.

'If it's not in here, then it must be out there,' he said drinking from his flask. 'Problem is, we're in here. And that's the last of the whisky.'

'That's it, Small!' I cried. 'You've got it.'

I spun the cap loose from the flask and threw the body in my pocket.

'It must work by reflection!' I said and breathed on the lid and rubbed it on the cleanest part of my trouser leg. Then in the stream of light I checked that the metal was suitably shiny and pushed it into the hole. It slotted into place comfortably, as though designed for the purpose, and then something remarkable happened.

There was a quiet click and a slight rumble and then the entire wall carving of the cat slid away from us. Only it was not a carving but, like its offspring, a statue, free standing, embedded in the wall.

'That's it, lad. That's it! You bloody genius. We're out. Move!'

The movement of the cat was near silent. Small, immediately alert to what might lie ahead, the continuing voices for one, readied his rifle and gestured for me to collect his satchel, and the all-too-light statuette. I retrieved the cap of the flask, too, and replaced it.

'You never know the scrapes the old Glenlivet'll get you out of, lad,' he whispered. He nodded at the metallic feline under my arm. 'Worthless, of course, but might as well take a keepsake by which to remember this whole affair. And you never know what some people will pay for an oddity.'

We stepped through the gap that had been created. A narrow tunnel ran upwards. The voices we had heard had not ceased their conversing, and the sound was travelling along the passage to our ears. In fact, they were significantly louder now, in part because there was no longer thick rock between them and us, but also because the conversation they were conducting had grown heated. It was undoubtedly a dispute.

Small entered the tunnel first. It was dark ahead.

'Light my way with that, boy,' he whispered, nodding at a torch which burned on the wall.

I pulled it from its fixing. Light flew up the tunnel ahead. Small had his rifle at his shoulder and frowned along its barrel onto our path. We edged slowly forwards. The men arguing, whoever they were, would surely not welcome guests, armed or otherwise; but a visitor with a weapon was more likely to depart in safety than one without, so I stuck to Small like a stamp on a letter.

We followed the tunnel upwards as it snaked first left then right, always allowing the rifle to lead us, lest we should happen upon the men. Their voices increased in volume as we grew closer: one was shouting now, the other rising somewhat, but still measured in comparison. At one moment Small murmured, 'Sounds like Shina,' but he did not deign to translate, for at that moment we reached a short flight of steps, at the top of which was a cloth hanging across our path, blocking our way. Light pierced through the drape and shadows moved on its surface like a Chinese play.

'We may have to shoot our way out of this. And there may be more than two in there. Even if not, reloading takes too long to fire twice. We'll have the surprise, but we need to be ready for a scrap,' Small whispered.

We moved as silently as possible. When finally our breath made the folds sway, Small stopped, removed his trigger hand from the rifle and raised three fingers. He lowered one, then another. When the third fell, he gripped the gun once more and pushed the cloth to one side with the rifle's barrel, and we stepped through.

26

THE LETTERS OF
SIR PAUL LINDLEY-SMALL

From a boudoir's parlour in
Kristiania, Norway

10TH JANUARY 1909

Dear Cyril,

Having successfully escaped the grips of a fiery-haired killer and an all-too-strong governess, I arrived in this land's capital city, Kristiania. There I reported the goings-on I had endured – at the hands of the killer, you understand, not the girl. A description of the dastardly chaperone's interruption would have warranted giving the officer in charge more whisky than I was willing to part with, so with Rød-Larsen's particulars passed on, I set about the business of finding the fellow I'm after.

Having lost any whiff of the Spaniard's trail, I was fortunate to encounter the maid Rosella who hosted my every whim at Dr Holm's. An enchantingly attentive girl, one of her many talents, it turned out, was being Spanish. While she was massaging out the knots of my frustration, I told her of their origins and in return she told me of a watering-hole in this city that is commonly frequented by both Spaniards and sailors. And so, my hunt recommenced.

Following the wee dram with the city official, I hailed a hackney cab to take me directly to King Knut's Tavern. However, the cabby, after passing his eyes over Crawford's handiwork, suggested that the establishment was not the one for a gentleman such as I. This initial resistance was soon quelled by my forceful manner and a hefty tip, however, and not long afterwards we arrived at a place the like of which I have rarely seen before. Such was its size that it seemed unlikely I would be able to identify a man I did not know among the heaving throng that presented itself when I opened the door.

I called it a watering-hole, but King Knut's Tavern is more of a reservoir, for it occupies the length and half the breadth of a rugby field, and it is arranged like an ancient, cobwebbed theatre. Indeed, my diamond-edged intuition once again served me faithfully, for I was subsequently informed that this is precisely the heritage of its heyday. Where once a stage had been, there is now a raised bar, manned by six men, each less than five feet in stature. They balance a dozen frothing tankards upon trays that are then lifted by women whose strength must equal that of the unfriendly governess. These remarkable women carry the trays above their heads with one muscular arm and hold aloft their heavy-skirted dresses with the other, noticeably less powerful. An amazing breed one has not seen in the inns of Britain for a century (and, I must say, it is to our sickly Motherland's detriment). With flashes of garter, these delicious wenches sally forth to stalls, circle and boxes, all filled with men and women and tobacco smoke, even at luncheon drunk on ale and the sheer good spirits of the toiling classes. You could not imagine better surroundings in which to enjoy one's pre-lunch drinking. Throwing my concerns aside, I dived in, prepared to wait all day for a glimpse of a strange circular beard.

As Rosella had promised, swarthy skin and Iberian accents were all around, but Spanish was not the only ethnicity to be found there. As I barged my way through the bodies, smoke and sweat towards the bar, I heard Russian and Polish, French and Italian, and all manner of African and Eastern dialects. Futures were being bought in darkened corners and pasts forgotten in song, but most of all my eye was caught by a vivacious lass who was swallowed into a swarm of admirers just as our eyes met.

They did not serve any kind of whisky here, let alone The Glenlivet, so on that first visit I partook of their watery ale and passed my time at the bar watching the crowds for the unknown face that had brought me hither. The following day, I carried with me a bottle of the good stuff. I arrived early in the morning and was among the last to leave. My appearance marked me out and I was invited to join a table at which I gambled a little, picking the minds of the sinister characters that constituted my fellow players. It passed the time, but they were too suspicious to be of help, and it was not until the morning of the third day that things finally got going.

King Knut's was experiencing the lull before the social tempest late morning would bring. I collected two of the establishment's smaller receptacles, empty ones, from the diminutive chaps at the bar, as well as a polite tankardful, cleaned them on my cuff without regard for Crawford's lambswool, and took them with a swagger to the table of the delightful wench I had spotted on entering the bar that first day. She was always in the place, it seemed, and we had joined eyes over the shoulders of her eternal suitors again when I was stuck at the card table, but it seems we were awaiting the right moment for what both knew was an inevitable meeting. This was it. She was sitting alone at a banquet table. I was happy to forsake the pleasure of more cards and mind-picking for her companionship, and took my place opposite her. If there is a thing that titillates my taste buds more than a tipple or a fresh encounter with a maiden of exotic descent, I should like to hear of it – though its existence would be quite as extraordinary as this tale. As with anything worth recounting, when finally the history of Diego del Fuego commenced, it was with one of the latter and several of the former.

Despite her dark hair, eyes and skin, she was, she told me as I poured our drinks, a native of this country. She did not share the blonde hair, blue eyes and fair features that most of her fellow countrymen exhibit because her blood was partially Sami. These nomadic northern people are known for their mysticism and enigmatic ways. I do not know if they are also known for their wantonness, but it was clear from the moment I joined this woman – and woman she was, no mere girl – that society's strictures held no sway with her. Indeed, by her third dram, when it came to the etiquette of the boudoir, she had detailed a string of possibilities so remarkable that I was quite willing to give up all else and spend the rest of my days sampling her *koldtbord* of delights. So it was just as well that a curious circular beard and its owner chose that precise moment to shuffle into the tavern and seat himself across the gangway.

An old man, he caught my eye immediately – for he was a character, and no mistake. What's more, he carried a sailor's kitbag, and when he sat down, I saw it was marked with the word *Syren* which, as you will no doubt recall, was the name of the vessel I had seen making its way into the Arabian Sea at Dwarka. This, surely, was my chap, for how many other Spaniards could there be aboard such a Nordic vessel – and with such a curiously circular beard to boot? Pleased to have finally found the bugger, my pleasure vanished when I noticed that his kitbag did not move an inch of its own accord. That is to say, it looked worryingly as though it did not contain a living beast.

The Spaniard glanced my way briefly and I back, but if he said anything, I missed it. As an obviously worldly man, so creased, weathered and brown was his face – I believed then that he was simply admiring tailoring at its finest, so I decided not to interrupt his appreciation. He could, I thought, enjoy a drink alone before I pushed my companionship upon him.

Knut delivered to him what looked to be a brandy, though I had seen no such drink on offer at the bar, and the man sipped at it as he methodically preened his funny little circular beard. Three inches in diameter, perfectly circular, each hair no longer than a fraction of an inch, the beard sat on the end of his sharp chin. It stretched up to the foot of his lower lip and down, under his chin, to the upper tip of his larynx. Hair grew nowhere else upon his chin, as one might expect it to – neither on his upper lip nor on his cheeks.

He was short and slim under the canvas deck jacket that hung loosely from his arched back. Indeed, so curved was his spine that his neck sprang horizontally from his shirt, and several inches lower than the gnarled ridge of vertebrae that pushed up through the thinning material of his coat. In an impressive feat of osseous geometry, however, his face looked out at the same angle as everyone else's, instead of facing downwards as one might expect. The bizarre, perfectly circular nature of his beard was at linear odds with the rest of his solemn-looking, asymmetrically scarred face and his crooked, pitiful body.

This was Diego del Fuego, the heated female informed me, noticing my distraction and cutting short her flow of possibilities; he was, she said, one of the most extraordinary men she had met in all her many and varied days. Fortunately for me, she had grown to know him well on his intermittent sojourns and he had bestowed on her the extraordinary tale that was his life so far, so she could further tell me why Diego del Fuego wore a woollen hat at all times, whether inside or out, warm or cold. It was, she said, to hide another bizarre and, to others, humorous dimension to his appearance. His head hair was perfectly normal, apart from one strange aspect. At the spot that is neither on the top of the head nor on the back, but between, and perfectly centrally, was a circular area precisely three inches across that was entirely devoid of hair, like the tonsure of a monk. Only here, unlike any recorded monk, in a strange example of complete growth equilibrium, the hair seemed to have been lifted from his scalp and transferred to his chin.

The beard's growth and the scalp's loss and their dual history were even more bizarre than their appearance, however. That very day, you see, on which he sat in King Knut's, occasionally taking time to appreciate the quality of the suit worn by the man at the next table, Diego del Fuego turned seventy-five years old. The half-drunk double brandy was to be his only celebratory alcoholic intake of the day and, indeed, it would be the last of his life. He knew it was to be so, for forty-five years ago to the day, he had made that choice.

Diego del Fuego's first fifteen years were spent in the mining town of Peñarroya-Pueblonuevo, near Córdoba. Rather than follow his father into the mines and continue to endure from him the physical abuse that had killed his mother on the eve of his fifteenth birthday, Diego del Fuego had packed a knapsack and travelled on foot to Cadiz. The journey of six days, made in the crisp winter sunshine, was an ample mourning period. By the time he reached the port, he had established that his mother, a firm believer in her Maker, was now in a better situation than ever she had been whilst living, and that her death had earned him his freedom, something she had frequently spoken of in hushed tones, even when her husband was several miles away and more than a hundred yards underground.

The young Diego discerned, therefore, that the best way to appreciate his mother's sacrifice would be to lead as free a life as he possibly could. With this thought forcibly placed to the forefront of his mind, he entered the thriving port town with his head held high, a skip in his step and dreams of an unknown, adventurous future with the Spanish Merchant Navy. The only thing that pained him as he drew away from his homeland in an enormous vessel destined for the worlds of spice, was the knowledge that his father, even though alone, even though hungry, even though unhappy, lived unpunished still. But, being the mature man of fifteen he had become both in fact and in feeling over the previous six days, he wisely considered his freedom and future of greater import. Besides, he believed the distance that the Merchant Navy was already providing would allow him to forget his father altogether. On this point, however, he was mistaken.

Diego del Fuego's next fifteen years aboard the *Odysseus* took him to all corners of the earth, made him many friends, saw him grow four inches in height and become a lean, hardy figure of a sailor. They bore him two children, one mothered by a sixteen-year-old girl on the islands of Vanuatu, the other by a forty-three-year-old Marseillaise of ill repute. He knew of neither child, since they had been born long after his departure. The fifteen years gave him ample opportunity to develop his serious mind. He discovered a passion for geometry and learned of many and different religions, faiths quite opposed in nature to his mother's. This fact caused him to cast to the ocean gales any beliefs he had held in a Greater Being, and though eventually he rose to the position of navigator upon the ship, he remained forever more a godless man.

It was at the end of these fifteen years, upon his thirtieth birthday, that he found himself in the town of Dwarka at the very westernmost tip of India, scrofulous and dirty, with a mane of hair and a Zeus-like beard. He was, in short, very much in need of a bath, a shave and a haircut. Taking leave of his seafaring comrades, who headed for the nearest saloon, Diego del Fuego wandered through the unseasonably chilly streets of Dwarka until he happened upon a small barber's shop that overlooked a small lake. It was tended by a small man, who sat in the barber's chair on the porch smoking a long churchwarden's pipe, apparently considering the flock of small pink and blue birds drifting upon the water's surface.

As Diego del Fuego approached, the small man leapt out of the chair, slapped its seat back and forth with a rag and proffered it to his new customer. He removed the pipe from his mouth, bowed to the floor and on returning to his usual height, adjusted his bowtie and grinned a grin of a thousand teeth.

'A haircut for sir,' he said.

American and English sailors passed through the ranks on the *Odysseus* from time to time, and they never spoke a word of Spanish. Job secured and at sea, these sailors would thenceforth claim not to understand a single word of the broken English the officers spoke to them, and in such a way they succeeded in shirking their duties. They would be dismissed at the next port with little or no pay, but full bellies. More often than not, the port in which they were dismissed was their intended destination anyway. If not, these resourceful knaves would repeat the process until they arrived where they desired. Irrespective of their inventiveness, however, it was from these men that Diego del Fuego, not yet an officer, had learned a smattering of English, and with it he explained to the barber that he also required a shave and, more importantly, a bath.

'Yes, yes,' replied the barber. 'First a bath and then to the hair. But first, tea.'

He showed Diego del Fuego into his small, unremarkable shop, in the middle of which were two chairs and a small round table, two cups, and a teapot steaming from its spout.

'Sit. Sit,' said the barber, and Diego del Fuego did so.

The barber poured the two cups full of a yellowish tea and sat in the other seat. He smiled as he sipped his drink and stared at Diego del Fuego, but did not say a word. Diego del Fuego did not feel like talking either. It was an effort to enunciate his English and this man would surely not speak Spanish. Instead, he drank his tea and relaxed, looking forward to the hot soak he would soon be enjoying.

The small wooden structure was whitewashed within, bright from the windows it had on two sides and the open door through which they had entered. There was a pot filled with razors, scissors and combs on one sill and on another sat a plant sprouting a long yellow spindly fruit.

As soon as his customer had drained his cup, the barber stood up.

'Come, come,' he said, opening a door on the wall against which the table stood.

Diego del Fuego followed the barber and through a barricade of exotic-smelling steam he saw a tub filled with hot water awaiting him.

'First tea, and now you bathe,' the barber said, bowing as he retreated out of the room, closing the door behind him.

The room was lit by a small window placed high on the far wall to preserve a bather's privacy, and there was no door in the room but the one through which Diego del Fuego had entered. As he disrobed, he saw that the water in the freestanding enamel tub was of a yellowish hue and decided that, though in far less concentration, the steam smelled much as the tea had tasted. It was not an unpleasant scent, just as the tea had not been unpleasant in taste. It was more that it was an entirely unrecognisable one. He did not linger on this thought for long, though, for as soon as he stood naked in the steam, he stepped into the tub and submerged his filthy body in the water.

It was delightfully hot. The heat eased its way into his flesh and entered his bones. It warmed him to the very marrow, to his very organs, in a way he had not experienced in all his years on the seas. Though one dressed to one's best ability, it was nigh on impossible to ever be truly warmed to the core on a boat in the middle of an ocean when the winds were high. Following a bath such as this, and with these soothing oils or salts in addition, he was sure that he would never again feel the bite of the sea air. The water was instilling his flesh and bones with an independent source of heat. While others froze on the deck, he would surely glow as if sitting by a blazing fire in the warmth of an inn.

He reclined in the tub and dozed until, he did not know how much later, a polite tap at the door roused him.

'Is sir ready for his haircut?' came the barber's voice.

Diego del Fuego stood in the bath and towelled himself down. Though he had certainly lain in the tub for some time, his fingers were not in the least bit pruned. In fact, quite the reverse was true. His skin was now so soft that it felt as though it had been replaced with that of an infant. Gone were the weathered cracks that he had developed. Where callus upon callus had formed over the years, his hands were now like those of a lady of high birth. His shoulders and neck, where the dry skin had been peeling through sun exposure, were now oily and moist. And it was not only externally that he felt fifteen years younger. As he bent to dry himself, where his bones had become stiff with exertion, he now found new bounce and suppleness. All his muscles, which after so many years of relentless toil had felt in need of replacement, now felt as though they had never been used, and were eager to work. He took a deep breath of air and steam, and as he exhaled he was sure that his lungs had doubled in capacity. As he bent this way and that, and took greater and greater gulps of air, his body continued to retain the unassailable warmth that the water had afforded him.

In short, he felt quite extraordinary.

Amazed at the rejuvenation of his body, he re-donned his clothes and, leaving the room surrounded by a billow of the steam, he entered the one in which he had drunk tea. The barber was awaiting him.

'Is sir very much refreshed?' he asked.

'Very much,' answered Diego del Fuego dreamily.

'And now I cut your hair and shave your beard,' was what the barber said, leading Diego del Fuego to the seat overlooking the small lake. 'If you allow me to do this, sir, I can make you very, very happy.'

These last are the very words the salacious woman from the tavern spoke to me just now, when finally she appeared from her preparations in her boudoir. And I, mere mortal that I am, find it impossible not to believe her.

So for now, farewell, old friend.

Lindley-Small

27

THE NOTEBOOKS OF CYRIL KING

1893

A Dead Man Dies Again

A small table stood in the centre of the room. On it a lantern glowed. To its right was a closed wooden door, before which stood Rustam Khan. His face was contorted with rage and in his hand, raised before him, was his long, clean dagger. What Rustam Khan's eyes looked upon with such unalloyed hatred was a second man, unarmed and to the left of the table. Perhaps nearing the end of his fourth decade, his hair and eyes were dark – a bearded native, dressed in a finely woven brown *chapan*, belted, and decorated with golden thread.

Their voices ceased as soon as we entered. The stranger flicked a sideways glance at our unexpected intrusion with shrewd, intelligent eyes that held no trace of fear. Given the circumstances, the poise he displayed was remarkable. Seeing the blade in Rustam Khan's hand, Small immediately pointed his rifle at the polo player, who appeared to barely even register our appearance.

'Don't fire, Small. This is the man who released me,' I said in as steady a voice as I could muster. 'Rustam Khan, what is happening here?'

'This is the man who murdered my family,' the polo player said between his teeth, without taking his eyes from the other man, jerking the dagger at him, his grip tightening. 'The one I must kill for doing so. This is not your country, sahib. Leave, as I told you. Go with your friend. Leave me to do what the murder of my wife and children demands.'

'Your wife?' I said. 'But—'

The other man spoke once more to Rustam Khan in the native tongue. He was the possessor of the calm and measured voice we had heard on our approach, and still he was not perturbed. Rustam Khan spat an answer back at him. Then, to me, he said: 'He admits it himself!'

The other man turned to us.

'Gentlemen. You have arrived in the nick of time,' he said, in English, and without a trace of native accent.

'I don't recall anybody speaking to you,' Small said. 'So whoever the bloody hell you are, you'll only speak when spoken to, d'you hear?'

The man did not appear concerned either by Small's rifle or his tone. Instead he raised a palm at my companion.

'Come,' he began.

'Y-you're English?' I interrupted. 'But you look—'

'Like a native? Yes. A useful skill in these parts, and one that has served me well. I was, however, born an Englishman. And if you would be so kind as to disarm this man . . .'

'Ha!' barked Small. It seemed that the soothing tones with which the fellow was attempting to defuse the situation had no effect on my companion. 'The words of the unarmed under threat if ever I heard them!'

Seeing that his nationality held no sway with the rifleman, the stranger turned back to Rustam Khan.

'Rustam Khan. Listen to me. You came here an outsider, as I did, and we have lived side by side for many years. You know me. Once I was a soldier, but even then I had walked too long amongst your people to consider myself an Englishman. I do not despise you as so many soldiers do, nor do I enslave you as those who walk the

halls of Calcutta. Have I not worked to return pride to the people
of this valley? Am I not teaching their young men how to be warriors, as their fathers were? They are my people, Rustam Khan, just
as they are yours. And your wife's. You found her here and with
her a new life. Lower your dagger, Rustam Khan. Do not bring
tragedy upon this wife, too.'

This time his words caused Small to react.

'A soldier, eh?' Small said, grimacing as he swung his rifle from
Rustam Khan to point it at the speaker. 'A bloody British soldier . . .'

'Enough!' Rustam Khan cried at all of us. 'For years I have lived
in shame because I could not avenge my family. And today I learn
that I have been living in the company of the very man who caused
their deaths. In the very place I found peace, I am sitting at the table
of their murderer, sharing his food. Laughing with him. I thought
him my friend! And all the time he knew who I was. What he had
done to me!'

'Rustam Khan,' I said. 'What are you telling us?'

He did not look at me when he spoke again, and I do not know
if his words were for my ears, or for He who would make the final
judgement.

'It was this man who accused my son of thievery. He was the
soldier who drew his pistol on him – a boy of four! And for what?
The crime of lifting a lost trinket from the dirt on the trail where
it had fallen. When the boy fled in fear and the soldier fired, horses
and oxen panicked, and wagons filled with people fell down the
mountainside. So many. He killed so many, and yet he pretends
he is of the people he slaughtered.'

'The Hunza trail,' I whispered. 'The massacre . . .'

'I was playing that day and so I was not there to protect my
family. Afterwards, his people told mine that he was dead. But
today you have proved them liars, and by the grace of Allah,
vengeance will be mine at last. Vengeance for the death of my wife
and my daughters, and for my son . . . Still I do not know what
became of him. Four lives, sahib, for one watch, carried into the
night by a child. A wooden case, I was told by one who survived,
with a stone upon it, in the shape of an eye . . .'

'But that man, Rustam Khan,' I said, stammering as realisation dawned. 'The soldier who caused the Hunza trail massacre. It can't be this man here. That was—'

'Tolliver,' said the man in the brown *chapan*.

He turned to look at me, lifting his left arm. The sleeve of his coat slipped back and where you would hope to see a hand attached to the wrist was a leather cup covering a stump.

I felt the blood drain from my face.

'My God!' I exclaimed.

'What's going on here, King?' Small demanded. This man, unarmed and with two weapons trained upon him, nevertheless seemed to have complete control of the suitation – a turn of events that left Small unnerved.

'But you're dead. They found your body.' I protested. In answer to Small's question, I hadn't a clue.

'My *jemadar*, Manraj Singh, found my body,' the stranger said. 'He led the search. It was unidentifiable, of course. How he obtained it, I do not know, but it was a simple matter to put my uniform on it. Once I was dead, and the blood debt of Hunza paid for, I was free to make my way back here.'

'You mean you're Tolliver?' Small exclaimed, lowering his rifle a fraction. 'Why, King, if that's so—' If, a moment ago, Small had been concerned, the realisation of this man's identity suddenly filled him with excitement, and that familiar sparkle returned to his eyes. I was knocked sideways by the revelation that before me stood a man I had thought was dead, but such trifles were meaningless to Small.

'*Except it is NOT paid for!*' roared Rustam Khan. 'Do not stand in my way, sahib,' he said, as Small swung the rifle back towards him.

'Yes, I am Tolliver,' said he to Small. 'And if you want what I imagine you have come for, then you must first shoot this man dead.'

'I'm afraid he's right,' Small said to me, and then looked back down the barrel at Rustam Khan. 'I don't doubt this blighter killed your family, man, and I understand. I do. It burns, and you want his blood. On any other day, believe me, I'd be more than willing to let you have his head. Why, any god would thank us for sending him on. But I'm not in the god-serving business, lad, and I say it can't happen today. I need him. And if you make the move, I'll shoot you through. So not another step, now.'

Rustam Khan did not hear him, however. His eyes were still locked onto Tolliver, but he was breathing freely now, relaxed, even, and speaking quietly, almost under his breath.

'*Mayra khandaan*,' he said, as if it were a kind of incantation. '*My family.*'

Tolliver backed away until he hit the wall.

I could do nothing but watch. Small was not so entranced. He had his mind on our goal. He tilted his rifle from Rustam Khan's chest to aim at his head.

'Careful, now,' Small growled.

Rustam Khan's voice rose, his words hissing out of clenched teeth as he stepped forwards. '*Mayra khandaan!*'

For the first time since we had entered the room, fear filled Tolliver's face. 'Shoot him, I tell you!' he demanded.

'Do something if you want him to live, King,' Small whispered. 'Or I'll consider my hand forced. We need this blighter!'

'*Mayra khandaan!*'

'Do it, man!' It was Tolliver. 'Shoot him and I will tell you everything you need. Everything.'

'King!' Small urged. 'I don't want to kill him, but—'

'Rustam Khan,' I blurted hopelessly. 'Please!'

But I was too late. His anger exploded, and he screamed at the top of his voice and lunged at Tolliver.

'No!' cried Small.

'Shoot him!' Tolliver shouted.

The rifle fired. The wood of the door splintered.

Rustam Khan's weight bore Tolliver backwards and I saw the dagger thrust beneath his ribs, once, twice, three times.

I dropped the statuette, the torch and Small's satchel and threw myself at Rustam Khan, barging him off his victim. We all three tumbled to the ground in a heap.

Small followed and as we disentangled ourselves he pointed the
gun at Rustam Khan's head.

'You bloody idiot, man!' Small said, to whom I did not know, for
though his rifle was trained on Rustam Khan he was looking at the
prone form of Tolliver. Blood was spreading fast over Tolliver's
chapan. 'We needed him.'

'You may kill me, sahib,' Rustam Khan said to Small, sitting up
as I released him. 'Certainly, if you do not, his people shall.'

Small was reloading the rifle.

'No, Small. There'll be no more death here,' I said, rising and
moving closer to Tolliver. 'Let him go.'

'Oh, there shall be more death, sahib.' Rustam Khan lifted himself heavily to his feet. 'You are a good man, Cyril King. After this
day I cannot live, but perhaps you can. If that is to be, in repay-
ment for your release I ask that you take Fahlhana from here.
Take her far from this place of death. She cannot now remain.'
He threw open the door and touched his hand to his chest, his
mouth and his forehead. 'Aleikum Salaam,' he said.

He turned and the darkness outside swallowed him.

*

'Well that worked like a charm, lad,' Small said, lowering his rifle
and taking his place at my side as we both considered Tolliver.
'Inspired. *"Rustam Khan, please."* Persuasive. Just brilliant. A real
day-saver! Wish I'd thought of it myself. Now, then . . .'

Small handed me the rifle and dropped to his haunches. He
lifted Tolliver by his *chapan* and threw him up against the wall.
Tolliver coughed blood into his face.

'Still alive then?' Small said, wiping his cheek with a sleeve.
'Good. You bloody fool. If you knew who he was, why didn't you
get rid of him years ago?'

Tolliver laughed weakly up at Small.

'Because I am not a murderer, no matter what you may think.
Besides, those who will kill him now would never have accepted
it. They love him. He is their hero, a polo player. A talisman. He

took one of their own as wife. It won't matter now, though. They'll both be killed for this. And you, too, if you're caught.'

'Well, let's get things moving then, and we'll be away. Get talking, man, and if you tell us what we need, I'll end it quickly for you. Wounds like that, you could bleed to death for hours. Tell us what we want to know, and I promise I'll end your suffering. One soldier to another. Now, speak up, man. Where's the damned loot?'

'Fools,' Tolliver croaked.

Small laughed and turned to me.

'The man's a lunatic, lad.' Then he turned back to Tolliver and jerked him forward so their faces were only inches apart. Tolliver winced in pain. 'There was treasure down there, and you found it when you first came here. You brought the eye of that statue back with you to Gilgit. Then you returned here for the rest. Where've you hidden it? What've you done with it, man?'

Small shook him, but more bloody laughter was Tolliver's response. Small cursed and released him. Tolliver crumpled to the floor and groaned.

'Well, long may you bleed, then,' Small muttered down at him, before moving away. Behind me I heard him kick at the wall in frustration.

I bent close to Tolliver's face.

'It does exist, doesn't it? I was right. I followed the trail, Tolliver. All the way here. I have the watch. Taqdir was wrong. I'm a watchmaker, too, but I was right.'

'A watchmaker?' he said.

'Adam-Khor is no legend, is he, Tolliver? He was here.'

'Adam-Khor? The Man-eater, you mean?'

His laughter was quieter this time.

'You imbecile, of course he's a legend. They're all legends. But there's no need of his story here, if that's what you've been thinking. These people have their own legends – hundreds of them.'

'Then what about Adam-Khor's protector? The statue at the end of that tunnel?'

'Half cat, and half serpent.'

'Yes. The legend says Adam-Khor created it for protection from rebellion.'

'He did not create it. He took it. The creature's a Suchi, a god these people believe shields them and their pantheon from invaders. It was beautiful. Covered from head to toe. *To please her, keep her strong, and strangers away* . . . You saw what used to be done down there in her name. They think outsiders will make them change. Take away their gods. Force them towards Islam, or Christianity now. A fearsome lot I stumbled upon, living up here in secret, until the Army destroyed their village and wiped out all their menfolk. Didn't know of the other place, though, up in the snow. Found the women and children when I came back. Fearsome enough, but too young to fight, none of them trained to be warriors. Made an agreement. I became one of them, showed them how to protect themselves, taught them as their fathers would have, to keep them safe from invaders. Manraj Singh and I . . .'

He was rambling. I was losing him. I shook him.

'Why, Tolliver? If you had the treasure, why did you stay? Why do you remain here? What have you done with it? Is it still here?'

'It's not the finding, boy. Not only the finding . . .'

Momentarily he drifted, leaving me to try and fathom the meaning of his words; then suddenly he smiled into the distance, this time with real warmth. I wanted to ask him to clarify what he had meant about the finding, but it seems a dying man chooses his own topic of conversation.

'Do you know why I returned to Hunza?' he said.

'No,' I smiled in my turn. Whether good or bad, sane or mad, any man so close to death is deserving of compassion.

'A woman,' he said. 'But I was too late.' A trickle of blood ran from his mouth. 'She carried my unborn child when I left. But her people killed her. Do you know what they think up here of a woman who bears a child out of wedlock? And when the father is a foreign oppressor? They stoned my woman and my child to death.' He looked up at me. 'The child was a boy . . .'

'Is that why so many others died that day on the Hunza trail?'

He sighed.

'A moment of madness. I was blind with grief and fury. I saw only killers and thieves, where before there had been women and children. I fired a shot to frighten the boy; I thought he would not give me back the watch. He ran, and I feared I would lose him in the crowd. I fired again to stop him. Then there was panic, a stampede, chaos. The soldiers fired to try and regain control. But that only made it worse. People and animals falling. So much death . . .'

There was a crash from behind me as Small gave the wall a final mighty kick before jumping round.

'That's enough!' he exclaimed. 'The treasure's been moved, we know that much. And you must still be here because *it's* still here.' Small had approached us. He grabbed Tolliver from me. 'I don't have time for your heartache, man! You're dying. You'll meet your son soon enough. But before that, is there anything you know that can help us? Do you know where it is?'

Tolliver's eyes were glazing, but he gurgled another laugh.

'You really are the most damnable pair of fools.' He touched his hand to his stomach and looked at the red on his fingers and frowned. He knew his time was near. 'Came here from the east with my men. Scouting. Found the statue. Stripped it,' he whispered, his breath short and shallow now. 'Thought this whole place was deserted. It wasn't. They came before we could get it away. Singh and I made it out. The others . . .' He looked towards the tunnel at the end of which lay what remained of his men. Then his eyes closed and he slumped.

Small shook him, rather more gently than before.

'Tolliver?' His voice was anxious. 'Tolliver!'

Suddenly the dying man's eyes opened again, and looked up at Small, as though surprised to find him there.

'So it was moved?' Small prompted him.

Tolliver nodded.

'Yes, but not by me. I watched them, saw where they . . .' His voice was almost imperceptible. 'You bloody fools. Been with you from the beginning. All the way through those catacombs. All the way along.'

He wheezed a final laugh.
'You damn fools,' he said again.
Then he turned to me.
'And you, a watchmaker . . .'

28

THE LETTERS OF
SIR PAUL LINDLEY-SMALL

From the locomotive Western Star
Norway

IITH JANUARY 1909

Forgive my scrawl, but I write in great haste, for the hunt is rushing onwards as fast and as surely as this train.

Diego del Fuego was sitting in the Dwarkan barber's chair, if you remember, glowing from his bath, awaiting a trim and a shave. He immediately noted the strange fact that there was no mirror before him, and therefore he could not see what the barber was doing to him. After such a bath, however, he was willing to relax and place his trust in the man who had infused his being with an apparently everlasting warmth. So with no mirror, he watched the pink and blue birds on the lake instead, as they occasionally took to flight and wheeled across the sky before resettling on the water.

As they took off for the first time, Diego del Fuego felt the barber pour a cool liquid onto his head. He could not see it, but he was sure that it turned instantly to vapour on impact with his warm skin. However, he was soon to forget that sensation, for it was quickly eclipsed by that of the barber delving his fingers through Diego del Fuego's thick and knotted hair to the scalp from which it grew. When all eight fingers and each thumb had found it, they began to rub, almost imperceptibly, the tips moving the skin on his head round and round, in tiny circular motions. It was intoxicating, though not like the inebriation of liquor, which he had experienced many times. It was more sublime than that, and had none of its accompanying aggression. He felt sleepy and yet was utterly aware of every tingle the fingers dealt out. As he closed his eyes and gave way to the barber's magical hands, he thought that perhaps he had been fed opium. Of all the exotic plants, herbs and drinks he had been exhilarated by on his travels, the effects of opium most closely resembled this trancelike state.

'You are a sailor,' the barber said, when finally he extracted his fingers from what was now an even more unkempt mop. It was not a question, but coming to, Diego del Fuego answered him nonetheless.

'A sailor,' he murmured. 'Yes.'

The barber had picked up a comb and was working the knots out of Diego del Fuego's black hair.

'You have come a long way, I think. From a land deep with holes.'

Though now facing him, the barber did not look at his client's face, but rather concentrated on the hair that he was currently drawing straight, over Diego del Fuego's eyes.

The Spaniard did not answer him this time. It was strange that the barber should guess such a thing, but Diego del Fuego was not perturbed. A man with such an understanding of his trade was sure to be able to see the telltale signs of a customer's roots, so accustomed must he be to working with hair from all over the world. A man such as this barber, one who served such an invigorating bath and apparently knew his trade inside out, could no doubt tell which nutrients and minerals had passed from food and water to hair. Indeed, what surprised Diego del Fuego more was that he should be the fellow's only customer that day, for surely he was keeper of quite the most remarkable establishment, even for these mystical parts.

'You are a religious man?' the barber asked, but Diego del Fuego did not know quite how to answer him. Without question he was not, but he had no wish to offend the Indian, himself almost certainly a devout Hindu.

'You think, perhaps, that it is only the man who must have an answer who can believe in the gods?' the barber said, guessing his client's thoughts.

The barber was correct.

'And you think this a weakness,' he went on.

'I am envious of the religious man,' Diego del Fuego finally and diplomatically answered. 'If you believe, what have you to fear?'

'Oh, very much,' laughed the barber. 'Very much. Only less than the non-believer.'

When Diego del Fuego said no more, the barber continued.

'The non-believer fears nothing,' he said as he combed. 'The believer fears the gods and their powers. The faithful man lives to please his gods. The non-believer lives for himself because the only thing he fears is nothing. He fears that when he is dead, there will be nothing.'

Diego del Fuego did not fear the nothing that he believed would occur once he was dead. Indeed, sometimes he delighted in it. He rejoiced that he was merely a meaningless organism in the enormity of the universe that he navigated by, and more so that all around him were the same, no matter what position they held.

'It is comforting to me that we are no different from the trees, the animals, the plants. That we are made of much the same thing as even the rocks around us,' he said carefully. 'We are just the fragile spire of a natural process, a spire that will one day grow so narrow that it will snap. I do not believe that we shall ever truly know where it is we have come from. We shall never know from where the earth came. From where the stars and the universe came. What the nature of the soul is. We can ask questions, but that does not mean we will ever know the answers.'

'The religious have an answer for all questions, but to have the answer you must first believe,' the barber continued for him.

'Yes. Believe in something you cannot see. To believe that God created all is to me a simple answer that requires no proof, only faith. It is the unassailable answer,' Diego del Fuego said, throwing caution to the wind. 'Giving comfort to those who cannot live with questions unanswered.'

It was rare that he was able to have a conversation on one of his favourite topics, for sailors are a superstitious bunch. Blind believers, Diego del Fuego thought, and anything that could be thought to bring bad luck was best avoided. Though he pined for such conversations, Diego del Fuego thought it best to forgo them rather than be thrown from the ship as a Jonah. Besides, this barber had instigated the conversation as though he knew it were a matter close to Diego del Fuego's heart and wanted to please his customer. It did not seem that he was in the least bit offended. Indeed, he looked more amused than anything, so, checking that this was still the case by looking into the barber's eyes as he continued intently with his combing, Diego del Fuego himself continued, satisfied that he could not affront.

'Can Nature perhaps be something that is not controlled, but something that merely occurs, that its process is a result of mere luck? Besides, how can I believe in any god when what a man in Rome believes in is different to that which a man in Jerusalem believes, whose god is a different one from that which a man from Mecca follows? And the man from Delhi has different gods again, so a man from Amritsar, so a man from Tibet, the Peloponnese, the Incas and the Norse. All ask the questions, and each has a different answer. There are too many. Too many to choose one man's god over another's. So they must all be false.'

'Ah, but each is a god, in that they are the same, and each answers your questions, but for you it is an answer that is created because the question has been asked, yes?'

The barber lifted the hair from Diego del Fuego's eyes. He was holding scissors now, and was considering the sailor's scalp.

'That is what I believe, yes,' Diego del Fuego replied. 'Perhaps I am wrong, but if I am, it means there is more than just this life, and I will be pleasantly surprised. If the religious man is wrong, he will be sorely disappointed.'

'But if there is the nothing that you tell me you do not fear, I will not be capable of disappointment.' The barber smiled and looked briefly into Diego del Fuego's eyes. He brought the scissors to the hair and sent the first lock into Diego del Fuego's lap, from where it slid off the muslin cloak the barber had draped over him, and onto the floor.

The barber was silent for a while as he snipped and Diego del Fuego feared that he had offended him despite himself. He had gone too far, he thought. It was foolish to talk of religion with anyone, be they religious or not, for it was sure to offend one or the other at some point. Diego del Fuego was sad to have upset this man. He seemed kind and well-meaning, and was taking pride in his trade.

The velocity at which the barber's fingers moved began to increase. He snipped rapidly for a while and hair fell all around Diego del Fuego like a dark blizzard. He cut from his head and then from his beard, readying it for shaving.

When the barber spoke again, it seemed that he was not downhearted, but Diego del Fuego noted that it was not of religion he spoke.

'You have left someone in this land of holes, I think. A man of whom you have a great fear and hatred.' He spoke matter-of-factly, concentrating on the hair before him.

In the fifteen years Diego del Fuego had been on the sea, he had frequently thought of his father. Indeed, whenever he thought of his mother, which was often, it was impossible not to think of the pain his father had inflicted on her and the fact that he had never been punished for the crimes he had committed against his family.

The hair fell around Diego del Fuego as he thought of him again now, and his body rose to an even greater temperature.

'You dislike this man. You would like to see him punished, I think,' the barber went on. 'Is it not so?'

'It is so,' answered Diego del Fuego.

'Were you a religious man, you would believe that he will be punished in the next life.'

'For that reason, alas that I am not.'

'Alas, indeed, sir.'

The barber came round to Diego del Fuego's front and lightly took hold of his chin. He moved his head this way and that to assess his work thus far. When he removed his hand, the barber again looked into Diego del Fuego's eyes.

'It is possible I can aid you in your desire, sir,' he said. 'I am a spiritual man,' as though this, in some way, would explain his claim.

Then he disappeared out of Diego del Fuego's line of vision.

'You shall live to an old age,' he continued. 'To ninety years. A very old age.'

When he had disembarked from the *Odysseus* that morning, Diego del Fuego would have laughed in the face of anyone who said those words to him, for he had never heard of any member of the Merchant Navy living to more than sixty, but since the tea, since the bath and since the rubbing of his head, he felt as though it were quite possible; indeed, he considered ninety years a conservative estimate.

'For only fifteen of those years, I shall see this man punished in your name,' continued the barber as calmly as before.

He then continued snipping away as though nothing untoward had been mentioned, but Diego del Fuego's head was spinning. Had this harmless, rather surprising and wonderful barber really said the words he had just heard? The barber was an old man, and should he even survive the journey to Peñarroya-Pueblonuevo, he could surely not overpower a man of Diego del Fuego's father's size; the latter was still only forty-eight years old. The desire to see justice done to his father was overwhelming, though, and he could not resist asking how the barber thought he could achieve his claim.

'How could you punish him? You do not even know who he is,' he said.

'I know,' said the barber from behind him. 'He is your father. He lives in the holes. He killed your mother, you believe.'

'And so it is!' Diego del Fuego exclaimed, distinctly put out by the barber's implication that this may not have been so. 'But how can you punish him? You are old and weak. He is young and strong.'

'I can punish him as easily as I can tell you who he is and where he is. As easily as I can read your descendency from the follicles of your head. He can be punished – do not doubt this. But do you desire it to be so?'

The snipping of his scissors continued apace.

'Do you desire it to be so?' he repeated.

He was once again facing Diego del Fuego. Putting the scissors down, he picked up a razor, then crouched to sharpen its blade on a strop hanging from the arm of the chair.

'And for fifteen years? What do you mean by that?' asked Diego del Fuego, curious now, as any man would be, and not a little perturbed.

'It is simple, sir. If you despise this man sufficiently for me to punish him, you must pay for my service. I am old. Older than you can imagine. I require more years. You must give me fifteen of your years. For that your father shall be punished. You shall live to seventy-five years. A very respectable age, sir.' He looked up at Diego del Fuego from the strop and razor. 'Moreover, sir, you shall not die before this age. You may be shot, you may be stabbed, you may even wish to take your own life, but in further exchange for the years you forsake, those left to you shall be of unerring good health. It will be impossible for you to die. Quite impossible. This is the first condition, sir,' he said, standing and testing the blade on the hairs on his arm.

'The first?' said Diego del Fuego. His desire was great to see his father punished, but if there were to be conditions to the affair, he could well do it himself, he thought, though really he knew this was untrue. Should he ever face his father again, he would be quite powerless to do him any harm whatsoever. Were this not the case, he would already have returned, for the desire had welled within him for fifteen years now.

'There are three such conditions, sir,' said the barber as he lathered soap in a dish and applied it to Diego del Fuego's cheeks, chin and neck. 'The second is that you will not again take a haircut or a shave until you are of the age of seventy-five. At that age, precisely forty-five years from this day, you must enter a barbershop and have your chin shaved. Never before, but neither your hair nor your beard shall grow any longer than I leave them today, so it is not so very much to ask, sir. But be sure, this is most vital. Should you fail in this, it will be very bad for you. All the evil that you can imagine shall befall you, and all that can be imagined. Very bad, sir.' He smiled at the confusion writ across his customer's face.

Never cutting his hair again did not really sound like a condition to Diego del Fuego, and he could not imagine what could possibly occur should he decide to go against the caveat.

'And the third?' he said instead.

'The third, sir, is very difficult. Very difficult indeed, sir. The most difficult of all,' the barber said as he shaved quickly and skilfully. 'You must never return to the land of holes. You must never seek this man, your father, to see if he is punished. If you do, the punishment shall be reversed, and you shall suffer instead at its hands. You must have faith, good sir.'

Having completed the shave of his chin, the barber moved to stand behind Diego del Fuego and began to put the final touches to the back of the neck with the razor. Having done that, he moved on to the area of the head that is neither on the top of it nor on the back, but in between. Under other circumstances, Diego del Fuego would have thought this very strange, and rightly so, but in the current situation he paid it no heed, for he was deeply engrossed in thought. Many questions passed through his mind – followed by the same number of calculations and ruminations – until he finally came to a decision. With the razor resting on Diego del Fuego's head, the barber paused.

'Do you accept the offer?' he asked.

'I do,' said Diego del Fuego.

At these words, the barber briefly put the blade to Diego del Fuego's head and swept it this way and that. He then returned to face his customer and grinned his thousand-toothed grin. The Spaniard did not return his smile, but felt a breeze at his crown as his eyes were diverted by the birds on the lake taking flight once again.

'And you will have faith that your father will be punished in your name? You will not attempt to discern if it has been done?' asked the barber through his smile.

'I will never return to my country to discover if what you say is true. I swear it,' Diego del Fuego said, without looking at the barber.

'But you will not have the faith?' the barber said, and then he thought for a moment before deciding. 'This is sufficient. Faith will come. But do not return, or what befalls your father shall also befall you.'

He then extracted two small mirrors from a pocket in the arm of the chair and held one to Diego del Fuego's face as he passed the other over his cranium.

Diego del Fuego looked into the glass and saw a man fifteen years younger than the one who had entered the barber's shop that morning. Despite sitting still for so long in the unseasonable chill and the breeze that met his newly shorn head, he still felt warmed to the marrow, his muscles and bones supple and ready for movement. The skin of his face was younger, and other than the strange circular beard that sat on the end of his chin, he looked like the boy who had embarked on a life of adventure fifteen years previously. His skin glowed with youthful verve. The beard, he thought, was a strange thing, but after looking at it from various angles he decided that he did not dislike it. The barber gave him the second mirror to better see the rest of his head. The hair was beautifully cut, not a hair longer or shorter than it should be. At the back, however, where hair should have been, there was a bald patch quite equal in size to the beard that remained upon his chin.

'It will not grow, and you must not cut it. Always remember, sir. And your father shall be punished.' The barber was grinning with ill-concealed satisfaction.

Though not so keen on the bald patch as the beard, Diego del Fuego had already determined to cover his head with a hat until the hair grew back and anyway, other questions concerned him more as he rose from the seat.

'When shall he be punished?' he asked the barber, who was

whipping hair from the seat in preparation for the next customer to come his way.

'Ah, my good sir. Is it not enough for you to know that he shall be punished? No more than that can I say,' replied the small man, swiping his cloth through the air.

'And how—?'

'It is too late for these questions, sir. You must now have faith,' the barber said with finality.

'How much do I owe you?' Diego del Fuego said, somewhat aggressively. He was keen to leave, the entertainment having gone out of this affair with the dawning knowledge that even though he would wear a hat for the weeks ahead, he would be unable to avoid the mocking of his fellow sailors aboard the *Odysseus*. It was also now time to hear what extortionate remuneration the barber expected for the imaginary service, the distinctive tea, the fine bath, the delirious head rub and the well-executed but quite bizarre haircut that now adorned him. And time to dispute it.

'Five rupees, good sir,' he said. 'Thank you very much, sir.' Speechless, for this was very little, Diego del Fuego crossed his palm with grubby notes and turned to walk down the three steps to the lakeside, quite surprised and not a little perturbed by the answer he had received.

'But good sir . . . before you leave.' The barber ducked behind Diego del Fuego and put his arms around him, holding the Spaniard in a bear hug from which he had no chance of escape. The barber arched backward and Diego del Fuego's feet were lifted from the floor. Then, with a sudden lurch, the barber partially dropped his burden, and then as quickly, lifted him again with a jerk. Diego del Fuego's spine made an astounding sound, like that of a child dragging a stick along an iron fence, as each of his vertebrae pulled away from the others. As the last did so, Diego del Fuego's feet hit the floor.

'Good God, man!' he exclaimed in his native tongue, not only out of anger, but also out of amazement and fear. The barber's trick had increased his height by more than two inches.

'Yes, sir,' the barber grinned. 'Very good day to you, sir,' and he waved to Diego del Fuego as the Spaniard walked down the steps and along the chill dusty streets to the tavern in which he had left his comrades.

Though excitement makes it difficult, I must sleep now. I left the delights of that temptress's boudoir in order to catch the night train to Bergen. It is now three in the morning and we shall arrive at our destination soon enough. When we have done so, and I await a more holy hour at which to visit a stranger, I will write again.

Good night, my friend.

Lindley-Small

29

THE NOTEBOOKS OF CYRIL KING

1893

The Slaughter of Kings

'But we looked,' I said. 'Tolliver, we found nothing. Tolliver—'

It was no good. His smile was fixed. He had breathed his last. Small cursed and dropped him, allowing his limp form to slump to the floor. By killing Tolliver, Rustam Khan had destroyed our only hope of finding any treasure, if treasure there was still; for surely Small had been right. Tolliver had told us the treasure had been moved. If that were so, and he knew where it was hidden, then he had taken the secret to the grave. More than likely some of the villagers knew; but why should they tell us, invaders who had brought about the death of a man who, if what he said was true, was regarded more or less as their protector? The adventure had been doomed from the beginning. Now Rustam Khan, the man who had allowed me to escape, who had saved my life, would be killed. And unless Small and I were to flee empty-handed, his good deed would be for nothing, for doubtless the villagers would come for us.

I turned to Small, expecting to see him as deflated as I. The smile stretched across his beard struck me dumb.

'You heard him, King. Been with us all along in the catacombs. We must've missed it.'

'We didn't miss a thing, Small. He must have been taunting us,' I said to him from the side of the dead man. 'It's no good. We've had our chance.'

'But that's what he said. You can't discount that. He was the man in the know if there's any. With us all along down there, that's what he said. What else could he mean by that? It's down there, all right, lad. Down there waiting for us. Come on. If that native of yours has returned to the village, they'll be up here any minute. We'll close the statue, grab what we can and make off from the other side. But we must go now. Before it's too late.'

Perhaps his thinking was sound, but I had been doing some of my own, and I had realised that the path of the righteous did not lead back down that tunnel, but through the door and into the village.

'It's a gamble, Small. You might not be right. And that man, Rustam Khan, he saved my life. I can't go back down there on a whim and make no attempt to do the same for him.'

'Of course I'm right. There's no question! And may I remind you that it was that lying native who told you there were no more stones? Or have you forgotten?'

'Helping Rustam Khan is the only decent thing to do,' I said.

'Decent?' he snorted in disbelief. 'What are you talking about, man? We came here for treasure, not heroics.'

'I brought you here, Small,' I said steadily. 'Any treasure so stained in blood is not worth having, if it's there at all. I did not come here to dig through corpses as you'll have to do down there. We must make a stand against these people and save Rustam Khan and his wife if we can. It is the only path open to us. The path of the Englishman and the gentleman.'

'Pah!' was his response. 'You're a watchmaker, I a wanted criminal – none would consider either of us to be gentlemen, nor will they ever. You may consider yourself an Englishman, lad, but I lost my country a long time ago, and I'm not about to lose my life to some ridiculous credo cooked up by a bunch of do-gooding toffs.'

His voice softened. 'My boy, contrary to what you say, what you suggest is the only course *not* to take. You are not considering the situation thoroughly enough for your own good. You hardly know the man. You helped him wreak the revenge he desired, and he was grateful. He wouldn't expect you to do any more. He certainly wouldn't want you to waste your life, the life he saved, in a vain attempt to save his. You heard him yourself when he told you to get out of here. We'd be wise to take his advice. Arm ourselves the best we can, head back down there, collect what we can and be away. I shall be sorry to lose old Bucephalus, and the rest of the whisky, but saving them is not worth both our lives.'

'I am considering the situation perfectly thoroughly, thank you very much,' I told him curtly. 'We shall die, Small, whatever we do. All we need to decide is how. Scrambling for wealth and without food in the cold of the mountain snows, or making a stand against the enemy, trying to rescue a good man and a beautiful woman.'

'It appears you are not thinking at all,' he responded. 'When these people discover that Tolliver is dead, what do you think will happen? I'll tell you. They will kill this Rustam Khan out of anger. Then they will look for you. If you stay they will find you. If you come with me they will not. The fruit of that green valley shall feed us until they are unsuspecting, and then when they sleep, we shall take from their food supplies and then retrace our journey.'

'And what of that man's wife?' I barked.

'Regrettable, I grant you; but unavoidable, I'm afraid. I do not deny that it is not the most ideal of situations, but we must make do with what we have. Perhaps we can take her with the food. Perhaps even Bucephalus, too. But I have not travelled so far only to run pell-mell into the jaws of death, lad. I came for the treasure, and that is what I am leaving with. We can be away from this place. Our task can still be a success.'

'I must do right by a man who saved my life, Small.'

'I have saved your life twice over!'

'And I would do the same if it were you out there!'

He sighed, shook his head, placed his hands on my shoulders and looked me steadily in the eye.

'I once asked you, lad, if you had thought how I happened upon you in the hills outside Gilgit. I told you that it was from your pipe smoke. I told you Abdul-Khaliq in the teahouse had informed me of you and your watch.'

Suddenly, what had niggled at my mind when I had first shown Small the watch came searing into my brain.

'I never showed the watch to Abdul-Khaliq, and yet you knew of the stone!'

'That's right; and that's not the whole of it.' A rare gravity had entered his voice. 'My young friend, you have no doubt learned that I am a brash character, one given to exaggeration. I would rather the company of a loose damsel and fine liquors to that of a dry scholar or a tradesman, but against my better judgement I have grown fond of you. How could I not after going through so much together? For that reason, I must tell you precisely how I happened upon you. If you must go to help that native, I must tell you why I cannot go with you. You will not like it, not a bit, but it is something you must hear. I have too much invested in this journey, you see. I have put too many thousands of miles into it to give up, too many scrapes and too many deceptions. I am afraid I must tell you that, from the very off, you have been had.'

I was speechless. I could do nothing but stare at him.

'My boy, you weren't to know. Let me explain it in this way: you believe in fate, I have learned, and that is a dangerous sport to play. By doing so, you let yourself be blown willy-nilly by its whimsical winds. That alone is risky enough, but sooner or later you will happen upon a chap devious enough to whip up a wind of his own. And that, I'm afraid, is what I have done.'

'I don't believe it,' said I, though the possibilities had already entered my reeling mind.

'It is so, my friend,' he said with a sigh. 'Cyril, you may think you brought me here, but I am afraid you'd be wrong. I first set eyes upon that watch long before you did, at a card table in Cairo. Forrester was there, and McNaughton. Forrester needed a stake. He offered the watch as surety. He showed it to us and told us that it would lead to a great find. I am sure I am the only one around that table who understood the writing, and though I never possessed the watch myself, I did not need to. It had been my intention to head south in Egypt, and return to Melancovic's stash, but when I heard of this hoard, I changed my course. There was no race for the former, whereas this – well, this was a case of now or never. Hoping to bargain with Forrester, I followed him back to his quarters, but he was having none of it. He won the pot fair and square and wanted nothing to do with the likes of me. When the Scot killed him and took the watch, I knew it would be only a matter of time before he learned where to travel. So I reported McNaughton to the authorities. It was a necessary delaying tactic. He was a criminal, but not a wanted one; not yet, not like me. He could have made his way to these parts long before I could hope to, and I couldn't have that. He only had to take ship and travel directly, whereas I had to go by lands where the British Empire held no sway. As soon as I was sure he was in custody, I left Egypt by way of Sinai. Through Arabia and Persia and then by way of the Afghans, I came at length to Gilgit. And when my old friend Abdul-Khaliq told me that an English watchmaker was seeking Ghalat Taqdir, I knew that you, too, must have learned something of the watch. I made it here in time to meet you, King; for that we can thank fate, and that you made it here at all, but for nothing more, I'm afraid. I must admit that it had been my intention to learn all I could from you and then do you in. But, as I say, I grew too fond of you. Besides, after the resolve you showed in the face of death in Gilgit, I knew that you would prove a useful stamp of fellow to have at hand.

'I don't expect you to forgive me, lad, so don't say a thing. But if you refuse to return to the catacombs with me, at least take my rifle. I fear you'll need it sooner than I.'

He passed the gun to me and a pouch of bullets. 'I'll take the bayonet. I've survived with less. But are you quite certain?' he said.

I was still speechless. This man, whom I had come to trust, who had saved my life on more than one occasion, as he had pointed out, had revealed himself to be a deceiver of monumental proportions. Quite suddenly, I was alone. If I were to do what I knew was right, I would have to face the villagers on my own. As long as Small had been at my side, throughout our journey over the mountains, through my delirium, through the catacombs, his daring had given me confidence, body and soul. All we had done together, all the scrapes we had found ourselves in, all our adversities had been overcome. Now, I felt my spirits shrink like a dying flower. I was terrified.

My voice shook, but I was determined.

'I have to do the right thing, Small,' I said.

'Very well, lad. And so here we part. I wish you luck.' He stuck his paw out for me to shake, but I did not take it. Suddenly my fear and sorrow manifested in a seething anger and instead I shouted at him.

'Stories, Small. All I have heard from you since the moment we met has been stories. Not an ounce of truth in any one of them. All fabrication!'

He shook his head and lowered his hand, saddened by my decision, as I was by his; but neither could now back down.

'Lad,' he replied. 'Who cares if I have lied? Does a tale have to be factual to be truthful? What should you care for how a journey is taken, so long as it is diverting? People lie for the good or entertainment of others every day. You shall have your own account of it if you live, just as I shall have mine. Have we not had fun together, you and I? Has this not been the adventure we both wished it? That is what matters. And it is not too late, lad. We can conclude it together and double our chances of survival. Come with me. Let us make haste.'

'I care!' I cried at him, before turning and throwing open the door. 'You're a coward, Small.'

'It's been said before, lad, and it'll be said again, because I will be alive.'

I slammed the door behind me and did not look back.

Below me, the village fires flickered. The underground tunnels had led us right through the ridge that concealed the upper, hidden valley from the lower, and I was on the slope outside that isolated hut I had seen high against the mountainside when Manraj Singh had brought me here earlier that day. The rifle in my fist, I stumbled through the snow from boulder to boulder, fearing my form would be seen against the white. The moon had long passed its peak and was beginning to dip. Soon it would be dawn, and now the village was alive and awash with torchlight. I did not know how I was going to save Rustam Khan, only that I must attempt it, come what may.

Not until I was some way down the mountain did I give in to temptation and turn my head in the hope that Small might have followed me after all. The door of the hut remained stubbornly closed, but that single glance was my undoing. I turned back just in time to see a furious face loom out of the darkness before me, and two hands held high brought a stone down upon my brow. Words were shouted, but I did not hear them. They receded into silence and I entered a consciousless sleep.

*

First came the throbbing of my injured head, then a blurred image of white and blue and green and black, then the realisation that I could not move. Rough stone dug into my shoulders and my back, and my arms were stretched uncomfortably behind me, my hands tied at the wrists. My vision cleared and the blurs turned to clouds and sky and grass and rock and snow. And before me, in the light of the rising sun, the dead Tolliver, laid out on a roughly hewn wooden bier.

I realised that I was bound hand and foot to one of the stone pillars I had seen when I first entered the village with Manraj Singh. To my left lay Rustam Khan, upon the stone table. He, too, was secured with rawhide ropes about his legs and chest, his arms stretched behind him beneath the stone, doubtless his wrists bound, just as mine were.

Before him stood Manraj Singh, his back to us, and slung over his shoulder was the rifle Small had donated to my gallant venture – a rescue that had failed before it had even got under way. On the other side of the grassy area, the villagers were assembled, that

group of perhaps sixty youths, women and children, each head bare
of scarves, many as fair as a Viking, all awaiting justice, every
one of them looking our way. Among them I spotted the beautiful
Fahlhana, her head bowed, still alive and free, but powerless.

'Rustam Khan,' I struggled to whisper. Rustam Khan slowly and
painfully turned his head towards me. His chest heaved for breath
beneath the restraints, but his eyes were calm.

'I hoped you would not awaken, Cyril King sahib. This should
not have been for you. You should not have followed me here.
Death for me today is inevitable. For you it should never have been
so.'

Then came another voice. Manraj Singh's. I did not understand
his words, but the villagers shouted angrily in response.

I glanced round as far as I was able. There was no one behind
us. My wrists were unseen by all. I struggled in my bindings. If I
could free but one hand, I was certain I could release myself. If
timed correctly, I could surprise Manraj Singh and take him
hostage before the villagers could cover the ground. I would have
the only firearm in the place. With Manraj Singh under my gun
and Rustam Khan leading our way, we could take Fahlhana and
depart. It was a desperate plan, but I could see no other. But the
timing would have to be perfect – the villages were a hundred feet
away at most.

I wriggled and twisted, digging the rawhide painfully into my
wrists. It would stretch, I knew – it is the nature of the substance –
but how long before I was free? I thrashed and twisted my arms
with all my might, pulling my hands against the leather, sinews
and tissue straining beneath my skin.

Manraj Singh lifted his arms above his head and a bloodthirsty
wail of excitement rose from the villagers. In his right hand he held
a representation of the serpent-cat, similar to the others we had
seen, except this one was made of a grey metal – steel, probably,
punched and decorated in the Indian manner. Its stylised body was
much the same size as the gilded statuette, but its head was larger
in proportion, and tilted backwards so that its fangs projected out-
wards rather than down. And what fangs they were – grotesquely

elongated and wickedly curved, they glinted where they caught the light, razor sharp, like knife blades set into the roof of its mouth. There was no doubt in my mind whatsoever that the sole purpose of this fearsome object was to kill.

He turned and came towards us, and halted by Rustam Khan. He said something further to the villagers, and was answered with another savage cry. In English, no doubt for my benefit, he announced, 'First the murderer. Then the intruder will die.'

A wild thought came to me. Of course! If only I was not too late . . .

'Listen to me!' I called out to the assembled villagers. 'These men are not what they seem. They are not your protectors. They are the men who had your fathers and your brothers killed. They came here only to steal your sacred treasure. Rustam Khan is no murderer – he has avenged you. He must not die!'

Silence greeted me, broken only by a cry of anguish from Fahlhana. I could see her surrounded by other women, pleading with them, struggling against the two sturdy youths who held her.

'A clever try, King sahib,' said Manraj Singh's voice in my ear. 'Alas, they do not understand you, so they will never know the truth.'

I could not save us. But Rustam Khan could – it was our only chance. I looked down to where he lay on the cold stone. 'Tell them, Rustam Khan!' I urged him. 'Tell them how these men betrayed them, how they have lied to them, who they really are. Tell them, for Fahlhana's sake if not for yours or mine!'

He turned his head towards me and opened his mouth to speak, but whether he was about to tell them, or whether he was so entirely resigned to his fate that he would not, I would never know, for at that moment, swift as a snake striking, Manraj Singh brought the fangs of the cat down on Rustam Khan's taut throat.

The twin blades bit into the hollow above his collarbone. Blood pulsed instantly from the two puncture holes, onto the stone, flooding it. The villagers yelled for a climactic moment as it poured onto the grass, into the stream that flowed beneath the table, and the water ran red down into the valley.

Manraj Singh then pointed at me and the voices rose again in anticipation. I doubled my attempts to free my hands. It did not matter now that all eyes were upon me. If I succeeded, I still had a chance, however slim. If I did not, I had none.

He came to face me, eclipsing my view of the crowd.

'And now you shall die.'

'B-but you're a soldier, of the Indian Army. A Sikh. Not one of these people,' I spluttered desperately. 'This is murder. Savagery!'

'Perhaps, but the savagery shall repeat itself,' he said. 'Unless . . .'

'Unless what?' I prompted, twisting my hands behind me with all my strength.

'Unless you speak. Tell me what you planned to do with the treasure. How shall you transport it? It is mine now. We found it together. I saved him after what he did on the Hunza trail. You have no right to it. I waited years for him to recover it, and now he is dead because of you. But tell me, and I shall release you.'

My mind was racing. This was an unexpected turn of events.

'Cut me down and I shall tell you all I know,' I said. 'I promise you that, but cut me down now!'

Unflinchingly we held one another's stares for what seemed like minutes. Then he tutted.

'You have no plan. I do not believe you even know where it is hidden. That is why you are willing to tell me all. You have nothing to tell; so now you must die.'

I fought frantically against the bindings, threw myself from side to side as best I could to upset his aim, but it was a fruitless endeavour. I could still hardly move.

His left hand shot out and seized my hair roughly, forcing my head back over the top of the pillar, exposing my neck. He held the cat high above me with his right. The villagers did not raise the same exultant howl this time, however. Indeed, they had fallen entirely silent.

My eyes were fixed on the metal beast that seemed to snarl above me, waiting for its plunge into my palpitating jugular. I saw it lift a fraction to begin the killing blow when there was a crack as though lightning had struck the very mountain.

The idol fell from Manraj Singh's hand. He released my head and I saw confusion ripple over his face. We both looked down at his chest. The rifle fell from his shoulder and before he collapsed, I saw blood spreading across the faded black of his shirt.

Beyond him, approaching me, was a smiling figure holding a pistol.

I was saved.

It was Major Flack.

30

The Letters of
Sir Paul Lindley-Small

From the Station Hotel saloon
Bergen, Norway

12TH JANUARY 1909

My friend,

It is half past six but I am quite awake. I will visit Kjellersmauet after a decent breakfast and once I have concluded for you what I saw and discovered in Kristiania.

Diego del Fuego left the barber in Dwarka with a curious, circular little beard and an equally curious and circular bald patch. He felt and appeared fifteen years younger, two inches taller, and departed with the absurd promise that for the next forty-five years, no matter what befell him, he would never require another haircut nor another shave, and that he would not die; indeed, that he *could* not die. On the day of his seventy-fifth birthday, wherever he might be in the world, he was to visit a barber and have his hair cut and his chin shaved, and on that day he would die. If he believed this, if it were true, he could also believe that something terrible would befall his violent bully of a father.

When he returned to the *Odysseus*, his fellow sailors mocked him, as he knew they would, and more than once they pulled his woollen hat from his head to see and laugh at his new monk-like appearance. However, when his hair failed to grow, his shipmates grew accustomed to his new look and became bored of ridiculing him for it. The lack of growth played heavily on Diego del Fuego's mind, though, and the more time that passed without growth, the more he had to fight the temptation to return home. He wrote letters for news of his father to all he could recall in his hometown, but replies never came. He inspected Spanish newspapers whenever he could, though he knew the death of a miner would not be reported. Could it be that the bargain he had made with the barber at Dwarka was real? Or had del Fuego's hair growth been restricted by the man's remarkable hair tonic in a vicious practical joke? And if the latter, then why?

Paranoia creeping into his logical mind, del Fuego decided that there was one sure way of finding out if he was the victim of a hoax. He would test the caveats of the deal. The second and third of the clauses declared that if he were to shave or ever return to his home, terrible things would befall him. Therefore he chose the first of the three – that which stated he could not, whatever occurred, be harmed. If he could be, he would know he had been tricked.

By the time I gazed at him across the gangway in King Knut's Tavern on his seventy-fifth birthday, he had been shot six times, once in the head, but had not died. He was stabbed eight times, once straight through his belly by a sabre, but had not bled to death. He survived four shipwrecks, including that of the *Odysseus*, which he scuttled in a desperate attempt to test his flesh. When wrecked, and on other self-imposed occasions, he had not eaten for weeks, but did not starve. He was attacked by carnivorous fish, but was not consumed. He had been underwater for hours at a time, but had not drowned. It was said that he had sunk to the bottom of the South Pacific Ocean, only to resurface unscathed by beast or pressure, and swim for eight days until he reached Tahiti, exhausted, but alive. He had even thrown himself before a locomotive and been ricocheted away, quite intact. In taverns he took on dockworkers by the dozen, and try though they might, they could do no more than make him bleed. He was, as the barber had promised, indestructible.

He had also retained throughout his life what was on that chill day in Dwarka a marvellous inner warmth. It had served him well in the colder climates of the world he sailed to, and they were many, but when he came to such places as the tropics and the South China Seas, he found it intolerable. His blood seemed to boil in his veins, and it proved impossible to cool himself in water or shade. There were times when he was certain both the heat and his indestructibility would drive him to madness, and indeed, the mind of the man I saw was not that of the thirty-year-old found walking in Dwarka forty-five years earlier. This one had become a man consumed by his own fate, driven to despair by words he thought absurd. Even when his father would have been dead of natural causes, so far gone was the mind of Diego del Fuego that still he had to fight the temptation to return to Peñarroya-Pueblonuevo; still he desired to know what had been the miner's fate, to prove beyond doubt that the barber had not duped him.

But he did not return to Spain. Instead, on the decks of the boats he guided over the oceans, he muttered to himself of all the possibilities, obsessively considering his father's fate under his breath, and his own. To his fellow sailors, he appeared driven to eccentricity by his constant staring at the stars by which they all made their way. This was an impression that doubtless would only have been exacerbated by the fact that he aged more voraciously than is the norm. Whether this was the barber's doing or that of del Fuego's self-abusive habits and mind, one cannot know; but though on embarkation from Dwarka he had looked and felt fifteen years younger than he was, by the time he was forty-five, his hair and beard, though of course the same length, were quite grey. By the time he was sixty, his body was that of a seventy-five-year-old. He was by then reportedly quite mad, but he had found the faith that the barber of Dwarka had said he would. With that, however, came something else to bother his deeply confused mind. He had faith, but what precisely did he have faith *in*? He could not say, for the barber could not have been of any religion he had encountered. This curse, as he deemed it now, was not the work of a Christian god, nor a Jewish one, nor Islamic, nor Hindu, Buddhist or Sikh. He believed in a power, in a god, but he knew not of what religion, and this, if it had the power to render a man immortal, must surely be the one true God.

It was with this question entirely occupying his addled brain that he returned to Dwarka when opportunity arose, hoping to call upon the barber for an answer before his forty-five years were spent. Since he was no longer entrusted with navigating, a kindly acquaintance took pity on him and admitted him aboard a vessel destined for Dwarka. Del Fuego spoke only to himself for the entire voyage and stepped off the ship a weak but excitable old man.

When he arrived at the lake, it still had the birds of blue and pink sitting upon its surface, but in the shack where the barber had plied his trade was now a seller of trinkets.

Deeply upset, he approached the seller and attempted to ascertain where the barber had gone, but was unable to make himself understood. Feeling sorry for this strange old man, the seller took Diego del Fuego into his shop and served him a cup of distinctive tea. Diego del Fuego recognised the tea instantly, for it was the very same in colour and taste as that he had drunk with the barber. He spluttered and gesticulated and spoke as well as he could, but was unable to ask the seller from where the tea came, or of what it was made. In frustration, Diego del Fuego sat on a stool in the shop, now dark with drapes and cluttered goods where more than forty years ago it had been so bright, and caressed the feline that arrived and coiled at his feet. When the cat bit del Fuego, he whipped his hand away.

After that, the seller was keen to be rid of the unintelligible old man, but as a token of good will, he agreed to part with the cat when Diego del Fuego offered money for it. It seems Dadri Landa did not know the value of the animal, or maybe he had simply grown to fear it.

So once again, Diego del Fuego left the lake in Dwarka the possessor of something new, though this time it was very definitely not what he desired. From there, he passed through the town and boarded the *Syren*. It was bound for the chill of Norway where his inner insulation had always proved bearable. As he made his way aboard, he rubbed his hand where it had been bitten. Bruises were blackening the twin puncture marks the feline's fangs had left.

When my attention was drawn away from the delightful dark eyes of the tale's teller in King Knut's Tavern, to Diego del Fuego as he rose stiffly to his feet, I saw – with glee, I'm afraid – that his right hand was now entirely blackened and wizened, just like those limbs we found.

Diego del Fuego did not seem to enjoy his final mouthful of brandy that he took in a single gulp once upright, and I was considering offering him a dram of the infinitely superior Glenlivet when he began to shuffle to the exit and the chill air beyond the door.

In two minds as to what to do next, I quickly secured the desirable company of the woman at my table for later that day, grabbed my satchel and whisky, and followed the old boy out of the tavern and down the road, hoping to find a moment at which I might request the information I had waited three days to garner. I could hear that he had begun to mutter to himself, however, and did not want to surprise him into silence, so hung back.

Fighting against the cold wind, del Fuego led me to a part of the city occupied by diminutive cottages built into a hill. The path was winding, with flights of steps up and down, and were I not a navigational natural like my lead, I should have become quite lost before he stopped at a southwest-facing cottage and ceased to jabber. After a pause, a deep breath and a look to the skies, he pushed open the door and a bell tinkled. As he entered, he removed his hat, and I saw the circular hairless spot just as it had been described to me. Within the dwelling, my hawk eyes spotted mirrors, seats, scissors, combs and razors. This small cottage was a barber's shop.

It was time to act, and fast.

I watched Diego del Fuego sit in one of the two barber's chairs. I followed him in and sat in the second chair, as though merely the next in line for a trim. He eyed me in the mirror with a frown, so I picked up a newspaper and feigned reading as we waited for the barber to appear.

If he were to die here in the barber's chair next to me, as he surely believed, now was the time to get the information concerning the feline from him. But how to address him? My arsenal does not include Spanish, and by the titillating woman's account, del Fuego spoke little English – but was there any other way to do it? I decided to test the water.

'Awfully cold up here, eh?' I said, folding the paper and looking at him in the mirror.

He looked back at me, his eyes sleepy, but nonetheless still frowning with irritation.

Just as I was about to attempt something a little more basic, a man young in appearance, but old in gait, air and velocity, shuffled into the room and, quite shocked at finding both his seats filled, attempted to enquire who was to be the first to feel the steel of his scissors. Before I could act, Diego del Fuego lifted his hand and the barber shuffled to his side. He hoisted up the chair by several inches, until the bald batch was before his very nose, and considered it for a moment before looking at Diego del Fuego's resolute face in the mirror and raising his eyebrows in question.

'A shave,' were Diego del Fuego's words, in English.

The young man nodded and reached for his soap dish, and with a flurry worked up a foam and spread it over the small beard with an oversized badger brush.

Diego del Fuego did not now pay me any mind, but stared at himself in the mirror as the young man plucked a razor from the counter under the mirror and began to sharpen it on a strop hanging from the chair behind his customer.

My mind raced for a solution to the situation. To shave del Fuego's beard would take little more than a minute and I had yet to request from him what only he could tell me: the whereabouts of the feline – the point of this whole damned journey. I doubted that he was going to die before my very eyes, but what if, by some unforeseen and unknowable power, he did? What if his mind had settled upon it? Then I would be in as bad a position as I was when I watched his vessel depart Dwarka. Worse, even.

Thankfully, the old grey matter being what it is, by the third stroke of razor on strop I landed upon a possibility and by the sixth, I had plucked pen and paper from my satchel and drawn a rough sketch of a cat, next to which I put a bold question mark. Hoping that I would be able to pass him the pen and paper before the potentially mortal razor was put to beard, I decided that an interruption was required.

So I started to cough. I coughed and I coughed until I was quite red in the face. Coughing when your body does not call for it is a hazardous business, and by the time the barber shuffled out of the room promising me a glass of water, I was very much in need of one. However, not allowing the importance of the moment to be superseded by my aqueous needs, as soon as the chap had left, I tore the page from my notebook and held it and the pen out towards the old man next to me. He turned and looked from the paper to my face, then back to the paper again. I stared at him with hope and pleading filling my expression and then, very slowly, a hand began to protrude from under the cloak the barber had put around him. It stretched forth until it took the pen and paper from my hands. Diego del Fuego then turned the page over to more effectively consider the drawing. Then, when the barber re-entered the room, the paper, the pen and the hand quickly retreated under the cloak.

The barber handed me a glass of water dense with minerals, and against my better judgement, I swallowed it down in a gulp, never taking the beseeching articulation from my face, nor breaking eye-contact with Diego del Fuego in the mirror.

'Please,' I mouthed.

The barber gave me a confused look, then picked up his razor, drew his thumb across it and, happy with its keenness, turned to his charge. Diego del Fuego looked away from me and into the reflection of his own distant eyes.

I watched as the barber leaned over the old man's left shoulder and took the first stroke of hair from the beard. As he did so, an extraordinary thing happened. At the very same rate with which he sheared Diego del Fuego's beard and wiped the mix of hair and foam on a towel lying over his left forearm, jet-black hair sprouted from the small bald patch on Diego del Fuego's head. At the second stroke another bizarre event occurred. Not only was black hair growing where there had been none for the last forty-five years, but also all the rest started to grow at an astonishing rate, and as it grew, it quite altered in hue.

When he had sat at that table in King Knut's Tavern, Diego del Fuego's hair had measured no more than half an inch in length. By the completion of the second stroke, which rendered his beard a third gone, his hair had grown to at least four inches and had turned from grey to black and was now beginning to show a tinge of red, as though an auburn dye had been added. And as if making up for the forty-five years on which it had missed out, the hair's growth did not slow, either, but increased in speed, and as it did so, it became redder and redder. At shoulder-length, it was not the ginger of Rød-Larsen, it was not a flaming orange. Diego del Fuego's hair had turned entirely red, to the crimson one sees on flags and on battlefields. I realised immediately what was occurring, but could do nothing but look on as the old man met his fate.

Initially, the barber managed not to mention this strangeness, since it did not appear to surprise his charge and he did not want to cause offence. I could, however, see absolute fear in his eyes now, and as he became more agitated, his shaving slowed. The cursed man in his chair was certainly not one to nick with a razor, for if he could make his hair grow with such astonishing rapidity and at the same time change its colour, imagine what he would do to a man who cut his chin!

Despite his terror and the subsequent wobble in his hand, it was not solely emotion that demanded this hesitation. You see, I now realised that it was not just the head hair that was so prodigiously and scarletly sprouting. Around the small beard that the barber had foamed and was in the process of shaving, it was the same story and the hair was now beginning to entangle the shaver's hand and razor. When he realised what was occurring, he leapt away from the chair. In so doing, he tore the hair that had entangled his hand from Diego del Fuego's chin, but the old man seemed barely to register it.

Diego del Fuego continued to look at himself in the mirror. All hair-growth had ceased. Then without moving his eyes, he spoke.

'Continue,' he said in a weak voice.

The barber moved back to the chair once more, apparently more scared of the man than his hair. He'd have done well to listen to his instincts telling him to flee from the hair, however, for what followed, though plainly not of his doing, will surely live with him forever.

He leaned over Diego del Fuego's shoulder and burrowed through the red hair until he once more came across the foam covering the man's chin. As he slowly scraped away more hairs, their red neighbours recommenced their speedy growth and entwined themselves first around the razor's handle, then around the fingers of the barber. In no time his hand was once more entirely engulfed by hair. He tried again to move from the chair, but this time he failed. I looked down. The red hair flowing from del Fuego's head had curled its way around the barber's abdomen and legs, holding him in place.

I looked at Diego del Fuego in the mirror. His eyes were as stony and resolute as they had ever been. Somewhere twinkling in their depths, however, as though he knew what was about to transpire, I perceived pity as he considered the barber, whose entire forearm was now swallowed by his beard, creeping ever upwards, towards his face. The barber's eyes bulged with fear and the effort he was making with the sum of his strength to control the razor, but it seems he was fighting a battle lost as soon as he had determined to complete the shave.

There was a blood-curdling scream. It emanated from the barber, and as it echoed through the shop a single tear fell from the beaten and scarred right eye of Diego del Fuego, and the Spaniard fell limp. With mighty fear giving him a strength he had not before possessed, and the hair loosening its grip, the barber wrenched himself from Diego del Fuego, pulling great locks of rich crimson hair with him. The razor flew into the air and due only to my famed agility and speedy reactions did it miss me by inches.

The barber fell to the ground and sobbed.

Diego del Fuego was dead. It had not, however, been the hair-cut that had killed him, but the barber, for where that young man had torn hair from chin in his terror, I could see a great cut through the skin of Diego del Fuego's throat. It seems the hair had taken control of the wretched barber's hand and made him commit this crime for the barber of Dwarka. I was astonished and looked to the young man trembling in the corner of the shop and back again. My amazement only increased when I inspected the wound more closely, for I saw that it was utterly dry. The razor had quite sliced across the jugular and yet the wound was entirely devoid of blood. There was flesh and sinew and tissue, but it was as though it had been cooked, and for quite too long. I defy you to believe me, but believe me you must for it is quite true – there was not a drop of blood anywhere to be seen. There was only the brilliance of the hair on the dead man's head and chin that draped into pools on the floor and on his thighs.

Gathering myself with the rapidity of a man who has seen things of such a nature with more frequency than most, and possessing the robust constitution you well know, I saw fit to check the poor man's pulse, though really it was quite obvious to one so medically-minded as I that having no blood rendered the chances of saving him extremely low.

It looked as though the hair had stopped growing – but one can never be sure in times of such peculiarity, so I readied myself for attack as I tentatively reached out. The assault did not come, however, and when I touched the body, the slight jolt I served it made a wizened and black arm fall from under the cloak. My pen fell to the ground, but still grasped firmly between equally wizened and blackened fingers was the page I had torn from my notebook and then forgotten about, in the amazement and horror of what followed. Slipping it from Diego del Fuego's dead hand, I gazed upon my now insignificant doodling. The feline was surely lost to me, and though annoyed by this turn of events, I could hardly hold it against the old wretch. However, when I looked at the page, I was filled with yet more amazement.

For below the roughly sketched cat and the boldly drawn question mark was an address which I have high hopes will prove to be the creature's current residence.

I left Diego del Fuego and the barber in the shop, but before I hailed a cab, I alerted an official to the gruesomeness that had taken place in that fairytale-like part of Kristiania. However, it is to you, Cyril, that I divulge the entirety of the tragedy.

Some say Diego had gone quite mad; others that he sold his soul to the devil rather than some years of his life to a barber. When I saw him, I thought him neither mad, nor evil. Simply that he was an old man succumbing to the venom of the cat. A man who was past caring and sombrely awaited the nothingness he had delighted in so many years ago.

His scrawl showed the Bergen address to be 43 Kjellersmauet. As yet, I am unaware of its relevance, but it is to this unpronounceable door that I shall now make my way.

Wish your good friend Lindley-Small luck. If his situation is to grow any stranger than already it has become, I fear he might need it.

Lindley-Small

31

THE NOTEBOOKS OF CYRIL KING

1893

Time Holds the Answer

'They just don't know when they're beaten, I'm afraid,' Flack said, holstering his firearm.

'But how—' I stuttered. 'How did you know?'

He laughed.

'Well, you'll not like it, but I'm afraid you have Captain Petts to thank.'

'Petts?' I gasped.

'Yes. He's a reformed character, just as I said he'd be – ever since we left Gilgit. Been concerned for your wellbeing everywhere we went. We're meant to be heading towards the Afghans, Chitral way, but Sir Mortimer was keen to come up here and see the lie of the land, so I allowed myself to be persuaded. Didn't think we could find you myself, but Petts tracked you down like a native. Led us straight here.'

He went first to Rustam Khan and cut his bindings. Beyond him a group of men in the uniform of the British Army were pointing their rifles at the villagers, who were tensed, ready to attack should opportunity present itself. I saw Corporals Finch and Crampers,

Lieutenant Fowler, the Sarge, a solid-looking man in civilian clothes who wore most impressive moustaches pointing sideways from his upper lip like a pair of stiletto spikes; and lastly, loading his rifle, Captain Petts on a piebald mare.

Rising from the polo player's side, Major Flack shook his head.

'He's still alive – just – but I'm afraid he won't make it. Lost too much blood.'

He crouched to cut my legs free.

His gun now loaded, Captain Petts descended from his horse.

'Still, you're more or less in one piece and you're the one we came for. You and my rabbit. Why on earth did you take off with him? Hostage, were you? He's a bad egg, you know. Damnably slippery – hell of a mover. Pops up here, there and everywhere. Where's he got to now?'

Major Flack stood and began to cut the bindings about my arms.

'You've had a time of it, King, by the looks of things,' he continued. 'We'll have you out of here in a jiffy.' I ignored his questions concerning Small, for I had been struck by something else.

'Major!' I whispered urgently. 'How did Petts know where to come? He couldn't have tracked us. We were completely lost. To follow our trail would have taken you weeks!'

He looked into my eyes.

'Eh?' he said, but nothing more, for then there was another crack and he too – that kind, valiant, trusting man – looked with confusion into my fear-stricken face as blood dribbled from his mouth and he slumped against my chest. He looked up at me.

'Awfully sorry, old boy,' he said and then slipped to the ground alongside Manraj Singh.

In a matter of moments I had gone from imminent death to safety and back again. Now I was not in the hands of vengeful natives, but the cruel ones of an Army officer with a twisted mind.

I looked up from Major Flack's body to see that familiar, snake-like smile approaching me.

'You bastard! You've killed him!' I cried. 'You are a murderer!'

'Keep those savages at bay, men – they're liable to jump you at any moment. Tolliver had them well trained, but now he's gone they'll be wild, and Fowler, keep your eye on Durand,' Petts said over his shoulder, utterly ignoring my fury. He removed his helmet as he walked towards me. Though every one of them also looked fearful and confused by this turn of events, the soldiers did not move their guns from the villagers, but for Fowler, who pointed his rifle apologetically towards this Durand character.

'By God, man!' Durand said, without a trace of fear, only out-rage. 'Are you completely bloody insane, Captain? Lieutenant, lower your weapon this instant! There'll be courts martial for this.'

Fowler wavered, but did not move his gun, and Petts did not hear his words, for the Captain was already addressing me.

'I?' he said, looking towards me. 'A murderer? Tut–tut. That will never do. One officer killing another? No no. Rather a crazed civilian killing the Major before his loyal captain could come to his rescue, I think, don't you? A crazed civilian your gallant captain was forced to put paid to; but not, of course, before he delivered what I require. I have exhibited to you already that my men shall follow their orders, and you can be sure that they will testify to my version of events, for who shall there be to say that it is untrue if they do not? Precisely. And all the way up here? Who is likely to embark on such a journey in order to determine the veracity of my tale? I am an officer. To doubt my word would be to insult the very fabric of the British Army. Yes, I rather think I have you quite where I want you.'

'Captain Petts,' came Durand's voice again. 'Do you not know who I am? Let me remind you, sir: I am the Foreign Secretary to Her Majesty's Government of India. Do you think you can just do away with me as though I were cannon fodder? Good God, man. You are a fool to think you can get away with this!'

Petts whipped round to face him.

'And who do you suppose will know where to look? To all who know, you are in these parts drawing up your secret border plans; you are headed to Chitral, and on to discuss the matter with the Amir. Perhaps the Afghan savages got you, or the Russians. I have

not yet decided, but it will matter little. For by the time they find
you, wherever I end up placing you, you can be sure that your mission will have failed. That you will be seen a failure. Your position
shall be filled by another, and you shall be soon forgotten.'

Shocked by Petts' logic, Durand turned back to Fowler.

'Lieutenant, as the representative of Her Majesty, I order you:
turn your weapon on this man!'

Fowler looked at Petts, terrified, but his rifle did not move an
inch.

'That's right, Lieutenant. *I* am your commanding officer. This
man is a civilian. The lieutenant follows my orders, Sir Mortimer.'

'This is—'

'Quiet!' Petts roared. 'Not another word or you shall be shot
immediately!'

The Foreign Secretary clenched his jaw and fell silent, and Petts
turned back to me.

I spat in his face as he neared and lunged at him with my free
legs, but he simply took a step back and wiped his cheek.

'That is really rather ungrateful of you,' he hissed. 'After all, I
have allowed you to live these precious moments more.'

He laughed mirthlessly.

'How did you know?' I demanded.

'Know?' he asked.

'Where to come, where I would be? You know these villagers.
You knew Tolliver.'

'Oh, yes, I've been here before. On all other occasions I came
alone, of course, but thanks to this fool,' – he kicked the inanimate
form of Flack – 'extreme times have called for extreme measures.
I was forced to tell him I knew where you were likely to be heading, and the whole party came along. But I wasn't expecting to find
this. No. The happenings here really are a most unfortunate turn
of events. I was quite relying on Tolliver, you see. And to find him
dead really rather angers me.'

He lingered on the last words as a smile slid across his face. He
dropped his helmet on the ground and began to pull his fingers
out of his gloves one at a time. 'Tolliver was mad, it's said, sent

over the edge by his experiences when he was first captured here in Ishkuman, and then killed up in the mountains after he fled the repercussions of his murderous outburst. They even found a body, rather fortunately pecked and torn to anonymity, but identifiable by his single hand.

'I say they; but really I mean Manraj Singh, for it was he who led the search. Of all the Army hereabouts there was only one who thought the whole thing wry – me. I had seen Tolliver work, heard his stories. He'd spent years here in the mountains, connecting with the natives, plotting maps, easing the British into the area. He was too mentally tough to have gone mad, no matter what befell him, and if there was ever a white man who could tackle these mountains alone, it was he. It was his bloody hobby.

'But for those above me, his death was the best possible outcome. With Tolliver dead, they could draw a line under his crimes, move on with the Maharajah, all without ever having to pay out on the reward offered to ensure his continued co-operation. If that had been the end of it, I should never have thought to investigate my suspicions, for if Tolliver were alive, he would be long gone. But when, some months later, I happened upon a report detailing the desertion of a native, my suspicions were aroused again, for the native was this one – Tolliver's *jemadar*, Manraj Singh.'

He nudged the Sikh's body with his foot.

'Not being an imbecile, I knew it meant Tolliver must still be in these mountains, that he was lingering, not escaping. It was then that I decided to discern whether or not I was correct, and, if I proved to be so, what precisely Tolliver was up to. The reward would still be valid, after all – the Maharajah was not yet fully seduced. There was only one place to start my search, of course – here, the place from which only those two men had escaped. The place which now, moreover, was devoid of torturous natives, so we thought, since Tolliver's description of their barbarity had led to a full assault, wiping out all trace of his kidnappers. And Tolliver, such a native lover!

'I was certain the reward would increase if I could prove not only that Tolliver still lived, but that, for his own nefarious reasons, he had engineered an attack which had led to the deaths of British soldiers. That is, of course, if I were interested in the reward at all once I found Tolliver, for what could possibly have inspired these actions of his? We both know the answer to that, now, don't we, King?'

His first glove was off and he whacked it across my face, as though challenging me to a duel I was incapable of fighting.

In an attempt to buy myself time enough to hatch a plan, I laughed at him. I forced myself to roar to the heavens, and the confusion on his face only caused my laughter to become genuine.

'Petts, you idiot,' I sneered at him. 'You have wasted your time as I have. We're too late. There is no treasure. There's nothing here at all. Tolliver played you, man, played you like a bloody sitar!'

I laughed again, but I stopped when I realised that he had joined me.

'Oh, really?' He looked round. All eyes were upon him. 'Then what do you call this?' he said triumphantly, plucking from his pocket a thumbnail-sized stone, blue, like a sapphire, but with three intersecting white lines upon it, as though a six-pronged star had been trapped within it.

'Time and again, King, you simply prove that you are as much a cretin as these others that surround us. Or are you merely feeding me lies? Desist, or you shall be dead before you know it. But speak the truth, and you will find me reasonable.'

He replaced the stone in his pocket and hit me with the glove once more, then began to remove the other.

'I arrived here and found Tolliver living as a native, ingratiating himself among the remaining villagers, training the boys to be fighters, persuading them that to keep themselves safe they must kill any who came. I must say it appealed to my sense of humour, that the man they had come to revere as their protector was the very man who had ruined them. What d'you suppose these fresh-faced lads would have done to him if they'd known?

'Yet he could not have me killed as he desired, since to insure my survival I had left a letter with my men, outlining his entire deceit, which they were ordered to open should I not return from leave, and act upon accordingly. If this occurred, Tolliver knew that he could expect either the entire Army to be out gunning for him, revenge on its mind, or else a pack of bloodthirsty hounds, greedy for gold. So I had to return to civilisation, and yet Tolliver could not allow me to do so without a cut, because he knew I'd reveal his whereabouts for the reward money. He simply had no choice but to include me in his plans.

'But I was to prove a useful thorn in Tolliver's side. It took time to find the treasure, as he told me it would, since the place to which the natives had moved it had been consumed by an avalanche, created by the gunfire of the battle he himself had instigated in order to ease his path. Of course, that would not have mattered had he not lost the map. Oh yes, King, there is a map. Of course there is a map. There is always a map. Did you not even consider the possibility? Tut tut – it appears you really are the fool you seem. Tolliver drew it himself, following his escape. He hid some-where up there in the snow and watched as the natives relocated the booty. Fool that *he* was, lose the map he did. In truth, I do not know how long it took him to find the treasure again, but it was near two years before I lost my patience and he deigned to sweeten me with samples such as that I have shown you.'

He had removed the second glove and carefully placed them together.

'But if he had found the treasure, why was he still here?' I said. 'Why didn't he take it away?'

'I asked him that myself. Why not take it further into the moun-tains? I would never find him. I could not stay in Ishkuman, since to do so I would either have had to turn deserter or give up my commission, and without the Army as my gambling chip, Tolliver could have done with me as he wished. Do you know his answer? He couldn't move it. And why? Because there was too much of it, more than he had bargained for. Tolliver was prisoner to his treas-ure, and ever since, it is I who have been planning its extraction, I who have been plotting a route, paying off officials, buying passage and blinding eyes, breaking these men to follow my every order, no matter what it may be. To plan the surreptitious movement of a train of treasure is no mean task, King, but finally I have done it. The fire was stoked when your friend Forrester came to town and now I am ready. Durand was to be our passport.'

He had tucked his gloves into his belt, and was now winding a strip of leather around the knuckles of his right hand, flexing his fist as he did so.

'I have given more years of my life to this interminable waiting than I care to consider, in that limbo town of Gilgit. I've been labelled a coward for remaining there, and been passed over for promotion. I could not sell the tasters Tolliver gave me – their quality would arouse suspicion. So I have toiled to establish an unbroken route of safety through this country to the sea, and invested every penny to my name, and borrowed more. I once had a wife in England, but I do not know what happened to her, for I have never returned there, so concerned have I been for my investment in a better tomorrow. Yes, King, I am angry, for it was a dream that remained alive only as long as Tolliver. Perhaps Singh knew the treasure's location, but he too is dead, thanks to you.'

Apparently pleased with the strap around his knuckles, Petts began to roll up the sleeve of his right arm.

'Tolliver said that weed of a man Forrester never made it here, but even so, I had to be sure that he did not possess the map. After all, why else would he be babbling about Tolliver and Ishkuman? If he did have it, it would have given me the chance to turn the tables on Tolliver and cut him out of the loop. But thanks to the bleeding hearts the British Army allows into its ranks, I did not have the chance to question him as I wished and find out what he knew. I shall not make the same mistake with you.'

I was thinking fast. There was a map. Tolliver had s it, but lost it. A thing so vital! His reaction to its loss was liable to be extreme, violent even; a reaction that could spread panic in the right circumstances. My God. What a fool I'd been. And I – a watchmaker!

Suddenly my cheek was struck, not by the glove but by a bony fist.

'Tell me, King. Where is the watch? Do you have the map? I can be reasonable. Speak, and I shall let you live. The treasure is all I am looking for.'

When I said nothing, his mouth twisted into that insidious smile and he sighed, before bursting into action and striking me again with full might. The edges of the leather bit into my face and tore the skin.

'Speak,' he instructed calmly, then struck me again. 'Where is the watch?'

He hit me again, and spoke those words, and swung at me a dozen times, each with more power than the last as his zeal grew, and he hissed that same phrase between each, with ever-increasing venom. I knew to tell him what I had realised would be fatal, so I set my jaw and counted the blows as my face swelled and opened. Fifteen. With every impact I prayed that he would not notice the string around my neck. Eighteen. Nineteen. He was exhausted and furious.

'Speak!' he screamed and served a final blow and I felt the watch swing around my neck.

He was heaving for breath, bent over, his hands on his thighs. He looked up at me, shaking his head.

'God damn you, man. What—'

He stopped speaking and looked down at my chest, frowning. Then his brow smoothed and he smiled. 'Of course,' he rasped, and his long, sinewy fingers extended towards my heart. I felt a tug at my neck and then a snap and I saw the watch in his hand. He held it up towards the sun, gloating.

'Shall I tell you how Forrester came by the watch in the first place?' he said. 'I gave it to him. I – what irony! I threw it into the pot as we played a hand in the Mess – I thought it a worthless trinket then. I took it from the body of a dead bandit. What reason did I have to suppose it was Tolliver's, let alone that it held the key? It was only later, after Forrester had escaped, that Tolliver told me how he had lost the map. That was when he described the watch to me. You can imagine, King, how I swore when I learned what it was I had let slip through my fingers.

'Speaking Forrester's name when you came to the Mess like a lamb to the slaughter had marked you already, but when you were fool enough to mention the watch . . . With that, you signed your death warrant.'

He opened the watchcase. 'It is not the watch itself, but what it contains, the secrets it holds,' he said. 'Did you not notice that it is running slowly? Did you never think to mend it – you, a watch-maker? Surely even in your position you can see the humour here. Had you thought to practise your profession, you would, I think, have seen that the cogs are obstructed. Tolliver drew his map, and placed it in a worthless watch he purchased, decorated with a stone to remind him such riches were real; thus transforming it into a priceless key.'

Petts was only a yard away from me. He turned the watch in his hand and showed me the face. He removed a knife from his belt, then laid the watch down and put the blade to its back.

'All shall be revealed by the simple flick of my knife.'

The rear of the timepiece popped and fell to the ground. Petts upturned the watch. Out of it, onto his palm, fell a tiny object.

'To the victor the spoils – to he who overlooks nothing. If only you had thought to leave a letter detailing my perfidy. Ah, yes. How foolish of me – you did not know. You did not know any-thing, and soon you must pay for your ignorance and lack of foresight. But first . . .'

He placed the body of the watch on the stone table next to Rustam Khan and nimbly unfolded the object. It was a piece of paper, no more than four inches by three. Craning my neck, I saw writing and sketches adorning it, but I could not make out their meaning. Its ink was faded and brown.

He turned the paper round to inspect it.

My God, how stupid I had been. Never to have inspected the watch, never to have queried why it ran slowly. So consumed had I been by living the life of an explorer that I had utterly failed to practise my profession, a simple act that would have led straight to the treasure. I cursed myself under my breath. And Tolliver had told me it was so. When he had said that the treasure had been with me all along, he had not only meant in the catacombs; he meant all the way from London, halfway across the world. Five weeks on a ship and I had never thought to open the watch for even a rudimentary glance at its workings. The journey to Gilgit, the trek across the mountains. Never. If only the watchmaker had come to the surface for a mere five minutes, then the hateful Petts would not now have held the map. It was no more than I deserved. It was he who was learning the location of the treasure, because he was not a fool, because, as he said, he had overlooked nothing.

As Petts intently read the map I saw movement behind him and a sudden glint of metal at his ear. It was instantly familiar.

'Petts,' I shouted at him, realising that a distraction was required. As he looked at me in surprise, the glint of metal moved very slowly over his shoulder and revealed itself to be long and sharp, and a hand was holding it.

'Your men follow your orders, as you say. They did nothing to stop you killing Flack and they do not arrest you now, though the Foreign Secretary himself demands it. You manipulated Flack, even Tolliver and these people. You have the Army in your palm, and the natives under guard.'

The burly paw holding the hilt of the knife edged the blade under the chin of Captain Petts, moving so slowly and steadily that I struggled to see it move at all. I held Petts' gaze.

'But tell me, will any of them come to your aid when you most need it? When finally you remember the single thing you have overlooked, will any care to prevent your throat from being cut?'

Alarm filled his eyes.

'What do you mean? I haven't—'

He could not complete his sentence, for another burly paw had braced the back of his head, and the one under his chin pulled the shining blade to his neck.

'The map!' I cried.

But Petts realised immediately what was happening to him, and despite his terror he closed his fist around the paper, scrunched it into a tiny ball, lifted it to his mouth and swallowed it. Small pulled the knife tighter against the soldier's throat. A drop of blood trickled down his neck.

'Small!' I spluttered. 'Stop! Don't kill him! Hold him, but whatever you do, don't kill him!'

★

'What do you mean?' Small said. 'I recognise him. Tried to kill us in Gilgit. Drop that knife now.'

Petts dropped his knife. Small removed the soldier's pistol from its holster and threw it to the ground, along with his sabre.

'That doesn't matter,' I said and looked steadily into Small's eyes. They were ready to kill, but ready to listen. He had returned; empty-handed of course, but he had come back, and my heart filled with all the confidence I had felt when he had been at my side. I threw his deceit to the wind and concentrated on the present. 'What he just swallowed was a map, Small. It led to the treasure. Only he saw it, so only he can lead us to it.'

'Map?' he said, his eyes widening. 'What map?'

'Oh, yes,' said Petts. His fear had drained and he was thinking now of survival. 'There's treasure here. Now Tolliver and Singh are dead, I am the only one left who knows where it is. Except perhaps the people here. By all means ask *them* to tell you where to find it.'

Small and I both glanced towards the villagers. Some of the youths among them had grown bolder, and had begun to taunt the soldiers. Finch struck one with the butt of his rifle; Crampers kicked another to the ground.

'Unhand me and we can commence negotiations,' Petts said.

'Negotiations, eh?' said Small with a snort as he pulled the knife harder against Petts' throat. 'You'll show us where, or you'll die. Negotiations complete. Understand?'

Another bead of blood trickled down Petts' neck.

Suddenly Small threw Petts' thin frame to the ground and flung himself across his chest, pointing the tip of his knife at his bloodied throat.

'Or better yet, I'll take it out of you, and then you'll be of no use to anybody.' Small ran his knife down Petts' neck. 'Can't have got too far. Let's see now . . . I've always fancied myself a bit of a surgeon. About here I'd say, wouldn't you, King?' He stopped his knife just below Petts' breastbone, then raised himself onto his knees and put his hand over the hilt of the knife, as though he was about to exert great force upon it, which would doubtless penetrate straight through Petts' uniform, skin, guts and bone.

'Whoever you are,' a voice came. 'Stop what you are doing this instant.' It was Durand, and Small looked up, scowling at the interruption. The Foreign Secretary no longer had a gun trained on him and was out of his saddle, approaching us. 'This man is our prisoner. He will return with us and be judged by martial law. These men are now under my command, and if you do as you propose, they shall arrest you a murderer.'

'Oh dear,' said Petts from the ground. Small looked down at him, spat, then up at me, his eyes smiling, and there was even a sign of a near-imperceptible wink before he turned to Durand.

'Who in hell are you to tell me what to do here?' Small said, not moving an inch. 'I just saved your skin from this bastard. Now then, through the breastbone, I should think. What do you say, King?'

'I warn you,' Durand said. 'Sergeant! Get over here.'

'Yes,' I said. 'Or through the belly.'

'I'll start high, and move down,' Small said, bracing himself for the first incision.

'I'll show you,' Petts gasped, terrified once more, and defeated. 'I'll show you.'

'I knew you would, old man. You see – Durand, wasn't it? – a little carefully judged persuasion can get things moving a treat,' Small said, pulling Petts to his feet. 'Though I do wish you'd not given in quite so easily, Captain. Now untie our friend here,' he continued, nodding at me. Petts struggled with the knots holding me in place – Small wisely declining to allow him the use of a blade.

I looked towards the village. Petts' men had moved between us and the villagers, at whom they were continuing to point their rifles. All, that is, but for the boyish Fowler, who had come to Durand, and was in the process of promising him that it was only Petts that had engineered any of what had happened, that he had been caught in the crossfire of the Captain's mania just as the Foreign Secretary had been. Durand frowned, but considering our circumstances, curtly nodded his acceptance of the apology.

Suddenly I dropped to the ground, my hands and knees sinking into the soft grass. I was free. I lifted myself to my feet and ran to the inanimate Rustam Khan's side.

'Not even a copper coin down there, lad,' Small was saying, as much to Petts as me, prodding the soldier with the tip of his knife. 'So I said to myself, "Small, old stick, you've a friend in need up there, and you haven't many. If you can save him and win his forgiveness, then for God's sake go and do so at once!"'

'Rot!' I said as I knelt by Rustam Khan. 'You knew the treasure must be up here somewhere.'

Small grinned.

'What do you take me for, boy?' he said, and then called suddenly: 'Lieutenant. Get over here and tie this blighter up, will you?'

Small lifted the watch from the stone table, considered it for a moment and then tutted.

'In here all along, was it? And you a watchmaker. Damn it all! I thought you'd be useful to have along!'

He replaced the watch around my neck. It was running perfectly. What an unutterable fool I had been.

Small nodded at Rustam Khan's body. 'I'm sorry, lad. You did your best, more than he'd have asked for.'

Rustam Khan's blood had soaked into the stone. His face was pale, his eyes shut. I felt for a pulse in his throat. There was none I could discern. I bowed my head.

'Rustam Khan,' I whispered into his ear. 'I'm sorry.'

'Sahib,' he croaked all of a sudden and opened his eyes wide, looking at nothing. 'My wife – she cannot remain here now.'

Rustam Khan tried to lift his arm, but failed, for that moment he breathed his last and died.

I looked towards the soldiers where Rustam Khan had tried to point. Through the villagers I saw someone making her hurried way. The soldiers raised their rifles.

'Let her come,' I shouted, and then the weeping Fahlhana broke from the crowd and was dashing towards us. She collapsed by her husband and howled with woe. I looked over at the dead Tolliver, the instigator of so much grief. I spat on the ground before turning to face the throng. All were looking at me from varying distances: Fahlhana from her husband's side, Small, Petts, Fowler and Durand, the rest of the soldiers and the villagers from where they stood.

'Now, Petts,' I said. 'Lead the way.'

32

THE LETTERS OF
SIR PAUL LINDLEY-SMALL

Twenty feet from my quarry
43 Kjellersmauet, Bergen, Norway

12TH JANUARY 1909

My dear Cyril,

I have told you how I came to this land, and I have related near all that has occurred since my arrival. And now my task is minutes from conclusion. When this letter is written, I shall rise from this bed, lift my bag and my remaining whisky from the floor, walk down a single flight of stairs, place the priceless creature into a gunnysack, and depart. But first I must wait an hour to make sure the coast is clear.

Kjellersmauet (meaning: Cellar Alley) was a residential street, it turned out, and the exterior of number forty-three was very much like the many other well-kept two-storey timber houses that line the narrow and steep lanes of Bergen. 'Unremarkable' is the word – precisely *not* the epithet you would choose for the creature I hoped it housed.

Ascertaining that the address next to my crude sketch of a cat matched that of the house before which I stood, I knocked upon the door and awaited an answer. The door was finally opened, but only a little way at first. When the old woman behind it saw me, though, she opened it wide and asked of me my business. Hers was a dear old face. Each wrinkle upon it seemed more from endless expressions of happiness and benevolence than wear, and her aged eyes looked upon me with a sparkle one rarely sees in such an old girl. She was dressed in colourful clothes and her short white hair was tucked behind ears decked with pearls. The small frame under this rather brilliant plumage, along with her somewhat abrupt movements and decent-sized beak of a nose, gave her the air of an excitable bird.

'I am here to discuss exotic beasts,' I said, smiling back at her from the doorstep. 'With your husband, perhaps?'

My grasp of the language being what it is, she recognised me instantly for the Englishman that I am, and responded to me in my native tongue, which carried only a hint of accent.

'Yes, he is very interested in exotic animals,' she answered in a sweet voice. 'It is something of a hobby for us. Do come in,' and she stood aside to allow me through.

Closing the door behind me, she led me through a small hall, where I set down my luggage. As I did so, she told me that she was Mrs Kleverud. In turn, I gave her my name and said how pleased I was to meet her. From the hall, we came into a warm and homely sitting room where she guided me to an armchair at one side of a fire. This was more like it. The room was decorated with paintings of the impressive surrounding landscape and photographs of family. One in particular, albeit briefly, caught my attention. It hung over the mantel and was of a healthy-looking man of middle age in solar topee and with a rifle in his hand. Under his raised foot was the body of a tiger. Her husband, I deduced. If del Fuego's tip-off was accurate, it was this man from whom I was here to buy, inveigle, or steal the King Cobra Cat, if he still held the beast. And I had reason to believe he might.

I say the photograph only briefly grasped my roving eye, for what diverted my attention the more was the abundance of animals in the room, posed as if in their natural habitat. In all the houses I have entered in this country, there has been a propensity for dead animals, though in most this trend does not go beyond the antlers of reindeer or the head of a moose. Here, however, each was a whole beast, and they were of wildly varying sorts. On the windowsill, I saw a weasel on a branch. Nothing remarkable about that. But climbing up a bookshelf was the brilliantly striped form of a mangrove snake. And standing by the coal bucket was a juvenile capybara. A fish eagle watched us from its perch above the door through which we had come, while a red kite flared its talons over another.

The couple were apparently keen and talented taxidermists, the ramifications of which hit me like Mr Bakkland's spade when I saw a basket placed between the fire and the armchair into which the old woman was lowering herself. Curled in this basket was a beige form, undeniably feline, a black figure of eight etched into the back of its head. I stifled a gasp of horror. How far I had travelled, and in so many different directions, only to discover that my prey had been slaughtered and stuffed like any common species. The Museum would take it, of course, but the eggheads in London who prop up the respectability of the Lindley-Small name do not possess pockets as deep as the princes of India, and what self-respecting Maharajah would pay through the nose for a creature of legend brought to them in this state? I sank into the other armchair and reflected upon my plight as the old woman spoke.

'I would dearly love to introduce you to my husband,' she said, taking up a photograph of the pair of them from younger days. 'For if you are a lover of animals as he was, you would surely get on uncommonly well. They were his passion, you see. You would have talked long into the night, I'm sure.' She looked at me and narrowed her eyes. Were they welling?

'But, alas,' she continued, 'you are six years too late. Can it really have been that long since we last spoke? Now all I have is the taxidermy we shared. And the animals, of course,' she added, and reached down to her side.

So her husband was dead. It was indeed sad that a woman who

plainly so loved a man was bereft of him, but I could do little to aid her in her troubles. Besides, I had my own to think of.

Having reached down, she straightened, and sitting on her thin lap was the cat from the basket. It was still curled as it had been in the basket and she stroked its inanimate form tenderly.

'Yes, at least I have you,' she said in Norwegian. It would be a sad sight to see a woman of any age caress and whisper sweetly to a stuffed cat, like an infant addressing its teddy bear, but the melancholy in seeing one of age do so was all the greater, for how could she escape thought of her own mortality? That the cat she was stroking was one I so dearly wished to see alive only tripled the sadness.

Then, quite suddenly, the cat stood and arched its back, a black tongue sliding out of its closed mouth between a pair of miniature sabre-tooth fangs two inches long. It was alive, Cyril – wonderfully alive! And its tongue, though wide, was distinctly forked! Only with my preternatural strength of mind did I successfully quell the desire to jump up and run around the place shouting, 'Bravo!'

Instead, I said, 'What an awfully fine beast.'

'Oh yes,' she said. 'The finest beast in the house.' She stroked the cat beneath its chin, between those mighty teeth, and its still outstretched tongue flickered in delight.

Behind my admiring grin, I was thinking that this was not so melancholy an affair, after all. The cat was alive, and her husband was dead. That I had to wrest the beast from the loving hands of this old woman alone halved the task before me. Surely she could not know of its background as her husband might have, for if she did she would not be stroking it so close to those fangs. From that thought, my mind leapt nimbly ahead to consider the best methods of obtaining the King Cobra Cat for myself. If this old girl were unwilling to take the healthy amount of money I would initially offer her for the creature, perhaps a replacement cat could be found on the street, free of charge, and left in its place. But no, I threw the idea from my mind as I watched her. Though sentimental, this woman was no fool. She would recognise an impostor immediately, for a common mog could never hope to replicate this extraordinary creature.

The cat was sitting on her lap, as I say, facing me with its tongue hanging out and its eyes blissfully closed, enjoying its grooming. It was perhaps a degree larger than an average puss, its sand-coloured fur slightly shorter and finer, and its ears stood higher. It also possessed a tail of rare length, which it flicked to and fro, belying the relaxation of its deep and contented purr. When the old woman invited me to stroke it, in order not to let on that it was anything but a common garden cat, I stretched out my hand.

I selected the haunches as my spot, since it was the furthest from its mouth that I could reasonably reach. However, I was never to get that far. My fingers inches away, the cat suddenly reared up onto its back legs. Its eyes were flashes of bright, alert yellow that tracked me as I threw myself back into my seat. Its ears and whiskers were flattened back against its head, its mouth open, hissing and baring those fangs in threat. Most remarkable of all, though, was its chest. Where before the skin on its underside had looked loose and slack, suggesting general laziness, it was now as taut as a drum and twice as wide, as though it had suddenly drawn ribs that had previously hung vertically up to the horizontal, stretching out the skin like an umbrella. Every muscle in its body was tensed and ready to strike as it began to swing slowly from side to side like the charmers' snakes. In my fascination, I leaned forward and saw that its lower jaw had moved backwards when it opened its mouth, as well as down, as though giving the oversized fangs room enough to effectively sink into the flesh of prey. Which was plainly what it considered me.

Remarkable, I thought to myself. To do such a thing it must be able to unhinge its jaw, just as a snake does. That way, it could bite into even the largest prey. The leg of a snake charmer, for example, or a torturer's victims. Also, where most snakes have pink and fleshy mouths, that of the creature before me was jet black, like its tongue. Having pulled myself together, I leaned further forward and saw that its hood, gratifyingly like that of a cobra, was thin and curved.

'This is even more—' I blurted out, before stopping myself. I did not want to give my intentions away, but I could not now doubt that the woman knew that she had something exceptional on her lap. But surely she could not know its true nature, for who would allow such a venomous beast so close?

'Is he not a spectacle?' the woman beamed.

'Quite,' I said, and shrugged. 'But I have seen his kind before. They are really quite common in the jungles of Burma. This, I must admit, is the plainer of the genera. Its cousins – the *naga felidae leopardis* – carry the most splendid spots, like that of a leopard.' With this brisk white lie I was hoping to lower expectations as to its value.

She stroked him again and smiled as he settled.

'Have you come far?' she asked abruptly. 'Where are you staying?'

I had not thought so far in advance as to take up lodgings for the night, and told her so.

'Then you must stay here with us,' she decreed, just as I had hoped. 'We will be able to talk of creatures and expeditions long into the night, just as you would have done with my husband. It shall be most enjoyable. Please say that you will stay.'

Things were going perfectly to plan. She was determined to have me and I was determined to stay, for if my persuasion did not succeed, a spot of midnight theft would be just the job. I said immediately that I would, thanking her for her kindness and stating that a home-cooked meal is always preferable to dining alone in a restaurant. That it was not is beside the point. I had not come here for culinary reasons.

Picking up my satchel and near-empty box of Glenlivet from the hall, I followed her upstairs to where I was to sleep. At the top of the stairs there were four doors. One, she told me, was her bedroom, one the bathroom, one the study and the last, to which she opened the door, was the room I now occupy. In it are the ghostly forms of two lambs frolicking, a sinister crow and a group of rats eating sunflower seeds, all stuffed. Before closing the door and leaving me, she said that we would eat in an hour.

I changed and washed in half that time and headed down with

my penultimate bottle, a good amount of Glenlivet being the least I could offer the woman. I also hoped that it would make her more conducive to parting with her companion or, failing that, sleep heavily enough for me to go off with it without her noticing. And anyway, I was in the mood for celebration.

After only two moderate fingers of whisky, which she seemed to enjoy almost as much as I, we sat down to a drab supper of potatoes and some form of fish, kneaded into balls, all doused in a thick and floury white sauce. Saying that so fine a tipple as the one I had produced could not be properly enjoyed with food, she insisted we save the Glenlivet, and instead brought a bottle of their harsh, but warming and tasty national drink, aquavit, to the table. It is, I believe, distilled potatoes, but should you ever have the opportunity of partaking of it, do not let that knowledge put you off. It cut through the stodginess of our meal admirably and we both left the table for our respective armchairs by the fire notice-ably tighter than we had approached it.

Then, with a good measure of Glenlivet in each of our hands, we sat and enjoyed the warmth of the fire on our toes. The cat, sleeping in its basket once more, seemed as inanimate as any of the other beasts in the room, but I was careful to keep my feet a good distance from it. Though she had been garrulous at the table, the old lady, presumably not so accustomed to the effects of distillation as I, now stared into the fire, deep in thought. Therefore, in the pleasant silence, I took the opportunity to appreciate the flavours trickling down my throat and looked around the room once more as I did so.

Presently, my eyes arrived on the mangrove snake. It really is an extraordinary-looking beast, deep green with electric yellow stripes running across the length of its body. Living in swamps, it spends much of its time travelling in the trees from branch to branch, and the position in which the Kleveruds had placed it did justice to this. It bent this way and that, up the side of the book-case and sharply around onto a shelf where its head lay, mouth wide, in front of impressively old-looking tomes that I had previ-ously neglected to admire.

Each one was of a different height, girth and colour, though all were leather-bound, poorly cared-for and well-read. Their faded titles were difficult to see in the poor light at such a distance, and through eyes blurring with flavoursome intake, but narrowing their lids, I succeeded in making out the first few before the old woman addressed me. *Incas Found* was one, *Aboriginal Skinning Techniques* another. The last was *Legends of the Hindooman*. Before I could consider these titles, my attention was drawn back to the woman. She was gazing at me with a slight frown, and gave the impression that she had been doing so for some time.

'Is it not bizarre,' she said, licking her lips, 'that you should happen upon my doorstep? I must assume that it was not entirely by coincidence.'

'You would be right, Mrs Kleverud. I must confess that I learned of you from a mutual acquaintance. One Diego del Fuego.'

'Ah, yes. Of course,' she said, her frown evaporating and the friendly smile returning. 'Diego is an errant fellow and must know many people. That is what makes him so suitable.'

'Suitable?' I echoed.

'Yes,' she replied. 'Diego was always on the look-out for beasts that he thought might be of interest to us. Wherever his boats took him, he would always return to us with something quite arresting. Even when, six years ago, my husband could no longer accept them, I took them from him, for how could I deny such a faithful fellow after so many years of loyal service?'

She smiled in memory before abruptly changing the subject.

'What brings you to Norway, Mr Small?' she asked.

'It is a fine country, Mrs Kleverud,' I replied. 'With many fine sights.'

'Is it to visit friends, perhaps? Or family, even?' she pushed.

'Alas, no, Mrs Kleverud. Though I have met many delightful people here, they have been fleeting acquaintances. I must admit to being somewhat errant myself, much like our friend Diego del Fuego, and not one to dally too long,' I said, hoping that a description of such a lonely existence would breed pity in her heart and make her more willing to part with her cat.

'I am also very interested in any kind of beast,' I went on, 'and this country of yours offers so many that are fascinating.'

'Yes, I understand you are, and so you will be pleased to hear that this little house and its contents are even more interesting than you know.' She tilted her head and smiled knowingly.

This threw me somewhat, because I did indeed know. But did she know? Did she know that I knew?

Was this a game she was playing with me? Or was she unaware that she was taunting me? Anger rose at the possibility, but uncertainty contained it and instead I tried to make her an offer. 'But I am particularly interested in this cat of yours. I was wondering, would you—'

'My dear fellow, I would never be parted from this cat,' she interrupted as though she knew my very thoughts. Her voice was suddenly stern and commanding. 'Though he is not what I expected him to be when Diego delivered him, he is really all I have, and I still have great hopes for him.'

'I would be willing to be very generous,' I said.

'Do you know,' she continued in the same unnerving tone, entirely ignoring my words, 'it was Diego himself who returned with that little vial six years ago?'

'A vial?' I echoed, my confusion doubling.

'Yes, a vial,' she said, smiling now, her voice softening as she remembered. 'It contained a particular kind of venom, extremely rare. I had never before heard of it, and if my husband had, his condition had become so very severe that he could not recall ever having done so.'

With that, she jumped to her feet, her sudden excitement lending her old legs a surprising agility.

'Come along,' she said. I was trying to gather my thoughts. She was not proving to be the soft touch I had hoped for. Plan B was called for, and that meant bed, so I rose, thinking she had just announced an abrupt end to the evening, and thank God for that, I thought to myself as I followed her up the stairs.

I had nothing to thank Him for.

On the landing, she opened the door she had previously told me led to the study, and into it she ushered me, announcing that it was her husband's room.

It was a smallish room, made all the smaller by the books that filled cases on every wall and an even greater number of stuffed animals than I had seen elsewhere in her home. There was a serval leaping from the ground to pluck a partridge from the air, which hung from a string; a pair of African Wild Dogs scrapped in one corner; a lanky and ugly secretary bird looked out of the small window; and a monitor lizard lay across the desk. However, what caught my eye immediately was the man sitting in the chair, apparently reading a book.

'Jon,' Mrs Kleverud said, 'this is an Englishman – Mr Small, wasn't it?' Then she turned to me and said, 'My husband, Mr Small. Mr Kle

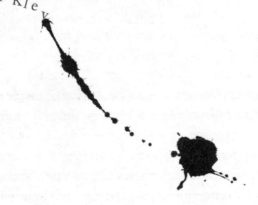

33

THE NOTEBOOKS OF CYRIL KING

1893

Into the Mountain

Small sheathed his blade. He retrieved his rifle from the corpse of Manraj Singh and prodded Petts in the back with it. Fowler had tied the prisoner's hands and the three of them started to walk towards the villagers, who were growing angrier and more restless by the moment. Small fired a round into the air and they stepped back a yard or two and quietened. I approached the stone table and pulled Fahlhana to her feet, but she continued to look into the lifeless eyes of her husband.

'We must go,' I whispered, and finally she nodded, wiping tears from her face. 'Come. Fetch horses. For you, me and Small. Go now.'

She dropped her husband's hand, broke her gaze and darted towards the huts across the slope.

I caught up with Small. As we neared the villagers, they grew jittery again. Murder was in all their eyes, but the soldiers split a path between them, shouting back at them as they began to shout at us, the bringers of so much bloody discord.

'We'll leave a couple of men here to cover them,' Small said as we approached the rest of the soldiers. 'Corporals, you remain here. You should be able to contain them in the bottleneck. When you hear two shots in quick succession, head down the trail towards them and find us. Understood?'

Crampers and Finch nodded their assent.

'Now Corporals, that's not the way, is it?' the Sarge barked from his saddle. His face looked gleefully at Petts. 'We've a new captain.'

'Yessir!' the corporals said in unison and jerked salutes at Small.

'That's more like it,' said the Sarge.

'There's no need for that, lads,' Small said. 'None of this rank rubbish. Let's just get out of here alive, eh?' He broke off, and in a delighted voice exclaimed, 'There's my girl!'

He was looking towards the village, where Fahlhana was leading four horses towards us. One was Bucephalus.

'Now then,' Small said, frowning at Durand. 'Who on earth *are* you?'

'I, sir, am Sir Mortimer Durand. Her Majesty's Foreign Secretary of India.'

'Well, pack my pipe and smoke it. Off your route a bit, I should say. A pencil-pushing bureaucrat's just what we need,' Small said. 'What're you doing here?'

'Government business,' Durand answered curtly. 'And you, sir. Who might you be?'

'Government business, eh?' said Small. 'Well, it looks as if it's been postponed.'

'Your name, sir,' Durand insisted.

'It's probably better you don't learn that, Foreign Secretary. For your own good.'

'Hmm,' said Sir Mortimer, frowning. 'Well, whoever you are, I warrant you've saved my life here today, so despite your tone I must concede that I am pleased to make your acquaintance.'

'Ha!' exclaimed Small. 'You may live to regret those words.'

'Whatever do you mean?' Durand asked, but Small did not answer, for then Fahlhana reached us with the horses. The fourth horse, I now saw, was loaded with food and grain.

Small went to Bucephalus and removed a bottle of his coveted whisky, uncorked it and took a long drink. 'Two more left to see us through,' he said, throwing it to me. 'And food, too. Nothing more to wait for. Mount up.' He prodded Petts again. 'I'll take you on Bucephalus. Up you go now.'

Small shoved Petts roughly into the saddle and then swung up behind him. Having drunk, I returned the bottle to its sheath and pulled myself up onto one of the horses. Fahlhana lifted herself easily onto hers.

'Now, which way, Petts?' Small said.

The Captain nodded up the path and Small nudged Bucephalus into a walk, through the gap the soldiers had opened in the crowd of villagers. Durand followed, then the Sarge, Fahlhana, Fowler, myself, and finally the corporals.

I looked back as we went forward. Beyond the corporals, beyond the villagers tracking our course with hate-filled eyes, we were leaving behind a gathering of corpses. The faithful Manraj Singh, the gallant Major Flack, the tragic Rustam Khan, and beneath the risen sun, being lifted from his bier by four fair youths, Tolliver. I only hoped what we would find would be worth the cost.

We moved silently and slowly along the path. The soldiers swept their rifles over the villagers at our stirruped feet as we rode through them, ready to fire at any sign of violence. At the head of the village, where the trail started, the corporals stopped, creating a barrier through which the villagers could not pass.

'Remember,' Small said to them from ahead. 'Two shots. It might take a while, but keep your ears open. And good luck.'

Petts led us on the trail for some minutes, but halfway down he brought us to a halt. There were voices at the front, but I could not make them out, so I squeezed my way along to the front of our caravan. There I found Small and Petts arguing.

'What's the matter?' I asked Small.

'This blackguard thinks he's taking us up there, into the snow where we'll all sink like stones and he'll make his break.'

'It's the truth,' Petts said to me. 'It is where we must go. It's up there. That I could have told you even without the map. The conundrum is not the where, but the how.'

'Very well, Small,' I said. 'Let him lead us on, but keep a good eye on him. You should be able to wing him before he gets far.'

And so we headed upwards again, towards a black wall of rock thrusting up out of the white of the snow some hundred feet. Petts led us to its base. Snow had been cleared here, it was plain to see, and what remained was compacted, but the wall was utterly featureless, one spot identical to the next.

'This was entirely hidden after the avalanche, as though wiped from the face of the earth by the wrath of God. It took them years to dig it out,' Petts said. 'I need to dismount.'

'Then get to it,' Small said. 'But watch your step, now.'

Small allowed Petts to slip from the saddle onto the snow. He fell to his knees. Small laughed.

'I can't walk like this,' Petts sneered up at him. 'If you want your treasure you must cut loose my hands.'

I dismounted. Small's laughter ceased when he saw me.

'What're you doing, man?'

'He's unarmed, Small. If he makes a run for it, by all means shoot him down with your rifle. He can't get away – not up here. And then you can get the map out of him.'

I spun Petts around and cut through his bindings.

'You will be killed if you run,' I whispered in his ear. 'But if you remain calm and do as we say, I promise you, you will go free.'

'How very charitable of you,' he sneered in my face. 'Fetch rope.'

He walked to the very edge of the wall, turned and strode back towards me, counting under his breath.

'Twenty-three,' he said and halted. Then he turned and started moving his hands over the stone of the wall. We all watched him as he stroked the black rock, like a blind man looking for his spectacles. But then his right hand stopped, stretched above him. Then his left one also ceased moving, a yard to the side of his right.

The forefinger of both his hands appeared to have vanished. 'The rope,' he said.

I passed him the rope which Small had uncoiled from his saddle, and when he reached to grasp it, I saw that his right forefinger had not vanished but been hidden by a hole barely an inch in diameter. He fed the rope into it, pushing it through until it appeared by his left hand. He pulled the short end through until the lengths matched and he passed one to me.

'Not the where, but the how. Now tie this to your saddle. We need another horse,' he said to Small.

Small tied the second line to Bucephalus.

'Now pull.'

We led the horses away from the rock face, until the lines grew taut. Small and Petts beat the creatures' haunches, jeered them on, and the animals' hooves dug into the icy snow. The rope creaked with strain, and looked ready to break, until first Bucephalus, then the second horse, suddenly moved forward. A great slab of black stone, six feet high, four wide and eight inches deep, slammed into the snow.

I turned to Small and Petts, the latter's excitement easily eclipsing the hopelessness of his position. He was suffering from that insurmountable thirst for discovery as we all were.

The rest dismounted and we all gathered around.

'Why, this is a cave,' Durand announced.

Small was looking into the blackness.

'Get the torches going, King.'

I pulled them out of the satchel on his back and lit them.

'Give one to Petts and keep the other.'

I did as he said.

'Now then. King, you and the Sarge come with me. The rest stay here. We don't know what we'll find.'

'You'll struggle to keep me out of there,' Durand said.

'Very well,' was Small's response. The Foreign Secretary's sporting nature appeared to be winning him over. 'But we'll all go after you, Petts.'

Petts pointed the torch into the cave and waved it. When nothing happened, he stepped in and was consumed by the darkness. All I could see was the flame of his torch and the side of his face. Small followed him in, then Durand, then I and finally the Sarge.

For the first twenty yards the way was broad enough only to

walk in single file, but then it widened and we were able to go two
abreast, until we were brought to a standstill by a junction of paths
ahead. Before us, three paths led each in its own direction.

'Which do you think?' Small said.

'I've no idea,' I answered. I had thought the treasure would
simply be waiting for us, that being hidden in a secret chamber
would suffice. But no, now we had to face a maze to boot.

'Men, if it is treasure you are after, I imagine gold would be part
of it, would I be correct?' It was Durand.

'Gold, silver, jewels. We'll take what comes,' Small replied.

'Well, if it were gold, it'd be weighty, take several to carry, and
so for convenience the widest route would be taken. That way.'

'That's good enough for me, man. Let's move on,' said Small.

After that we came across other divisions in the path, but since
the tunnels were blacker than night, and lit only by our weak
torches, we did not see them until we were upon them. Following
as we were Sir Mortimer's theory, it was only the final one we
arrived at that presented any obstacle; though at first we did not
realise that there was a fork at all. Something else had drawn our
attention.

There was the faintest glow of light from the tunnel ahead.

'That must be it!' Petts said, striding forwards. It was fortunate
for him that Small moved with him, for he was able to grab on to
the Captain's cuff before he fell into the great hole that lay
between us and our path, eight feet across, a pit leading to the very
bowels of the earth. Small took the torch from Petts, barged him
back towards us, then leaned cautiously out over the lip of the abyss
and peered into it. I edged up next to him.

'Some kind of fissure,' he murmured. 'Must have been caused by
ice.' He crouched and threw a stone into the darkness of the chasm.
We heard it strike the wall as it fell, and again, and then a third time,
fading into silence. We did not hear it land. 'As deep as Hell.'

Small stepped back and then, as though it were a javelin, he
launched the torch over the hole towards the tunnel from which
the glow was emanating. Travelling through the air the flames lit
the cavern for a moment and I briefly saw that immediately next

to the one in which the torch clattered to a landing, there was another tunnel that continued in darkness.

'No way round,' I said. 'The sides are sheer.'

Small's eyes sparkled in the flame of my torch. He was grinning again.

'How's your long jump, lad?'

I didn't have a chance to answer him, though, for he turned to the Foreign Secretary.

'Sorry, sir. Can't have you risking your valuable neck here. You are a passport, after all.' Then to the Sarge: 'Take him back up. Then look around. If we're on the right trail, this must have been crossed before. Wood, rope, anything that might be useful. If there's something there, we won't be able to jump back with the loot. If it's gold, we'll struggle to throw it, but if you find nothing we'll have to try. Off you go, now.'

'Yessir,' the Sarge answered, rather pleased to be about turning. 'You heard the man, Foreign Secretary, sir. No place for you.'

This time Durand didn't argue.

'Jump?' I said to Small when they had gone and only he, I and Petts remained. 'It's eight feet at least.'

'Well, you're nearly six, lad. Put your arms up and you're eight. Where's that spirit got to, eh? You keep an eye on Petts,' he said, handing me his knife. 'I'll go first, show you how it's done. Then you, Petts, and lastly you, lad. Just aim for the light. As simple as that. Stand back now.'

With that he tightened his satchel on his back, secured his rifle, let out a banshee's wail and sprinted towards the pit. He took off at the very last moment, springing his foot off the very cusp of the endless fall and disappeared into the darkness, his bulk cutting out the light of the torch he had flung across. Only when his yell ceased and on the other side I saw him pick up the torch and brandish it did I know he had made it.

'Now you, Petts,' he called. 'Couldn't be easier.'

'Off you go,' I said to the soldier, flicking the blade towards the hole. 'And remember what I said.'

'How could I forget such saintly words?' he spat, but when I raised the knife to his face, he bit off further retort. 'Very well.'

He backed up against the rock of the tunnel. He too screamed as he went, but when he took off he did not eclipse the flame of Small's torch. His holler ceased and I heard him land but I could not see him next to Small in the yellow glow. Petts grunted in the dark, there was the sound of scrambling and then of footsteps running.

'Small!' I shouted. 'Have you got him?'

'The blighter jumped to the left, King. Into the other tunnel. Get after him. Aim a few feet left of my torch. Throw yours over. Quick, man.'

I hurled my torch in the direction that Petts had leapt. It landed in the tunnel, but rolled backwards until it dropped into the pit. I watched it descend, down and down, until fathoms below, it was swallowed by a darkness that not even the light of fire could penetrate. My landing strip was sloped, towards the cavern. I backed away from the edge of the hole.

'Quick, man!' Small shouted.

I braced myself against the stone and looked on into the darkness. This was surely suicide. I saw Small's face glowing angrily next to his torch, but Petts had utterly vanished. Even the scampering footsteps of the rat had died.

'King! Get a move on!' Small's voice came again.

I let out a scream, more terrified than either that had gone before, squeezed my eyes tight shut and ran forwards as quickly as my legs could carry me. After only four strides I pushed off the ground and opened my eyes. I saw Small's torch flashing by, a glimpse of his concerned face, and then my breastbone hit rock. My arms were in the tunnel along which Petts had disappeared, but my body, the great majority of my weight, was dangling into the chasm. I flailed my arms around the tunnel, slapping the smooth stone, panicking for a handhold, but there was nothing but hard, flat rock to grasp. Loose pebbles moved me backwards like an archaic conveyor belt. I kicked against the wall of the chasm, digging the toes of my boots into the rock, but the protruding stone on which the leather of my sole gripped merely

crumbled, broke free and fell into the natural throat that was waiting to swallow me. The incline of the tunnel was too steep. I was
slipping.

'Small!' I cried. 'I'm falling! *Small!*'

I saw the swish of his torch not three feet from me.

'I see you, lad. Hold on!'

I heard him struggle with something, but not quickly enough.
Only the friction of my forearms against the rock was now delaying my fall. The stones tore at my skin, but I pushed down with all
my might, for the pressure was slowing my descent.

'SMAAALLLL!'

'I'm here, lad. You feel that?'

There was a prod in my armpit.

'Don't tickle me, man!' I cried.

'It's my rifle, lad. Take hold of it. I'll swing you here. Just don't
pull the trigger or we're both going down there!'

There was nothing else I could do. As the last of my fingers
slipped from the ledge, I lunged into the darkness and flailed. I felt
the gun, and grabbed at it. My fingers closed round cold metal, but
the sweat of my palms made them slip down to the polished
wood. I felt the trigger guard. If I had not grabbed it, I would have
fallen. The shot rang through the chasm, echoed its way down,
and the flash of light showed Small above me grimacing, flinching,
fearful.

'Good God, man! What did I tell you?' he barked. 'You've taken
half my ear off, you fool!'

But I was not falling. I had gripped the gun and despite the shot,
Small had taken the weight. There was a lurch, and I found myself
dangling in the darkness. Then Small began to hoist me up.

'You're heavier than you look,' he said.

He gripped my hand in his and with a final mighty heave we fell
backwards into the tunnel. I landed on Small's chest and gasped for
breath.

'This is all very nice, lad,' Small said. 'Cosy, but what say we look
for this damned treasure now, and find it before that detestable
Petts, hmm?'

We crawled forwards and got to our feet as we rounded the bend. Small removed his turban from his satchel and wrapped it around his head, binding it to gather the blood from his wounded ear. The ice that had split the rock to form the tunnels we traversed must once have broken out from the mountain, or into it. I am no geologist, so cannot tell of the movement of ice; but that it had once forced a passage to the light of day could not be questioned, for the source of the light we had seen from the other side of the chasm was the sun. An angled beam shone down through a crack in the roof above and illuminated a broad cavern. It was neither the cavern nor the light that stopped the pair of us in our stride and caused me to grab Small's wrist, however. It was what the one contained, and the other illuminated.

'By God, lad,' Small whispered as he leaned his rifle against the wall of the tunnel and walked slowly forward. 'We've found it!'

★

He was not exaggerating. Indeed, what I beheld outdid all my fantasies, melted them under its brilliant glare. It was a sight difficult to describe with a mere pen. I should struggle even with an artist's easel.

We stood on an intricately woven carpet, large enough for twenty men to occupy. Before us, bathed in that shaft of light, was a man, eight inches high, on a gilded plinth. He was red, as though of ruby, but for a hand which was the very yellowest of golds. Around him, in relative darkness, on similar plinths spaced no more than six inches apart, were more figurines, hundreds of them, of every description conceivable – human, animal, chimera and many more still that bore no relation to the physical world at all – each intricately carved and glittering with decoration. The walls of the chamber were gilded, too, and the plinths did not sit on the ground but floated on a sea of ingots, nuggets, necklaces, bracelets, brooches and crowns, goblets, platters, shields, swords and jewels of every colour imaginable that flowed onto the carpet. To my left, near the entrance to the chamber was a collection of wooden rifle crates, each marked with the emblem of the British Army. Only these did not contain firearms. Ribbons of gold spilled out of them, like licking flames solidified burning from a nest of gems.

It was a collection more unutterably beautiful than I had ever imagined possible, the likes of which I was sure even Small had never seen. The boxes were Tolliver's haul, I knew, that he and his men had stripped from the statue of the Suchi. The rest had been here longer.

'This is a temple,' I whispered.

'My God, the turn Tolliver must have got when he first walked in here, expecting to find only those boxes!'

'That's why the natives let him dig – they wanted their temple back.'

'No wonder he couldn't move it,' Small commented. 'We're eight and we'll struggle. There's an idol here for every bloody day of the year. The sun, it must choose a different god each morning.'

'If that's the case, their placement must be terribly intricate.'

He had waded into the sea of riches and picked up a figurine of a naked human female with the head of a dog.

'Well, then we'll do the right thing and leave their stands, eh? They're only leaf.'

'Have you ever seen anything so lovely, Small?'

'Saw something a bit like this one in Egypt, actually,' he was saying. 'Funny how ideas travel, eh?'

'I can't believe it!' was all I could muster. And I couldn't. After so long, so many miles travelled, so many scrapes, fantasies and idiotic mistakes, I really could not comprehend that what my eyes told me was true.

Small lowered his figurine and his face grew serious.

'We've found it, lad,' he said. 'But that doesn't mean it's ours – not yet. We still have to get it away from here.'

'What the—? Great Scott, sir!'

The voice came from behind me. It was the Sarge.

'In some ways, yes, my man,' Small responded. 'A crossing is made?'

'Yessir. But how—'

'Good. We'll form a chain. Cyril and I will bring the boxes to start with – to the other side of the crossing. Leave a torch there to guide us. From there you and Fowler carry it to Durand and the woman. Empty saddlebags, put food in blankets. Transfer the loot. We'll need all the bags and sacks we've got. Only two of these boxes can come with us – one either side of the riderless horse. Then bring any receptacle you can down here and we'll pluck the best from the rest. We'll never be able to take it all, but we'll do our damnedest, and now we know where it is, we can return. Now go.' The Sarge tore himself away, excited greed filling his eyes, and then Small turned to me. 'And we won't do anything so stupid as bringing the Army into it.'

There were six boxes total, and it took both Small and me to move a single one. Even then it was slow work. Half carrying and half dragging, we reached the chasm to find a great beam of wood, like a railway sleeper, forming a bridge across the void. Rope was attached at either end, stretching upwards and disappearing into the darkness above. Pausing to raise a torch, we saw that the rope fed through a series of pulleys and then ran down the wall to be tied off just feet from where we had leapt. The crossing had been hanging above us. It just required lowering. Our impatience had got the better of our reason; we had only had to look about us for the solution.

Carrying the chests over the bridge was wobbly work, since the beam was barely as long as the gap was wide, but we managed to take two to the other side before the Sarge and Fowler returned. They carried saddlebags, a few sacks, even the Glenlivet belt. When Small saw that, his eyes widened in fear.

'What on earth do you think you're doing with that, man?'

'You did say to bring everything, sir,' Fowler said.

'Don't worry, sir!' the Sarge said. 'Whisky's as valuable as any gold in these parts. The bottles are outside as safe as can be.'

Small slapped his back.

'I like you already, man! Get moving, and put this back in its rightful place!'

By the time we brought another box over the bridge, another had been taken and an empty returned, and so it went. After three more, we returned for the last filled crate, after which we intended to start filling the others, but as I went to take a grip, Small spoke.

'Lad, fill some bags. We can carry at least a couple with us, then return for more. The fewer trips, the quicker we'll be. Take the jewels – God knows we've already gold enough to keep us in clover for the rest of our days.'

He was right. He began filling the sacks and I took up the saddlebags. I slipped a goblet in, a crescent crown, and I was about to wedge in the ruby red figurine, but paused with him in my hands.

'It's remarkable, Small.'

'Eh? What is?' he said without looking up.

'All this. It's gold and jewels, yes, but it's so much more than that, too. The extraordinary stories that must lie behind every one of these figures. Gods whose existence was known of by no man beyond this valley until today. Fantastical myths, but also the history of a people. Small, we are real explorers, you and I.'

Now he looked at me, and I passed him the figurine so he could feel the moment as I did.

'Whatever you say, lad, but that's not ruby, I'm afraid. Quartz. Cornelian, maybe. Not worth taking whatever it is. The hand's gold, though. Break it off if you want. But leave the rest.'

He threw it back to me and continued his rapid work.

I caught the statuette, but I could not do as he suggested.

'But don't you see, Small? Don't you see?'

'See what?' he demanded, looking up in irritation at my time-wasting.

'It may not be ruby, but in a way this is the treasure more than any riches. This, the Suchi, these people's beliefs. You said yourself it's funny how ideas travel. Myth, folklore, fact, it didn't matter a jot. All through this journey, I have been—'

'Like I said, boy.' I was not operating as Small desired. 'So long as the destination is the right one, who cares if truth and fact diverge? This stuff is both. As is the monetary worthlessness of that figurine. Also both true and factual is that we need to move, so work while you talk.'

I had felt what had drawn men such as Forrester here. Men like Small and Tolliver, though, were made of sterner stuff. I pushed the figurine into the bag, and did not speak another word as I worked. When the bags were full, I slung them over my shoulder. Small did the same with his and we took up position on either side of the box. He was himself again.

'Do you know, lad,' he said as he crouched. 'For a soldier, that Sarge chap's not entirely despicable. You hear the way he talked about the 'Livet?'

'It's only a pity we're not all quite so malleable.'

The answer was not mine. It was Petts. He was at the mouth of the tunnel and was pointing Small's rifle at us. His face was contorted by a repulsive grin. He giggled like a demon. In the excitement of discovering the treasure, neither one of us had given Petts another thought.

'Some of us are downright greedy, so I'm afraid you'll be taking the last of that out for me.'

Small stood and the bags slipped off his shoulder. His eyes were blazing. 'If you think I'll help you get away with our loot, you're madder than you look,' he said between his teeth.

'And if you don't, then you shall die,' Petts hissed.

'Very well!' Small shouted, striding forwards, allowing the muzzle of the rifle to poke him in the chest. 'Shoot away, you black-hearted fiend. You'll never reload before King has cut you open like a fish.'

'Do you really think he is capable?' Petts replied derisively, before crying: 'I'll shoot!'

'Do it, man. I told you to. Shoot away, you worm.'

Petts raised the rifle to Small's face.

'I will!'

'Do it!'

'Small,' I said, but his blood was too high to hear me.

'Shoot, damn you!'

'You're a dead man!'

'Small!'

'It's you who hasn't the belly to shoot a man in the face. I can see it in your yellow eyes. No stomach!'

'*SMALL!*' I cried.

'What is it, man?' they both said at me at once.

'Listen!' I whispered, and then they heard what I had heard. Gunfire. Distant, but certainly gunfire.

'Well, we'd better get moving then, hadn't we?' Petts said, lowering his rifle a fraction. 'You may have your use after all.'

Small turned his back on Petts and returned to me at the box.

'Come on, lad. We'd better get up there. You take the front,' he said loudly. 'And slip me that knife now,' he mouthed at me under his breath.

'You go ahead of me,' Petts said, gesturing with the rifle.

'But of course,' Small replied with a dangerous civility, smiling at me as I slid the blade up his sleeve. 'With pleasure, Captain.'

With difficulty, I took up the front end of the chest, Small the back and we made our way along the tunnel under the watchful eye of Petts, who picked up the torch. Though it was cold in that place, sweat dripped down my face as I walked slowly into the darkness. Eventually we reached the bridge, on the other side of which I could see the Sarge's torch lying on the ground. I stepped gingerly forward. Step after precarious step, we made our way across, until finally I placed my foot on rock again and I felt the chest stop behind me.

'Move along!' Petts shouted.

I looked back. Small nodded and looked down. I believe he smiled before suddenly pushing the chest and me forwards. I lurched onto the ground. I hit the torch and it went out. The chest tumbled into the chasm. There was great shouting, Petts waved his torch, and then the scene was motionless once again. Both Petts and Small were on the bridge, facing each other now. Small's arms were outstretched, wobbling for balance, the knife in his right hand. Petts bent his legs. In one hand he held the torch, in the other the rifle, which he pointed at Small.

'So you thought you could throw me down there, eh? You bloody fool.'

'You're the fool, Petts, if you thought I'd let you have it all.'

'You leave me no choice, Small. That's your name, isn't it? And how fitting it is.'

Petts raised the rifle and stretched forward his thumb to cock it. As he did so Small lunged at him. The Captain could not fire before the two of them went crashing back into the tunnel. The torch Petts had held flew into the chasm, the rifle into the tunnel beyond the pair. Before his opponent could gather himself, Small leapt to his feet and cut through the rope that secured the bridge. In the same movement, he kicked the beam of wood from its perch on the lip of the chasm, and it followed the crate of treasure into the blackness. Small moved so quickly that he was on Petts before the Captain had even got to his feet. It was no contest. Small was a bear of a man, and he was beating a rat. Petts cried out as Small pounded his face and body, and then, suddenly disgusted, with himself or Petts I could not say, Small rose and picked up his rifle. He spat at Petts and stamped on his ankle. I heard the gut-wrenching sound of splintering bone and then Small approached the chasm.

'Lad,' he called to me, more serious than ever I had heard him. 'It's entirely dark. I can't see a thing. Light that damned torch and hold it up or I'm sure to drop.'

I grabbed the torch, and returned to the edge of the chasm as I pulled my matches from my pocket. The first broke; the second died instantly. Only the third did I succeed in putting to the torch, and the flames grew to light the tunnel at whose mouth I stood.

'Now catch, lad!'

The rifle appeared out of the darkness and I caught it.

'And now me.'

He backed up slightly, readying to launch himself across the chasm, but he was stopped by Petts grabbing his ankle.

'Don't leave me here!' he whined. 'I'll starve!'

'Probably,' Small answered steadily. 'Hopefully. A most painful death, I hear. Or you can try and jump it again, but with that foot you know you'll not succeed. But it'll end it quickly, down there wherever that hole'll take you.'

Small kicked the squirming form away from him and then ran towards me. He came tumbling down from his leap next to me, rose and brushed himself down. He put his rifle over his shoulder and lifted my saddlebags from the ground. With his other hand Small took the torch from me, pointed it to the ground and turned to Petts.

'Don't leave me!' the wretched creature begged.

'It's no good, man. I'd've killed you in the village if I'd been able. I'm not a fan of soldiers. You know, you're a bloody fool. You had only to keep your mouth shut, take the watch, get the map and return and all this could have been yours. All your years and work would not have been for nothing. Surely even under the circumstances you can see the humour? After waiting so long, it is your impatience that has killed you. This is your end, man. The cost of your blackguardry. It's a revenge most sweet for all that you have done to us and to countless others, though it is a kinder fate than you've given many. Now accept it as the man you must once have been.'

With that Small extinguished the torch on the ground and we were plunged into complete darkness. The chasm had disappeared and on the other side all that could be seen was the silhouette of Petts, on his knees, beseeching. All that could be heard were his screams for mercy, all the way to the mouth of the cave, for the gunfire from the world outside had ceased.

*

'Now, what was all that noise about?' Small said, dropping the bags to the ground.

'Coming from the village, sir,' the Sarge replied. 'Think the natives must be giving the lads a time.'

'Well, get all this stuff onto the horses, then. This is as much as we're getting. The bridge is gone. Then we can get the corporals out of there and all of us out of here.'

'And Petts, sir?'

''Fraid not. It was a simple case of him or me.'

The Sarge smiled.

'Don't be afraid, sir. No, don't be afraid.' He pointed next to the boxes and sacks and saddlebags. 'And there's your whisky.'

'Good man.'

Small picked up a bottle and drank from it as Fowler and the Sarge started moving the bags to the nearest horse.

'The belt's back in place, but not the liquor! Now what good is that? Why, you haven't even started loading up yet, by God. What have you been doing?' Small's tone was jovial, but it was lost on Fowler.

'Transferring, sir. But we're all ready to start now.'

'Get on with it, then,' Small said to Fowler, but the wink was for me.

Sitting beside the beasts were Fahlhana and Durand. The latter was getting to his feet.

'Everything's all right,' I said to them. 'Now we leave.'

'I shouldn't be so certain,' Durand replied. 'Look!' He pointed along the mountain, in the direction of the village. There, dashing towards our group, on foot, his face and shoulder bloodied and shouting at the top of his voice, was Corporal Crampers.

We only heard him shout, 'Bandits!' once before a force twenty strong came over the lip of the mountain, their horses at a gallop, the men firing their guns.

'My God!' I cursed. 'When will this end?'

Crampers threw himself down the mountain and landed at Small's feet.

'They ambushed us!' he puffed. 'Seventy of them at least. They got Finchy. I tried not to lead them here, but . . . but—'

'All right, lad. You help load up the horses.' Small was loading his rifle. 'Lieutenant, King. Get over here.' He fired off a shot. 'Fire at bloody will.'

I grabbed a rifle from one of the saddles and started shooting, but my aim was hopeless, and reloading took me an age. Fowler and Small managed to hit a good number, but there were too many of them, and firing was too slow.

'Bloody Petts!' I heard Small mutter as he reloaded. 'So busy pretending to track us, he didn't think to cover his own trail.'

We would soon be within range of the bandits' inferior weaponry and then, if not through accuracy, by sheer volume of bullets fired, they would hit us. Even if they failed in that, we would never be able to shoot them all before they got to us and put their swords to use.

I looked back. Crampers was injured. Durand and Fahlhana were struggling. The Sarge could not do it alone. I dashed over to them and threw my rifle at Crampers.

'Shoot, man!' I shouted over the gunshots and grabbed the other end of the chest. The Sarge and I hoisted it onto the back of the horse, but it went straight over, and collapsed on the ice, the wood splintering, the valuables pouring into the snow.

'No!' we both cried.

'My God!' Durand exclaimed, seeing the booty for the first time.

As I rushed to the saddle bags, a sound came to my ears, over the gunfire, over the thundering of approaching hooves for which I first mistook it. Holding the bags in midair, I froze.

At first it was a creaking sound that I was not sure I had really heard, but then it grew in volume until it became a distant, tremendous rumble that was unmistakable. I looked up the mountain, beyond the bandits. A whiteness was rising into the sky, but I knew instantly that it was no cloud.

I dropped the saddle bags and rushed to Fahlhana. I grabbed her and threw her onto the nearest horse.

Fahlhana looked at me, and must have seen the fear in my eyes, for she instantly looked up the mountain and saw what I had seen. I sprinted towards Small.

'Small, we must go now. Now!'

'Is the treasure packed?' he said, firing and reloading.

'Small, we can't. It's too late.'

'There's time, lad. There's still some distance between us! Maybe we can't take all of it, but load up what you can and stay alert – they'll be within range soon.'

'No, Small. You don't understand. We can't take anything.'

He turned to me.

'What do you mean, man?'

I pointed up the mountain.

'Avalanche!'

He reacted immediately.

'Retreat, lads. Avalanche!' he shouted, leaping to his feet.

When all had seen it, things happened very quickly. We were on our horses in a moment and following Fahlhana. The rumbling consumed the world and only at the last moment did the bandits realise that it was the snow, and not them that we were fleeing. By then it was too late for them. The thundering snow dashed all that remained of them against the surface of the mountain at a blistering pace. The limbs of men and horses bent at every angle as they were hurled down the mountainside, their bodies dashed to limpness. Then the snow simply swallowed them. That terrible sight spurred us on and we beat our horses for all we were worth. The snow was roaring towards us. Behind us, it rushed over the black rock face, stifling the last of Petts' cries. The gold and stones were thrown into the air and briefly the white of the speeding snow glittered with all the beauty of a rainbow, but only for an instant before that too was consumed by the mountain. Fowler panicked and headed straight down the mountain instead of along. The snow was smashing at the hooves of the horses and then, in an instant, it overtook us. But it did not swallow us as it had the bandits. Only by the very skin of our teeth had we gained sufficient ground along the mountain to avoid it. We pulled our steeds to a standstill just before the great plunge into the pass and turned to see Fowler galloping valiantly downwards at the tip of the rush. But an avalanche can be outrun by neither man nor beast, and we watched helpless as that pitiful wretch disappeared from view.

As quickly as it had come to life, the mountain was silent once more, the snow smooth and untouched. Near all of our band had survived, but the treasure had not. It had been scattered and buried beneath tons of snow and ice, hugged to the mountain's frozen bosom for all time, as Fowler had been. This time it would never be found. We had come so close, but now there could be no doubt. It was over. Gone.

Small put his ear to the wind and listened. Then he turned to us. 'Looks like we're digging again,' he said.

He kicked Bucephalus into a trot and started to make his way over the snow once more. The Sarge and Crampers followed him. I rode after them.

'Small, are you mad? There's not a hope in hell of finding it,' I pleaded with him. 'Not a hope in hell. I wanted it as much as you did, Small, but it's gone, man. Gone.'

We reached the spot where the black rock face had been, now as smooth and white as porcelain, and he dismounted and started to dig with his hands.

'I believe you wanted it, lad, but not as much as I,' he said without looking at me. 'Or you'd be down here digging with me.'

'Small, we found it. It was real. That must be enough for us now. We could be here years and not find a thing.'

Another sound came to my ears. This time it was less awe-inspiring than an avalanche, but I knew it would prove just as dangerous. Crampers had said there had been at least seventy bandits. Only twenty or so had been killed by our rifles and the snow. Over the horizon of the mountain came the rest.

'Small! Look!' I cried, pointing up the mountain. 'The rest of them!'

Small glanced up but then continued to dig, more furiously. His eyes were sparkling again, but not with thrill or glee. This time madness was upon him.

'Small!' I cried, pulling my horse around.

He looked up at me. I saw in his eyes that he was not going to follow me.

'You're a fool,' I whispered, but there was nothing left for me to do. My duty lay elsewhere, a hundred yards away. I cantered to Fahlhana and Durand. When I reached them, I looked back up the

mountain towards Small. Crampers and the Sarge were firing at
the bandits now, but Small was still digging.

'Lead on,' I said to Fahlhana.

*

Fahlhana kicked her horse into action. It reared and then dashed
downwards, towards the mouth of the pass. Durand and I followed her, around boulders, the horses slipping and bucking, until
finally we came to the narrow trail that led between the valleys.
We threw our horses into it and made our way as fast as possible.
When cracking came from above, I looked up to see bandits lining
the top of the pass, looking down at us. Not all had gone to see to
Small, it seemed. Others had split off and were now shooting at us
like exotic fish in a long, narrow barrel. I pointed my gun upwards
and fired, but I knew it was hopeless. The best we could do was
gallop onwards, but I knew the pass was too long. We were
doomed just as Small and the remaining soldiers were. Had we
remained together, as a single force, there would perhaps have
been a chance, but divided there was none.

I kicked on nonetheless, determined not to give up until my last
breath, and was followed by Fahlhana and Durand. The very moment
I looked back to check that all were with me, the Englishman's horse
was hit and threw him to the ground. I pulled my beast to a skid-
ding halt. Fahlhana dashed on. I leapt from my saddle, and ran to
Durand's side. I pulled him up and dragged him to my horse, but
before I could hoist him into my saddle, I was hit in the shoulder
and thrown to the ground.

Lying helpless on my back, I looked up at the bandits. It did not
seem possible that the tiny flashes so far away could be the end of
me. But one of the men was not so small. He was larger than the
rest. Indeed, he was growing. I could even see his face. He was fearful, screaming. By God, he had been shot and was falling towards
me. I rolled out of his path in the nick of time, only to hear gunfire
close by.

I was thrown back into my saddle. I looked behind me and saw the uniforms of the Sarge and Crampers, firing up at the bandits now, and the grinning beard of Small. Durand was seated in front of him on Bucephalus. With one hand, Small pushed Durand down to hug Bucephalus's neck as he ducked the gunfire of the bandits following us down the pass. Shots now came from back and above, but I was not alone. We were united once more. We rode on.

★

'Move it, boy,' Small shouted at me. 'There's nothing for you to do here! Get out!'

I saw Crampers slump in his saddle and fall sideways to the ground. Small pulled to a halt and turned and stooped for the dead soldier's pistol. The Sarge stopped and turned, and both of them started to fire their weapons back at the marauding mob bearing down on us. Durand reloaded and the bandits fell like flies, the speed and accuracy of our pistol fire the superior of their unwieldy rifles in such a space. Then they started to move along the pass again and Small and the Sarge alternated firing backwards and upwards. Then Durand grabbed my rifle before Small gave my horse an almighty slap on the haunches and the beast broke into a gallop. Barely conscious, I left Small, Durand and the Sarge and seconds later burst into the green valley where Fahlhana was sitting in her saddle, anxiously waiting in the ruins. Seeing my state, she grabbed my reins and led me quickly beneath the trees where the canopy of the forest protected us from view. She pulled us to a standstill and as we and our horses heaved for breath, we waited and listened.

The gunfire continued.

Screams, groans and yells echoed from the stone corridor, and then, quite suddenly, all fell silent. As I waited for Small, Durand and the one remaining soldier of Flack's company to emerge from the passageway, my heart beat heavily in my ears. Seconds passed that seemed like minutes, but nobody, not even bandits, arrived.

They had fallen, every one of them, slaughtered in another trail massacre. Small, who had returned to save me yet again from certain death, had this time paid the final price. I looked at Fahlhana and bowed my head. Blood ran from my shoulder and soaked my shirt. I had led this woman only to death in another place, in another way, for surely now, after losing so many of their own, the bandits would not hesitate to kill us. The villagers would not welcome her back, if indeed any remained; and were we to escape and continue into the mountains, without sufficient food we would perish there as surely as at the hands of our pursuers.

I had failed, after all.

34

THE LETTERS OF
SIR PAUL LINDLEY-SMALL

Awaiting a boat in sub-zero temperatures at the dead of night
Bergen, Norway

13TH JANUARY 1909

By Gad,

That was a close call.

Let me explain why at the end of my last missive I cut from the retelling of this riveting tale so abruptly.

The woman had just introduced me to her husband.

As you can well imagine, I did not know what to say. This strange old bird had told me that her husband was dead, and yet before me I could not deny that there was a man of sufficient years to be her spouse. He was far more tanned than the man in the pictures downstairs. Indeed, he had turned the colour of an Indian, and his flesh had wizened somewhat beneath the skin, but unquestionably it was he. And he did not look dead.

'Mr K-Kleverud,' I stuttered, 'it is a pleasure.'

I awaited a reply, but none was forthcoming. He did not even see fit to look up from his book. I was becoming irritated. It seemed as though she was playing games, after all. Why had she lied about her husband, for instance? Or was she just senile? Whichever, I cared not a jot. I had a job to do, and as you know, with one in hand I like not to be distracted from it by piffles.

'Do not worry,' she told me as I stared at her husband, wondering when I could reasonably retire. 'He is not being rude. He cannot move.'

As she said these words, their meaning came tumbling into my mind. I had agreed to spend the night in the house of a woman, mad to the core, who had stuffed her dead husband. In her madness she believed him to be alive still.

'Mr Small, you must think me quite mad, talking to a dead man and introducing you to him,' Mrs Kleverud said, reading my mind. I declined to answer her, but it must have lain in my eyes, for she continued in that authoritative tone again. 'But you must understand that he is not dead. He is merely very still. He cannot move, but he is quite capable of seeing and hearing.' She turned a page of his book. 'He always did read voraciously, so I turn the page once a day. It's unlikely he can manage more. Reading without moving your eyes must be such an effort, don't you think? But really I cannot be sure, for how can he tell me?' she added with a sad smile, her façade cracking slightly.

I was speechless and stared at them, her arm around his shoulder, to all appearances the picture of a happily married couple.

'Mr Small, I see you are still not convinced. Come,' she said, holding a hand out to me with the same kindly smile. 'Touch him on the brow.'

I moved backwards, to the door, disgusted at the thought of doing such a thing. Taxidermy, you see, is a nasty business. To stuff an animal, you must first skin it entirely before adding the stuffing and carefully setting it into position. Then there is the treating of the skin. This woman, requesting that I approach her, must have patiently followed the gory process on her very own husband, and was now asking that I admire her handiwork. I was, as I say, disgusted and rather than granting her request was wondering if I could flee the room, gather the cat and the bottle and be out of the house before she could get to the bottom of the stairs, but her next words broke through my repugnance and presented to me a possibility.

'He is quite warm,' she said.

I paused with my hand secretly on the knob of the door.

Did not the legend of the King Cobra Cat speak of victims being rendered wholly immobile, but alive, and quite capable of seeing, hearing and feeling?

'Come,' Mrs Kleverud said.

I realised it was quite foolish of me to be so fearful of a harmless, sad old lady, and being the valorous character that I am, with no thought for personal safety, I bravely edged forward and delighted the mad old woman.

She took my hand and laid it upon her husband's forehead. As she had promised, the skin was warm and soft. I moved my fingers to his neck as Mrs Kleverud grinned at my amazement. There was no pulse, but the muscles in his arms, though wizened, were soft and supple like those of an active man, not hard and dry like those of a long-dead corpse. He was unquestionably alive, or at the very least, not dead.

'What was in the vial?' I asked, drawing back.

'Venom,' replied Mrs Kleverud. 'The venom of the Cobra Cat. It is a remarkable substance. He has gone rather darker than I had hoped he would but that is a small price to pay.'

Then she embarked upon a detailed description of the stuff, which I will not set down here, for I myself have already told you what it is capable of, and besides, her words were so filled with obscure chemical terms that I am sure it would bore anyone not savvy to their meaning as I am. As she spoke, I bent to look into the man's eyes. There, sure enough, was the twinkle of life.

She had received the liquid from Diego del Fuego six years ago, when he had returned from the East. There, he had discussed the plight of his friend Mr Kleverud with a medicine man who had subsequently supplied him with the vial. He said that to swallow the substance in hugely diluted form was used to aid sleep, but if passed pure into the bloodstream its effects were quite different. In what doctors had said would be the last days of Mr Kleverud's life, Diego del Fuego had arrived in Bergen and the desperate Mrs Kleverud, being told what the results of the injection would be and incapable of imagining life without Mr Kleverud, had pushed the liquid through a syringe and into her husband's arm. His fatal ailment had been cured, but he had fallen instantly into the state in which I now saw him.

'I inoculated his favourite dog with the last of it,' she said, pointing to a basket next to the fire she was stoking. It contained a skinny, content-looking Setter. 'Before I injected my husband, I promised to set him at his desk with a book, and said that I would supply him with company. He thought me foolish to believe that he would need company in this state, but I am sure he is aware of having another living being around him, and that it makes his life a little more bearable. But really, after six years with only the dog, he is so lonely.' Returning to her husband, she carefully straightened his swept-back hair and mused a moment. 'Diego tried to find the medicine man again whenever he returned to India, but he never succeeded. He looked the world over for the cat the venom came from, but he has never succeeded in that either. I so wish to give my dear husband more real, living company. This last time, Diego was convinced that he had finally found the beast, but alas, he had not.'

'What do you mean he had not?' I cried, for even though she was plainly mad, she could not fail to realise that one such beast lay down a flight of stairs in her own home.

'I am not even sure that the thing ever existed. Perhaps I only wished to believe in the legend. I think it quite possible the medicine man made the venom himself and sold it as that of the Cobra Cat to garner a greater price. But try as I might, I cannot emulate it in a test tube. I fear my husband shall never have his company.'

Something leapt into my mind.

'But my dear woman, the legend is certainly true. The King

Cobra Cat exists and I can prove it.' I rushed her to the fireside downstairs, thinking it high time we left this room, and on my way plucked from my satchel the skull I had taken from the catacombs and carried with me. Sitting in her chair, she held it and gawped. The skull was very like the head of the cat in its basket at her side, though perhaps slightly smaller. She turned it upside down and inspected the teeth.

'You are right, Mr Small, it must exist. Or once have done so. But this is not the skull of an animal of the same breed as mine. Tell me, where did you find this?' she said, without moving her eyes from the skull.

'Not the same!' I exclaimed. 'Why do you say that?'

'This beast has fangs, with holes at the tip,' she said, stroking the skull's canines with a forefinger and showing the route the remarkable substance would have followed. 'It would have deposited venom held in glandular sacs behind its whiskers through the fangs and into its prey. My cat has no such holes. When Diego first delivered him to me, I held a rag doused with chloroform to his muzzle and inspected him with the utmost care. He does not have fangs. His are merely very large teeth.'

Once again, I could not believe what I was hearing.

'But Mrs Kleverud, surely you have not failed to notice the other similarities?' I said, attempting to coax her back into belief. 'The figure of eight, the tail, the tongue, the black mouth, the hood?'

'You are right, of course,' she said. 'They are traits not found on an ordinary cat, but let me put this to you. Is it not possible that the man from whom Diego obtained the cat had chosen one that looked particularly like the Cobra Cat of legend? They are a rare combination, but you will surely agree that cats must exist with both the correct markings on the back of the head and the long tail and black mouth, and also that tongues can be cut.'

'It is certainly possible,' said I, but she had forgotten its most singular trait. 'But what of the hood? I have only ever heard of a cat like that in the legend.'

'Ahh,' she said, pulling the now docile cat from its basket to her lap once again. 'Come and look.' She pulled at the skin that formed the hood, now flaccid and loose. 'There is much scarring here. I think the cunning man has implanted the bones that lift the skin.'

I could see that there was, indeed, the scarring that she spoke of, though whether it was from surgery or battle was impossible to say.

'And what of his owner, the snake charmer?' I said instead. 'I myself saw him in Calcutta, and he was quite as in stasis as your husband.'

'Mr Small,' she said, again choosing to ignore my words, 'the animal is a wonderful imitation, there is no doubt, but I am afraid that is precisely what he is. A well-trained imitation.'

I remained unconvinced. I was not prepared to take the word of a woman so mentally touched as this one. Even if it was an imitation, the Maharajahs would not know that, and they would still compete to pay me a pretty penny for it. I was unwilling to return empty-handed after so long a hunt.

'In that case,' I said, 'allow me to take him off your hands. It must be a terrible burden to keep him.'

'Quite the opposite, Mr Small. Quite the opposite. As my husband lies in warm state, I require protection from any pillagers that might try to steal from me, and the cat is quite sufficient for that. And besides, he may not be the Cobra Cat, but he is not without interest. His may not be the venom I wished for, but he is still a poisonous beast. It is his spittle,' she said, her eyes widening and my ears twitching. 'This man you speak of, the snake charmer, he had been bitten?'

'On his leg,' I said eagerly. 'It was black to the thigh. And he was as still as a stone.'

'Diego had also been bitten. And repeatedly. Yet his wounds were only blackened around the incision. I think the cat's poison reduced in power quite rapidly once it had been removed from its source.' It seems she was not savvy to Diego del Fuego's curse, however, and surely a man who cannot die would be less affected by the poison than the rest of us.

'Its source?' I queried nonetheless.

'Mr Small, I wonder, are you familiar with the Komodo Dragon?'

I could not help smiling at this. She was willing to believe in something so fantastical as dragons, and yet could not believe that she held a King Cobra Cat on her lap.

'It is a very large Indonesian monitor lizard found only on a handful of islands,' she said. 'It is a meat eater, and though it is large, its prey can be disproportionately big. It can kill a buffalo, some fifty or a hundred times its weight. Do you know how it achieves this remarkable feat? It merely bites it, and yet it is not venomous like a snake. Its saliva is alive with the rancid bacteria of years and years of decaying flesh. When the spittle enters the buffalo's bloodstream, it poisons it. The dragon leaves the buffalo to itself for some days, following its scent with its tongue. The buffalo then dies of blood poisoning and the dragon will feast. That, Mr Small, is how this little chap has become poisonous. Though the bites Diego received seem not to have been nearly so potent as that which the snake charmer suffered, subsequent tests I have conducted have shown that his spittle is still poisonous. However, unlike the substance that keeps my husband alive, this is not a venom, and its effects can be cured by the application of iodine or surgical alcohol. They kill bacteria most effectively. If left untended, however, the infected flesh would certainly turn black, and death would be slow.'

Mrs Kleverud cleared her throat as though this speech had wearied her, and I gallantly produced the Glenlivet and poured her a livener. She immediately looked brighter, and launched forth on the conclusion to her argument.

'At first, the cat's spittle was very weak, but I have since been experimenting with all manner of diets. Unsurprisingly, considering the Komodo Dragon, the most effective seems to be rotting flesh. With the addition of a chemical compound of my own invention I am hopeful that the poison will act in a similar way to that of the real Cobra Cat, but alas, I have nothing to test it upon. I have run out of animals.' She paused, and sipped again at her whisky. 'The logic is sound, but one cannot be certain that anything will work as logic dictates. I am, therefore, very unwilling to allow the beast to bite anything I value as yet. However, without this chemical addition of mine, I am certain that the cat's saliva would not render a man static. Quite the opposite; at the height of its potency, a single bite would have served a man slow but excruciating pain for some days before rendering him dead and cold, and that is surely what the snake charmer must have been.'

'Not at all – quite the opposite,' I riposted in imitation of her words. 'He was quite as alive and warm as your husband, as I have told you.' I was getting irritated by the old woman's insistence that the creature was not my prize whilst also being so unwilling to part with it. The rubbish about the dragons had merely been a diversion, for I could not deny what my eyes had seen. The two men, Ashvin Landa and Mr Kleverud, were certainly in the same state, only the poison had travelled all through the body of the latter. As you will understand, her insistence that her husband had been injected with the venom, but that Ashvin Landa could not have been, was a source of powerful frustration.

'The only conceivable explanation is that he was meditating to slow the spread of the poison,' she said. 'An impressive feat, for the festering must be a deeply uncomfortable sensation.'

I sighed at her disbelief.

'I fear, Mr Small, that your long and arduous journey has been in vain. You have followed this beast to Norway, have you not? That it is not the one you desire must come as difficult news. I too have searched for it for many years. You can be happy that you are merely without the remarkable beast you sought. I, on the other hand, shall one day not far away be dead, while my husband shall live on, indefinitely, with only a canine for company.'

It was her turn to sigh then, and she drained the last of her whisky and rose.

'And now, I must sleep. I am sure you will be quite comfortable in your room, and I look forward to talking more in the morning, for you are such good company.'

And so finally we went to our rooms and I lay in my bed fully dressed, thinking that an hour would be ample time for her to fall asleep. I'd use it to write to you, I decided, and after that, as I told you, I would gather my things, slip the feline into a sack and head off, hoping to find an evening ferry to take me away. However, while I am quite capable of tolerating the inebriating effects of Glenlivet better than most, a decent quantity in addition to the aquavit is liable to make one drowsy. Couple that to the fact that I had slept only a few hours the night before, and it is no surprise that I passed out mid-sentence. What a fool I was to even lie down!

I awoke I do not know how much later with a jump, furious with myself for having dropped off. However, it was of no matter, I thought, for it was still quite dark outside, and Mrs Kleverud was sure to be sound asleep. I drew back my covers and made to rise.

In the darkness I saw an ethereal figure standing at the foot of my bed.

'Mr Small,' Mrs Kleverud whispered through the shadows, for it was she. 'I am afraid your company is far too valuable to allow you to leave. My husband will enjoy you so much. You cannot take the beast, but you will by all means remain with it here.'

With that and the same kindly smile, she brought the feline, which she held by the scruff, into my view, and threw it towards my face. As the cat flew through the air towards me, its mouth agape, I deftly rolled to one side and the creature plunged its fangs deep into my pillow. Before it could retract from its feathery prey, I had grabbed it by the tail and thrown it from whence it came. Of course, though a clever old witch, physically Mrs Kleverud's reactions were no match for mine and the beast landed on her chest where it dug its claws into her nightdress and plunged its fangs into her drooping breast. She had time only to widen her eyes and yelp in shock before she fell to the floor, stock-still. She experienced none of the convulsions that she said would result from the spittle of the cat, and since I found no sign of dalliance with chemistry as I searched the house for a sack to put the cat in, I can only assume that her belief in the alterations she had made to the venom were born of a mad mind. Or of a plain and devious liar.

The cat successfully in the bag, I dragged the inanimate woman into her husband's study and sat her in another chair on the opposite side of his desk. There I set her eyes towards her husband and his towards her. I then immediately departed for the quayside from which I now write to you.

It is possible that she merely fainted and will soon awaken, with only a slightly blackening breast, which she will douse with the surgical alcohol she spoke of, and that she will be none the worse off, but I very much doubt it. For I am as sure as ever I was that the beast writhing in the sack next to me is the King Cobra Cat. Mrs Kleverud said that there were no venom-delivering holes in the cat's teeth, but she did not show me, and besides, if that bore Darwin has taught us anything, it is the power of Nature to change and adapt. And she made no attempt to explain the existence of those sabre-teeth, the likes of which I have seen on no other cat. Mrs Kleverud also claimed that the scarring on its chest was the result of surgery. I say it is from battling. She said that Ashvin Landa was meditating in Calcutta, slowing his death, but he was a snake charmer, not a fakir.

So desperate had she been to give her husband company, that mad old Mrs Kleverud had tried to convince me this was not the cat I sought. In doing so, she hoped I would relax and drop my guard, and give her the chance to set the beast upon me. According to her theories, though, in a matter of months my corpse would be rotting and the worst company imaginable for a man alive but in stasis. Would she want to torture her husband with the stench and vision of a chap rotting on the other side of his desk? I think not. This is the King Cobra Cat and she very nearly succeeded in her intentions, but thankfully she had not bargained on the unmatchable reflexes with which I was born and which I hope will continue to extract me from narrow squeezes for many years to come.

Even though the hunt is over, I hope you will still, and always, consider me,

Your friend,

Lindley-Small

35

THE NOTEBOOKS OF CYRIL KING

1893

Full Circle

My heart sank as I debated the best way in which to die. Its beat gradually grew louder, faster, until it was thundering irregularly in my ears, the decision facing me too much for my injured body and mind to contemplate. The moment I realised that the sound was not my organ's pumping, but the clatter of hooves on rock, I looked up to see Small and Durand burst from the pass. Small was bleeding from his left thigh, but still grinning like a maniac. Even Durand could not help but laugh at the excitement he had just partaken of.

'Small!' I cried as they dashed towards us.

'No time for celebrations, lad,' he shouted back at me from his saddle. 'We bagged as many of them as we could. It was like a wall of the dead. They couldn't get over and we legged it from those above. The Sarge fell, but that's a soldier's lot in life. We will too if we don't get moving. They'll be through any second. The river, lad – head for the river.'

Fahlhana had already kicked her horse into action and was galloping headlong downhill, weaving her steed in and out of the trees with all the skill of her husband. Small galloped past me, Durand close behind him on Crampers' horse. I belted my horse with my heels and followed suit. I did not look back, but allowed my horse to carry me after Bucephalus, straight down to the water's edge. She splashed into the river only moments after those I followed, clattering through the water until Small intercepted us. He was pointing his rifle downstream. On the banks stood a crowd of people, unarmed and dirty.

'Bandit women and children,' Small said. 'Waiting for the men to get rid of us. They'll take the village. Any who've survived up there are bandits now.'

He kicked Bucephalus into a walk, levelling his rifle at the unarmed gathering.

Durand, Fahlhana and I followed.

The women and children did not move as we approached, just watched us, until a single child broke from the restraining arms of a woman and came running towards us, pointing at me, jabbering. The woman followed him out until Small trained his rifle on her, then she stood ankle deep in the water, watching the child, calling to him. The child, deaf to her words, came onwards, pointing up at me. He was perhaps seven years old, maybe ten, with brown eyes and skin, black hair stiff with dirt, his little *chapan* stained and torn.

'You'll take nothing,' Small said to him.

Gunfire again came to my ears from the forest.

'Now get out of the way,' Small shouted, turning his rifle at the child as he passed him.

I stopped my horse as the boy came close, as did Fahlhana. Small and Durand continued on.

'What does he say, Small? Why is he pointing at me?'

The boy gestured at me again, at my chest, and spoke, this time in stuttering English.

'You have – is mine.'

'What?' I said.

'King, we need to move!' Small said from ahead.

The child pointed at his own chest.

'Is mine. Is mine.'

'I don't understand,' I said putting my hand to my chest. I felt the watch, outside my shirt, and held it.

'Is mine,' he said again. 'Give. Is mine.'

'This watch?' I said. 'Yours?'

'Yes, mine.'

'Small!' I said. 'Do you hear what he says?'

'I don't care, lad. His father and his pals are nearing.' He turned and looked towards the sounds of the rushing bandits, readying himself to fire as soon as they came into sight.

'He has no father amongst those men. Nor a mother amongst these women. His parents are dead. So are his sisters. He's Rustam Khan's son, Small.'

Fahlhana had realised it too, for she had dismounted and was talking very quickly to the child.

'What if he is?' Small responded. 'If we stay here a moment longer, it won't matter if he's Allah himself, they'll still shoot us down.'

I moved towards the boy and Fahlhana and pulled the watch from around my neck, breaking the weak fragment of material that held it there.

I placed the watch in his outstretched palm. He held it to his chest and Fahlhana continued to speak to him.

'Come on, King. We haven't time for a tryst with a bandit child. To the other side. We're sitting ducks here. At least from cover we'll be able to make a go of it. How many rounds do you have, Durand?'

'No.' It was only the second time I had heard Fahlhana speak my tongue. She was trying to hold the boy in her arms, but he was resisting her. When she succeeded in embracing him, she rose with him and mounted her horse, and the woman came running from the shallows. 'Down stream. We take horses down stream,' Fahlhana continued before speaking pointedly at the bandit woman.

Small frowned in confusion for a moment, but as quickly smiled and looked over his shoulder.

'By God, I think she's right, lad. Of some use after all. Get going!'

He galloped off along the shallows, Bucephalus throwing up cascades of spray, Durand on Crampers' horse following.

'We must go,' I said to Fahlhana.

The bandits appeared from the trees behind us.

'He come. He is son of Rustam Khan,' Fahlhana cried. 'Tell him he come.'

The lad spoke in his native tongue to the woman as she reached Fahlhana's feet and fell wailing to her knees in the water. The only word I could discern from either child or bandit woman was 'mamma'.

The thundering of hooves was approaching. Small and Durand were already some way downstream.

'Fahlhana,' I said. 'We must go. You cannot stay here. Come.'

Fahlhana looked down at the weeping woman, the child's adopted mother, then at the son of Rustam Khan, the vanishing child that had brought the secret of the treasure of Ishkuman into the world at large. Then gripping the boy tightly to her, Fahlhana turned her horse away from the bandit woman and rode on down the river. I kicked my horse and lashed it with the reins.

Very quickly the water became too deep for our horses and they were forced to swim. I looked at the child. He was staring back, beyond me, tears in his eyes, waving. Behind me the woman was for a moment alone in the water, her arms reaching to the sky, her cries audible, and then her menfolk dashed past her on their horses and she disappeared from view. They fired at us and the river burst with water-bound bullets.

'Lad! Woman! Dismount and hold on,' Small called from ahead. 'It's damned cold, but let the current carry you! And protect your beasts or we haven't a chance!' He had already pushed Durand from his horse into the water, and now plunged in himself. Fahlhana was already in the water, holding on to the boy. I gripped my reins and slipped into the freezing water. It ran into my bullet wound, a new kind of pain.

There was a period of a minute when the shots threatened us,

when the bullets zipped around us, but we succeeded in retaining
hold of our horses and the bandits did not move forward, and as
the water grew rapid with current, that miraculous deep green
valley led us to safety.

*

We have travelled far since that day, and now rest, wounds mend-
ing and bellies filled, on a train travelling through the deserts of
Rajasthan. We pulled ourselves dripping from the water long after
the bandits had escaped our view and left that green valley on
horseback when night next fell and we considered it safe to venture
from our cover. We dressed our wounds and headed south across
the country, and the going, in our weakened state, was difficult.
Eventually, we made it to Gahkuch. Fahlhana knew the territory
and guided us, and besides, Durand carried a map. The food we
succeeded in saving managed, with prudent rationing, to carry us
that far, and in Gahkuch we restocked.

When we were at our very coldest, Small revealed to us that all
was not entirely lost to the avalanche and produced a single bottle
that had survived. When he had unearthed it in the snow, and
had seen it lying there, unbroken, shining wet in the sunlight, he
took it as a fateful sign; a signal he should flee. 'More valuable than
any gold,' he quoted the Sarge. That remaining whisky, measured
even more carefully, and shared only between four, saw us over
the mighty Indus, to the Babusar Pass and to a town called Gayal
Gah. Then we followed the river to Srinagar, where Small picked
up another case, and the intoxicating, alien scent of wild flowers
filled the air. Snow was replaced by fields of crops, the running
water of rudimentary irrigation and the smiling faces of people for
whom such luxuries were standard. From there we boarded a train
bound for Lahore, where, of course, I expected to continue on to
Marwar and that Faddhuan Clock.

In the compartment from which I write, through the window
to my right is the arid sea of sand. To my left snoozes Durand,
disguised as a native, who, since this episode concluded, has

become very fond of Small. 'You told me that I may live to regret being pleased to make your acquaintance,' he told our criminal companion on our long journey. 'Well, thanks to you I am still alive, and regret is the feeling furthest from my mind. I shall be forever indebted to you. If there is ever anything I can do to aid you, you need only speak your mind.'

In the opposite corner of our compartment to this curious example of spirited English bureaucrat sleeps Small. Bucephalus is in the horse car, with the other horses, but above his head is the Glenlivet bandolier, near full, and his face is the most relaxed I have seen it. I nudged him when Durand spoke as he did, and suggested a royal pardon. On hearing that such a thing might be required, the Foreign Secretary demanded the whole tale of Small's past. On Small's conclusion that a mere pardon would not stop the Army hunting for him, Durand twisted his moustaches thoughtfully.

'I'm inclined to agree,' he said. 'The Army does not forget as the rest of us do. They rather put one in mind of a bull terrier. Once you're between their teeth, there's no escaping. If they can't have you, even if I clear your name, they will not cease to sully your reputation, I'm afraid. You'll continue to struggle to show your face anywhere. I don't doubt you're already blackened to the gutter. Even my word for your gallantry would be ignored by them, I fear. No, no. That won't do at all. Something more is required, as you say. Something quite transformational. I shall think upon it, and by the time we arrive in Calcutta, I will have devised a plan that will see you wholly exonerated and free to walk the Empire at your will. Perhaps not the higher halls of London, nor the clubs and barracks where you might be recognised, but elsewhere – and certainly your more usual haunts. Yes, I am sure something can be done. I shall go with you to Calcutta and return to Kabul later in the year.'

And that is how the Foreign Secretary of India came to decide upon travelling as a native, with a known criminal, into the heart of the jewel in the crown, instead of marching into the nearest outpost and demanding passage. Small was pleased both by

Durand's promise of assistance, and that he proved a man game for such a journey. It occurred to me, however, that Small had perhaps forgotten our back-scratching bargain.

'Sir Mortimer, I am afraid we cannot take you all the way to Calcutta, for we are to head south to Marwar, for the Faddhuan Clock,' I said. 'It is small consolation for missing out on the great riches of Ishkuman, but nonetheless Small and I are very keen to seek it out as soon as possible. Aren't we?'

Small coughed on his whisky.

'Well now, lad. Let's not be hasty. A trip to Calcutta might do all of us the world of good. A bit of rest and relaxation on Her Majesty. And Marwar's no place for them.'

He jerked his head towards Fahlhana and the boy, the latter of whom, named Nasir, we had learned, now sleeps with Small's substantial frame as a pillow. He is further comforted by a protective paw holding him to it. He and Small have become firm friends. Small is convinced that the child possesses magical abilities. Though I am sceptical, it seems Small is a great believer in such things, as is Fahlhana, and they both chide me at every opportunity for not sharing this belief. Though I am certain he is too sensible to share such superstitions, Durand merely smiles on as Small attempts to train the boy's mind. Within the last two hours, Nasir has accurately described the number, gender and garb of all the eight people in the next compartment. He also told us which toe on which foot Small is without and how he lost it. Considering his record, it is hard to tell whether Small was being truthful when he said the boy was right, that it had indeed been gnawed at by a juvenile crocodile in the night, and then removed by a one-armed child surgeon for fear of gangrene; and when I learned that the adjacent compartment was reserved for females only, containing eight seats, I thought it highly likely that all its occupants would be adorned with saris. Still, I must confess that I no longer doubt the value of the talents the boy displays. That is not to say I am a convert, you understand; but I am only too pleased for his mind to be diverted by childish exploits from the harshness he has doubtless endured in the company of the bandits. He is feral, certainly, and now, like

an animal, clings to Fahlhana for protection as before he reached
for the woman in the river, but I think he is good-hearted. When
he is entertained by Small, he laughs like a normal child, which I
hope he will eventually become. Small, on the other hand, feels his
wild nature will be a marvellous addition to our team, though I
fear the influence that so seasoned an adventurer may exert upon
so young and impressionable a mind. And with Rustam Khan
gone, Small and I must accept the privilege of becoming paternal
figures. I shall do my utmost to live up to this challenge responsi-
bly, and act as a counterweight to Small, but I suspect the loving
envelopment of Fahlhana will eclipse either of our attempts.

She sits opposite me, watching as we pass trains of camels bearing goods and nomads. She has just awoken from her sleep. She is,
I have no doubt, devastated by her husband's demise, but neither
her face nor her conversation reveals it. Her statuesque poise has
only once collapsed into the despair you would expect. She wept
for him onto my shoulder late one night as the others slept. Since
that sole act of mourning, when both of us remained utterly silent
and awake into the night, she has even raised a smile or two, for
it seems Small is capable of being charming as well as bawdy.

'Calcutta's the place for them, lad.'

'But you told me they would make invaluable members of our
team,' I replied. 'We've the map. Why don't we head to Marwar
first, then go and see Sir Mortimer at his convenience?'

'The lad could help, I said. And I don't deny it'd be the making
of him. But it's no place for a woman. None at all. If you've her
best interests in mind, you won't be taking her to Marwar.'

I do have Fahlhana's best interests in mind; and not merely
because Rustam Khan told me I must take her from that village of
death, for that I did many weeks of travelling ago. I had expected
Fahlhana and Nasir to leave us at Gahkuch and I was overwhelmed
with joy, not when she said that she could not return to her people
with Nasir, that there was nothing for them there in the northern
provinces – no future or hope – but when she demanded to follow
wherever we led. To Marwar, I had thought. I accepted her
demands immediately, as did Small, but he told me in no uncertain

terms that she and the boy were to be my responsibility. I shall do all in my power to keep them safe from harm, be it foohardy or dangerous.

Small had told me that this Marwar was to be found in the very south and west of this enormous country, that it lies in luscious tropical lands of bounteous and beauteous natural wonder. He gleefully promised danger, excitement, adventure and the most pulchritudinous women the subcontinent can offer. The woman into whose wondrous eyes I now look precludes me from believing the latter, but I was nonetheless keen to head there for the former.

'They are my responsibility, Small, as you told me. Let us conclude our bargain and hope that the south proves more fiscally fruitful than the north.'

'Lad,' said Small, that uncharacteristic gravity filling his voice as he delved into his breast and produced his fistful of papers and scraps of hide. He unfolded the map we were to follow. 'This chart. Do you see any of what I described to you upon it? No, you see camels, Thebes, pyramids. And these others – why they came from Forrester's very own rooms in Cairo. You see, lad, my deception of you stretched far and wide. This map shows the route not to the Faddhuan Clock but to Melancovic's stash, which as you know is in Egypt, which as you also know is in Africa. It is an adventure and a story for another day. Today Calcutta has been made a very much more tempting destination than Karnak and Luxor. I was seeking a watchmaker and the Faddhuan Clock was my bribe. And we'll be passing through Marwar any hour now. A dry and dusty place, quite the reverse of what I told you. I had to have some way of judging the extent of your knowledge hereabouts, lad. The Faddhuan Clock told me you were a watchmaker, Marwar told me I could lead you wherever I pleased. Do you know what it means, Marwar? The Valley of Death. Not a place to go if you've nothing to go there for. The clock does exist, though, lad, do not doubt that, but I'm afraid I have no more idea of where it is hidden than you do.'

To explore is to be lost, I have discovered, for being lost in every way conceivable is what has made this an adventure, and I an explorer. I have been lost to the mountains; I have been lost to cultural nuances of which the kindly Karachi soak Captain Spicer had warned me; I have been lost to delirium and imaginings of cannibal kings, and of treasure and to greed; and I have been lost to deception. Over my time with him, Small has proved himself to be nothing if not a scoundrel, a deceiver and a swindler, but the sheer extent of his deception no longer angers me, or hurts me, as it did in Tolliver's hut in Ishkuman. Faddhuan Clock or none, with him by my side I found the adventure I craved. Indeed, it was a deception of my own, a self-deception, that was to blame for our failure, if that is what you consider it.

In all the weeks that I was on the sea, and journeying from Karachi to Gilgit, thence to the Ishkuman valley, I never once thought to inspect the watch as a watchmaker would, for I had convinced myself that I was an explorer. Had I done so, undoubtedly I would now be travelling accompanied by untold riches, but perhaps not by friends. Had I opened the watch and discovered the map, I might be a wealthier man, it is true. But would I have encountered Small, or Rustam Khan or Fahlhana? And was it not these characters, Taqdir, Tolliver, Flack and even Petts among them, who have made this journey what it is? So if, for me, it was the fantasy of adventure that made itself real, how could I reasonably reprimand Small for his deceptions, which themselves have served to bring about the excitements I have related?

I am no longer lost, and in truth I now feel more the watchmaker than the explorer. I have decided to return with the woman and the boy to my shop on Chancery Lane, where we shall be able to live in safe if frugal peace. They shall struggle to adjust, I know, but each of them wishes to accompany me rather than go with Small to uncertain destinations, and I know over time they shall succeed. Nasir is but a child, and Fahlhana – well, I am certain London shall fall under her charms just as I have. My rooms on Amwell Street are not capable of housing us, of course, and since I have sold my collection of antique timepieces, to secure more spacious quarters will be difficult; for what remains of my funds shall carry us only as far as the shop's front door, where McNaughton first eyed me through the tear in the blind. Not that I doubt that we shall manage. Besides, there is a great distance between here and there, and I have learned from Small that much can occur during its traversing. It may not have been fate that brought the two of us together, but it seems we were fated to become friends, and I would not exchange him as my companion on this adventure for all the treasure in Ishkuman. Lahore shall see our parting of the ways, however, for while I go west to England with Fahlhana and Nasir, Small shall head east to Calcutta with Sir Mortimer Durand. I suspect that his restless spirit will not hold him there for long.

'I'm sorry, lad,' he said rather sheepishly as he refolded the thin skin of the map and returned it to its place at his heart, but I had already forgiven him his additional and apparently characteristic dishonesty. Then he passed me his flask, freshly filled with Glenlivet, and delved into his knapsack. From it he removed that bizarre feline skull he had taken from the catacombs. He briefly considered it with the studied precision with which a watchmaker inspects a timepiece and then he grinned, stretching that scar wide across his cheek at the thought of impending adventure.

'So you're not just a legend, eh?' he said to the skull, and then turned to me. 'There's cash here. I can smell it – the very sweat of Maharajahs clashing in a bidding war over such a beast. After all, lad – how hard can it be to track down such a singular creature?'

36

THE LETTERS OF
SIR PAUL LINDLEY-SMALL

Cabin 148-2, the vessel Nabijawar
En route from Bergen to Bombay

LOCATION AND DATE UNKNOWN

Cyril, old friend,

This morning I was shifting the sack holding the cat, prodding it to be sure that it still lived, and the fangs pierced through the gunny and even through the tight threading of Crawford's weave. I have been bitten, and the puncture wounds are discolouring.

Have I been duped by people at every turn? Had the fakir previously heard that I sought the King Cobra Cat and constructed for me a world in which it still exists? Were Ashvin and Dadri Landa merely accomplices playing upon my wish to encounter the beast? If so, why send me to the icy climes of Scandinavia, to serve me their devilry cold? Or were they all as genuine and honest as they seemed, and unknowingly sent me to my fate?

Can you unravel the final mystery? I fear it is beyond me. I am rapidly weakening, though I do not know if it is due to the poison or the antidote I apply. I am following the practice of the only

European snake charmer I ever met, you see. He was a one-handed Irishman I met in Ceylon whilst gun-running to Sumatra, and long years of experience brought to his attention a remedy no *sapera* had unearthed. When he fell foul of his creatures' venom, he swore by whisky, to be administered both externally and internally, the stronger the better. And so that is how I employ the last of my 'Livet. At least I will spend my final hours basking in the pleasures of Scotland's finest.

Whatever the truth of my journey, this marks the end of my great adventure. It has carried me far and wide, and you have been savvy to more of it than any other. Our paths merged on that Gilgit mountainside, and now they must part once more. But before that happens, my only friend, I ask that you carry with you as you continue two nuggets of advice. The first, Melancovic taught me: enjoy the hunt, or what you seek shall be a sore disappointment. The second I hope I have taught you: Truth be damned! Death is death, and life is life, and neither need be burdened by the dull.

I only hope I have proved diverting.

From this life or the next, I will remain always,

Your dear friend,

Paul Small

AUTHOR'S NOTE

'They don't make 'em like that any more' was supposedly being said of the film version of Kipling's *The Man Who Would Be King* – to which this book owes much – even as it was being made in 1975. It was a sense that such stories were no longer being written, and that I would read them if they were, that led me to write this one. In the golden age of adventure and 'lost world' fiction, the books of Kipling, Rider Haggard, Conan Doyle, Stevenson and the rest told readers what the unknown might hold. These days, you need only look at a device in the palm of your hand to see a satellite image of any point on earth. What has not changed is the desire for entertainment. In the twenty-first century as in the nineteenth, people want to escape the daily grind by enjoying themselves. I did while writing this book. I hope you did while reading it. If so, further material can be found at www.thelostkings.com

In bringing *The Lost Kings* to your hands, I would like to acknowledge the efforts of my agents, Luigi Bonomi and Molly Sterling of LBA; and of Simon & Schuster UK, most especially Sally Partington, my editor. Thanks must also go to my parents, ever supportive, as well as to Dr Vladimir Metzinoff and Martin Shawcross. Highest gratitude, however, must be reserved for Mona, the list of reasons too long to fit here.

B.H. 2010